Shadow of the Twins

A novel by A.J Kelly

Dedicated to my wife, parents and family and to the Jack Regans of the world who stand between their loved ones and danger and refuse to move.

"Instead of a man of peace and love, I have become a man of violence and revenge."

- Chief Haiëñ'wa'tha, 1525 - 1595

Table of contents

Hear who I am.

I do not beg nor cry for your morning light
Daybreak can keep its natural calls
I prefer the scream of man as I strike in darkness
And blood bellows its silent fear

I do not beg nor cry for your hope
Fervour springs lighter in darkened hate of cloudy skies
I prefer the feel of death on my blood-wet hands
Drier than my soul can ever be

I do not beg nor cry for your joy
None such sentiment lives now in your blood
I prefer salted tears on weathered cheeks
Proclaiming fear has danced nearby

I do not beg nor cry for your honour
It flowed freely with your blood and sacrifice
I prefer your soul for I am Death
And I beg nor cry for no man.

Jack C. Regan, Somalia 2004
Poem scrawled on the wall of his cell before his escape.

The President held the stare of his friend for longer than was polite or necessary. Longthorn was more than a political friend, if such a being existed in the politically darkened halls of Washington, he was a long time financial supporter and his money had put this President into the White House. His plea for help could not fall on deaf ears and it was not going to. The problem was that the help that the man was looking for did not exist, at least, not in the public domain. The help, the only true resolution to the problem at hand, needed to be 'Swift and Final.' The motto of the men, the men whose existance the President could not admit to, would ensure that Longthorn's daughter would be returned.

Looking into his friend's eyes, seeing and feeling the plight of a man who feared for his daughter's safety, the President agreed with his inner voice that had reprimanded him for responding so slowly.

He took his friend's shoulders in a firm grip and reconnected with him through the windows of the soul. The President's calmness was veiled by an excited glint in his eyes, a child showing a friend a new toy. He turned to his Secretary of Defense and sternly uttered the words Longthorn had prayed to hear.

"Send an Envoy."

The employment of an Envoy meant one thing, an unquestioned need for the immediate conclusion to an unsavory situation and the Secretary of Defense dialed the four digits that would get him an immediate response.

"Petersen." The voice was calm, steady and primed to respond.

"We have a situation, we need to move."

"Who, where and how many?" The timber of the voice unchanged by excitement.

The details were passed quickly before electronic communications took over the rest of the task.

"Mr. President, they are moving."

"Do we know who is taking the lead on this?" the President asked still holding his friend firmly.

"Regan, Sir. Jack Regan."

The President smiled then turned to Longthorn. "Those are the two words you wanted to hear."

1

Jungle Dance

The pupil contracted gently as focus tightened on the heavy-set, panting target. As the moment drew nearer body functions began to slow down in the anticipation of action. The dull sound of blood being pushed through the veins flowed through ears that had closed to all outside sounds and concentrated solely on the commanding voices within his head. His breathing was slow and gentle, breaths every ten seconds so that the sensation was comfortable but the intervals were long enough to allow the focus to last without the interruption caused by the movement of the diaphragm. Muscle memory was playing its part too, the signals had passed through the nerve pathways and muscles down to the finger that would answer the command to action. Slowly the eye, in unison with its weapon, moved from target to target and back again creating a minute dance that would culminate in death. The movements and thoughts were as natural as the Colombian rain forest that was to witness the silent dance of death.

Fifty feet away the party of five that was making its way up the mountain path stopped for the umpteenth time. The heavy rain had stopped but it had made the mountain path unstable to all but the locals who climbed up and down these mountains every day as part of their daily labour. As in this instance, the labour was not always innocent and it was rarely legal. The lead man in the climbing party fingered a packet of cigarettes from the chest pocket of his sweat-sodden shirt and flicked a smoke between his thick, wet lips. His head tilted sideways against the non-existent breeze as he lit the crumpled cigarette. Once lit, he drew deeply pinching the butt between his fingers to maximise the effect. As he exhaled with a contented grunt, the back of his head exploded outwards.

The eye and the finger had expressed themselves in unity and now acted quickly together to encounter the remaining three targets. As the first body was falling to the muddy ground the second target was acquired and dispensed with in the same bloody manner. The third man in the party was only beginning to comprehend what was happening and tried to turn his head towards the man behind him. The sudden movement slightly upset the targeting of their attacker and the third bullet careened off his upper cheekbone before exiting through the top of his head. The body crumbled vertically as the knees gave way to the dead weight above and his blood flowed from the efficient hole in his head onto the feet of the fourth member of the group. The man's body had frozen to the spot as his mind screamed for an explanation for the silent carnage that he was seeing. He saw the young lady stand limply before him and his mind raced back to the fun they had had with here in the previous days. His eyes had fixed on her body as he began to fall, not understanding why he was falling or that he was already dead.

The girl stood in silence as stared wide-eyed at the death surrounding her. Her fingers, wrinkled by the damp, heavy air, clawed at her cheeks as she fought with her sanity to muster a scream. Around her floated a sticky red mist of blood that had exited the heads of her captors and seemed to silence any noise from ruining the moment. Rachel Longthorn's scream finally shattered the silence. It was a scream of such pleading intensity that she thought her lungs would rip through her chest and create another red, eyrie mist to hang with that which was already settling on her pale skin.

Birds screeched and fluttered nervously as the intruder to their territory screamed and screamed at her surroundings. Rachel could not, at her young age, figure out what had happened. She ordered herself to stop screaming so that she could try to understand what was happening but that was a useless endeavour. Her mind was in a spasm of turmoil as it tried to absorb the death that was before her. How could the four men who had manhandled her up the mountain path suddenly be dead? She had seen her father hunt on their estate and so knew that guns made noise. There had been no noise from the men she had been with and there would certainly be no noise from them now. As these thoughts were molesting her mind a blur of mottled green and black caught her attention as it moved from the heavy foliage. Her response was to scream again.

He covered the fifty or so feet to the contact in a matter of a few short seconds. He had hoped that she would not notice him in her moment of panic but she had turned just as he had started his run and by then it was too late to stop. Within six feet of the girl he pushed his weapon to his back and aimed one hand to her lower back and one hand to her screaming mouth. He required silence as much as she required security.

She realised he was human only when she felt his hand enclose her mouth. It was firm but not rough and his second hand had grabbed the top of her cargo-pants and the lower section of her shirt to hold her steady. She decided instantly that she would not struggle. If this individual had killed the men who had moments before being holding her captive and now holding her in his arms then she would be better off staying still until something was said. She allowed her eyes to look upwards.

She saw nothing, an invisible man. His face was the same colour as his surroundings, a blended mixture of autumn browns and summer greens. His clothing was the same from neck to boots. Her first thought was that the jungle had taken offence to her mistreatment and had taken human form to attack her assailants. But the jungle could not have had the eyes that she was staring into at that moment, eyes that, while intense, were lifeless and devoid of the ownership of the death their owner had caused. No emotion leaked from the pools of grey-blue as they seemed to check her over for signs of abuse and injury and found nothing externally threatening. As she began to shake uncontrollably he spoke just four words, which caused an eruption of joy and tears.

'Your Dad sent me.'

He pulled the scarf away from his neck in order to finger activate the communication set strapped around his neck. He squeezed it gently and spoke clearly.

'Palace, this is Envoy. Do you copy?'

There was a moment's silence before the response came through his earpiece.

'Envoy, this is Palace. We read you Five by Five. What's your sit-rep?'

'Diplomat is with me and we are ready for extraction.'

'Targets?'

The response was unsettling to the young girl awaiting freedom.

'They are sitting on a log eating ice cream. Would you like to say hello?'

'We can give that a miss, Envoy. Be advised that the paymaster requires proof of...contact. Please bring visual and DNA proof.'

The Envoy's hand slid into a side pocked and withdrew a slim micro camera and he began to quickly take photos of the dead. Once done, he pocketed the camera and drew his knife in order to gather DNA samples.

Rachel looked in horror at the matted black sheen of the knife.

'What are you doing?'

'Turn away, Ms. Longthorn. Your father requires proof.'

Her mind screamed an explanation, which she didn't want to hear and so she turned away.

With her back turned the Envoy sawed rapidly through the skin and bone of the right thumb of each corpse. The noise of the brutal field surgery was muted only by the sound of Rachel as she vomited in unison to the sounds she heard. She could not fathom the brutality of the act. To her death was sacred and not a thing to be interfered with. To the Envoy death was a way of life.

Once done the four thumbs were bagged and pocketed by the Envoy. He looked skyward for the approaching helicopter as he wiped his bloody hand on the chest of one of the corpses. He then placed the mutilated hands onto the respective chests, withdrew his camera again and took eight more shots.

'We are done here. Are you ready to go home?'

She couldn't answer. What more brutality was she to see before she reached home? She didn't want to know.

The radio broke silence as the Envoy waited for a response from the young girl.

'Envoy, we have a situation here. There is a group heading your way. The image is mottled by the latent heat of the surroundings but we are talking fifteen, I repeat fifteen, non-friendlies heading your way. Be advised that we are five minutes out and will be coming in weapons hot. Retreat to predetermined LZ and lay the ground for our friends.'

Slightly over two hundred miles over-head, one billion dollars worth of equipment, a KH 11B reconnaissance satellite, passed over the area of jungle now being occupied by the Envoy. The satellite, providing real-time images, tagged as 'expected' by the National Reconnaissance Office, relayed to ground stations via Milstar relay satellites and those images were advanced to the Dark-Eye base. Instantaneously, the images were then sent to the helicopters hovering outside the kill-zone awaiting instruction from the Envoy on the ground. Moments before, the satellites low-light-image intensifiers, usually used to provide night-time images, identified the differential thermal inertia of further targets on the mountain. The heat of the targets, drifting from their bodies, through the leaves of the trees and the growing dusk of the late afternoon, was enough for Dark-Eye's hidden eye.

The Envoy turned to Rachel and spoke directly to her.

'There are more of these men behind us. Are you able to stay calm just a little longer?'

She nodded agreement while staring at the bloody corpses that lay before her.

'Will there be more of these before we get away from here?'

'Yes. I am afraid it is necessary. Try not to look at them.'

He leaned over the body of the first killed and jammed a small device under the back of the neck of the dead man. Stepping over the bodies of the other men he quickly pinned eight ice-hockey puck sized objects into the foliage at equal intervals of three feet. The ground was laid for the oncoming group. He then grabbed her arm just above the wrist and guided her towards the landing zone for the incoming helicopters, which was a hundred meters away from the bodies. Once there, he gently positioned her behind a fallen tree stump and told her to close her eyes. Things were going to heat up very suddenly if the approaching group moved any quicker.

'Palace, this is Envoy. Now would be a good time!'

The message being relayed was interrupted by a concerto of explosions.

Moving up the mountain path at pace, the fifteen men had heard the screams of Rachel Longthorn. A mixture of men, some were locals and some were former military, all were armed. The pace halted rapidly when they came across the bodies of their fallen comrades. With no leaders among their ranks they didn't take any precautions when milling around the bodies; all were curious to see what had happened and how the men had died. The idea that the smaller group had been ambushed had occurred to no one. Bullet wounds were obvious but that could have happened if the girl had grabbed a weapon and opened fire. They needed a closer look. One of the men crouched and went to turn the body of one of the dead to examine the wounds. Pressure was released on the transmitter under the dead man's neck.

Once released of pressure, the transmitter carried out its two functions within microseconds of each other. The relay transmitter spat a command to its neighbouring charges before using the remaining power to detonate the phosphorous-based charge compacted beneath the tiny but efficient electronic brain. The explosion, while small, was fatal. The searing white flame had engulfed the arm of the curious one as the other charges detonated around them all. The effect was terrible in its efficiency.

The eight devices acted as one, fanning a flaming web of phosphorous micro-stars across the path of the men. Before the heat could burn through the clothing and bare skin, the secondary explosions peppered the area with thousands of star shaped metal projectiles. A bloody swath was cut through the men as they huddled around their fallen comrades. Flesh and bone fragments were scattered over a wide area as eight of the men were engulfed in fiery death. The others were left with varying injuries as they staggered around, blinded and deafened by the explosion. Their ears could not have hoped to pick up the sound of the low flying helicopters as they swept in low and fast. Weapons hot.

'Envoy, keep it down. We have you eyeballed and we are clearing your zone.'

The three HH-60G Pave Hawk helicopters circled-in like angry sharks as gouts of flame poured lead into the kill zone from their Miniguns. The result was final. The remaining men who had been left standing were cut to pieces by the hail of bullets without having a chance to engage an enemy that they had never heard nor seen.

Once the threat was neutralised the guns stopped their screeching spin and the helicopters hovered menacingly overhead. They seemed to sniff the air for danger before one dropped lightly down and touched the ground briefly as the Envoy and his package bolted to the lift to freedom. The down-draught caught the young lady off-guard as she tried to reach the door of the helicopter but the Envoy caught her arm and boosted her onto the craft. He turned to look at the carnage that lay only a hundred meters away and felt nothing. He did not know any of the men that had been killed nor did he want to know about them. There lives had no bearing on his except for the fact that he had killed the majority of them. He turned back around and jumped into the awaiting craft. Time to leave.

The rotors clawed at the thin Colombian air as the engines gained power and lifted the passengers away from the contact site. They reached the altitude of the other awaiting craft and circled the area once more. Two of the helicopters peeled away while one stayed to clear the evidence.

Aboard the remaining helicopter the pilot positioned his craft above the contact point where the nineteen bodies were strewn in ghoulish slumber.

'Clear to drop, clear to drop.'

Behind him an Envoy released a barrel-sized package through the open door, which released a small parachute as it fell. The barrel dropped rapidly, slowed marginally by the 'chute, onto the bodies below before settling in the soft mud.

The pilot dropped the nose of his aircraft and powered away from the area in chase of his wingmen. Behind him the barrel of napalm detonated and the ball of sticky fire engulfed the bodies and a small part of the jungle.

The evidence was wiped away and a regenerating jungle would consume what was left within weeks.

2

Searing Words

Once up in the air the pressure began to bleed off. The Envoy handed over his weapon to a crewman after he had cleared the chamber and leaned back onto the metal airframe of the aircraft. The tension was crawling from his skin into the air around him but the adrenaline induced shakes would take time to ease. Rachel Longthorn looked up into the face of her saviour.

'What's your name?'

The words passed through his ears without creating any urge to reply. He never spoke to those who had been rescued. He didn't even look at her.

'Hello! Can't you speak? Hello!'

He turned and looked at her with dead eyes. He was wiping the camouflage paint from his face with a wet cloth that had just wiped the blood from his hands.

'I asked what your name is. Any chance of a reply? I would like to know whom I have to thank. That would be polite.'

'Wait until you get home and thank your father. He was the one who sent me.'

He was annoyed now at her arrogance which was a vast change to the terrified little girl who had been crying and vomiting just a few short minutes ago. The security of the helicopter and the presence of a protective force around her had brought her back to life. With that awakening came the arrogance that had been a continuous part of her life. She wanted conversation and wanted it from the young soldier who was sitting before her. She was not used to being ignored and didn't like the sensation of having the authority of her family brushed aside either.

'I just want to know your name. What is the problem with that? I have met many soldiers and security types like you before. You are all the same.'

The Envoy was trying to come down from the adrenaline high and was not in the mood for small talk.

'Please be quiet or I shall gag you. Do not test my patience, as I do not have any for spoilt brats. Shut up or be shut up, I get paid either way.'

Her reply made him wish that he had controlled his temper.

'They gagged me when they raped me. I didn't feel too spoiled then.'

Her eyes burned angrily into his, challenging him to reply. She continued to stare but he did not reply. He watched as her anger burned through him and then burned itself out. Her eyes became visibly softer and began to moisten with the approach of tears. Only then did he reply.

'I didn't know. We were informed of your location and the possible number involved. We didn't have time to involve ourselves any further. I am afraid that is the nature of our business.' He paused for a moment and breathed deeply before carefully continuing with his apology. 'I am sorry that they did what they did but they are all dead now. You saw that and so I hope that will help with you're healing. More than that I cannot do or say.'

Her words clawed through his ears, eagerly burying themselves deeply into the darkness of that part of his mind, the part which held only death.

'You didn't get them all. You didn't get the one who organised it all.'

His mind shuddered with frustration at the perceived failure as he fought to control his own physical response to her words. He had known that the mission had been set up too quickly. They had been given only the necessary intelligence that would enable them to extract the girl from her developing predicament on the mountain. The team could work with that intel but their motto was 'Swift and Final' and so they always endured, battling to finalise a situation, to bring closure. His mind commanded him that this situation would be no different. As if in a physical response to the command, his hand slipped down to the pocket, which held the severed thumbs of those he had just killed, and he toyed with one between his finger-tips and his resolve emboldened.

'Who is left?' he asked gently, the tone of his voice leaving no doubt that his intentions were dark.

She could not bring herself to answer. Her body shook as her tears erupted and poured freely from her shattered spirit. She longed for a human touch that would take away the memories of those who had abused her. In seeking that touch, she turned and buried her head into the chest of the young soldier who had saved her.

He had never been moved by death. Those whom he had saved before had never had the opportunity to thank him. Now he had a young girl crying on his chest and he didn't know what to do or say. The Envoy opposite him shrugged his shoulders knowing too well that he as well wouldn't know what to do in the same situation.

'My name is Regan.' he offered.

The helicopters left Colombian airspace and flew steadily to a US Navy ship off the coast, circling in its predefined waiting point in the Caribbean Sea. Once refueled, the helicopter took off once more to Panama where the pick-up of the young lady was to be affected. The flight was uneventful for all involved and especially so as adrenaline levels had dropped since leaving Colombian airspace. All the pent-up tension onboard had eased somewhat and even young Rachel had slipped into a deep sleep. She was exhausted from her ordeal and had effectively cried herself to sleep, her head resting on the chest of the man who had saved her. He, meanwhile, did not sleep. His mind no longer was on the action that had just been endured, but instead his mind had already started to work out the closure to the mission that he defined as a failure. He wanted to know more about the man who had organised the kidnapping. So many questions were starting to take root in his brain as he ran the details over and over through his head. He knew as well as any soldier that the best-laid plans went South with the first contact with the enemy. But this situation was different. The unit was created to react to situations in an instant without the constraints of months of planning and red tape. The unit did plan but it was more like intense brainstorming combining the minds of intelligent men who understood war and death. In this situation the goal had been achieved but the knowledge that the organiser of the action was still at large galled the young man.

As the three helicopters approached their landing zone the radio chatter between ground and air became more intense. Information was being passed in code between the pilots and air controllers on the ground. The information was reporting that everything was in order. The craft were intact and the crew, soldiers and package were unhurt. There was no need for anymore than the necessary ground crews to be available when the helicopters swept in. The mission was secret and so the smaller the number of people on the ground to witness the return the better. It was necessary to keep such operations under such secrecy because there was the small matter of having just completed a minor invasion of a sovereign country and killing its citizens. All within the loop understood the situation as it was and accepted the realities of their actions.

The helicopters swept in and alighted on the darkened landing strip. The helicopter carrying Rachel Longthorn was centred between the sister craft, a sign to those who had the mind to notice that the cargo was valuable and was going to be protected at all costs. The mission was not over until the package was handed over. To one man on board the middle helicopter, the mission was far from over and he had to command his mind to focus on the handover and leave the rest locked away for another day.

The doors of each chopper slid open as the engines powered down and six men alighted swiftly from each and took defensive positions at the compass points of each aircraft. Once the men had been positioned the pilot of the centre craft flicked the landing light as a signal of clearance for the group to be approached. The team did not want to be approached by anyone not on their 'expected' list and were ready to add any uninvited guests to their own very special list. Memories were still fresh from the landing from their first mission. The unit had completed a snatch and grab from a neo-Nazi group based in the mountains of Montana. The targets, a group of fascists, had never expected the governmental response. As a group of people, they had never expected hell to be visited upon them in the manner that it occurred. The Envoys had 'neutralised' the mountain holdout and cleared off of the mountain with three infants that had been taken from a military hospital earlier that morning. The success of the event had turned sour as a unit of army Rangers approached the helicopters as they landed ten miles south of the contact zone. The snatch team had not been advised of the approaching group and had reacted as trained. The Rangers team had been cut to pieces as they approached the choppers and the fact that the Rangers had been there to collect the child of one of their own had made no difference. The team had literally seen through the night and had reacted. From that night the un-named team had been christened by some of the toughest soldiers around who had just seen them in action. They were to be called Dark-Eye.

3

A Sister's Screams.

On the far side of the world, in middle Italy, a new front was beginning to open onto the War on Terror. Italy had experienced mixed luck in dealing with terrorists in recent decades but had, since 9/11, had become much more efficient. Any hope of using Italy again as a staging post for attacks into Europe had dried up. The army and police had become cleaner and tougher and a new sense of direction had been followed. The intelligence services were working around the clock checking all types of leads that they were picking up themselves and from the various international agencies they now worked with. There was a palpable sense of pride among the services as they achieved their goals. Al Qaeda had had units operating within Milan and Rome until anti-terror units had hit them. The assaults had not made the news, as the operations didn't officially happen. It became the unspoken word that such assaults would occur in a way that would exclude the public eye and therefore public opinion. The world's most sought after terrorists were no longer to have a base in Italy.

Others didn't need a base. Italy was already their home.

The sounds of an Italian spring morning crept into her conscience as her mind struggled against a drug-induced sleep. Her head felt heavy as she tried to wake. There was no understanding yet in her mind except the sickening rumble of danger that crawled in her stomach and made her heart sink. Pain began to pierce through the drowsiness and she realised her hands, feet and neck were bound tightly to a cold metal pillar. And she was naked.

They walked in together looking at her form that was tied roughly to the metal upright. They could see that she was beginning to wake from the slumber that they had induced some hours before and they wanted to be there to see the effects. They enjoyed their work and wished to see the results once again.

She was new for them. A new short-term toy, one which they had decided to capture and to destroy. She had written about them in a small paper, a short piece that had been hidden discretely in the foreign section of a Rome edition.

She had written in an attempt to warn her new home of the dangers of a developing threat. Her editor, and worse still the Italian authorities, had ignored those warnings. She had handed to the police a file that she had compiled in the previous months on the lives and developing tendencies of the two men who stared at her now. The file had been stored away after being ignored by a young detective who had bigger fish to catch in the turbulent sea of terrorism. He did not believe that the file was worth reading while the mopping up of Al Qaeda was ongoing. He had not had the success that his young colleagues in Milan had and wished for it. The file disappeared as well as the hope for the life of the young reporter. As events were to unfold the file would have to re-emerge. But events had not come to that point as yet.

He had been born just minutes before his brother and held that fact as a point of authority over his younger twin. They were identical in every sense and used that fact to avoid trouble at a young age. Both were tall, powerfully built young men, each with a shock of pitch-black hair. They turned the heads of the young girls and received the envious glares of their male peers. However, they ignored both as irritants as they understood that there was more to their lives than petty differences. They were born to terrorise and were becoming efficient. Mauro and Marco Gasco had started small-time and had decided not to enter the world of the Cosa Nostra. It was too corporate for them. The wanted to start their own 'business' and to develop their own special trade, their own special calling card. They enjoyed suffering and mutilation and inflicting those twin horrors onto others with a sadistic glee.

That was what the young reporter had discovered and as she woke from her slumber her fears were starting to burn through the drug haze. She was beginning to realise what had happened and the terror began to ferment within her mind. She knew even before she looked up that she would be facing the twins. As her head lifted, her heart sank. They stood before her smiling and nudging each other in wicked anticipation of their impending fun. Each held a long jagged blade that seemed to empower them, their eyes dancing dangerously as they visually ravaged her naked body. Their eyes didn't rest to enjoy her breasts or her intimate parts. Instead, they seemed to dilate with joy at the mottled bruising around her neck and wrists where the ropes and held her. They really enjoyed pain. And now they were going to inflict more.

'Good evening, miss ' he giggled. His English was word perfect with only a trace of the rolling Italian accent.

'I hope you realise the length we have gone to give you a real interview. I did not like that fumbling little article in the paper. It wasn't concise enough. I, and my brother, like things to be concise.'

She tried to hold her head up and stare him in the eyes but her muscles would not respond. She hung from the pillar in an almost crucifix-like pose and listened to her captors.

'Time to die, my cute little friend. Time to die.'

He walked in front of her and lowered his head to look into her eyes. Her's still held a trace of defiance, which galled him into action. His hand shot to her neck and his fingers dug deep into her soft flesh. She gagged as she tried to scream but his fingers had dug deep into her neck, cutting off the flow of air. Her eyes danced and surged out of their sockets as if trying to breath for the air-starved body that was writhing beneath the manicured nails of her attacker. He let go.

In deep gulps her lungs greedily inhaled the air that was once again allowed to pass through its natural path. The effect was dizzying to a mind already uncertain from the drugs that had been injected into her veins the evening before. She fought the haze that had settled upon her mind but she continued to seek a solution to a situation whose end she already knew.

Mauro saw no more defiance and decided to be more adventurous. His hand, gently this time, slipped onto her breast and he squeezed it without causing pain. He looked mockingly into her eyes as he caressed her with his soft hand.

'I think you are becoming more affectionate towards me. What do you think? Shall I pleasure you?'

A solution. Where was the solution? In the back of her dazed mind a blur of something gave a trace of hope and strength.

'Go ahead,' she offered with a wry smile.

Mauro screamed in rage at the further act of defiance and his fist lashed out at her unprotected head. He connected just below the cheek line with a sickening wet slap as flesh, gum and teeth merged into a pain of equals.

Where was the solution that seemed to be fighting to clear the fog of her mind and announce itself? It was there, moving to the forefront of her thoughts but it seemed that it hadn't enough time to surface.

Mauro again moved his hand to her body but this time with singular determination. He groped his way down to her side, just above her hip, and roughly grabbed a handful of flesh.

She looked up through puffed cheeks into his eyes asking without words what her fate was to be. The glint off of the blade of the knife as it moved swiftly towards her was answer enough. Time slowed as she saw the blade pierce the skin that had been stretched out in Mauro's hand and her senses warned of horrendous pain yet to come.

The double-edged military knife carved through her flesh without hesitation and before the pain had been fully registered in her brain, Mauro was holding a handful of her flesh in front of her face. Blood dripped between his fingers and cast a red hue in his quivering eyes.

'You might say that I got my pound of flesh in the end, my dear.'

Pain could not fight its way through the horror that was being played out before her. She now was begging for death to be visited upon her quickly but that wish was an internal one and not one that was going to be expressed vocally to the two bastards standing before her. The solution was driving itself through her veins and coursing to her tongue. But it still had not announced itself.

Marco stepped forward to get a closer look.

'Enough. Let's put an end to this.'

Mauro was not happy as he wished to continue but decided, as ever, to heed his brother. Just one more little play. His hand toyed with the gaping wound in the young girl's side, which caused her to convulse in agony. From there his hand slid through the streams of blood and he smeared her pale skin with his bloodied hands. He danced his fingers back up her torso before gliding them around her neck to the back of her head. His sticky fingers now gently caressed her red curls before he roughly grabbed a clump of them violently pulling her head towards his face again before unleashing a flurry of well placed blows to her stomach. The bout of fury lasted only seconds but broke the young girl. As she felt herself fade the solution surged forward from her brain to the pit of her stomach and from there outwards in a guttural scream.

'Jack.........Jaaaaccccckkkk!'

Marco and Mauro were taken aback. They couldn't understand how she could even move after the abuse she had suffered. Marco, slightly shaken, grabbed her head in his hands and looked her deeply into the eyes.

'Who is Jack?' he asked gently.

The final ounces of energy were used to answer the men who were to kill her. They were men of flesh and blood and so they could be made to be frightened, they could be made to bleed. After all, how could they possibly know what was to come. Through bloodied lips and teeth she spat the answer at them.

'Death,' she answered, "Jack is death, and he will come for you. He will come for all of you.'

Marco's hand darted straight upwards and the blade made it's final passage through the girls body, passing through her lower jaw and upwards into her brain. She quivered for a moment before the ropes took her full weight.

The twins had no realisation that they had started a war that would have no boundaries. They really had no idea.

Donato Izzo sat at his desk staring into space. He had missed the connecting bus that would have brought him to the train station and home to the comfort of his bed and his beautiful wife. That was not the only bus he had missed in recent months. The whole flurry of activity surrounding the capture and closure of terror groups in Italy had passed him by. He really felt at a career low as he watched his colleagues in Milan and Rome make the breaks in the larger crimes while he rotted in the backwater towns and cities watching his police career dry up before his eyes.

He leaned back in his comfortable leather chair and drew deeply on the cigarette that hung from his lips. It would be another hour before the next train and so he thought that he might as well hang around in the station talking football and tits with the other officers. It beat getting soaked walking to the station in the unseasonable rain. Truth being told, he loved his job. He hated criminals and loved the police. Therefore his bitching always fell on deaf ears. Everyone knew that Donato Izzo was a career police officer and that was that. He knew his break would come some day. It had to. He wished and wished for the big break, not for promotion but for satisfaction. He loved to see the smug smile wiped off their faces when their little crime worlds fell apart. It was a wonderful feeling. He just hoped that his big break didn't involve children. He hated crime that involved children.

Izzo was a powerfully built man. The stocky Sicilian neck separated the brains in his head from the ropey muscular body. His eyes were constantly alert for anything out of the ordinary and his ears clued in to all conversations. His thirty-two years sat easily on his body even though his wife wanted him to quit smoking and drinking but he gently rebuked her by telling her that she had married a real man and not a pretty boy from Milan. She always smiled when he joked with her in that way and it made him smile now just thinking of her.

He jumped from his daze when the phone rang. He reached for the receiver and answered lazily.

'Izzo. Who is this?'

'Donato, it's me, Gigi. Turn on your computer. I have sent you some photos from a scene we are at. Quick, quick. I think your case has come.'

Izzo leaned over and switched on his computer muttering quietly to himself. The PC had just been upgraded and so it whirred into life quickly. He clicked on his photo view software icon and waited a few more seconds for the pictures to load. It didn't take long and the first close up image popped onto his screen.

'Jesus, Gigi. Where is this? Who is this?'

'We found her an hour ago. It seems that she was just dropped here and Donni...' There was a pause on the other end of the line.

'What is it, Gigi?'

'....The wounds are horrific. The wounds are horrific.'

It had just dawned on Gigi that the young girl was dead and that she had suffered horrifically. It was no longer a scoop for Donato. The girl was dead.

Donato was half way out the door before he realised that he hadn't hung up the phone. It was swinging from its cord over the edge of his desk and the barely audible sound of Gigi's cries could be heard. Donato skidded down the invalids' ramp and nearly landed on the bonnet of his captain's car. As no other car was available he reefed the door open and slid into the seat to avoid the pouring rain. There was no reason to frantically look for the keys as the captain always left them in the ignition. The captain wrongly believed that nobody would be bold-faced enough to steal his car. He hadn't counted on one of his officers being in one hell of a hurry.

Donato tried to drive carefully as he possibly could but the desire to get to the crime scene was too much for him. Twice he nearly became a statistic himself as the car tyres lost traction on the slippery roads. However, minor slides apart, he made it to the given directions ahead of schedule. The number of emergency personal and vehicles reawakened his natural curiosity. This was big.

From the end of the short country lane Gigi saw his friend absorb the sights and sounds of his surroundings. He always did that in order to get what he defined as a 'feel' for the scene. He then lumbered down the uneven surface of the lane towards Gigi.

'So?' he asked quietly while extending his hand.

'She is over there. Behind the screen.' He replied taking the offered hand.

'I'd better take a look.'

'Donni, it is horrible. The pictures could not have possibly prepared you for what you are about to see.' He paused and tried to swallow. 'She really suffered.'

Donnie walked towards the screen accepting the muted greetings from the other officers. They all held their heads low muttering among themselves smoking frantically and shielding themselves from the heavy rain. Some were shielding themselves from the horrors that lay behind the screen.

He walked up to the screen and put his hand on the entrance cover to pull it back. The sky lit up with a bang and a tremendous flash as a bolt of lightening snapped viciously out of the clouds and all around nearly jumped out of their skins. 'Welcome to Hell.' He thought to himself. Then he walked through the opening.

The sight that greeted him was indeed a sight from Hell. His eyes transfixed themselves onto the body before him but just as his brain was processing the images his mind and heart went cold. It wasn't the coldness that went with lack of emotion. It was that professional coldness that pushed emotion aside so that work could be done. Work that he already knew would have to conclude with the capture of one sick individual or maybe even more than one. That thought shook him a little as he continued to look at the body before him.

The broken body lay impaled on an old metal fence that was surrounded by rough scrubb foliage. Two spiked uprights of the fence had protruded up through the back and had exited through the lower abdominal region. Even now, the body was slowly shifting down the metal bars in a slow procession of death. To Donato it seemed that something evil had dropped the young woman carelessly from the sky and she had fell back first onto the metal fence.

He leaned over and sought the obvious signs of death. The wound to the lower left side was horrific but not, he thought, immediately fatal. It was, however, obvious that death had come from the wound beneath the chin.

'A knife.'

Donato turned to put a face to what had to be a medical voice it was that cold and matter of fact.

'A large hunting knife was used to carve her side and then driven, with immense force, under her chin and into her brain. You can see where the hilt of the knife bruised the flesh around the entrance wound. This was an act of aggression. Nothing sexual here. Oh, excuse me, my name is Dr. Reno. Please call me Marco.'

Donato offered his hand and the doctor shook it vigorously.

'You are saying that this has no sexual motivation what so ever?'

'Oh, my first impression was that it was sexual. However, the wounds seem to indicate that this was an act of punishment. Retribution for some injury caused or perceived. There are no violent marks on the neck except the marks of the rope that restrained her. Cuts or scratches on the neck would have indicated a sexual nature to the attack. However, we shall inspect her thougherly before we commit to the cause of death. Off the record, however, this young lady was tortured to death.'

'My God. Who would be sick enough?' asked Donato with a voice of desperation. He knelt down closer to the body and placed his hand on hers. It was cold and wet and obviously lifeless. He looked into the dead eyes and felt a surge of sadness through his body. He could see that the young woman was not Italian. The patches of sunburn that were visible in the areas not crusted by blood gave that impression. He leaned closer to her head until his lips could feel the closeness of her cold flesh.

'I will find your home and send you there. I will find those who did this to you and send them away too. I shall give your soul peace, young lady. I shall give your soul peace. That is my promise to you.'

He gently let go of her hand and stood to walk out leaving the medical Examiner to do his work.

His work would have to be just as detailed if the killer was to be caught and that was the conclusion that he wanted to this case. The image of the girl's body, arched onto the metal fence, would stay with him forever. There was no way of taking that image from his mind. He promised to himself immediately that he would not describe what he saw, ever, to anybody. Why spread images like that into clear minds. He knew that it wasn't going to be a topic of conversation at the dinner table with his wife or while sipping on a light German beer while watching his beloved Juve on the television with his friends. No, this was going to be discussed with nobody except his colleagues. And, of course, it would be discussed with his conscience.

He walked to the command vehicle and sought out his friend Pietro Marrone. He really needed this case kicked off quickly knowing that unless leads were picked up quickly and cleanly within the first twenty-four hours, the case would have the tendency to grow cold. That, he promised himself, was not going to happen. He mind was already in gear for a long night and it once again silently asked, *'Why do you care?'*

Marco froze at the question as it bubbled silently in his brain. *'Because you know her!'* He stopped in his tracks and allowed the rain to massage his skin. The questions started to run around his head chasing answers. His memory kept flashing images of young women to his minds eye where they were instantly matched against the body on the fence before being dismissed. The image of the young girl was too powerfully imprinted onto his brain and was not allowing the other images to push through.

He was still thinking while trying to light a smoke in the rain when a soft voice accompanied a light tap on his shoulder.

'Detective Izzo?'

He turned and looked at a young lady standing before him with a small recorder reaching out towards his face.

'My name is Valeria Rocco. I am a reporter for ....'

Izzo was sprinting towards the tent before the lady could identify what paper she worked for. She knew by the reaction of the detective that there was a story worth waiting for.

From within the middle helicopter ID codes were passed between those who had just arrived and those who were waiting.

'Dark Eye this is Socket. Area is clear and we are ready for approach.'

'Socket, this is Dark Eye. Ready when you are.'

'Be advised that her father and his people are approaching as well. They know the procedures and will keep out of the way.'

'They better.'

Regan moved back towards the door of the chopper and placed a hand on the shoulder of the young girl that he had rescued. She had dosed off after she had cried and was still asleep when he shook her shoulder. She awoke with a start and, not recognising where she was, screamed. Regan crouched down to her quickly and grabbed a firm hold of her shoulders. Just as he was about to reassure her of her new found safety, he remembered that he hadn't removed the camouflage paint from his face. Rachel was again looking into the face of death and her body began to shake uncontrollably. All the horror of the previous days came flooding back to her tormented mind and she started to lose control.

'Rachel, come on, girl. You are home safe now. Hold it together.'

She looked into his eyes and accepted his comfort. The belief of rescue was now creeping back into her world and her fears began to drain away.

Regan offered his hand and she took it without argument and he picked her up onto her feet. He looked at the young lady knowing that her world would never be the same again. Even her father's money would never be able to buy away the memories or the dreams that were yet to come. Yet, he had to put all of that out of his mind now and hand the package over to the owner. That was how he had to think of it, leaving only orders in his active intellect with no room for emotions. He knew that in this case things might have to change a little. She had told him that all involved had not been on the mountain. That thought had been with him even as he had been dropped onto the mountain in advance of the action earlier. While concentrating on the primary task his mind ran over the secondary information of the mission. That was all he needed now. He wanted to have the mission closed on the tarmac as the girl was handed over. That was not going to happen now. The girl was only moments away from her father's arms and safety but the repercussions would continue as far as Regan was concerned. They had to close the mission in a nice tidy box with nothing sticking out of the sides. That would come in the after action report.

'Let's go,' he advised gently.

Two black transit vans pulled up in front of the helicopters as Regan and the girl stepped out of the side doors of the chopper. All the other members of the unit held position around the choppers watching and ready for anything.

The slide door of the first transit was opened as the van eased to a halt and Trevor Longthorn jumped out. He remembered the advice given to him as he got into the van and urged himself not to run to his daughter in case the movement was seen as a threat. He had told his personal security officer to stay in the van and wait but the same message was never passed to the four in the van directly behind. As soon as they saw their boss move they decided to move as well. They had no idea who the Dark-Eye unit was but they were about to find out.

On the driver's side of the van, Steve Epps drew his weapon as his left foot hit the tarmac. His three comrades, all ex-military like himself, moved in a like manner with weapons drawn. They were going to converge on their boss in a show of the new force and protection that he wished to display for his daughter. He hoped that the show of force, ignoring the advice of Dark-Eye seniors back in the hanger, would make up for not being there when she was kidnapped. He was wrong.

Regan was first to react to the sight of a gun, the weapon being drawn by Epps. He slipped in front of Rachel while drawing his own pistol from his right hip. Before the weapon had reached his eye-line he saw that his men had reacted just as quick and twelve laser beams danced on the heads of the bodyguards, waiting to guide home death. The heavy humidity of the local air allowed all to see the beams of warning that were being emitted from the laser sights of the weapons and the bodyguards froze in unison. Longthorn himself was left standing alone between the two groups not knowing what had happened or what was to happen.

'Drop or be dropped. Right now!' roared Regan at the group in front him. He was milliseconds from opening fire and knew that his men were the same. The situation needed to be defused but not until the weapons were dropped and cleared.

'It's ok, man. We are with Mr. Longthorn as security,' offered Epps as an explanation looking at the silent dance of the lasers as the moved from head to chest of each man beside him. The one standing shielding the girl looked like he didn't care whether the weapons were going to be dropped or not. He didn't have any expression on his face. Nothing.

Regan said nothing and Epps took that as the final warning.

'Drop them, guys…slowly.'

They were all professional enough to know that the manner in which they lowered their weapons would save them from a serious physical patting down and so they all bent down slowly, placed their weapons on the ground and stood back up. They each, then, took two paces back to show that they understood the situation and knew what to expect next.

The Dark-Eye Envoys moved quickly towards them, guns still aimed for headshots until they covered the few short meters to their targets. Once there, the weapons were kicked backwards and the bodyguards roughly but efficiently put to ground. The way was now clear for the hand over.

Trevor Longthorn never took his eyes off his daughter during the commotion. He watched the young man shield her from danger and wished that it were he instead who had that ability to protect. Longthorn was now a man racked with guilt and anger. Most of it aimed at himself. He knew that he had failed in his fatherly protective role and that none of the damage caused could be forgotten. He just hoped that in the immediate future that his daughter would forgive him.

With the area clear, Regan now made his way to Longthorn. He had holstered his sidearm and held Rachel by the hand as he walked towards her father. Just a short few feet away he let go of her hand and she flew into her father's arms. Tears and words of joy and love could be heard coming from that moment of happiness as the two were reunited. Longthorn was a large man and his powerful arms were wrapped around his daughter holding her tightly to her chest as hot tears streamed down his face. They were tears of joy and love, tears of release. He had his daughter back and he was going to do everything in his power to ensure that evil would never reach out and touch his child again. He pulled his face from her soft head of hair and looked at the emotionless face of the man who stood before him.

'I owe you for two lives, young man. I would have died if your operation had not been a success.' He continued to caress his daughter's head to his chest and she maintained her grip on him. 'I will never be able to thank you enough for what you have done for us. I will ensure that this unit will never want for anything. I will budget each year for a special donation to be made to this unit so that you will always be capable and ready to hit people like those bastards who took Rachel. Sir, I thank you from the bottom of my heart.'

Regan was slightly taken aback and reached to grasp the extended hand that Longthorn was offering and by doing so, he cemented the future, financially at least, of Dark-Eye. Longthorn was known to be a tough competitor in business but more so he was known as an honest man. Regan could feel that in the handshake and felt relieved that such a man as Trevor Longthorn deemed the operation a success.

'Thank you, Sir. Maybe we should move to the hanger and have Rachel checked by our medical team and we can go over some of the points of the contact with you.'

'Good. Back to the hanger then.' Longthorn took his gaze from Regan and looked at his bodyguards. ' What about them? Are the allowed back on there feet?'

A smile broke out onto Regan's face as he looked at the bundle of men on the ground. He was quiet sure that they felt embarrassed enough as it was without making them feel any worse in front of their boss. They hadn't done anything wrong just that Dark-Eye had done everything very right. He walked over to Epps and offered his hand as an aid to get up. Epps took the pro-offered hand and raised himself slowly upwards until he was at full stretch. He shook himself down as he watched his men get up in the same careful manner and felt in awe at the man standing before him.

'You would have killed us if we didn't drop the weapons quick enough,' he asked.

'Yes.'

'Delta?'

'Better.'

'No shit. I believe you.'

'Come on to the hanger for the debriefing. You will need to hear the details of what happened so that you can be prepared for the next time. After that, maybe tomorrow, we can show you and your men a few tricks of our trade.'

In a few quiet words and in his own way, Regan had just advised Longthorn to keep the men as bodyguards. Longthorn hadn't missed the subtlety of the act and admired the young man even more for the gentle and intelligent way that his men had their egos nursed back into shape.

They arrived at the hanger within five minutes and were met by senior officers and a medical team. Everything had been set up to deal with the girl as soon as she was back in safe hands.

'Rachel, you can go with these people and take a shower and get checked out. I will be waiting here for you when you are ready to go home. Don't worry, honey, I am not going to go anywhere and you will be safe with these fine people.' He kissed her on the cheek and she allowed herself to be taken through a door to a shower and medical area.

Longthorn turned to Regan as soon as Rachel was out of earshot. His eyes burned with a fury that only a father could muster.

'Show me the proof, young man.'

Regan reached down to the pocket where he had placed the bag of thumbs and withdrew them out and put them on the table. Next he plugged the small micro-camera into the powerful laptop that was on the table and downloaded the images in seconds.

The look on Longthorn's face did not change as he looked at the severed thumbs on the table before him but the images on the screen of the lightweight laptop made him take a step back. The images were of real men, men who no longer lived or breathed but who were now a part of a remote Colombian mountaintop. The first image shown was of the first killed by Regan. On his back, with his freshly butchered hand on his chest, his eyes gazed into a darkness that was unknown to the living. The wound to his hand seemed a lot more gruesome than the perfectly bored hole just above the right eyebrow. The rain that fell so frequently on those mountains was not responsible for the dark puddle that the head lay in and Longthorn did not need any confirmation of that. The rest of the pictures gave all the confirmation that the man required.

'Five in all?'

'No, sir. The initial number, as far as our intel was concerned, was five. However, the time constraints involved, coupled with the speed at which this mission had to be carried out, caused an oversight. As we were dealing with the five holding your daughter, a second group arrived on the scene. The total killed was in the region of eighteen. I will go over the tapes from the choppers and give you an exact number.'

Longthorn held his chin in his hand as though deep in thought. 'Eighteen in all. Maybe more, maybe less. You killed these men a few short hours ago and there is very little in the way of emotion or even elation that the mission was a success. Why do I feel that you are not telling me something?'

'In effect, you are correct. The mission was not a complete success if you view it from a point of view that we wished to have no loose ends. We cleaned the area in question and the jungle will take care of the rest. However, the fact that Rachel believes that the organiser of the kidnapping is still at large puts a whole new slant on the situation. I shall be reporting to my seniors that the mission is not complete.'

'Not complete?' Asked Longhorn.

'We will have to discuss the details with Rachel as she will, I hope, be able to identify who was responsible. From there we will view what we can do about closing the book on this mission. I want to do this, Mr. Longthorn and I am sure that both you and Rachel feel the same way as well. As soon as she is willing and able to discuss the matters in more detail I hope we will have the opportunity to do so.'

'I will do whatever you will advise, Mr. Regan. I will do and pay for whatever you advise.'

'You have already paid, Mr Longthorn. The mission will be closed on our account. And we will close that account, Sir,' the soldier assured.

4

Make it right.

Izzo slid the last few meters through the mud to the flap of the tent. His mind was racing as fast as his feet as he clawed the flap back to reveal the body of the young girl once more. He didn't want to look at the body again but he knew he had to. Being questioned by the young reporter up the slope caused a brain rush, which he could swear was almost physical. The dead girl was a reporter who he had spoken to some months ago. He now had a rush of information to deal with as his eyes tried, again, to deal with the image before him. It was becoming clear.

The doctor looked up as he was scraping samples from the nails of the young girl.

'What's up detective? I didn't expect to see you for a few days.'

'I know her, Doc. I met her some time ago in my office. I can't remember exactly what she wanted but she had been quite vocal,' replied Izzo.

'Where is she from then? What is her name?' asked Reno.

'I can't remember but I know that she is, was, a reporter in Rome. She herself was Irish if I remember correctly. She had a fantastic smile and beautiful eyes. This was no way for her to die. Christ, it is no way for anyone to die,' he corrected.

He now knew where to start looking and at the very least he knew where to send the body of the young lady. But first he had to contact the Irish embassy in Rome. Or was it British? Did the Irish have an embassy in Italy. He knew very little about that little island up north except they had a great midfielder playing for his beloved Juve back in the early eighties. He would find out a lot more in the time to come. He would have to, as he knew that there was something big about the case that was clawing at his mind. He knew that things were going to change.

'I have to phone the embassy and advise them of the situation. I shall keep you updated, Dr. Reno.'

'Thanks,' he replied as he continued the grim task of taking samples.

The following morning at the door of a large house in a southern suburb of Dublin, a tall officer of the Garda, the police service of the Republic of Ireland, pushed the doorbell and heard the ring from deep inside the house. He was hoping that there was nobody at home as he did not wish to deliver the news that he had for the occupants of the house. Even having the sobering effect of the elderly priest beside him did not take away the horrid feeling. Nobody liked to deliver such news.

The door opened quickly and an elderly man looked impatiently at the two men standing before him. It was obvious that the man standing before them held their uniforms in no great reverence.

'What can I do for you two gentlemen?' He asked with clear precision of a man for whose time cost money.

'Mr. Regan?' asked the young Garda.

'Doctor Regan, young man. Now what can I do for you and your serious friend? Will it make it easier for you if I ask you both in? I am sure, by now, that I know why you are here.'

The priest finally spoke and accepted the offer to step indoors. 'I am sorry that we have to disturb you, Dr. Regan, but I am afraid that we must speak to you and Mrs. Regan.' He hoped that Mrs. Regan was not a doctor as well and thus fall into the same trap as the young Garda.

'Mrs. Regan is dead. Please step into the living room.' The reply was surgically cold and concise. He said it with the same emotion as one describing the weather or the flavor of a dull wine. This was going to be a difficult few minutes.

The three men entered the living room and Dr. Regan pointed to a dark leather couch where his two guests could be seated. There was nothing jovial about their host and that situation was not going to improve any time soon.

'Father, may I offer you a drink? I am sure that the young officer must refuse as he is still on duty,' Dr. Regan finally offered with a hint of a smile on his face.

'No, thank you' Replied father Jim Thomson. He did not drink and wished to get the news delivered.

'Relax, Father. I know why you are here and I am sorry for you both that you have to pain yourselves with delivering news of such a selfish person.'

Father Jim and the young Garda could not help but trade glances with each other. This was not going well and worse, how could he know already that his daughter was dead.

'Selfish seems quiet harsh when one is defining one's own flesh and blood. Correct?' he asked pointedly.

Garda Mike O' Brien didn't know how to answer. The man before him was obviously angry at life and now had lost his daughter as well as his wife.

'When you raise a child and they disappear without reason anger is a strong factor in your life. I am sorry that I may seem cold and uncaring but I have been waiting for two men like you to call at my door for the last six years. More if you consider the actions of that fool. How did my son die?' asked the doctor.

'Your son?' Garda O' Brien asked with a confused look on his face.

'Yes, yes. My son. John Cathal Regan. How did the young fool die?' the doctor asked impatiently as though trying to finish the chapter in some disturbing book.

'We have not come here to discuss your son, Dr. Regan. We have come to speak to you about your daughter.' Replied father Jim.

'Kathy? Why would you want to speak about Kathy?' His world began to fall apart before his eyes as the recognition of reality hit home. 'What is wrong with my little girl?'

'Dr. Regan, I am afraid that your daughter died in Italy yesterday. We have, with the help of the Italian authorities, identified her remains and shall have them flown home as soon as possible. I am so sorry to be the bearer of such news. I cannot imagine how you feel.' These were the words of comfort from the priest. Not one of the words passed through the ears of the Doctor.

'My little girl is dead?' he asked incredulously. ' No, no, Sir. You are wrong. Kathy is not dead, you fool. I spoke to her only a few short days ago. How can you say that a hard working loving girl, a young mother, is dead?'

There was no reply from the two guests. They knew that the hardest was yet to come for the man that sat before them. His life, as he ever knew it, was now ruined and the remnants lay in the hands of God. And one other.

Izzo sat in his office, his heavy head held in his manly hands. The image of the young Irish girl was imprinted on his mind forever and he understood why. It was his fault. There was no other way to look at it but that it was his fault. The heavy bound folder that she had dropped on his desks a few short weeks before sat staring him accusingly in the face. He understood that his world was now turned on its head. His desire to join the hunt for terrorists in his country was now going to come true. True to the terms of that ancient Chinese proverb, he had wished too hard for something and it had happened. Except it was horrific and he, now, had to deal with it.

'How did she die?' he asked.

'We, at this point, Sir, are still unable to answer that question. We are still awaiting reports from the Italian police that will ultimately pass through the Irish Embassy onto ourselves. And then to you,' answered the Garda.

'Kathy is dead. Jack is alive, I suppose, and Kathy is dead. It doesn't make any sense to me. Why has she died and he still lives. There is no sense to it all.'

'Who is Jack?' asked the priest.

'Jack is my only son. He is probably dead but I will never know now. Kathy was his only world. She was the only thing that would have brought him back. If something bad had happened to her it was the only way that we, I now I suppose, could be sure that he would come home. He loved her with an aggressive passion. No, not aggressive, more a true brotherly love that he could not show to his parents. Not towards me, at least,' he added as his voice began to break under the strain.

It wasn't to be the only thing to break under the strain. Deep within his chest the lining of his heart was stretching under the pressure of the heavy flow of blood that was being pushed through the already weakened aorta. Something had to give and unfortunately, in front of his two guests, it did. He blacked out and slumped to the floor as the blood from his ruptured aorta flooded his chest cavity.

The two guests were quick to react to the obvious heart attack that was occurring before their eyes and an ambulance was quickly called to the scene.

The elderly doctor had not much time left but an attempt would be made to save his life as he had done for others in the past.

The sleek black Mercedes slipped into the empty parking space in the car park of Blackrock clinic. It wasn't out of place there as the rest of the cars parked in that secure zone were of the same quality or above. Blackrock clinic was the private hospital to the wealthy in Ireland. If you couldn't be treated successfully there then you would be expected to make your peace quickly with God before he called you.

The man who withdrew himself gracefully from the Mercedes was twenty years younger than his client who was lying in a bed in the cardiac unit inside the clinic. He was twenty years younger but looked younger still. His bearing was of a man who knew what he was doing and knew where to do it. Yet, he did not want to see this client now. His client had become a good friend and now death was calling him. With a heavy heart Steve Watson closed the door of his car and walked to the main doors of the clinic.

Dr. John Regan was lying in his bed in a private room with an army of doctors and nurses checking everything and anything that may have been overlooked after his surgery. The procedure was carried out with cold professionalism of a young surgeon who had trained under Regan. He said that it had been an honour to carry out the operation. However, while he had physically put the elderly doctor back together he didn't hold much hope for his survival. He could feel that the man did not want to live. He had heard the news after surgery that young Kathy was dead and that was the final straw for the man who had given so much to everybody. He didn't think that Dr. Regan would last the week. Infact, he was not to last the night.

Steve Watson approached the bedside wary of the tubes that seemed to have grown out of the man who lay before him. He looked down at the man who had befriended him ten years ago in the very same clinic. Watson had arrived in the clinic under orders from the senior partner. He had won his first case in Dublin after arriving from a large firm in London. The celebrations were going well until Steve felt a sudden discomfort in his chest. The unbelievable was happening, or so it seemed. The senior partner was quick to drive his expensive new junior partner to the Clinic for tests with his own personal surgeon, Dr. John Regan. The results were to draw smiles from all departments. Steve Watson had nothing worse than a bad case of indigestion. The change from his usual diet in London to the fat filled cholesterol time bomb that was the Irish diet had confused his digestion system.

However, the surgeon was not convinced and had spent time talking to the young lawyer seeking to find any other problems. There was something that just wasn't coming out in the conversation. Doctors were paid to notice these things even though the most professional of liars would never think or realise that. Dr. John Regan was about to discuss that fact again with Steve Watson.

He came out of his deep sleep still in pain. He understood all the sensations that he was feeling at the moment and felt regret. He knew that he was going to die. Not because of the quality of the surgery but because regardless of the repairs done to his damaged heart, it was already too late as the death of his daughter had already broken his heart beyond the abilities of any heart surgeon. He was ready to die now but he wanted to speak to his young lawyer before he died and so he had instructed his former colleagues to contact his as soon as possible.

'How are you?'

'Great. How do you think I am, Steve? I am dying. That much is clear to me. My daughter is dead and that much is clear to me too,' he wheezed.

'I am sorry, John. The news is starting to break about Kathy. I tried to contact a few friends in the papers and television in an attempt to close the stories down. It seems that I have been unsuccessful in that front and I apologise for that.'

'Time to cut through the shit, Watson,' the dying man wheezed. "I want to clear the air of a few problems before I die and you are going to do that for me. I am going to be direct with you and I ask you to be the same with me.'

'Of course, John. I ...understand what you are saying and know where you are coming from but you are far from dead yet.'

'Are you a fucking doctor as well as a spy now Steve?' he spat through clenched teeth.

Watson was taken aback and didn't know what to say. A thousand lies formed from years of experience, rushed to his through in defence.

'Don't even bother. I have known for years what you have been looking for. I could never give it to you but you can have him now. I want you to bring him home so that he can face his past. He will also have to deal with the realities that face him now. There is no one left to mind Kathy's little boy, Jack. He will have to do that. But, yes, you can have him now,' he said sadly.

'John, what are you saying?' Steve asked incredulously.

'Damn you Steve you know what I am saying. From the moment you came in here with your chest pains I knew that you were looking for my son. I knew that no matter where he went after what happened here that someone from your side would come looking for him. It has been my recurring nightmare. You were just to bloody fit and healthy for anything to be wrong with you. When I questioned you on your lifestyle your answers were inconclusive, you stuttered from one implausible answer to the next.' He had to pause for a breath and then continued. 'Did you come here to catch him or kill him, Steve? What would you have done if he ever had come home? Would you have come to the home of a friend and shoot his son on the doorstep or would you British secret agent types have used some other method to exterminate the enemy?'

Steve Watson looked at the man who really had become his friend in recent years and decided to be honest with him.

'Yes, John. I came here to find young Jack. I was just to find him and identify him to your police force. I didn't come here to kill him, John. Just to find him. Anyway, we lost interest in him as the peace process advanced and the trail had just gone dead anyway.'

'Are you really a lawyer at all, Steve?'

'Yes, actually. I was recruited from Oxford and trained as a corporate lawyer at the same time that I trained with SIS,' he answered truthfully. 'It was a hell of a time for me jumping from one life to another trying to keep it secret from my family. Bloody nuisance actually.'

'Well I need you to be my lawyer again. My will remains much the same except that the majority of it now goes to baby Jack. I want him to be secure for the future as he is going to grow up without parents or grandparents.'

'We can do that now if you wish in the presence of someone else here. Maybe one of your surgeon friends.' Offered Watson.

'That would be good. I want that aspect closed before we go on to further issues.'

'What would that be then?'

'I want you to find Jack. I want you to find him but not bring him home. I want you to…unleash him on those who killed Kathy. I want him to clean the slate by cleaning their slates. I want revenge, Steve. I want bloody, horrible, awful revenge and, in the name of God, that little bastard is going to get it for me. He is going to make up for all the shit he put me through and he is going to do it. I know that you can find him somehow and let him know that his father and sister are dead. He won't particularly care about me passing on but he will care that some little prick in Italy has killed his sister. I need for him to know that. I need for him to know that at the end I was thinking of him and that I wanted him to do something for me. In that way, and only in that way, can he have my forgiveness. No other way can he gain my forgiveness.'

Steve looked at his friend as the life began to slip slowly away from him and decided that for once he would put his friends before his Queen. He drew up the new will immediately in front of two surgeons and had his friend sign it in front of them. That part of the deal was to be the easiest part of the man's desires. The rest was to pull him into a world of death and deceit where only tragedy would exist. He was smart enough to know that.

The first names to an international death warrant had been signed and as the ink began to dry the first casualty of the new order was taken. Dr. John Regan, surgeon, died with his wishes to be fulfilled by an English agent and a son who might have been dead for all that anyone knew.

Chapter 5.

Finding Shadows

On the far side of the Atlantic discussions were under way in a secured room in a seemingly disused army base. All the men and women seated around the table were experts in their own specialised fields and, in many cases, in others fields as well. The voices were all steady and controlled as this was not a political meeting but a meeting of military minds.

The discussion centred on the mission to Colombia to rescue young Rachel Longthorn. Not all in the room agreed with the mission but all were happy that it had been completed without casualties on the side of Dark-Eye. They had been in operational existence for nearly two years and had not suffered casualties in combat. That would not last forever and all those in the room knew that. None more so than the young man who had grabbed the girl from the jungle.

Regan was seated in the second circle surrounding the inner table where the chiefs sat. He was listening to the conversation coming to its conclusion and felt the anger beginning to brew. He felt that the unit was going to close the book on the Colombian encounter so that no details would emerge in the press. The fact that the girl had been taken had never reached the news and that was the way that Mr. Longthorn wanted it to stay. He didn't like the way that the mission was to be concluded and urged himself to speak.

'Is the mission over?' he asked quietly.

'Yes. There is nothing left for us to do on that subject. It was a success and trying to tie up the loose ends will cause the fabric of secrecy to fray,' replied one of the senior officers.

'With all due respect, Sir, fuck secrecy. We are not confined by government and should not act like we are. Ms. Longthorn advised me that we didn't get the leader. She has the details we require to identify him and we should do that. We can snatch him from wherever he is at this time and make him disappear. Make the whole issue disappear so that there will never be the possibility that it might return to bite us. We owe it to ourselves and to what we believe to do this, Sir.'

'We can talk about this later, soldier. Let us conclude this meeting like gentlemen.'

Regan stood up, faced his commanding officer and saluted. He turned briskly in his heel and left the room. He left in a cloud of anger that was palpable in the room.

'Is he under control?'

'If not, he will be.'

Dark-Eye was going to feel political interference for the first time in its existence and that did not bode well for future operations.

Izzo was sitting at his desk tapping his pen against the glass paperweight resting on one of the many files spread on his table. He could not remember where the file had gone to or what he had done with it. Had he passed it onto someone else or had he binned it? He hoped to God that the latter had not occurred. He wanted that slim file back in his hands so that he could get a start on the investigation. He had already been in contact with the newspaper where the girl had worked and had gotten her name and contact details quickly enough. He had called his colleagues in Rome to pass by the apartment and collect an address book or something like that so that he could find out who they could contact in order to collect the girl's remains and belongings. He knew that the Irish embassy was also doing that but he had to do something even if it was duplicated effort.

The phone buzzed him out of his thoughts and his hand darted across his desk and grabbed the receiver. It was one of the detectives from Rome with news that would further complicate the investigation. The girl had a young child. Izzo felt sick.

'I will get back onto the embassy and see what they have to say. Thanks for all your help.' He hung up.

Steve Watson walked down the footpath from the graveyard to his car holding the arm of his fiancé. His eyes had welled up at the end of the ceremony as the body of his friend had been lowered into its final resting place. It had been a small ceremony but one that he would never forget. He had been thinking of the pact that he had made with John Regan before he had died and now wished that he hadn't made it to the hospital on time. That sentiment shamed him and he squeezed his fiancés arm for support. She had known Steve long enough and decided not to ask any questions until later. She never understood the relationship between the two men but never inquired any more than she needed to in order to seem politely interested. There was a lot more to her man than she was really willing to know or understand. She was, for the moment, happily and blissfully unaware of the troubles that were in Steve's mind.

He on the other hand, was trying to build a mental framework for the task ahead. The search for Jack Regan had gone cold with the French Foreign Legion where it was rumoured that he had died in combat while trying to save the life of a friend. If that story had been true why had it never reached the papers? Why was it only available to those who were really seeking the whereabouts of Jack Regan? It was available because it was untrue. Regan was not dead. He had disappeared into the world of Black Operations. He was a betting man and he would have bet his life that that was the truth about the disappearance of Jack Regan. He had to find him and he knew where to start the hunt again.

Except now he was hunting a man who, in his mind, was now a 'Black bag' soldier. He was no longer the young idealist that had wandered into the arms of the Provisional IRA. This was going to be a tough number to deal with and he would have to back to London to start his inquiries.

They were back at base now that the post operation meetings had been dealt with. The helicopters had landed without any fuss and the men had disembarked with their kit bags and jogged to their holding quarters. There, those who had not been on the mission looked at the men who were coming in and knew that the mission was a success.

'How did it go?' one asked from his bed.

'Cleanly.' Came the reply.

'Good, good.'

The mission was never discussed. It was understood to be the best way in dealing with security. A mission was never discussed after the fact unless under the supervision of a senior officer. Girlfriends and wives knew very little of what the Envoys did and the men never discussed the missions off base. It was better that way.

Jack Regan dropped his kit bag onto his bed and turned to walk to the armoury to check his weapon. He was in a dark humour and wanted to be free of any discussion.

'Hey, Regan, how did it go? Bring any souvenirs back for me?' came the cheeky voice of Stephane, Frenchie as he was known to the rest of the squad. He knew that Regan would not ignore his old friend from the Legion.

'Sorry, Frenchie, the had nothing worth bringing back to you kids. The chocolate back there was worse than that shit you call chocolate in Paris. I wasn't in Switzerland unfortunately, where they make real chocolate,' he replied knowing that he would raise his friend by berating French chocolate.

'Ha! You would not know quality unless it came out of a beer keg you uncouth Irishman,' came the French reply. He loved his French chocolate as much as Irishmen liked their beer but would take the ribbing without losing his famous temper. It would not be good to lose his temper now as he saw the look in Regan's eyes. He could see that something was wrong and decided to let the man go on his way.

'Go on your way Irishman and clean your little gun. I might let you pay for a beer later. I haven't decided yet,' was the last comment from Frenchie.

'Funny little Frenchman,' smirked Regan as he left the room.

He walked over to the armoury unloading his weapon as he walked. He wouldn't allow his mind to wander to the evening before because he needed to rest and dwelling on that evening would prevent that. He would check in his weapon and call it a night. He would get some sleep.

'Just checking my baby in, Max. I won't be a minute,' he told the Sergeant at the desk. He signed his name beside the release date and handed the sniper rifle back in. It would be cleaned and recalibrated in the machine room within the hour in case it was required to speak the mind of its guardian again before the day was over.

Once finished in the armoury, Regan decided that a beer would help him sleep and so he decided to chance his arm for a very late one in the mess. That was not really going to be a problem as the base was open 24-7. Just finding a quite spot in the mess with a cold beer was good enough for him. He didn't need conversation this early in the morning, he just needed to wind down.

He walked through the door and straight up to the bar. The mess itself was far from empty as the other men on the same mission had the same idea as he had. The men were in small groups playing cards, pool or just chatting among themselves, simple conversations from complex minds. Some nodded in his direction others winked an acknowledgement at him. They all new that he preferred to be alone after a mission. In fact, they all knew that he preferred to be alone in general.

'A bottle of whatever is cold please,' he asked. He took the bottle and walked to the TV room. As he expected, the room was empty and he sat into one of the comfortable chairs and swapped his bottle for the remote control. He flicked onto the Discovery channel and wished he didn't. *'How the Towers fell'* was been screened again and it made for terrible viewing. Regan could not help but to watch the planes fly into the Towers from the many different angles and the collapse and the mayhem that followed. His head slipped back into his hands as the horror of it all crept back into his soul. The pressure of the moment was being pushed to breaking point within his head and he hated the sensation. The feeling of failure over the evening before was combining with the sense of futility that he felt at the mention or the sight of the Twin Towers. His eyes gave up and the tears of frustration rolled down his face. He tried to control it but the dam had burst. He could not, like with targets, place them at different levels of importance. A target was a target was a target. He was never on the team that was hunted Bin Laden but understood the frustration of getting near and yet being so far to closure. His tears crept their silent path down his face.

'Regan?' asked a quite voice as he heard the door close behind him. ' Are you ok here, Buddy?' asked his commander, Stan Petersen.

Regan wiped his eyes quickly and looked up at Petersen the anger and confusion taking the place of his tears in his solid eyes.

'Just hard to watch it again, Sir, and not feel helpless. We, you guys I mean, could have stopped it. The signs were there that the bastard would try again. Sir.' Petersen looked at his most respected soldier, a young man who had no country and no family. He could not help but feel fatherly towards him.

'Let it go, son. We all have to let it go and live on. We can only win in that way. Not all the battles are in the field or on the streets. Hell, you aren't even an American.'

Regan looked up with a pained look in his eyes that cut to the soul of the man before him. The reply left no misunderstanding as to where the loyalties of the young soldier lay.

'We were all American that day, Sir.'

The following morning a meeting was convened in the communications bunker five floors beneath ground level. The room was large and spacious to make up for the lack of natural light but yet felt crowded to the ten men who sat around the oval marble table where the decisions of each day were made. Dark-Eye was more than Top-Secret; the existence would never be admitted, could not be admitted, as the targets were highly sensitive and politically ruinous in certain cases. DEVGRU, the supreme anti-terror task force was still held as the ultimate weapon of counter terrorism along with Delta Force and the British SAS regiment but EYE, as the insiders called it, was one step beyond. The men involved were all dead, officially. They were not away on official business or tasked to special force units elsewhere. They were all officially dead. They had all been buried with full military honours in their respective countries, with a couple of exceptions when the body could not be recovered.

Regan was one of those who had not received a military funeral and he was now the centre of discussion of the men who were around the oval table. Secretary of Defence, Paul Borden, was one of those men.

'How is he, Petersen? Has he developed as we expected?' asked Borden.

'Sir, he has developed beyond what we expected. He is the mould we will use for the development for the others and those who will follow. He is the complete soldier. He thinks on the ground like a general playing chess and fights with control and precision. It is my opinion that the young man in question if far beyond our expectations and initial hopes,' came the reply.

'How about his past? Does that effect him and will it come back to haunt us?' was the next question.

'It is my belief, Sir, that his past is exactly just that. His past. I understand that he keeps himself up to date with all that is still going on in Ireland but only as much as he does with everything else that happens in the world. It may be,' he paused to ensure that the answer was sufficiently clear, '...judicious of us to inform the British some day as to what happened to their most wanted man but to date we have all the indications that they believe that he is already dead. The incident with the Legion should have secured that.'

Borden then dropped his bombshell.

'They are actively looking for him again. We have received an inquiry, through the usual intelligence sources, as to his whereabout. The British were not that quick to leave the scent behind or, if they were, they are back on it again. The President is concerned and hence I am here. What do you suggest?'

Petersen was momentarily taken aback but his mind was equal to the task.

'It is my belief, Sir, that 'Plausible deniability' is no longer plausible. We either allow the Brits to know what happened or we smoke screen,' came the levelled reply.

'We might just let it go for a while and see how far they are willing to push. The French continue to assert that there was no body in the field but that was not extraordinary, as seven of their men didn't return that day. I believe it was a hell of a fire fight,' he answered.

'Any indication why they are looking for him? Has something happened that gave them the idea that he is alive and well and back fighting? Christ, worst of all, do we have a leak?' came Petersen's reply.

'No leak. We just have to keep it in mind.'

Steve Watson sat in his office sifting through old reports that made interesting reading even though he had read them until it seemed that the ink had been worn off the pages by his eyes. The young man that he felt was still alive had been quite a bit of work in his time in Ireland. The more he looked at the report the more he knew that Regan was alive. But who had him and why?

The 'Why' aspect was easy enough. Regan had to have been taken under the wing of some specialist operations group or even the intelligence community of some country that identified his skills as those that were been wasted under the control of the Foreign Legion. Watson had read the reports of how Tenant, when head of the CIA, had recreated the paramilitary section of his organisation. The Special Operations Group, SOG, was back in business and the forerunner in the tracking down of Osama Bin Laden. Would Regan have been drafted into that unit? He wasn't an American so the answer had to be no. It could have been the French but that seemed unlikely as they had a distrust of foreigners. The British? He laughed at that idea. He had been sent to kill Regan before and not to arrest the young man. Who was it then?

A new attachment to the file stared at him as he sat staring into space. His eyes wandered down to it and the first creeping of an idea came into his tired mind. He took the sheet of paper into his hand and read.

'Garda and Irish Military intelligence sources are still attempting to unravel the circumstances surrounding the killing of five suspected FFI terrorists in an isolated farmhouse outside the small town of Kildare in the Republic of Ireland. Only one member of the unit survived the attack which was brutal in its speed and precision. The survivor, John Maher, was hospitalised with minor injuries that were not ballistic in nature. Three days later the FFI announced that it was disbanding, as it believed that its war had ended. A week later a large cache of weapons was discovered and destroyed by the Irish armed forces.'

Watson had a sudden desire to interview Maher, who was locked away in a high security prison in Portlaoise. The report that he had just read was from the Irish Times and had added that the PIRA had, in order to further its own role in the continuing peace talks, wiped out the unit that had been killing around the border counties. However, Watson's contacts within the PIRA had denied the incident though one had expressed his wish that they had been indeed involved.

Watson had initially believed that it had been the SAS but that line of thought had drawn a blank. He wanted to talk to Maher and knew the man who would let him. He had a favour to pull.

Two days later, Steve Watson walked into the office of the Warden of Portlaoise High Security Prison. It had been a while since his last visit and he was amused that the place had received a fresh coat of paint. The Warden, Jeff Dunne, strode confidently to him and warmly shook his had.

'Steve, it is so good to see you. How are you?' Dunne asked with genuine delight.

'Still pulling the Devil by the tail, as you Irish love to say. I like the paint job,' he smiled.

Steve Watson had played a critical role in the return of Jeff Dunne's youngest daughter who had been kidnapped by a Dublin gang wishing to have one of their own released. Watson had walked into the house where she had been held and negotiated her release. The three men holding her walked out after him without their weapons and quickly surrendered to the armed Garda unit that was waiting outside. Getting into the Garda car one of them had turned to Watson and said 'You crazy bastard.'

It was never known what he had said to them.

'What can I do for you, Steve?' asked Dunne, knowing that he would do anything the man asked.

'Cutting straight to the point, Jeff, I need to speak to John Maher. I need to speak to him straight away and in isolation. No recorders, no guards, no one but him. He may have something I need and I am going to get it from him.'

Jeff Dunne picked up his phone and called a senior guard.

'Bring Maher up to my office straight away, Ray, with as little fuss as is possible,' he ordered politely down the line. 'This will be as private as you can get, Steve, Ray will walk him through the door in two minutes and I shall leave you to alone. I don't need or want to know what is to be said and I trust you are not going to run away with him,' he smiled at his friend.

In two minutes there was a soft knock on the door and the senior staff guard poked his head around the door and nodded to Dunne.

'He is all yours, Steve. Just press the red button on the dial when you are finished and I shall come back.' He walked to the door, took the handle in his hand and glanced once at Watson before walking out.

Watson took Dunne's seat behind the large oak desk while listening to the murmurs from outside the door. He sat back into the comfortable seat and prepared himself.

The door opened and Maher, without cuffs or chains, walked slowly into the room and turned to face Watson.

'And who might you be, Sir?' he asked in a soft Northern accent while his eyes darted around the room.

'Take a seat, Mr. Maher, make yourself comfortable. I am going to be very quick as I do not wish to waste your time,' replied Watson in a voice void of emotion.

'Englishman, sure I have all the fucking time in the world to waste in here. It is not that I have any where to go, is it?'

Watson beckoned to the chair before him and Maher stepped lightly into it.

'I want to know about the night that your friends were killed, Mr Maher. I need this information quickly and I really don't care how I get it.

'Ah, go fuck yourself backwards, Englishman,' spat Maher with venom in his voice.

Watson's hand moved in a blur of motion and Maher barely recognised the danger for what it was before he felt the silenced round splatter off his ear from the pistol that was firmly held in Watson's trained hand. He buckled in pain and screamed in shock, as he understood what had happened. He was about to raise his head but it was grabbed from behind and reefed back and upwards into the glowering eyes of Watson.

'You shot my fucking ear off you crazy bastard. What the fuck did you do that for?' he asked through clenched teeth.

'Count yourself lucky, Maher, I was aiming for the other one. Now you are going to be a nice fellow to me, aren't you dear boy,' came the chilling reply.

Maher nodded his agreement as the silenced barrel of the Sig Sauer pistol slid down to his groin.

Watson walked back to the desk as Maher struggled somewhat with the blood pumping from his ear. The necessity of the violent action was not lost on Watson. He was not a violent man by nature but he had to get the information quickly and Maher understood violence. He hoped that it was going to be worth it.

'So, who did it?' he asked politely.

'It was quick. Whoever did it was professional and so as I lay on my back with a boot in my neck I figured it was you boys, or at least the SASmen. It was only when the one with his boot in my neck started to speak to me that I figured it was our own guys. Not PIRA, or anyone like that, but I thought it was the Army Rangers. They were professionals and, as good as PIRA were at one time, they were not as good as these guys. He was Irish and so I thought that Dublin had grown a pair and ordered the Rangers out after us. The boys were dead before I understood what was happening and I was wondering why I was alive,' Maher replied.

'You think he was Irish?'

'Am certain of it. You can't mistake the accent but it was a clean accent. Educated, like. He was a big man, not like a body builder but fit. He couldn't speak to me through his respirator and so he took it off. I thought he was going to kill me then because when you see the faces of those Special Forces you can generally believe that they are not going to let you stay around to identify them.'

'What did he look like?' asked Watson as he tried to hide his excitement, feeling that he was getting closer. He had felt as soon as he believed that Regan was alive that he had somehow been involved in that raid. Maybe it was his way of paying back for his past. Cleaning out his closet.

'His face was blackened but I suppose that I would recognise it again but, to that extent, I hope I don't have to. He leaned into my face and told me that my war was over. He said that if he didn't hear that notification in two days he would walk into the hospital and shoot me in front of my family. After the declaration I was to wait a week before identifying our weapons bunker. He said that would save me. That, and only that. He said that there was no use in complaining about what had happened, no use complaining to the authorities. He said that he and his men were the new authority in the world of terrorism and the rules had changed. No more sending messages. He was a serious fucker.'

'So you followed his orders. Simple as that?' asked Watson now even more interested.

'I had no other choice. One of the others going through the pockets told him to shoot me but he smiled and said 'No'. It was at that point that I really felt frightened. He was able to smile after what he had done and speak with absolute authority to the others. Yes, in that moment I thought that I was going to die. What a fuck-up. He broke my two legs instead. He said he couldn't let me off without some warning and so he broke my legs with his bare hands and knocked me out with one blow to the head. I am surprised that I am still alive,' came the end of the admission.

'So am I, Mr. Maher, so am I. Is there anything else you feel I should know?'

'Yeah, the guy who suggested that he should shoot me wasn't Irish,' he offered.

'Well?' came the question in anticipation.

'It was an American accent.'

Chapter 6.

Through Darkened Eyes.

There was no loud hailer or siren. It was a simple vibration felt on the wrist of each active soldier. It was an electronic signal that announced to all on duty at that moment that something was going down somewhere and that they were being called into action. The bracelet was their pager and the first sign that action was imminent.

Regan was lying on his bed when he felt the electronic vibration and he was on his feet in an instant. He activated the video screen by his bedside and saw the flash traffic scroll across his screen. He read the first report and made his way to the armoury while mentally digesting the information that he had. This was not a drill and he could see others making their way to collect weapons as well.

Eight minutes later nine men were waiting between two Black Hawk choppers that were already heated and ready to move. A whole stick was to be used on this hit and so he knew that the target was important. They boarded without any comments and strapped themselves into their seats as the choppers lifted off.

'Gentlemen, we have a situation. We are flying eighty klicks due North to what has been identified as a camp for our Eastern friends. Intel has identified four individuals in the camp as being highlighted on the President's list. We are not going to interrogate. Repeat, this is a clean strike. We are dusting these individuals and sending the images to their bosses. On our time, gentlemen, but not on our ground,' came the cool order from the squad leader.

Regan understood what was being said. They were going to make the camp disappear and those in it were going to exist no longer. He sat back into his seat and tried to rest knowing that the camp in question had gotten too close to theirs and so the order was clear. Nobody was to know about Dark-Eye and these boys had gotten too close.

Each chopper had a tactical display at the front section that the men could observe. A real-time satellite view was being displayed at that moment and the men were seeing what they were going to attack. The plan was very straightforward. The men were going to be dropped two clicks downwind of the small compound. From the drop zone there were going to have to make their way, on foot, to the target and prepare for the clean up. The main firepower of the operation was going to come from the two Black Hawk helicopters. First the air power, then the ground assaults. After that, the men inside would make their peace with who or whatever they deemed God to be. Swift and Final.

'Dark-Eye are on the ground, Sir' the young lieutenant informed the Commander.

'Bring up the images on the screen. I want to see this and tape it for the Boss,' came the reply.

The Boss was a reference to the President who would want to see the latest step against terrorism and it was for the Commander to produce the evidence. He agreed with this type of operation as being necessary. There was no emotion being felt towards those who were about to die. They had not shown any emotion towards his wife when their comrades had flown an airplane through the North Tower where his wife had worked as a futures trader. He was still waiting and praying that something real of her would come from the rubble. Something that he could bury.

He watched as the nine images from the satellite image moved swiftly over the ground as dusk approached. He silently wished them God's speed.

The image was now focused to watching an area one thousand metres square. The attackers could be seen making their plans.

Regan decided to send Johnson and his sniper rifle to the rear of the compound in order to give cover fire in case anyone was to exit the building from the rear. Johnson was the finest shot he had ever seen and had the confidence in him to control the rear in case anything was to go wrong. Mark Hall, another cool customer under pressure, took position just eighty metres from the main door to cover the main assault as it was to enter the building. He decided to wait five more minutes before calling in the two choppers and their fearsome chain-guns and rockets. The darker it was the more like Hell the firestorm from the chain guns would seem. The psychological effect was like having extra fifty men. Time to open the communication links with base and all the men.

'Palace, this is Envoy 1. Birds, this is Envoy 1. We are ready to move. Birds, launch and hold at two clicks. Repeat, two clicks. Palace, Dark-Eye is GO,' came the calm voice of action of Regan.

'Envoy 1, this is Bird 1. We are holding form with Bird 2 at two clicks.'

The final order was in Regan's hands and he was ready.

'Target is clear. Roll in Birds 1 and 2. Weapons hot.' Came the order.

From two kilometres out the two choppers dropped their noses and increased the engines to full power. They would make contact in just over a minute.

Johnson, as one of the snipers and overall lookouts, had the right to eyeball a situation and call halt to an assault. Like the others, he had direct communication linkage with the choppers, the base and the rest of the men. He, therefore, knew that he had to call off the assault as he saw a vehicle approach the compound.

'Abort, abort, abort. We have visitors arriving from the southwest. I am spotting them at this moment. Abort,' he urged into his mike.

Regan slipped his night-vision goggles over his eyes and focused in on the visitors. He had already given his approval to the command from Johnson, as he knew that sniper would not have given the command unless it was entirely necessary.

Back at the base, Petersen ordered the zoom of the satellite image to be retracted so that he could see what was going wrong. He didn't realise that it was going to get worse. However, just as a precaution, he alerted the second team to be air-borne within five minutes and ready to join Team One if the case required.

Sam Cohen, the Israeli born pilot of Bird 1, was as prepared as any pilot for this mission, his first for Dark-Eye. He was recruited from the Israeli Special

Forces for his flying skills and went eagerly to the new team. He wanted the job more than anything and had proven himself a dedicated soldier as well as being an exceptional pilot.

Now, at close to one hundred and fifty kilometres an hour he had to pull his chopper away from the target before the noise could alert those in the camp. It was then that a barrage of warning lights lit up the cockpit.

Regan didn't have to look around to see if the others had halted their advance. He knew that they had all settled down in places of cover in order to wait for the all clear.

Their visitors halted in front of the main door of the building and that is when Regan decided to call base for reinforcements or at least time to affect a tactical retreat. A bus with at least twenty passengers had arrived and Regan knew that they had not come to go sight seeing. He would request back up.

What Sam Cohen did not know he was soon to find out. A multiple system failure was about to cripple his chopper at fifteen hundred feet and he was going to require all his skill to land. He knew from the pull on the controls that the aircraft had lost power to the main engines that ran the rotor blades and a surge of power had bleed into the rear stabiliser rotor. The chopper was doomed as the increased yaw caused it to bank uncontrolled, the rotors separating from the drive shaft, into a horrifying, screeching cartwheel.

'Bird 1, we are in the shit…we are going in…oh shit….'

Regan spun his head at the sound of straining metal and saw the chopper plunge to earth. The fireball lit the skyline and outlined the shapes of the men to those who had dismounted the bus carrying weapons.

Bird 2 came over the comlink. 'We have a Bird down. Repeat, Bird 1 is down.' There was no emotion in the voice. There would be time for that later as in that moment there were men on the ground who would require more assistance that the three comrades on Bird 1.

The plan had gone to Hell and the inevitable was going to happen. Dark-Eye was a counter-terrorism team. It was created to hit quickly and disappear. The pitched battle was not meant to be on their cards unless all support was cut off. The situation they were in now was going to test their ability to adjust to the situations they met. They were going to be out numbered at least three to one if they were to count those within the building but yet they were professional soldiers and all had seen combat. Two factors were going to be of real importance; one was the level of training the terrorists had received and of course, there was still Bird 2 to be brought into the equation.

Amir Dagher was a man the same age of his counterpart who was about one hundred meters away. He would never have heard of Regan but the two men were mirror images of each other. Amir had grown up in a wealthy family in Jordan and had trained to be a lawyer under the tutelage of his father. He had spent time in Yale and had been offered a job in a law firm in New York. He lost his job after 9/11 being a victim of race fear. He never loved America before then but he didn't hate it. Now he did. He no longer felt sorry for what had happened on that fateful day. In fact, he now wished that it could happen again. That was why he was back in America. He had survived Afghanistan and now was back in the belly of the beast. He was ready to fight and he believed in the military training he had received was as good as he could have received anywhere. Indeed, that was true. Before starting his studies in Jordan he had completed his military service and those who had trained him were Green Berets. American Green berets. He was ready to meet Allah and he was going to take as many infidels as possible with him.

Amir, at the sound of Bird 1 going down, instinctively drew his weapon from the holdall he was carrying and rolled back behind the engine block of the bus. He had no night vision aids but the flash had imprinted the outlines of the enemy on his mind and he opened fire in the direction of the men who were advancing on the building. The others with him were as quick to respond. Amir trained them and hence he expected no less. Those still on the bus knew that they would jam up the door getting out and so the kicked out the windows and started to fire in the direction that their leader was shooting. The air quickly filled with the sound of chattering AK-47s, a one sided battle for the moment.

This was it. There were defining moments in time that many people and groups could look back at after success or failure. For Dark-Eye, this was that moment in their time. The tide had turned against them in an instant and they had to react or be overwhelmed. For Regan there was no choice. He knew how to fight against the odds. The crashing helicopter had bought back memories of Northern Ireland to him and in an instant his mind ordered him to put those memories aside. It was time to fight the enemy.

Johnson knew the importance of his role and took pleasure in that feeling. He buzzed off the feeling of working for Dark-Eye. He felt proud of the fact that he was one of the extremely dark eyes, a sniper, of Dark-Eye. Now was his time to repay that feeling and the payment of that debt was passing through his mind, down the muscles of his trigger arm and into the trigger finger. That particular finger had an incestuous relationship with his left eye. Anything that passed between them was automatically fucked. Now they were being called into action again.

When the first Bird had hit the ground Johnson knew that things were going to get rough for the first time for Dark-Eye. It had to happen at sometime and so he tossed orders out of the window. Special Forces had a habit of doing that. They were intelligent men, all educated in some way or another. Orders fulfilled a certain task but when they went wrong, the intelligent soldier took command of himself and his surroundings. That is why they were Special Forces. They were able to think for themselves when the shit hit the fan. This was one of those times and the fan had a thick covering.

Johnson saw this moment as one of those times too. He slid through the grass like a snake on speed and took up a new position far to the right of those who had exited the bus. Far, of course, meant a different distance for different people. For Johnson and his rifle the distance was not far at all. He was close enough to smell his target and that was what he could do. Cordite from the 7.62mm rounds exiting the AK-47s mixed with the smell of vomit and urine that was wafting from those within the group who had squeezed a trigger in anger for the first time. The smell told him that the situation was real. He opened fire with Dark-Eye's first shot in anger. The effect was final.

Regan had no feeling from the chest down. It was a strange feeling as he heard his men return fire in what sounded like a scene from Dante's Inferno. His head was spinning as he realised that he was not dead but he had been hit. He had been hit in the chest but the Jacket had saved him and now he was pissed. He did not want to miss this fight and did not want to miss the opportunity to lead his men into combat. He rolled onto his stomach and then pushed himself onto his knees. His breath came back and he spun upwards towards the enemy with his night goggles back down over his eyes. The mottled green image of a target passed into his vision and he released a double tap. The image of the head of the target expanded immediately in his sights and he knew instantly that his first kill of the night had been recorded. He did not realise that the score was two – one in the first ten seconds of combat. Sergeant Mark Hall had become the first combat casualty of Dark-Eye while Regan had been grasping for breath.

Bird 2 had held back for long enough and was now racing into the fray. The pilot had decided to hold fire until he was certain of his targets. The bus was the centre of fire at that moment and he advised his weapons officer of that much. He wanted to close that target as quick as possible in order to even the odds for the guys on the ground. He felt confident that small arms fire was the only fire to be expected and so he decided to hover his craft two hundred meters from the bus and unleash hell. He was holding position as required when he depressed the trigger for the side mounted Minigun on each side of the chopper. The scream of the rotating multi-barrelled weapons could be heard over the rotors and the ugly flash poured death into the target zone. He could barely see the bus due to the muzzle flash from both sides but he was able to walk the tracers into the vehicle. Glass, rubber and steel mixed with the flying body parts as the bullets did their job. Eight of those left on the bus were shredded by the bullets before the fuel tank gave way and exploded. The fire added its own personal carnage as flames and bullets engulfed five more outside the bus. Lady luck began to shine on Dark-Eye in the form of Black Hawk Bird 2.

Regan radioed up to the chopper.

'Bird 2, hold fire and position. We need to regain our positions here.'

'Roger that, Envoy 1.'

The night vision goggles were no longer needed for the moment as the flames from the bus gave out ample light and Regan took a quick glance around. His men had gained the upper hand outside the building and the vast weight of fire was coming from Dark-Eye. Concentrated firepower was defeating the enemy quickly but the main targets would still be in the building. Regan decided that the remaining assets from the chopper would be better used on the original target, the building.

'Bird 2, re-target to original point of contact. We shall employ the remaining combatants outside with force. Hit the building, repeat, hit the building. Bring the fucker down, Bird 2.'

'Heads down, Dark-Eye. We are going to unleash Hell,' warned the pilot. And he did.

Amir Dagher shook the sound of the explosion from his ears and tried to figure up from down. He had been tossed like a rag doll by the explosion of the gas tank of the bus. He felt a searing pain in his side and could feel the warm creep of blood on his stomach and down his leg. It took a moment for him to realise what had happened and he tried to reach for his gun but his lower body wouldn't respond. The realisation that he had severe injuries dawned on him along with the immediate feeling of failure. How could Allah have allowed this to happen after all he had been through? Their plan had been compartmentalised and so nobody but the men in the compound knew what was to have been visited on the Americans. It was all to go to waste.

He pulled himself along the ground but had to halt due to the weakness through loss of blood. He heard the whoosh of rockets as they tore into the compound and exploded.

Bird 2 had unleashed her HEAT rockets in anger into the by now unprotected building. The High Explosive Anti-Tank weapons tore through the walls of the building and exploded inside. Sixteen rockets in all ripped the building apart. Those inside suffered the same fate as the building as they were torn apart by the molten lead shrapnel. It was a horrific sight but there was nobody left alive in the building to witness it. For all intents and purposes the battle was over and with it a bloody plan to attack America again.

Regan came slowly to his feet for the second time and ordered the men to cease firing. The battle had been won but not without casualties. He ordered his men to advance to the building as he walked over to the body of Mark Hall.

Hall lay slumped over his weapon, killed by a lucky shot. The bullet had passed through his forehead leaving a pool of blood on his back. Regan knelt beside his fallen comrade and gently turned the body over. Hall's eyes were still open, staring at enemies that were no longer on this earth either. To his right were three empty casings. Such a good shot was Hall that Regan knew that each bullet had found a mark. Three of them for one of his was not a fair trade. But such was war.

Regan closed Hall's eyes and stood silently and said a short prayer. He then turned and walked to his men.

He was beckoned over by Johnson who was standing over the body of a terrorist who still seemed to be alive. It was Amir Dagher.

'What shall we do with this guy,' asked the large sniper.

Regan pulled his sidearm and shot Dagher twice into the face.

'Make your peace with Hall, motherfucker,' he hissed through clenched teeth and then turned to Johnson while holstering his weapon.

'He has nothing else to say.'

'Fine by me, Regan,' came the reply.

'The same for any others that you might find. No prisoners,' he added as he walked to the building.

Johnson could not help fell a shudder of fear in the presence of his team leader. There was a hole in the air when he passed that took feeling from the body but you had to respect him. There was no BS with Regan, he considered each fight on its merits and the targets were simply targets. That was the reality of war.

The house was smoke filled though it was not burning. The men had already swept through the building and checked the two floors finding the remnants of those who had been unfortunate enough to be there when the rockets had smashed through the building. No one had, as expected, survived.

They carefully entered the cellar and found the smoking gun that they had been expecting to find.

Amir Dagher had worked hard on his plan and had come so close to seeing it come to fruition. In the basement over the previous three months he had developed a plan for a new weapon of mass destruction. On three separate tables were twenty-five completed suicide bomber units, jackets laden with explosives and ball bearings. Further inspection later would show that cobalt and sesium had been mixed with the plastique. The plan had envisioned twenty-five fighters to disperse through downtown Manhattan and at mid-day, the height of lunchtime human traffic, detonate themselves and their radioactive weapons. Dark-Eye had arrived with less than twenty-four hours to go before the attack was to be launched.

Regan felt a rush of his relief as he fingered the keys of one of the computers that were still running. This was Dark-Eye's major hit, it's first major mark against terrorism and a sense of pride swelled in the men as they reality of what they had stopped.

'Take photos of the dead, remove their teeth, then take the hands and feet for print-filing and stack the bodies down here when we have all we need out of here,' he said to the soldier who was examining one of the bomb units.

Outside, Team Two arrived in their two choppers and landed upwind from the smouldering wreck of the bus. Bird 2 stayed aloft guarding the sky not wanting to land. The pilot had not had his fill of death after the downing of Bird 1 and wanted to be ready in case anything else went wrong. He had checked the systems twice since the firefight had ceased and understood that there was nothing wrong with his bird. What had happened to Bird 1 was just an accident. The Black Hawk helicopter was a formidable aircraft and not prone to system failures. This incident would be written off as just one of those things. He continued to circle the kill-zone passing over the charred remains of the crash site of Bird 1. The smoke couldn't hide one of the crew that lay prone fifty meters from the point of impact and the sight wrenched at the heart of the pilot. Images of Somalia skidded through his conscience as he battled the urge to land his craft and hold his fallen comrade. He had had the same feelings in Somalia.

On the ground by the building he could now see that Team 2 was helping with the clean up. The men were working in two groups; the first was dealing with the bodies of the fallen while the second group were clearing away the weapons and bullet casings. It was necessary that all traces of what existed in the eight hundred square meters of the compound would disappear. The isolation of the area would aid the matter and there was very little chance that people would come snooping about.

Two hours later all the hands and feet had been bagged and tagged. Beside the gruesome stack lay a smaller bag filled with the teeth of the dead. It was a necessary act of cruelty onto the dead, as the DNA would be documented deep within the vaults of Langley, Virginia, of those who had come to do harm. The information would be added to the banks of computers and all activity and transactions of the dead would come to light. Maybe this would help trace their training grounds or suppliers. It was always the little things that broke a case and this would be no different.

Regan had, by this time, sent Team 2 back to base. They would stand down to condition three on their terror barometer. It was a level of alertness that proclaimed that the unit was ready to move out from the base, if not yet ordered to assault a target. Level two was when they were on route to a target and level one was what had happened just over two hours before. They would return to their billets to read, play cards or listen to music with the constant reality of their jobs waiting to vibrate on their wrists. Team 1 was off rotation as it had been used. They would finish the job at hand by burying the dead and destroying the compound and then they would bring Hall and the chopper crew home.

It took just over an hour to collect what they could from Bird 1. The charred remains of the co-pilot and gunner had been the hardest to face. Jan Fisher, the co-pilot, had been a giant of a man in every way. He could not help but smile and the others joked that he couldn't fly night ops because his white grin could be seen like a strobe in the darkness. Now his entire life was twelve kilos of ash and bone, a part of his helmet and a pin from his knee from his football days. The gunner, Sly Fabre, was a heavy loss as well. He was the kind of man that all soldiers respected and wanted standing behind them. He was the one who controlled the cover fire when the crap hit the fan and he was a firm disbeliever in friendly fire. He had cleared the zone for Regan during the extraction of Rachel Longthorn and was going to be missed as an integral part of Dark-Eye.

Finally, Regan walked to the crumpled remains of Jacob, the pilot. His body was twisted in a horribly unnatural position, his face angled awkwardly towards the sky. A trickle of blood had crawled a path down his cheek and had hardened across the bruising on his face and neck. It was not the way for a proud warrior to have died. He had not even had the chance to get a shot off in anger at the enemy, an enemy that was as close to him as any man. Regan knelt down and for the second time that day, closed the staring eyes of a comrade.

'It is the end of your fighting, my friend. Let us finish the battles for and in our victory will be your lasting peace.'

That was a promise that would take time to fulfil but, then, from that moment, Jacob had all the time he could wish for.

It was after midnight before Team 1 was ready to move out. Bird 2 had been returned to base and a lumbering Golly Green Giant had come as its replacement. The bodies of the four fallen men were loaded gently on board in their body bags and were lined together by the front of the massive aircraft. The rest of the men waited for Regan as he did one last check before going to the pilot side of the craft to speak to the pilot. The pilot handed him a black satchel and Regan turned and walked back to the building. At the remains of the door he turned and beckoned his men to come over. They, in unison, jogged over and came to a halt behind him.

Regan opened the satchel and removed, to the men's amazement, the Stars and Stripes and the Star of David, both folded into the familiar triangle form, and lay them on the door step one over lapping the other. Then he removed a flag that had the Shahada embroidered on it and placed it in the middle of the two flags. The fabric with the Islamic creed lay gently on the soft cotton of the flags of two great nations.

'Those who died today fought as soldiers, regardless of their beliefs. We send them to God and to peace,' he said gently to his men. He then took a laser designator from the satchel and set it on its tripod, the laser beam secretly touching the damaged support beam above the door.

'Move out, gentlemen,' and in the same breath into his radio, ' Fly 1 and 2, target is clear. Start your runs.'

Thirty thousand feet up and eight miles away two F-22A Raptors traced an invisible path across the sky towards the compound. Each one activated their passive radar and the seekers sought the laser beam that was still miles away. The doors on their bomb bays opened as soon as the target was acquired and all the systems worked as expected to recognise their target. The complexity of the aircraft's design merged with the intelligence of the targeting systems and from each plane a single JDAM fell, acquired the targets and began their whistling dive towards the door frame, thirty thousand feet below.

The men had boarded the chopper and were now strapped into their seats ready to move. Within seconds of the "all clear" the engines powered up to the maximum and the chopper lurched upwards. They were going to fly south as the Raptors flew in from the north with their loads. They large rear door was left open so the men could see the final result of the night's battle.

The electronic brains of the free fall weapons had immediately zoned in onto the laser dot that had been painted onto the target. Small adjustments were being made to the angle of the fins of the bombs as they hurtled to the ground to take into consideration the weather variables. Even if a heavy wind had been blowing the weapons were to fly true to their mission and they did just that. Each one flew into the building, delaying detonation for a split instant until they exploded simultaneously. Two thousand pounds of explosives vaporised everything in the building with a hellish roar. The bodies in the basement were no more in existence as much as the building that they had been stacked in.

From over two miles away the men in the chopper watched in awe as the target zone erupted in a bright flash and was no more. They didn't hear the blast over the sound of the powerful engines that were powering the craft back to base. They had all watched except Regan. He sat impassively, staring at the bodies of the men who had not made it. The losses had been heavy yet he knew that the losses to America would have had been greater if they had not been successful in their execution of the operation even when it had gone to shit. However, again he felt as though he had failed even though he had done nothing wrong. He had lost men although only one in direct fire and even that had been a lucky shot. His thoughts wandered back to Colombia and he vowed to himself that he would rectify that issue as soon as he could, with or without permission.

Two months later, had anyone passed by what was the compound, they would have seen that the grass had grown on a clean piece of government land. In the middle of the large square of green grass four simple white marble headstones stood firmly in the gentle rain. They each had a plain oval shaped piece of black marble inlayed near the top. Each stone was faced into the other in a neat circle and each had a small blue ribbon attached. The ribbon represented the Congressional Medal of Honour that had been awarded to each man, posthumously, by the President when he had heard of the sacrifice made on that tiny piece of land and represented not just the mission passed, but the unspoken missions the men had endured as soldiers before they died. Each dark marble eye watched the other within the circle as was expected of the men in life as in death. Dark-Eye took care of it's own.

Three days later all at the base, at least those who were able to, attended the funerals of their fallen comrades. The body of Jacob had already been interned during a small Jewish ceremony. Now the caskets holding the bodies of

Hall, Fisher and Fabre were being lowered into the ground to join that of their pilot comrade. It was a large funeral for such a small community of men and women and when the final prayers had been uttered over the graves Commander Petersen spoke to his people.

'I watched footage fom New York on the TV this morning. There was a program about how well those people have bounced back from 9/11.' His voice was calm, measured and yet full of sadness. 'I saw young kids marching to school holding their parent's hands, young couple's kiss before parting ways to go to their respective jobs. I saw a vendor sell his wares, a broker screaming into his cell phone. I saw all that and much more. And the most important thing I saw?' His voice was was holding on to his emotions as he stared at those listening, and they were all listening. 'I saw no fear in their eyes. I saw no furtive looks over their shoulders. I saw no terror. And why?' It seemed that his eyes challenged everyone to answer.

'Sacrifice. That is why. The spilling of blood that is not civilian to prevent the spilling of that which is. That is our job,' he paused and looked up at his troops, ' in fact, no, not our job but our vocation, our lives, our chosen path. We may not have personally chosen the path here but we have been nudged onto this path by a force stronger that ourselves. We are the thin line between the simple wishes that civilians wake up to each morning and the complex beliefs of those who wish to inflict terror. We are the all-seeing Eye of understanding in the world of terror and we will be victorious. We will see an end.'

Silent looks were exchanged between those at the graveside before the Commander continued speaking to them.

'I feel a huge loss standing over the caskets of our four fallen men. The call came and they answered without question and we are better people for having had them with us even if it was for such a short while. That is why my voice is quivering and my eyes are filling,' he explained as emotion was beginning to show, 'our loss is our country's gain but we must absorb the blow. We can grieve at our loss but we must fight on. We must remember our dead but not let the memories hinder us, but make us stronger. We will stand and face terror and we shall not back down until we have victory. Our loss shall make us stronger and that will weaken our enemy. God damn it,' he urged, ' we will be victorious.'

'Take aim.' The order was barked before the millisecond of silence, time for those unused to the crack of gunfire to brace before the final command. A firm, clear shout 'FIRE', and the shots honouring the dead were fired.

The shots rang out over the graves of the fallen soldiers followed by two more volleys and put a close to the mourning. It was then time to get back to War.

Chapter 7

Empty Black Bags.

The British Airways flight touched down punctually on the runway of Charles De Gaulle. Onboard Steve undid his safety belt and released a silent gasp of relief. He never enjoyed landing as much as he enjoyed the take-off. He waited for the plane to come to a complete halt before standing to get his case from the overhead. It was a small case as he only expected to stay one night if plans worked out they way he hoped. It had been some time since he had seen his old friend and hoped that the meeting would bear the fruits that he required.

He walked out of the airport quickly, passing through all the checks with ease using his clean diplomatic passport. A white Mercedes taxi was waiting for him and he quickly got in.

'First time, Sir?' asked the driver.

'For what exactly,' came the reply in agreeably fluent French.

'To be driven by a senior CIA officer,' came the reply as Tom Hutch lifted the peak of his cap and winked a hello to his old friend.

'Damn it, Tom, don't you ever stop?' Steve asked frustrated that he had been lifted.

'Old habits die hard. How have you been? Still chasing the Irish? Why can't you leave those poor lads alone?'

'It is because of a poor Irish lad that I came to see you, Tom.'

Only for his training he would never have noticed Hutch tense up. He knew that he had come to the right man.

'Let's go get a bite to eat and catch up on old times. Some decent food wouldn't go astray on you, Steve.'

Izzo walked through the plastic folds that acted as doors in the mortuary. He had come to collect the autopsy report an hour earlier but felt the need to see the remains of the young girl. He felt a certain responsibility for her death and wanted to stand before her and apologise. The mortician accepted his explanation and escorted him down to the basement where the cold room was.

Once inside he felt like a trespasser. This was the room where, in a sense, death lived. There was ample lighting but yet the room felt dark to him. Death had an overwhelming presence in the room that sense was almost palpable. It was real. It was real for those who were unfortunate enough to be in the cabinets that held the dead.

With the guide he walked to the cabinet that was numbered 207 and stood before it waiting for the examiner to open it. He was suitable impressed by the gentleness with which he opened the cabinet. It amazed him that after all these years and all the bodies that had passed through the room that the man had not yet lost his human touch.

The body was covered in a light blue sheet and Izzo could not help notice how well the colour went with the shock of red hair. The examiner pulled the sheet down to the girl's waist to reveal the extent of the injuries that had ruined her body and that had taken her life. Izzo's eyes wanted to close in revulsion at the image that raped his vision. It all looked worse now than it did when he had viewed her at the crime scene. The tranquillity of her surroundings now made the horror all the worse. He whispered a small prayer and a promise, again, into her ear.

'Thanks, I have seen enough,' he told the examiner.

He turned and walked away with the report in his hand deciding to return to the station instead of bring the images in his head home to his wife.

The small restaurant suited the needs of the two men both in the seclusion and the quality of the food. Hutch had the physique of a middleweight but the appetite of a Sumo wrestler and so his order came as a "large." Steve decided to follow suit as he enjoyed French cuisine and was absolutely ravished at that moment. Two full plates and a chilled bottle of white were promptly placed before the two men.

'So, Steve, what can I do for you?'

'I am looking for a young Irishman who seems to have disappeared off the face of the earth and I am wondering if you can help,' came the reply through a mouth full of food.

'I thought you boys knew where all the ex-PIRA men had gone, Steve. Why would we be interested? We have bigger fish to fry at the moment,' added Hutch.

'I never mentioned PIRA, Tom. Why do think I mean those guys?'

Hutch looked up from his plate knowing that he had walked himself into the situation he was now in.

'Get to the point, Steve. I really have no time for games at this time,' he added with a little anger in his voice.

'Jack Regan. Where is he? He was supposed to have died fighting with the Legion but I don't believe that crap. He out-thought the SAS for long enough not to walk into a stupid ambush. I want to know where he is.'

'What do you know, Steve? What do you need to know for? That dirty little fucking war is over, remember? You couldn't catch him before and now you think you can! Jesus, Steve, leave they guy alone. He never targeted civilians, just troops and you guys. He played fair and got out when the peace began. Why the fuck do you want to start chasing him again?' asked Hutch with more frustration than anger in his voice.

'I need to speak to him, Tom. It is important,' came the reply.

'Important my ass, Steve. You want to settle a score and that is that is that. Christ, Steve, what even makes you so fucking certain that he is alive?'

'Let me just say that a little bird told me that Regan and his American friends paid a visit to a dissident Republican meeting and killed them all except my little bird,' he informed his friend in a painfully low voice.

'How come the 'little bird' had so much to say?' asked Hutch.

'I shot his ear off and he decided that it was prudent to answer my questions.'

'Steve, birds don't have ears,' grinned Hutch.

'Well, this one is special and he has only one ear now,' replied the equally grinning Steve.

'Let me explain, my friend,' conceded Hutch. He began.

'It was decided some time ago to merge the best assets that we have in personal to create a new agency/military hybrid unit. We thought that we could take the best from Delta and the Ops guys from The Farm and create a super unit.

However, both sides agreed to disagree as it would pull important assets from each side without benefits that would be seen for a couple of years. It was decided then to create a unit that would operate independently of, but always with, the military and government agencies. New people were required and we decided that they did not have to be necessarily American personal. Therefore, we went looking for talent abroad. We went to Germany, England, Israel, Australia, France and so on. Those we deemed as suitable we tried to recruit. The numbers were small but impressive. We did, in the end get a couple from Delta, some from your SAS, fine men, and a couple of others. Then we heard of your boy. We watched him in action and were knocked over by what we saw. He became the standard after that. Jack Regan is the prize asset of Dark-Eye, Steve, and God help you if you try to go after him now. He is no longer the wide-eyed kid that was in PIRA. He is anti-terror now and there is no going back for him. He pulled that stunt outside of Dublin as a payback for his past. As far as we are concerned he is clean,' he explained.

Steve released a gasp of surprise. He had been right but still couldn't believe it. He now had a conduit to Regan after all those years.

'So he is alive and well in the land of the free. What will it take to get a message to him, Hutch? His world away from all of this shit has changed for the worse, some thing bad has happened.'

'Explain, Steve,' replied Hutch as he felt something was about to ruin his day.

'Regan's father has died at home in Dublin. As we had no way of contacting Regan, the funeral went ahead without him,' Steve explained.

'How did young Kathy take the news?'

Steve didn't expect Hutch to know her but he should have known better.

'Kathy is dead, Hutch. She was killed in Italy. It was that news that killed her father and that is the news that I have to get to Jack. I made a promise to his father to find him and tell him. That is why I am looking for him. There is no other reason.'

'My God, how did it happen? Was it an accident?' asked Hutch with genuine hurt in his face.

'It was no accident, Hutch. Somebody killed her. Her body is still in Italy and there is no one to claim it as yet. It was in the papers there and in Dublin too but not with all the details. She was brutally killed from the scant details that I have received do far.' He paused for a moment, 'She has a kid, Hutch. That is why Regan needs to come back. Regan is all that kid will have as family in this fucked up world and I am going to make sure that he comes back.'

'Shit. Once he finds out there is going to be a bloodbath. He never lets anything pass him by. This is going to be hard to control.'

'Can you get a message to him. Ask him will he meet me in Dublin. I can arrange to have his life resurrected. It will be the end of his career with your new unit but, then again, from what you have said, he has paid his debts to society,' added Steve.

'I'll get the message to him, Steve. When he returns, and he will return, make sure you keep an eye on him or we will be selling body bags to the Italians and I don't want to be responsible for the bill.'

The two men shook hands and parted ways.

Regan walked to the door of his commander's office and knocked gently. He had to explain his feelings about the previous days to his commander and seek advice.

'Come in, Regan. It's open,' came the reply to his knock.

'How did you know it was me, Sir,' came the obvious question.

'I could tell by your face at the funeral that you had something to say to me. So, what is it? My head tells me that Colombia is on your mind.'

'Sir, I need to finish the job. The organiser is still out there and I want to close him out before he does it again or even worse for us, before he starts to look for us and opens us up to the public,' added Regan.

'No go, soldier. That issue is going to be dealt with by other means. We are off the case. Period. Am I making myself clear here?

'Sir, we..'

Petersen jumped to his feet and stared Regan straight into the eyes.

'This is not 'We', Regan, this is 'You'. You want closure and it is not an option. Other assets in the field are dealing with Colombia. Dark-Eye will not be risked any further for a political favour or a perceived personal vendetta. Am I clear, soldier?' he roared.

Regan was not used to be spoken to in that manner by anyone and was momentarily taken aback by his commanders reaction.

'With all due respect, Sir, I close out the target or I close out my time with Dark-Eye.'

'What the Hell are you saying, Regan?' asked the commander, himself now the one taken aback.

'I am closing Colombia with or without my unit, Sir. That is our motto. I will add the 'Final' to this equation. We have already lost the 'Swift' aspect.'

'Are you threatening to resign your position for some piece of shit in Colombia? Are you fucking crazy, Regan?' asked Petersen in disbelief.

'Sir, yes, Sir!' came the reply

The secure fax started its rapid print sequence and both sets of eyes darted to it.

'Regan, get the fuck out of my office and go lose some of the Irish temper of yours on the range. That's and order, Son. We shall talk after five hundred rounds,' Petersen added with a voice that was suitable for diplomatic negotiations.

Regan saluted and left the office still seething. Petersen reached for the fax and read it while still shaking his head at the intensity of Regan's argument. He had nothing but admiration for the young man but his temper was a handful. The information on the fax caused him to look again at the fax header. The number was that of the direct line from CIA headquarters in Langley, Virginia. Regan's world was about to get turned on his head. In fact, not just Regan's world.

Regan took his commanders advice and walked to the firing range. Loosing a few rounds always worked when his temper was getting the better of him and now was going to be no different.

When he got to the range he noticed that all the lines were full and so he jogged to the Gunnery Sergeant, Lee Williams, to see who was ready to leave. Williams was a powerfully built man, a career soldier who greeted everyone with a beaming smile that belied the man that lay beneath. Regan received the same smile.

'How do, Regan?

'Hi, Gunny. Whose time is up? I need to shoot,' came the reply.

'New guy from Bragg has been there ages. Been shouting his mouth off about how good a shot he is. I now know why they call it Fort Bragg,' added Gunny with a smile.

'Call him off, Gunny. I need time.'

Gunny buzzed the soldier on line six and advised him that he was causing a traffic jam. There was no reply from the soldier and both men were angered to see him reload and start firing again.

'Fuck this, Gunny. I'll deal with this.'

Gunny sat back and smiled. He knew that this was going to be interesting.

Regan walked up to the soldier on line six, pulling his Beretta from its holster as he approached. He tapped the man on his shoulder as he was still firing and put him off target.

'What the fuck is your...' came the beginnings of a challenge but Regan stepped in front of him and opened fire on the target that was twenty meters beyond the one being peppered by the new guy. He hoped that the man would get physical at the insult. His blood, by now, was boiling.

Each bullet was hitting the head kill zone when the large hand landed on Regan's shoulder and spun him around.

'Like I said, what's your problem, man? I am not done here.'

Regan didn't give the man a second glance but turned back to resume firing. Again the large hand grabbed his shoulder, more forcibly this time, and spun Regan again. Except this time the soldiers left hand was making the shortest journey directly at Regan's head.

As he was being turned Regan holstered his pistol and stepped outwards with the pulling motion of the attackers hand. In Regan's mind he was being attacked and he was going to use force to cease the attack. His left arm swiped away the gripping hand of the soldier while his right arced up and outwards to parry the direct face shot that was being aimed at him. Regan then stepped into his attacker with a left elbow to the nose before locking the neutralised left arm with his right and executing a powerful leg sweep, taking both legs from under the soldier.

He had thought that his punch would have reached the target but the concern that it didn't did not reach his brain until it was trying to understand why the sky and the brown earth were spinning in the wrong directions. He landed with a lung deflating smack onto the ground and felt the heavy knee of the smaller man that he had tried to hit weigh heavily on his chest. Worse was to come.

The other soldiers on the range were all now watching Regan's particular lesson in Dark-Eye manners and firing line etiquette. All were glad not to be in the new man's position.

Army Ranger Steve Beck knew that he had met more than his match with the man who was leaning on his chest and decided to call quits. However, surrender was not an option on offer at that moment. Regan had pulled his weapon again as the young man under him began to raise his hands in submission but he had not done it fast enough. Regan drove the barrel of the pistol firmly into his mouth, splitting the lip and breaking a tooth on its way. Then Regan spoke.

'Now we have a difficult situation here, Mr. Army Ranger man. I am so pissed off that I am going to return you to your mother unit but only if I have no bullets left in my pistol.

Beck's eyes widened in fear at the realisation that Regan was going to pull the trigger and was going to scream when he heard the trigger click softly. He began to shake uncontrollably as the gun was pulled from his mouth and a look of disappointment crossed Regan's face.

'Would you fucking believe it? It's empty,' he snarled at the young Ranger. 'All of that for nothing. Your lucky day, I guess.'

Regan stood up and saw a couple of controlled smiles from the men around him. Most had seen him eject the clip as he was pulling the pistol from his holster. Most, that is, except Beck. He was sobbing quietly on the ground holding the blood from his mouth trying to shield his embarrassment from the men who were to have been his new teammates. Except that he fucked up.

Regan felt a pang of regret at shaming the young man so early in his time with Dark-Eye and realised that only for his temper the young man, who had already been pushed to the limits to get that far with Dark-Eye, would have finished his shooting without the unnecessary force. He leaned over and offered his hand to the young man.

'Take my hand soldier. I only offer it once.'

Beck did as he was told and was pulled to his feet. He didn't know what to say and turned to walk to the barracks to get his belongings. Regan called after him.

'And where do you think you are going now, soldier? He asked. 'We are not done here.'

Beck didn't think that he could take any more abuse but he turned anyway and spoke through his bloodied mouth.

'I am being returned to my unit, Sir. I was going to get my bag and get the hell out of here before I lose any more teeth,' he added with all of his self control mustered to create a smile of defiance in the face of the man who was sending him home.

'Regan is what I am called by my teammates here in Dark-Eye. So what is it to be? He asked with the beginnings of a grin on his face.

'Sir?'

'You passed the final test, Beck, you are in,' he added as the rest of the men cheered and applauded.

Petersen was watching from where he could keep his distance yet see what was happening. The final test for Beck was due to have been preformed the following day but Regan had pre-empted the ritual. The injuries would have been pretty much the same, in some cases even worse. He remembered Regan's jaw hanging off his face after been broken at the joint. He had kept getting up to fight even though he should have stayed down. The mentality of the final test was to give the men the understanding that they were not invincible and that they could be beaten. Regan, however, kept getting up believing that he was fighting for his life after Petersen and two others had jumped him after a live fire test. It had gotten to the point were it came down to Regan and Petersen, face to broken face, and Petersen knew that he was beyond explaining to Regan that it was a test. At that moment Petersen also felt that he was in for a struggle for his life and that Regan was not going to stop until he wore himself out. Regan then collapsed forward, as if in dire fatigue, and Petersen for a single moment dropped his guard and moved forward to catch Regan before he fell on his broken face. Regan's feint worked and he powered up from a falling motion into a powerful upward motion catching Petersen squarely on the chin with the crown of his head. As Petersen stumbled back Regan pulled the commanders gun from the leg holster. Petersen landed on his rear and looked up in stunned silence as Regan aimed the pistol at his head and pulled the trigger. There was no emotion on his face. Nothing. The pistol was empty from the free fire training and it was only that that saved Petersen's life.

Now Petersen had to tell the man that his sister and his father were both dead.

He walked up to the group of men, brothers in time of trouble, and called Regan over. Regan looked over and acknowledged his boss, patted Beck on the shoulder and told him that the first round of drinks were on him in the bar later and then walked over to Petersen.

'A day early but he earned his place, Sir.'

Petersen cut straight to the point knowing that the Dark-Eye was about to lose its finest soldier.

'This came for you from Langley, Regan, I...I am so sorry, son. There is nothing I can really say,' he added.

Regan took the fax from the outstretched hand and read down through it then crumpled it in his hand and threw it on the floor. His face was contorted in a mixture of livid anger and sheer desolation.

'I should have been there.'

'He would have understood, Regan,' offered Petersen.

'For my sister, not him.' Regan said staring through his commander before walking away towards the weapons rack.

His mind turned in a tide of emotions as he pulled a MP-5 from the rack and walked to the firing line. A million solutions, second guesses and feelings attacked his very soul as he reached the line twenty meters from a full sized target that had been made in the shape of Osama Bin Laden.

He, while the rest of the men were watching in some confusion, raised the weapon and settled the butt firmly to his shoulder and cut loose on the target, splintering it with thirty rounds of lead.

He then dropped the weapon and ran at full speed at the target, launching himself into the air just three meters from the wooden structure before demolishing it with his outstretched right leg. The target collapsed under the weight of the assault and both Regan and the image of Bin laden crashed onto the ground in a cloud of brown dust.

The men were shocked and a few concerned looks were traded as they watched Regan pummel the wooden board with his bare fists. Then he seemed to collapse onto the remains of the target in a form that resembled a Muslim at prayer time. They understood what was happening when they saw his body heave and shake. He was crying.

Petersen did the only thing that he could do for his friend in that moment and that was to give him privacy with his tears. He roared at his men.

'Dark-Eye, about face!'

The men jumped-to, spread out and faced away from Regan. They faced away giving him the privacy of sorrow but not one man walked away. A Dark-Eye Envoy would not leave one of their own when he was injured, regardless of whether the injury was physical or emotional.

What Petersen also knew that day was that Regan would fold into his own world again. Dark-Eye had made him retreat from the grasp that history had on his soul and now he would return to that grip that, Petersen thought, was almost motherly to the young man. He knew that Dark-Eye had not made Regan the man that he was. It was a combination of many factors that had occurred in the man's life. However, above everything else, Petersen knew that soldiers were not made. They were born and some were born into the life of combat of different levels and intensity. Regan would have always been good at conflict because his life was conflict. It would have found him regardless of the career he had chosen.

Sitting in his office Petersen was flooded with conflicting emotions for the young man. The overriding fact that came back and back again into his train of thought was that Regan was going to cut lose on every field he could find. Colombia was, without doubt, going to be his first move towards the new role that fate had handed him on a bloody platter. The kidnapper was now going to be in his sights, the first target of many that Petersen knew would fall at the hands of Regan until his desire for revenge could be sated. He also knew that Colombia probably didn't represent anything any more for Regan, as the hunt for the killers of his sister would now be the only controlled goal in the man's mind. Colombia now would represent one thing, and one thing only, for Regan. In the violent opera of his life, Colombia would simply be a rehearsal.

8

Rehearsal

Regan had slept. He still was able to sleep even though his world was back in turmoil once again. He was awake now and staring at the blank wall in front of him. He had no pictures on the wall, unlike the other men who adorned their walls with images of naked women and fast cars. He preferred to imagine pictures on the walls when he was on his bed resting. Now the blank wall was filled with mental images of the plan that was forming in his mind.

Over the door his mind had traced the images of those who were coming into his line of sight, his new targets. By the window, where the early morning sun was creeping through, his mind had placed the image of his smiling sister and the serious demeanour of his father. Across the other walls came discrete plans of action, dates and times, weapons and contacts and images of place names in Colombia and Italy. On the blank wooden door his mind had created a clock. The second had had already started its sweeping motion, commencing the attacks.

Regan jumped out of bed and went straight for a shower. He let the cold water flow over his body as his hands and fingertips massaged his head. He knew that his career with Dark-Eye was over and that made his demons mass in the pit of his stomach. He had found his place in life and now it was been taken from him again. What else was fate to take from him? How much more could he take before the stretched elastic of his mind would snap? He had to hold it together and he knew how. Just follow the plan, his mind advised. Just follow the plan and everything would fall into place.

He was drying off when his beeper summoned him to the office of his commander. Petersen was to Regan as much a father figure as his real father. He had guided him in the right direction when the path seemed to disappear in the greyness of his emotions. He did not want to let Petersen down. He would tell him of his plans but not mention Colombia or the complete plan for Italy. He would seek Petersen's advice and seem to accept it. It would work.

Petersen was sitting on his desk flicking through an old paper file that had to be added to the computer systems when Regan knocked on the door for permission to enter.

'Come in.'

Regan walked in on command and closed the door behind him. The reaction of his commander surprised him.

Petersen dropped the file onto the desk and walked over to Regan and without saying a word, placed his two large hands onto Regan's shoulders, squeezing hard. He then took the head of the young man between his hands and held him gently while staring into his eyes.

'You are going to hold it together, Jack. You are going to control these emotions and channel them in the right direction. This is not going to break you. Do you hear me? This is not going to break you.'

Regan was lost for words. He did not expect this from Petersen and now his need to lie to the man evaporated in a mist of loyalty.

Petersen took his hands away and turned and walked back to his desk. He sat down and pulled out one of his Cuban cigars and lit it with a tarnished old Zippo that had followed him in every combat zone that he had visited.

'Now, tell me honestly. What is your plan?'

Regan could not help but smile at the Churchillian image before him.

'I am going hunting and I want, sorry, need a licence from you. I am going to go anyway but a licence from you will make it easier to accomplish the task before me. I wish not to give you any specifics but you do understand that what I am going to do is going to bend a few rules,' came the honest answer.

Petersen nearly choked on his cigar. 'Bend?'

'Well, completely shatter would be more precise but I did say that I did not wish to give you any specifics.'

Petersen smiled and nodded gently before speaking. 'This is what I am going to do for you. From midnight tonight you will have five days to target Colombia. One shot, one target. On that I must make myself very clear. You take out the leader and then take yourself out of Colombia. Do not try to clean up the whole country. One target only, Regan. If, after five days, you cannot make the target, you get out of there and go bury your sister. I mean that. I can cover you until then but after that you are on your own. What happens in Italy after that is your own business but I do expect you to behave like a soldier. Don't just go blowing the shit out of anyone you suspect of doing something to her or being involved. Acquire your targets, study them, get a feel for them and then, with my blessing, waste them. Keep it all clean and you can come back to Dark-Eye. That is my offer. There is nothing to negotiate.

Again, Regan was taken aback by his commander.

'Why, Sir? Why are you going to help?'

'Because I would do the same as you if the situations were reversed and I know that you would, without question, help me,' came the fatherly answer.

Regan nodded his agreement as Petersen continued to speak.

'I know you have the ability to fulfil your goal and take your targets out of existence but at this time you are not the only one chasing in Colombia. Word of what happened was passed to the Boss and he has intervened in the game. By his order, we have nothing else to do with what is going to happen in Colombia. He has impressed onto us the need for our focus to be directed at the domestic threat form AQ and their people. Therefore, a team from Delta have been infiltrated into Bogotá in order to work with our local intelligence unit,' he didn't have to say CIA, 'and together they will close the book. I discussed this fact earlier with Mr. Longthorn and he expressed his wish that we were to carry out the closure to the operation. So much so that he has given us permission to meet Rachel again and to glean whatever information we may need from her. She may be tougher than we originally gave her credit for.'

'Will I go and speak to her?'

'Yes. Here is the plan and you may alter it as you wish over the next five days. Go and speak to her, find out what you need to identify the target and then make your way to Colombia. Longthorn, in fact, insisted that if anyone was to speak to her that it was going to be you. He may not be a soldier but he is a man of action. If he has something to say, hear him out.'

'I can't thank you enough. This was a lot more that I could have expected from you. I believed that I was coming here to hand in my resignation and that was tearing me up. I will go and exorcise my demons and I will come back and continue my service until such time that you decide that I have no further use here. Again, thank you.'

'Just remember what you are, why you are the way you are and why you do what you do. Come and see me after you speak to the girl as I will have a good luck charm for you to carry.' Petersen said that with a glint in his eye and Regan smiled as he walked out the door.

Later that evening Regan touched down on a small private landing strip just north of Washington DC. The flight had been smooth and the service discrete as one would have expected on the private jet of one of America's richest men. Regan had taken advantage of Longthorn's offer of the use of the jet as he had considered the time frame that he had would not support flying into Washington's main terminus.

Once the plane had landed and taxied to a stop, Regan unclipped his belt, thanked he crew and walked through the open door and down the steps to the black Lincoln that was waiting to bring him to the Longthorn residence.

Standing in the slight drizzle, holding the door of the car open for him was Steve Epps, Longthorn's security chief.

'Mr. Regan, good to see you again. I hope I can stay on my feet this time.'

Regan smiled and shook Epps outstretched hand. 'From what I heard from the base, and the training you did with one of our instructors, you will be staying on you feet for some time to come. It takes a lot to impress that guy and you did it in style.'

'I believe you are here to see Rachel. Will you be visiting anyone else while you are here? I would be insulted if you didn't let me drive or at least take you for a beer with the boys. We owe you one.' His offer was sincere and Regan knew it.

'After I speak to Rachel and her father I will be straight back here, I am afraid. A lot of unfinished business to attend to and I can't ask you to drive me there. Thanks for the offer, though,' he added with slight smile. The understanding of the situation was not lost on Epps and he didn't push the issue.

A short while later the car eased up the gravel drive to the main residence after passing through the main gates. Regan noticed the security presence and figured that he hadn't seen it all. Epps was doing his job and was going to make sure that the young lady was never going to meet danger again. Everyone had to learn from mistakes and Epps was doing just that.

The car slowed to a gentle halt outside the door of the enormous house and Regan saw the tall figure of Longthorn standing waiting for his guest. He turned to Epps and thanked him for the lift before stepping lightly out of the car. Just before he shut the door, Epps called him.

'Regan, if you are going to have to go back and finish the job please say hello to the prick from me. I know you can't say anything but just in case. And ...thanks for everything and good luck.'

Regan didn't say anything but winked at Epps and shut the door of the car.

Longthorn watched the young man as he walked lightly up the steps onto the porch. He was, again, impressed by the man's demeanour. He seemed at ease yet alert at the same time a skill, he presumed, that was inherited and not taught.

'Mr. Regan, you are indeed very welcome to my home. I hope the trip was agreeable.'

'Sir, it is not often that a mere soldier gets to fly in a private jet. I should have stayed in college longer,' he said, shaking Longthorn's hand.

'Please, call me Trevor. "Sir" is an expression that you guys use and I am no soldier. Please, come in and join us for dinner. Rachel shall be down soon and she is looking forward to seeing you.'

They went to the kitchen instead of the dining room as Longthorn said that it was more comfortable and that Rachel preferred it there. There was already a small buffet laid out for the guest and Regan filled a plate and sat by the fire. The feeling was indeed homely and Regan felt at ease for the first time in days. Although a serious man, Longthorn had a fatherly friendliness about him and he began asking questions of the young man.

'Can I call you Jack?' he asked while biting into a chicken wing. Regan nodded his consent, as his mouth was too full to answer.

'You have a hint of an Irish accent. Is that your part of the world, Jack?

Regan swallowed his mouthful of cold beef and sipped from a glass of iced water.

'Born and raised there. I can say that I am Irish but it is no longer home. I don't really have anywhere that I can call home now because of what I do but that is the choice that was made a couple of years ago. I came from the French Foreign Legion into the unit I am with now. I plan to stay where I am now if everything works out well for me.'

Longthorn looked thoughtful as he spoke to the young man before him. 'An Irishman in the Legion? What did you do to deserve that?'

'Sometimes it takes a thief to catch a thief. In this instance, my life, it took a terrorist to catch one. That is why I am now with Dark Eye,' he answered honestly.

'IRA?' added Longthorn without skipping a beat.

'I am afraid so,' he answered honestly.

'Want to tell me more? I mean, did you kill people?'

'Sir, I am twenty-eight years old. I have been killing since I was seventeen. There is too much to tell,' Regan replied. He didn't really want to explain himself to the man sitting in front of him but there was a need to explain to the man what had happened. 'I got involved at a young age and got out with my life. I agreed with the peace process and felt that things were going to change for the better. I was on the verge of leaving but one more mission was required. I needed to do what I did because then it felt right. I lead a small unit that ambushed a SAS team that had been picking off our people over the previous months. I killed two of them and blew up their support chopper as it came in to pick them up. Five men in total in one operation. When I got back to Dublin some time later it was made clear to me that while the political momentum was going to succeed, I was to get out of Ireland if I didn't want to be paid a visit by friends of those who had died. I left and went to France, joined the Legion and died in Africa.'

Longthorn looked deep in thought as Regan finished his brief recount and then at Regan with a concerned expression on his face.

'How many innocent people died because of you, Jack? Did you kill for the sake of killing or had you really an objective in mind?

'I killed soldiers, Trevor. I was expecting to be killed myself by them or the other side but it turns out that they were not as lucky as I was. I didn't target any civilians, nor were any killed or injured because of my actions. I mean that. I was at war with the British army and they were at war with me. We each saw death and destruction on a scale that should never have been allowed to develop in a Western country. We all saw stupidity and waste, especially the waste of young lives. Looking back now, I can't understand why it went on so long. Maybe we forgot what peace and normal living is like. Maybe we just liked to fight and didn't know how to stop. Too many reasons that then seemed valid and now seem futile. I am kinda hoping that the work I do now will, in some way, make up for what happened in Ireland.'

'Do you have any sense of remorse for the young soldiers who died at your hands?' asked Longthorn.

'Seventeen names are etched onto my brain. Seventeen families, wives, loved ones, fathers and mothers, comrades, children and friends. I see every one of them in my dreams when the nightmares take over. I have seen the burials on the newsreels, heard the fathers call me 'Paddy bastard' or 'Murdering Irish pig' and have heard young children cry for their daddy when I knew that it was me who caused their father to die. I heard a young English girl pray for my soul and asking her dead father to forgive me because she said that I would be as lonely as her. I had all this before my twentieth birthday.' Regan said this looking straight into the eyes of Trevor Longthorn and the man was moved by the intensity of the words.

'Why, Jack? Why did you do it?' he asked silently.

'I was sixteen years old and driving with a friend up to a concert in Belfast. We took a shorter route that took us through the countryside and off the main roads as we were running late. We drove straight into the aftermath of an ambush just outside a small village where a unit of the IRA had driven through the town in the back of an open backed truck shooting their weapons into the air. They had been losing people in recent months and had wanted to display a show of force to the locals. Well, as we turned the corner we saw the truck burning and bodies on the ground. I could see the soldiers retreat into an open field where their helicopter was waiting to whisk them back to their base.' Regan's voice remained steady. 'My friend stopped the car upwind from the flames coming from the lorry. We jumped out and ran to the driver's door of the lorry to see was there anyone still in the cabin that we could pull out. The door was open and there was a young man hanging out, his legs still caught in the dashboard. He had been shot twice in the head and his blood was dripping onto the road. I reached in and pulled his legs free and he dropped to the ground. The sound of his shattered skull hitting the ground still echos in my ears. We pulled him clear of the flames and turned to see could we do any thing for the others. Well, they were all dead. Seven in total but one in particular stays with me. He was slumped against a tree but only for his arms and legs I was unable to tell that he was human. He was shot to pieces and there was very little left of his head and torso. And there was no weapon by his side.' Regan added.

'What happened then? What did you do? What could you do?' asked Longthorn incredulously.

'The chopper was waiting for two more soldiers to cross from the far side of the road but they ran up to us instead. My friend was on his knees vomiting on the ground and I was frozen to the spot in front of the body that was against the tree. One of the soldiers spun me around and grabbed me by the neck. He looked at me for a second, figured I was a civilian, and threw me to the ground. He told me not to bother calling an ambulance but to call a priest instead 'for the Fenian bastard'. I screamed at him that the boy wasn't even armed and he just laughed and turned and jogged to the chopper with the other soldier.'

'My God, Jack. That was nothing for a young boy to see. Were you hurt?

'I pulled my friend up and we say the last two soldiers load themselves onto the chopper and they turned and waved as the chopper began to lift off. Something just snapped inside and I screamed at my friend to run to the car and get ready to get away from that place. As he walked over to the car I ran to the rear of the truck and picked up a weapon dropped by one of the dead men. I had no idea how to work it but I had seen enough films and read enough books to know that you point one end at the target and the other end into your shoulder. The chopper was just clearing the fence of the field when I opened fire at it. I could feel and hear the chatter of bullets over the sound of the helicopter and could see the sparks fly of the belly and tail rotor. I was shocked that the weapon worked and even more shocked that the bullets hit. I ran back to the car and jumped into the passenger seat. My friend was laughing so much he could hardly start the engine. His nerves had gone a bit weird, as I couldn't see the funny side of what we had just seen or of what I had just done. I looked out of the car window when I heard a high-pitched screach of metal and saw that the chopper was in trouble. Somehow I had managed to damage the chopper and it was coming back around to the field from where it had taken off. It landed heavily but didn't seem to be too damaged. We got ourselves out of there as fast as my friend could drive and made our way through an unauthorised crossing and then home.'

'That's one hell of a story,' came a voice from the doorway.

Both men turned to see Rachel leaning against the doorway, her arms crossed and her head cocked to one side.

'How long have you been there?' her father asked gently.

'From the beginning of the story. I mean, maybe I should have said something but I just wanted to know something about you, Mr. Regan. You did save my life, remember?'

'Kind of hard to forget, Rachel,' replied Regan rising from his seat to greet the young woman. 'How are you feeling now?'

'I am working on it. I realise that what they did to me was not my fault and not something I allowed them to do. I am still me and I will have to work hard to put everything behind me. I have to thank you for what you did back in Colombia, Mr. Regan. Knowing that men like you and my father still exist gives me strength and courage to face the outside world. It will be put behind me with time.'

'I am certainly glad to hear that. For all I have been through as a soldier I will never have to deal with that which you endured. I do believe that you are tougher than me and definitely than a lot of my men,' answered the smiling soldier.

Rachel smiled back at the man who had saved her life in the Colombian mountains. Then, he had seemed to be an uncaring killing machine, an arrogant soldier who cared nothing for civilians. Now, however, he looked relaxed and at ease in the surroundings of wealth. He was a real chameleon, fitting into his surroundings and blending. She found herself staring at his hands as he twisted the glass between his fingers. He had hands like a piano player, which struck her as odd as they were the same hands that carved the thumbs off her attackers as evidence for her father. He seemed so at ease talking to her father. She had seen powerful men wither in the presence of her father and now this soldier, hardly the social class her father was used to meeting, impressed her father like a young suitor. Her father's head was cocked to the left, a real sign that he was listening, as it was his good ear. His head stayed straight up when he cared little for what was being said.

A few short hours later the informal party broke up as Rachel retired to her room and Regan stood to leave the house and return to the hotel where he had been booked in for the night.

At the door, Longthorn took his hand and once again shook it firmly.

'I still feel that I owe you so much and maybe I shouldn't expect you to go down there to finish the job.'

'I have other fish to fry at this time but those can wait until I clear the slate in Colombia. All the information you have supplied will ensure that the program will be followed and finished.'

'I am sorry about what happened to your sister. Petersen told me in confidence but I could not just let it go without saying something,' added Longthorn. 'If you want to leave Colombia for some other time I would entirely understand. In fact, why not wait a few weeks. Go back to Ireland and settle things over there and in Italy.' The reply clarified for him the true concept of fear.

Regan turned to go but left a chilling comment hanging in the air. 'Sir, I will settle affairs in Italy. Colombia will be,' he tilted his head slightly and breathed out heavily in concentration before finishing his sentence, 'practice.'

9

Slippery Steps.

The alarm went off at exactly five thirty. Regan reached over and tapped it into silence. He was already up and showered and had just set the alarm as a final precaution. He had never been awakened by an alarm clock but that didn't mean that he would always wake before the buzzer.

Standing in front of the mirror he checked himself over as he towelled down. His lean frame glistened with droplets of water on his tanned skin. Some fine lines denoted where surgery had intervened after one or two fire fights that had gone unexpectedly wrong. Other scars were more brutal looking only because the tender hands of a surgeon had never stitched them up.

He shook his head clear of those thoughts as he began to dress himself for the day ahead. He knew that mission time was coming up and so his almost monastic preparation was automatically setting in. The anger within was beginning to coil itself into a spring and the tension would build until he was ready to release it. It was always this way. He was content and driven by his natural anger towards injustice.

Once dressed he checked the contents of the matt-black Samsonite briefcase that lay on the bed. Within the case were a choice of two Sig-Sauer pistols, eight Flash-Bang grenades, two hundred rounds of hollow point bullets and a collection of passports. All of this inside a case that had, as Regan did on this occasion, diplomatic cover. In fact, all Dark-Eye operators carried the same case on all flights now since 9/11. If anyone thought that they could take a flight captive now they were in serious trouble if a Dark-Eye Envoy was on board.

After double-checking everything Regan left the room with the briefcase held firmly in his left hand. He walked down the two flights of stairs and went to drop his keys at reception.

The young receptionist smiled at Regan when he handed over the key to her and he returned the smile.

'Are you leaving so soon, Sir?' She asked politely.

'I shall be back in a couple of days so please hold the room for me. I have left some belongings there for the time being. You have my credit card details so there should be no problem,' he added with another smile. He could not but appreciate her pretty looks and half wished he were ten years younger.

'Sir, a gentleman left a package for you from the office of Mr. Longthorn.' She handed over the padded envelope and Regan took it with a nod of gratitude and popped it into the inside pocked to his light overcoat.

'See you in a few days, Miss. Thank you.'

He could barely hear her say, 'I hope so' as he walked through the revolving doors.

Longthorn sat in his office viewing a copy of the file that he had just sent Regan. The pictures of the young man who had planned the assault on his child was now between his fingers and he knew that by his actions, sending the information to Regan, that he had effectively sealed the fate of the man who stared at him from the picture.

He had met the individual once during his short term as ambassador to Colombia. He remembered the firm handshake of the man who had promised to protect him and his daughter at all costs. He had felt the comfort that the man's confidence had given him and now he felt the hatred run through his veins.

Longthorn had earned his place in the world through hard work and hard decisions but had never destroyed any man in order to get what he wanted. Now things were going to change. The horrible sense of power that he now felt for having ordered the killing of the man was making him shake uncontrollably.

He turned just in time and vomited into the waste paper basket beside his vast desk.

Regan was at ease in his seat. The flight was already an hour old and he was sitting back in his first class seat with his Jacket off and his sleeves rolled up. The file that Longthorn had given him was opened on his lap and his brain was absorbing the file and pictures of Carl Williams.

Williams was a former member of the elite Navy Seals, Team Six. An impressive service record showed that he had served well in numerous conflicts ranging from the Gulf War to Bosnia. He had retired after being injured in Bosnia and took up a Diplomatic Security Service role at the Department of State. He was well regarded and well liked by his peers and there was nothing in the file leading Regan to believe that the man in question was a psychotic rapist and killer. Yet, the evidence in the latter part of the file began to throw question marks over the perfect record. The more Regan read, the more he realised that Williams had been getting away with murder, literally, for some time.

'That's all going to change real soon, Mr. Williams. Real soon.' He whispered to himself.

He finished reading the file, closed it and put it back into his case. He than lay his head back and closed his eyes as if to sleep.

The young air hostess who was walking by saw the contented face of a man at rest. If she could see into his mind she would have seen death develop from an embryonic state into full manhood in the mind of a perfect soldier.

Three hours later Regan waved his Diplomatic passport like a magic wand and walked unhindered through security at Bogotá airport. He had already switched his mind into Spanish mode and eased his way to a cab rank and waved for a driver.

He opened the back door and threw his bag onto the back seat. He closed the door and opened the front passenger door before sliding in beside the driver.

'More leg room, my friend,' he advised the driver who shook his head in apathy. Regan preferred the front seat for many reasons not least being that he was closer to the mirrors and if anything serious happened he could dump the driver out the door and drive himself.

The journey to the hotel took less than half an hour but Regan was not counting minutes. He was getting closer to his own private 'Zero Hour' and his mind was barking orders to the rest of his body.

The cab slowed to a stop noisily at the main entrance of the hotel and Regan stepped out of the car after paying his fare and leaving a tip. He grabbed his bags from the trunk and walked nonchalantly into the main foyer.

Regan approached the main desk and booked a room for a week, paying cash up front. All going well, the room would be vacant from early the following morning. All going well, that is, in the world of mice and men.

The receptionist was an over helpful busy body and inundated Regan with details of their fine dining hall and service. If there was anything that the Señor wanted all he had to do was phone down and Señor Muñoz would be ever so pleased to help. Regan slipped a twenty-dollar bill into his hand and assured him that if he required any assistance he would call.

He then turned and walked to the lift and retired to his room.

Three miles away across town Carl Williams was starting to breath a sigh of relief. Nothing had come back to his doorstep to implicate him in the Longthorn kidnapping. He was safe.

He still needed to know what had happened up the mountain but he assumed that FARC had intervened in his plan. Well, fuck them. He was still a million dollars short of his goal and he would get it by hook or by crook. He was as confident of that as he was confident in everything that he did.

He rubbed his temples with his fingers and decided that he had done enough for one day. He would go home, shower and hit the club. A few beers with the boys and a couple of those young Latino types would ease the stress that had built within his chest and ever-active mind.

He was smiling to himself as he walked out the door of his office. He was a very lucky man in every aspect of his life and could see no reason why that would change now. As Head of Diplomatic Security he had the security clearance to check everything and, in many cases, direct questions away from himself and his few chosen men.

Yes, he would relax this evening and a new plan would offer itself to replace the money that he had lost through bad luck. Bad luck for the men who had died on that mountain and just an inconvenience for him.

The laptop purred gently as Regan uploaded the virus and sent it the reception desk computer at Club Paradise. Señor Muñoz had told him that the club was very elitist and that there was always a queue a block and a half long.

Entrance into the VIP section took a miracle and a healthy wad of greenbacks. Regan had the money but not the time to smooth talk his way in. The virus he was now passing to the club's mainframe was going to do the smooth talking for him.

Exactly ten minutes later Regan called down to Señor Muñoz and asked him to call the club and confirm his booking under Walters. Table for one.

Señor Muñoz called back two minutes later completely flabbergasted. The table was booked for the respected señor Walters and a bottle of his favourite wine was already chilling.

The virus had opened the books to Regan and he had altered their files to show that he was a valued patron of five years who, even though his visits were rare, left a sizable tip and spent freely.

The virus would delete itself at midnight and no trace would exist of the booking. Cinderella was the perfect name for the micro-virus.

Regan then showered and changed and prepared the weapons for the evening. He was going to carry one pistol that he had disassembled and cleaned twice since his arrival, three clips and four flash-bangs. It was going to be more than he needed but it was better to be over prepared than under prepared and he fervently believed in the old Marine saying that they were not paid to bring home bullets.

He then went through the plan once more in his mind and commended its simplicity. Distraction to the left and action to the right. Like a magician except one man was not going to see the funny side of the trick. Indeed he would not see the funny side of anything anymore after Regan had his way.

Carl Williams sauntered past the doormen of the Paradise Club with a beautiful young Latino girl on his arm. As professional as the doormen were in that club they could not help but look at the girl in awe. As for Williams, they knew not to cast a glance in his direction. His reputation as a man of action was becoming legendary in the city and those who had crossed him in any way knew to keep away from him or suffer the consequences.

Williams occupied the same table every evening that he visited the club. It was a matter of pattern that he followed so that he knew always what was happening on his turf. He could also see the best looking women from the vantage point that he held at his table.

Tonight he shared the table with a few close friends, his drinking buddies and their girls. He had no reason to be concerned in the surroundings of the club and relaxed back into his seat his arm draped around the young girl's shoulder and his hand toying with her ample breast.

His senses did not pick up on the solitary figure sitting at the window table sipping chardonnay from a crystal glass.

Regan had arrived an hour before Williams and, after presenting himself at the entrance, was pompously ushered to his seat by the fawning manager. Regan was amused by the managers insistence that he was delighted at the Señor's return and that his visits should be more regular. Regan had thanked him and sat at his table with as little fuss as possible.

After viewing the menu Regan ordered a salad and fish for main course. His favourite bottle of white wine had indeed being chilling since Cinderella had booked his table and he poured himself a glass while waiting for his meal.

The club was filling up with couples and groups and that, combined with the dark lighting and décor, suited the plan that Regan had in mind.

Ten minutes before Williams walked in the door Regan noticed two young men at the bar request the table that was two from him. Generally that would not have been a concern except Regan had noted that they walked like soldiers and worse still, they were carrying side arms. The slight bulge under their Jackets was barely noticeable, but noticeable nonetheless.

For a moment Regan had thought that they were the Delta boys that Petersen had told him about. However, the fact that Regan had noticed them so quickly meant that they were not. Delta boys were only visible when they wanted to be.

Ten minutes later Regan's questions were answered when Williams walked in with his girl. Just before sitting down he cast a glance at the two men at the table and gently nodded to them.

Bingo, Regan thought. Williams was not stupid enough to not have his back covered in some sense. No matter, Regan had that planned into his mission.

Regan ate slowly. He wanted to prolong the time as a diner so that his target would loosen up more, be more relaxed and fuelled by alcohol. From his viewing point all was going well and Williams seemed to be enjoying himself and his last meal.

Regan leaned over to take a look out the window and while doing so tipped more wine into the potted plant on his right. He had sipped a glass but the rest was going to the roots of the palm tree. Strike time was getting closer.

Williams got up to go to the bathroom and Regan noticed him stagger slightly while removing himself from the grip of his girlfriend.

Strike time.

Regan raised himself from the chair and placed his napkin beside his plate. He began to move towards the bathroom after Williams and moved carefully but intently. It was going to be swift. He would follow him in and take him down in the bathroom. Then the plan went to hell.

'Hello, handsome.' The grip on his arm was firm and the voice very sexy and Regan knew in an instant that the bathroom option was in jeopardy. He turned to face the lady and only his training stopped him from jumping out of his skin.

'Rachel, what the fuck are you doing here,' he spat angrily as she stood before him with an impish grin.

'It's a long and complicated story and I don't have time to explain,' she whispered in his ear. He looked at her in amazement as she stood there before him. Her black wig and heavy make up was hiding her from Williams's memory but not from Regan's.

'Kid, I have a job to do and you are wrecking my plans. I don't want to know how you got here but I do want you to leave now.'

'Not until I see him die. I must see him die,' she insisted.

Regan hadn't time for this and he knew it. Any further remonstrations with her and they would start attracting attention.

'Rachel, wait for me at the bar closest to the door. When I move, you move too. I mean it. You have fucked things up and this might yet go south on us. Now go!'

Rachel turned and walked to the bar.

By now Williams had returned to his seat and Regan felt the rising sense of frustration. Fuck it, he thought and decided to use plan B. The men from the table down from him had noticed him speaking to the girl and here now looking in his direction. It was time to move. *Showtime*, Regan said to himself as his adrenaline kicked-in at full speed.

Regan pulled a packet of smokes from his pocket, unwrapped the cellophane and pulled out the metallic paper tab. He took out a cigarette and rolled it onto his lips. He then exaggerated a patting movement on his pockets looking for a light before looking around for someone with a lighter.

He stood up and walked to a young lady chatting to her friends close to the table where Williams's men were sitting. He made a striking motion with his hand to the girl in a silent question for a light. The body-hugging dress the girl was wearing revealed everything but the presence of a lighter and Regan smiled at her negative reply to his quest. He then turned to the two at the table.

'Got a light, guys?' he asked with a sheepish smile.

'Yeah, sure, man. Here,' replied the bigger of the two.

Regan leaned across the table, cigarette between his lips, to have the smoke lit for him. While exaggerating his lean he was able to drop a small flash-bang at his feet and gently kick it under the table.

'Thanks, guys,' he added and walked away from the table unbuttoning his Jacket.

From the moment he dropped the charge he had eight seconds to clear the zone. He did that easily.

Three, two, one...the flash was as blinding as a bolt of lightning and everyone turned except Regan. The bang that followed made everyone hit the floor. Again, except Regan. He was now ten feet from Williams and behind a pillar. The two men who were sitting at the table were now jumping to their feet trying to douse the flames on their legs with beer and water.

Williams was staring at the commotion across at the window when a large figure stepped into his line of view.

'Get the fuck out of my way, shithead,' he roared at the figure before him. His roar was all the louder now that the music had stopped but it drew no attention as everyone was looking at the two men trying to put out their personal fires.

Regan stood before Williams with his pistol aimed at the man's groin. Williams had no time to respond or react to the threat standing before him.

An orange lick of flame spat out twice from the silenced weapon and hit Williams squarely in the groin. A sheet of red spread angrily through the cotton of his jeans and he screamed in agony.

Regan raised the pistol to aim at Williams's face and smiled coldly at him.

'Rachel Longthorn sends her regards,' and he fired twice into the unprotected but protesting face.

Blood and brain tissue splashed across the table and Carl Williams slumped onto the lap of the girl who was seated beside him.

Across the floor Rachel watched her nightmare being put to rest. She had not blinked when she saw Regan pump the bullets into her attacker. She did not flinch as the mist of super heated blood hung in the air nor at the face of the girlfriend as her lover's blood erupted onto her. No, Rachel felt nothing. Not even joy.

Regan was in no doubt that Williams was dead. In his mind he registered the death as one would count points in a good basketball match. He had achieved the closure that all had wanted and now it was time to leave.

He spun on his heals and slipped the gun back into its holster under his left arm. He didn't wait to see the death he had just caused slip down from the seat onto the floor. Regan was walking away quicker than the blood that was pouring out of the head wounds and pooling itself under the ragged remains of the head. Regan was making a direct line for Rachel before the initial shock evaporated from those who had witnessed what had happened. He didn't want some wannabe hero make a move and so he had to move fast and get out of the club.

Rachel was moving towards the door when Regan caught up with her. He put his arm around her waist and ushered her towards the door. It would not be long before someone figured out what was happening.

'Nice work', Rachel offered.

'Thanks.' More than that he did not know what to say. He felt like laughing at her comment but could only manage a smile.

The screaming had not abated and the security staff had switched on all of the lights in order to see what was happening. By the time it was clear to some what had happened Regan and Rachel were clear of the exit and walking arm in arm down the street, a carefree couple out for a stroll.

A large bouncer had ran to the aid of the screaming girl just before the lights had come on and had slipped in the puddle of blood that was spreading from the body of Williams. The lights came on just as the bouncer landed on his backside into the puddle of blood and he flayed in panic in the sticky warmness as he realised what he had landed in.

The two minders who had been sitting near Regan before he had set them alight had been knocked to the floor and the flames put out. They were now being attended to by a swarm of do-gooders who had gone to their aid and it was evident that their wounds were not life threatening. Regan had never intended killing them and so their lives had been spared.

Regan and Rachel had flagged a taxi just as the first of the police cars and ambulances came speeding around the corner. Regan intended on returning to his hotel, collecting his belongings and getting the hell out of Dodge as quickly as possible. He had no intention in staying around to be a part of any investigation into the death of a US diplomatic security agent. Especially since he was responsible for the attack.

Rachel had nothing to say. She had seen another man killed by the young soldier sitting beside her and she felt nothing. Staring out the window of the taxi at the streets whizzing by she could not remember why she had decided to follow Regan to Colombia. She had wanted to see justice done and, to an extent, she was glad of that. Williams had died in the way she had wanted but it did not make her feel any better. He had raped her but she was alive. He was dead. This inescapable fact began to sink into her very conscience and she wondered quietly how Regan was able to continue with the life he had chosen. How was he able to take life so easily without it affecting him? Why did it not seem to matter to him when people died at his hands?

Regan's mind was wandering as well before he grasped it and placed it firmly back on path. He wanted to know how Rachel had gotten into Colombia and how she had found out where he had been going. He would deal with that later when the got back Stateside. He glanced over at her as she stared out the car window.

'Hungry?' he asked. She started laughing and shook her head in amazement at the question and at the man who had asked it.

On entering the hotel Regan took Rachel's hand in his so that Señor Muñoz would not start questioning him on the pleasantness of the evening. If it looked like he had 'scored' then he would be left alone in order to avoid any embarrassing questions. As the walked through the foyer Señor Muñoz nodded his good evening to Rachel and winked conspiratorially at Regan. The wink said, 'Good catch, Sir' and Regan could not help but smile to himself.

On entering the lift Regan let go of Rachel's hand and hit the button for his floor.

'Sorry about that. I just didn't want him asking questions and I thought if I held your hand then he would have guessed the answers to his questions,' he explained.

Rachel laughed and smiled back at him. He had to explain everything so that there was no misunderstanding. She found that endearing.

'Just a pity you had to let go,' and walked through the opening doors of the lift as it arrived on the required floor.

Regan smiled and walked after her.

10

Mirrors and smoke.

The police had arrived in force as soon as the manager had called them, informing them that there had been a shooting in his club. As soon as they had arrived they had instructed that all patrons be interviewed before being allowed to leave. The local chief had arrived on the scene and was busily instructing his men to close the doors and start the interviews as soon as possible. Neither he nor his men noticed the two men by the bar slip under the bar flap and out through the staff exit. They did not want to stay around and be questioned.

The two men in question were both Colombian and both had worked for Carl Williams. He was their bread and butter from a forbidden menu and they had just seen their extra pay being shot to death and they wanted payback. They were both soldiers and they had fed information to Williams about troop movements in the mountains where he used to keep his victims. Now they were going to be soldiers again.

Just as the commotion had ceased one of the men had used his mobile to call their friend outside in the waiting car advising him of what had happened and to keep an eye on a tall foreigner who was exiting the club. He was ordered to follow at a distance if necessary but he was not, under any circumstance, to make contact or more importantly, lose him.

Regan could not have known that he was followed back to the hotel. No plan could ever be planed to perfection and unfortunately Regan's plan fell into that category now.

He was now back in his room and sitting on the comfortable couch by the large window opened onto the muggy city. He was cleaning his gun and repacking it into the case for the flight back home. And he was thinking.

Rachel was sitting opposite him combing her hair after removing the wig and was humming to herself. She was now over the initial shock and felt happier in herself. She also felt happier being close to Regan.

Regan looked up from his task at hand and caught her staring at him.

'Now what?' he asked with a mock look of concern on his face.

'You are a very attractive man, Mr Regan,' she answered back with a smile. The smile hit a switch inside Regan and he felt a surge of mixed emotion surge through his body. Rachel, with her head tilted to one side and that cheeky smile reminded Regan of his sister. He had known all along that Rachel reminded him of someone but his mission mind would not allow him to wander to far from the problems at hand at the time. Now the Colombian mission was over and his mind was free to seek answers.

Rachel saw the hurt in his eyes and felt that she had over stepped the mark.

'Regan, I am sorry. I didn't mean it that way. I mean...' and he cut her off.

'You smile like my sister,' he explained softly.

Rachel stood up and walked over to where Regan was sitting and kneeled before him. He did not flinch as she took his head in her hands and looked into his eyes. She sought some form of emotion but saw none. She leaned closer until her lips brushed off his and she could nearly taste the anger from his breath. Her heart was thumping with fear and excitement as she fought the desire to kiss him and to pull him onto her body. He was coiled up like a deadly snake ready to strike and she felt the tension as she slowly moved her hands from his face to his chest. Yet there wasn't a blink from the grey blue eyes that had locked into hers.

Regan felt like he was going to explode. She had entered his zone and now he had to decide where to take this situation. Only watching as she walked out of the elevator had he allowed himself to realise how beautiful she really was. That made him glad that he had killed Williams. Now she was kneeling before him with her hands on his chest and he really had no mission plan for this situation. He nearly laughed at the absurdity of the situation. A mission plan for a woman! He had been away from women for too long.

Rachel leaned in closer and kissed him. She felt a weight on her chest, a pressure that needed to be released, and she kissed him harder. Her body felt warmer and tenser than it had ever before and she wanted him. He still had not reacted but his eyes were still locked into hers. She leaned back a little; still holding his stare, and took her hands from his chest. Slowly she unbuttoned the top three buttons of her blouse and pulled one side away to reveal her naked breast. Finally, he reacted.

Regan reached out to touch her, his hand steady and controlled. His hand hovered over her naked flesh and she could feel the tingle of heat from his hand on her breast. He reached closer but not to touch. Instead, he drew back over her blouse and buttoned it closed.

'Not now, Rachel, not....' And a knock on the door interrupted him. 'Thank Christ,' he said and raised himself from the couch and walked to the door. Rachel released a breath of tension followed by a quite giggle.

He reached for the door handle and had the door half opened before he felt any danger. He felt something in the air and had been too distracted by Rachel for his own good. He let out a breath of relief when he saw Señor Muñoz at the door.

He picked up on the danger as soon as he saw the look on Señor Muñoz's face and he heard the hammer being cocked on a pistol. Señor Muñoz was standing in a puddle of his own urine and looked terrified to death. Then the side of his head exploded outwards as a silenced round paid a quick visit to the inside of his head.

Regan was already rolling backwards and drawing his spare pistol before the body hit the ground and as the body hit the ground with a wet, splashing sound, Regan had fired twice into the light socket. He needed darkness. He then fired at chest height down the length of the wall before completing his roll back to the table where his briefcase lay still opened. His left hand released the empty clip from his Sig as his right hand grabbed a fresh clip from the briefcase. There was no fumbling and his eyes had remained on the door for the brief moment it took for him to change clips.

Reloaded, he opened fire at waist height again down the length of the wall with his left hand while short fusing a Flash-Bang with his right before throwing it, bouncing it off the opened door so that it would roll into the hall onto those out there. It was times like this that he wished that he had stored an automatic weapon of some variety in his case. He needed to reload again and tossed a second Flash-Bang just in case while reloading.

In less than twenty seconds, which felt like an eternity to Rachel as she hid behind the couch, Regan had tossed three Flash-Bangs and had emptied three clips of thirteen rounds each. Then he stopped. The flurry of activity ceased in a cloud of smoke and cordite. Regan had been unleashed in a blur of controlled violence and now he needed to check the damage.

'Stay down until I call you and don't move,' he advised her as he made his push to the door.

Once at the door Regan used the laminated plastic of his credit card to get an idea of what was happening down the hall from his door. By the reflection of the card he was able to see one body in the hallway and possibly one or two moving down by the end of the hall by the elevator. The situation had to be viewed as a whole picture and not just the situation in the hallway and Regan knew that he had to make a move immediately. It was going to be a reaction based on skill and experience and not on planning.

He was about to make his move when he heard the sirens from outside and knew that there was no more time left for inaction. Fuck, he thought to himself as he prepared to act. He had two pistols fully loaded and decided not to use any more Flash-Bangs. His worry now was that the local authorities would view this as a terror attempt and seek assistance from the US Embassy. That would mean that the Delta boys, who were already in Bogotá, might be called to defuse a possible terror incident. That was the very last thing he wanted to do and so he moved. He stepped into the hall and started firing.

Downstairs in the foyer there was a hive of activity as police and soldiers crowed in to assist those held on one of the upper floors. The call had come in on a military waveband and so all knew that it was real. It was known that a foreign national had a woman held in a room in the hotel and that it was probably the same individual who had killed an American Security Agent in a club in the centre of town. The Colombians who had worked for Williams were now doing a fine job in turning the whole of the police force and the army against Regan. The clock was ticking.

Through the smoke Regan could see the outlines of two men at the end of the hall. It was not a considered action when he opened fire but a systematic reaction to what his eyes told him was danger. He engaged his targets and both fell within an instant of each other. He knew that the first had been squarely drilled through the forehead by the two rounds that he had squeezed off but he felt the second may not have been completely neutralised. He stepped to the body of the target that had been downed in the initial assault and shot him twice in the head with his second pistol while keeping the first trained on the two at the end of the hall. He was making damn sure that none of the three attackers would move again. He jogged to the end of the hall keeping his weapon trained on the two bodies, sweeping from one to the other in a swift and controlled motion. Once at the bodies he saw that both were dead, shot them both in the chest to be sure, and then kicked their weapons away. It was then that he heard the orders come in on the radio that was protruding from under the hip of one of the men. It was time to get Rachel and get out of the hotel.

Rachel was where he had left her and he was glad to see that she had not decided to move. He slammed the briefcase shut and looked calmly at her.

'It is time to get out of here. I don't know exactly how just yet but we have kinda outlived our welcome here. Plan B was to make my way out through the mountains but that was not with you being part of the plan. You wouldn't have a spare helicopter anywhere, would you?' he added with a grin.

'Yes.' Came the answer, which he did not expect. 'There is a helicopter on the roof of the Palace Gardens Apartments. My father bought a suite there when he became ambassador. The helicopter is his as well. Can you fly?'

'Yes, but, oh what the Hell. We need to get out of here first and consider the rest of the issue after that. Grab the case and lets go.'

Rachel took the closed case and Regan took her hand as they walked back to the two bodies by the elevator. Once there, Regan picked up the radio from under the dead man and listened for updates on the situation. While listening to the chatter he glanced down at one of the bodies and an idea came to mind. It was a slim chance but he needed to get out with his cover intact and this seemed lie the only way to do it. The dead guy was his size and build so it might work.

Plans A, B and C had gone to Hell. Maybe this one might work.

Downstairs in the foyer the police chief and an office from the army were in a head-to-head. They wanted to resolve the situation without needing American assistance. They had their pride to consider too and the offer from the US Embassy to lend the visiting Delta Team had not been rejected but instead, put on the long finger for the time being.

They were standing by the communication systems listening to the chatter and to the gunfire further up in the Hotel when the direct line to one of the soldiers upstairs came alive with screams. A frantic voice, obviously in pain, came on line.

'I have the girl. I have the girl. I am coming down with the girl. We have two men down in the hallway. One dead, one with head wounds but he is still breathing. The target is injured but not dead. Repeat, not dead.' There were further gunshots and then more shouts on the radio. ' I am hit. I am hit. The girl is safe but I am hit. We are making our way down in the elevator. Please have rescue services available.'

The army officer replied to the frantic request for help.

'Soldier, we have emergency services on stand by. Please advise of target. Is he down? Repeat, is he down?'

'That's a negative, Sir. He is still shooting. He seems to be injured but he can still shoot. I advise that you assault from the fire well and not the elevator as he seems to have his back to the fire escape. Sir, I am coming down with the girl and one of my men...' and the line went dead.

The doors of the elevator opened and a girl rushed out screaming and pointing to the others seeking assistance. Behind her, the soldier who had just been on the radio to his officer, staggered out of the lift carrying his fallen comrade on his shoulder. It seemed that the weight of his man was too much and his knees buckled and he fell as medics ran to his assistance. The body of his comrade rolled off his shoulder and onto the ground, landing on his back, his dead eyes looking upwards at nothing. The medic closest to him could see that their time and expertise would be wasted on him as he was already dead and they turned their attention to the hero who had brought him down. They saw him on his knees staring at the body of his comrade and the blood still pouring down his face.

The young medic slid in on his knees to grab the soldier before he fell any further. It seemed to the medic that the young soldier had come through Hell and it was now in his hands to ease the rest of his journey.

At the same time the Officer and the police chief approached their man seeking information but the medic pushed them away. It was obvious from the bloodstains on his clothing that he had used all his effort to get down to the foyer and now there was nothing left in his reserves.

The soldier was placed onto a stretcher and another medic assisted the first. A drip of blood expanders was administered to the left arm and a heavy sterile cotton bandage to the head wound. The soldier then groaned and coughed out a splattering of blood and saliva. Judging by the blood flow from the head and now the fact that he was respiring blood, the medics decided to work the head wound and keep his air passage free until a surgeon could work on him at the hospital. The other wounds did not seem to be life threatening.

The body of the other soldier was now being carried out to an awaiting ambulance, covered from head to toe in a white sterile sheet. The blood from his head and chest wounds was seeping through the virgin white of the sheets and the medic threw his red jacket over the blotches to hide the image from the camera crews that were beginning to gather outside. News of this type travels fast in every city and not just in Bogotá. The crews were waiting for the scoop on the story of the week. The killing at the club was now old news as the excitement had now passed to the hotel where the live action was.

The two medics lifted the stretcher and began to carry it to the ambulance when the young lady the soldier had rescued rushed to his side.

'Is he going to be ok? Is he?' she shouted at the first medic. The medic nodded vigorously, not understanding English, and turned the question onto his more educated colleague.

'He speak English, he speak,' as he nodded towards his colleague.

'Is he going to be alright?' She asked frantically.

'Miss, I don't know, it is a head wound and it is hard to say. Please let us get him to the hospital.' He was serious about his patient and he wanted to get going.

'I want to stay by his side. I want to thank him when he wakes. Please let me come along.'

The medic looked at the girl and then at his patient and knew that he hadn't time to argue that she couldn't ride in the ambulance. He decided on the quickest route to the hospital.

'Come on. Lets go but you must not interfere,' he added in a serious tone.

'I wont and thank you so much,' she added with a smile.

As the stretcher came rushing out the doors of the hotel to the awaiting ambulance the cameras started flashing and reporters started hollering their questions to those carrying the stretcher and the policemen surrounding it. At the same time a team of Colombian Special Forces were entering through a side door and making their way silently up the stairs to engage their target. Their orders were to engage and kill.

The stretcher was pushed into the back of the ambulance and a helpful hand helped the young lady, who was covering her face, into the seat. The doors were slammed shut and a shout to the driver gave the ok for the pedal to hit the floor and the siren wailed into life.

Rachel sat in the back of the ambulance giddy with excitement. The plan had gone down so well that she wanted to bust with joy. She smiled over at the medic who was attending the wounds of their patient. He nearly had a heart attack when the patient sat up and pointed a pistol directly between his eyes.

'Hi,' the polite greeting whispered from the bloody face.

Regan had decided to brazen his way out of the hotel and the only way that was going to be successful was to become one of the men that he had killed. Once he had swapped clothing and now bore the blood and holes in the Jacket, he pulled a tiny slim razor file from the strap of his watch and slashed a gaping wound into his forehead just above the hairline. The pumping blood would be real. He then nicked his gum just below his front teeth allowed the blood to fill his oral cavity, an effect he used to good effect when he coughed up blood in front of the medic. Overall he was a convincing victim. Now, he was a soldier again.

The medic was frozen to the spot where he sat and watched in disbelief as the man before him ripped the drip needle from his arm and pulled the bandage from his head.

'Got anything smaller than this? Never mind, I'll find something.

He rummaged through a drawer and found a smaller bandage, one suitable for the cut on his head and not a bullet wound. Rachel washed his head and face with sterile water ensuring that his hair was clean as well. All the time Regan kept the gun trained on the medic who didn't move an inch nor utter a word. He figured that whomever the man before him was he didn't want to piss him off.

The driver of the ambulance was oblivious to the happenings in the rear and was speeding along until there was a tap on the separation window. He reached back and opened it without looking and asked was the patient all right. He felt the cold end of a pistol just below the jaw line as a reply and then an accentless babble of Spanish which advised him to slow the ambulance down and to turn off the lights and siren.

'Now what?' he asked once he had complied with the demand.

'Pull over by that tree and kill the engine,' came the reply in a cold, calculated voice that spoke volumes of the intent that it exuded.

The ambulance pulled over and the engine idled to a stop. The driver felt like making a run for it but he didn't want to leave his colleague alone in the back with whoever it was that had just hijacked his ambulance. As he was contemplating his next move a large bandage, doused in chloroform and held in a powerful hand, covered his mouth and nose and he quickly passed out.

Regan pulled the drivers body through the separation window and onto one of the stretchers. There he bound him with restraining straps and checked his victim's pulse in the same way as he had done with the medic seconds before.

He had no intention of hurting either of the two men but he didn't exactly want them to be free to call in their ordeal as soon as they woke up.

'Rachel, reach in and pull the receiver from their radio and see can you reach the keys.'

The Special Forces team in the hotel had reached the target floor and eased their way down to the room that had been identified as that being the room of the instigator of the two attacks. It was an eight-man team that had been well versed in counter-terrorism warfare by Delta Force. They had formed a working pact after the capture of the head of the Median Cartel some years ago and that pact had stayed intact through thick and thin.

Now they were ready to pounce onto the lone attacker who had killed on their turf and wanted to do it without outside help, to show that they could as opposed to indicating that they didn't need help anymore.

The young captain and team leader edged his way to the door and with his extended mirror, peeked into the room. It seemed empty but the lights were off and so he wasn't quiet sure. He decided that shouting a warning was something the police did and not the job of his strike team. He was going in with night goggles down and had signalled his intent to the other men behind him. They all signalled acknowledgement and the captain ran in and to the left sweeping his weapon to the left hand side of the room while the second soldier, who was directly behind him going through the door, dropped right, scanning that part of the target room. It was clear to the soldiers as soldier three and four charged in covering the centre point of the room that the target had already fled. Had he been in the room he would have had a nasty surprise but, as things stood, no action was needed by the soldiers and from that point, unless the unlikely happened and their target re-emerged in the hotel, the matter would now be a police issue.

The young captain radioed down to the commander on the ground floor advising that their man was already gone. His disappointment was clearly audible.

Regan was trying to think his way out of the problem that faced him now. It was not going to take the authorities long to figure out what had happened and then the net would start to close on them again. Rachel was baggage that he had not intended on carrying but he could not let her go and fend for herself again in the same country where all this shit had began. The helicopter was out of the question. He could fly one but it would not take them as far as they needed to go. Then it came to him. They had brazened their way out of the hotel and they could do the same with the international airport. He decided to use Cinderella again.

Rachel was now just along for the ride. She felt totally at ease in the company of Regan and knew that he would protect her at all costs. She also knew that she had the way out as well. A way much quicker than Regan's. She turned to tell him and hoped he would not be angry.

'Epps came down with me on my fathers jet. I told him that he was to wait at the airport and that I would be back with you. See, I am useful.'

Regan nearly had a fit but he knew that it was the quickest and safest way out.

'I'll deal with Epps when we get you home. How did you give him the slip after what had happened? Jesus, he was supposed to shadow you until all this was over.'

'I told him that you had given the OK after speaking to my father. He believed me.'

Regan nearly smiled

Forty-five minutes later the taxi carrying Regan and Rachel slid into the taxi rank unnoticed. Regan paid the fair, much to Rachel's annoyance, and the two walked through the large sliding doors into the main concourse. Epps was waiting there for them.

'I can't believe you let her come down here again.'

'You didn't OK this with Mr. L. Oh, Jesus. Rachel, are you trying to get me fired? Regan, I am really sorry. With everything going on ….I just didn't want to question your call on this.'

Regan eased off and turned to Epps again. 'The day you stop asking questions is the day something is going to go really wrong. Now, have you Rachel's passport?'

Things were going to be all right.

They were all sitting on the private jet within twenty minutes and Regan decided that enough time had been spent in his least favourite country. The pilot advised them that there was going to be a delay as the tower was trying to allocate clearance for them. Regan didn't like that news. He was not sure that Cinderella would be able to negotiate with the airport's mainframe fast enough and he really felt the need to get out of Dodge as quickly as possible. He flipped open his case of tricks again and pulled out his laptop. He was going to go Governmental on this one and favours were going to be pulled. Cinderella gave him immediate access to the US Embassy and he dialled the phone number that appeared on screen.

'United States Embassy, good morning,' came the reply.

'First Sec, please. It is urgent.'

'Sir, the First Sec is busy. I shall, patch you through to his assistant if you wish, Sir.

It was a Marine on the other end of the line thought Regan. Who else would use 'Sir' so frequently in a conversation?

'I am talking to a US Marine am I not?'

'Sir, yes, Sir.'

'Listen, Marine. Check your Red List. Under the Counter Terrorism heading there should be a name and a code. I am going to match those codes now. Do you understand?' The Red List was a detailed and codified list of those who could call into the Embassy at any time of the day or night for immediate assistance from the US Government. Now was one of those times.

'Go ahead, Sir.' came the automatic reply from the young Marine.

'Code, Alpha seven, Delta four, Dark-Eye.'

'Codification matches, Sir. I shall patch you through immediately.'

The phone rang once before being picked up. Mike Davies, First Sec, answered in his impeccably polite voice.

'Yes, Davies speaking. How may I be of assistance?'

'Davies, you know who this is by the code line being used. I don't have much time so I want you to listen very carefully. There is a private Lear jet on runway 4 at the airport. This plane needs to take off now and I do mean now. I want you to advise them that it is a FG flight carrying diplomats. That's it. I want to be off the ground in ten minutes.'

'That is impossible. Do you know the shit we will have to go....'

'That is not my problem. You understand that this flight will be designated 'Foreign Government' and we will be taking off in ten minutes. Otherwise there will be such an international shit storm that you will be wishing that you grew wings and came and flew us out yourself. Our engines are heating up and our pilot is good to go. Make it happen and call me back in five minutes.' He closed the phone and switched off the laptop.

'This better work.'

Regan was waiting for the cell phone to ring when he heard the engines power up and the pilot shout back to them that they were cleared for take off. Regan smiled to himself and thanked God and Davies for their intervention. It was a very close call. The cell phone rang at that moment and he answered it immediately.

'Yes.'

'I did it. You are clear to go as FM-2.'

'Sir, if I ever have the pleasure to meet you, dinner is on me.'

'I have to ask you a question. In fact I have been ordered to do so. Were you involved in the...action... taken this evening against unnamed individuals? Unnamed American individuals?'

'Sir, we can discuss all that at a later time but basically the answer is yes.'

'Safe flight home.'

'Thanks.'

11

Enigmatic Encounters

President Steven Malcolm was a patient man. His second year in the White House had been a difficult one. The war on terror was still ongoing. Of course it was because it was one of those 'wars' that needed to be. The wars on drugs and on organised crime were the same. Open-ended.

He had been awakened early by a call from his Secretary of Defence and hoped to God that something terrible had not happened. He did not put much hope in that.

Sitting in the Oval office waiting for him was Paul Borden, his Secretary of Defense. Borden was also his life long friend and closest advisor.

'Good morning, Paul. What has gone wrong in the world today?'

'Mr. President, we have had a situation develop in Colombia and I believe it in our interests to get to the bottom of it.?

'Paul, there is nobody else in here, drop the Mr. President crap.'

'Steve, we lost a man in Bogotá last night. He was the head of security for our embassy down there and he was assassinated in a local club while out with friends. It seems that our Colombian friends had the killer cornered in a hotel but he escaped after a brief gun battle. It is a messy situation....the man killed was Carl Williams. We had him under investigation over the Rachel Longthorn kidnapping. If you remember, Dark-Eye was used to get her home. They were not too happy to have left Williams alive down there. They may have gone back to finish their job.

'They were told that we were going to deal with Williams by other means. Do you think that they really went and finished the job? I mean they have a very free reign but the have to pay attention when we tell them not to do this shit. Look, are we sure it was them?

'Steve, it seems so. We received a call at the Embassy requesting assistance to get air clearance for a plane at the airport. The call came in under a Dark-Eye code. It was them.'

'Petersen is still in charge of Dark-Eye. Get him on the phone immediately. Then I want to speak to Longthorn himself.'

The day was young but the problem would make it old as already the Ambassador from Colombia was trying to call for an appointment.

It was pouring rain back at the Dark-Eye base and the dark clouds hanging over the large base matched the humour of the commander. Petersen was sitting at his desk clicking his way through the intelligence reports that were already trickling their way out of Colombia. The death toll was, for the moment, five. He knew that things had gone wrong for Regan otherwise there would have been only one death. A knock on his door interrupted his thinking.

'It's open. Come in.'

Regan walked through the door.

Petersen didn't know what to say. He was delighted to see his man back in one piece but he also knew that he was going to be the cause of a word of trouble. The fact that the young man had not yet had his chance to unleash hell in Italy was now starting to be a matter of concern for the commander.

'What happened down there, Regan?' He asked with as much poise as he could muster. He already knew the answer but wanted to hear the answer for himself.

'Rachel Longthorn turned up just as I was making my move. I had to alter the plan. It all went to shit.' He explained as bluntly as he could. 'Williams had better cover than I had allowed for and we were followed back to the hotel. There, his men killed the concierge while he was standing in front of me. I cut loose and, well, here I am now. I had to pull diplomatic assistance from the embassy in order to get the plane clearance for take off. That's pretty much it.'

Petersen listened to the explanation with out saying a word. What the Hell could he say? He had cleared the Op and now he was going to have to take the heat for it once news of it hit the political seniors. As his mind was working through the mist of lunacy that had been explained to him the red light on his phone console lit up aggressively. The White House was calling.

'Well, this is a little earlier than expected.' He allowed a smile to breach his serious demeanour as he reached for the phone.

'Petersen.' He answered coldly. He listened carefully for a minute before he had the opportunity to answer. 'Yes, Mr. President, I understand entirely. No, Sir, he has not reported back to base yet.' Another pause then, 'Thank you, Sir. Good morning.'

Regan looked sheepishly at his commander waiting for a berating. Petersen pulled a drawer open and pulled two diskettes from a plastic box.

'This is the little thing I had to give you. The blue disk is a list of contacts that we can use in Italy. They are non-government individuals so you can trust them. The main character that you can utilise is codenamed CREDIBILITY, ex-CIA and a good person in a storm. Credibility works for us but has not been actioned in a while. Anything you will require, and I mean anything, should come from this source and this source only. The red disk must remain within a metre of the blue at all times. If not, the electronic connection between both will be cut and all the information from Blue will be lost. Use the passports in your possession until you get to Italy. After that, depend on Credibility for new ones.

Regan took the two diskettes and slipped them into his chest pocket. He didn't know what to say. Petersen had, however, more to say.

'The President wants you put on hold for a while. He wants you to be removed from active service ASAP. That is due to Colombia. We may have overstepped our mark a little.' He allowed a grin to stretch across his rugged features again. 'Regan, as much as is possible I shall protect your tracks. However, remember what I said before, this is not a free for all. Take your targets down and get the fuck out of there. We will see then about making you reappear here.' He paused and looked deeply into the young mans eyes before finishing. 'This is your home and I want you back when you are ready.'

Regan took Petersen's hand and shook it warmly. His chest was bursting with pride and no little sense of love for the man who had become his father figure. He would come back and be a part of Dark-Eye again. Be apart of this unique family.

'Thanks you, Sir.'

'Get outta here, you crazy Mick.' Petersen felt the moment becoming too emotional for him. Regan walked to the door and opened it.

'Regan.'

'Sir?'

'I never got to say goodbye to my wife. They never found anything at Ground Zero that I could bury. I can never got closure. Bury your sister then bury your demons. Good luck to you.'

Regan stepped to attention and snapped a perfect salute to his commander.

'Sir. Yes, Sir.'

Steve Watson was sitting at his desk mulling over his options. The Americans were not going to give any information on Dark-Eye and that was final. He wanted to meet Regan and see what was going to happen and, in doing so, he needed to fulfil his promise to his dead friend knowing that he would carry that monkey on his shoulder until the promise was fulfilled. The phone rang and without knowing it, his life was going to ring a different bell as soon as he answered it.

'Watson.' He always answered in the same way giving only enough information to the caller that they knew that they had reached the intended person. The caller already knew that the intended person had answered the phone.

'Mr. Watson.' The voice was void of emotion. 'You have been looking for me.'

Steve Watson, for the first time in his life, was fazed and, indeed, he felt fear. The voice was Jack Regan's.

'Jack Regan. To what do I owe this honour.' He almost instantly regretted his flippant reply and wished to pull the words from the line. He knew also that he had not masked the surprise and, worst of all, the fear in his voice. He was talking to a man that had killed his countrymen, a man that he himself had been sent to kill. That man was dead and he was now talking to his reincarnation.

'It is no honour, Englishman. I wanted to put you out of your misery.' Regan didn't realise the effect of those last words and could not see the look of desperation of Watson's face. 'I think that I may need your help.'

Watson coughed in surprise and struggled to gain control of the conversation. 'You have a lot to answer for over here, Mr. Regan. Are you going to face your past?'

'I face it every day, Mr. Watson. Do you? The reply was a challenge.

'I remember those men that you killed. I remember the families that were ruined by your action. Don't you dare speak to me about the past.' Watson was becoming angry but the voice on the other end of the line did not seem to care.

'I need to see you. Let me know when you are capable of being an adult again. See you soon.' The line went dead.

Watson swore at himself and knew that he had blown a real opportunity to settle things with the young man who had taken so much of his life; a life spent hunting a ghost. He was leaning against the kitchen wall with the phone still in his hand when the doorbell to his apartment chimed. 'Who the fuck is this now, Bin Laden?' He muttered angrily to himself. He was attempting to recall the number that had just hung up on as he opened the door.

'Fuck!' was all he could say when the door was opened.

12

Shadow boxing.

Regan had done as his commander had ordered and moved quickly to leave the States. He had decided to fly to Dublin and make arrangements for his sister's funeral. The idea of going home was strange to him. He had been home once before but that was to put an end to the FFI group. He had not landed in Dublin Airport for that piece of work. In fact, like all Dark-Eye missions, that matter was carried out without the knowledge of the Irish government and they, of course, did not know that they had been invaded by a foreign power for a matter of a couple of hours. It was better that way.

Now he stood at passport control for non-EU persons. He was carrying a US passport and was travelling under the name of Jeff Holms, a contractor from New York.

'Business or pleasure, Sir?'

'I have business in the Dublin and then a couple of weeks travelling around. I am looking for any living relatives. I believe that there may be some down in Cork.' He smiled his big American smile.

'Well, welcome to Ireland, Sir. Enjoy your stay.'

'Thanks, I will.' He took his passport and walked into the main luggage collection area and waited briefly before his bags arrived. He really didn't fell like he was home but that was to be expected. He approached the ForEx and changed his Dollars to Euro and walked out to get a cab.

'Where ya headin', bud?'

'Just drop me into the centre and I shall find my way around from there. I am sure that I will find a room without much bother.

'American, eh?'

'Yeah, kinda.'

'What brings you to our over-priced little country? 'Tis not the fuckin' weather anyway. Fucking terrible shit we have been havin' these last few days.'

Regan smiled to himself. He had forgotten the pleasures that foreigners first encountered on visits to Ireland. Dublin taxi drivers were vocally gifted in a way that made Colin Farrell seem like an alter boy.

'Just taking a break from the hustle and bustle of New York. See can I find a few Irish relatives to have a pint with.'

'New York, eh? Jasus, how does it look now? I mean, after what the fucker Bin Laden did. Christ, I am really glad ye got him. Should have strung the fucker up by his balls and give him a good kicking. Kick the Jihad out of his scrawny little arse.'

Regan actually laughed at the image and took an immediate liking to his driver. 'I am sure that a lot of New Yorkers would agree with you, Sir. We were glad to get him all right. He would have given his trigger finger to have been on the DEVGRU team that hit the Abbottabad compound.

The conversation continued in the same vein until they reached O'Connell Street, the main thoroughfare in Dublin. The taxi driver then charged Regan thirty-five Euro for the journey and Regan gave him fifty. 'Now I know what you mean by over-priced.'

'Cheers, bud. Enjoy yourself.'

Regan found a quiet hotel on Camden Street and booked in for a two-week stay. The girl on the desk was polite and friendly and she smiled as she took his details. It was a no fuss hotel and catered for those who wanted a break from the hustle and bustle of the city centre hotels. It was also a five-minute walk from Watson's apartment and that was close enough to a man who wanted Regan dead.

His room was on the top floor and Regan sat on the window looking out onto the busy street. There were numerous stalls selling fruit and flowers on their private patches up the street and customers were strolling in and out of the busy pub across the road. The girl at the desk had mentioned that Flannery's pub was the place to go for a good pint and the best of banter with the locals who frequented the place. Regan decided to give it a go later after his unplanned meeting with Watson. He believed that he might need a drink afterwards.

He got up, pulled a light Jacket from his bag and looked at the weapons that had arrived in the diplomatic pouch. He decided against bringing any to the meeting and pushed the bag under his bed. He would forward it on to Italy in a couple of days. It was time to meet his nemesis.

Watson was lost for words but not for actions. In a single fluid motion he stepped back from the doorway and pulled his pistol from the holster that was attached to his belt and levelled the gun squarely into Regan's face. Regan didn't flinch but his eyes danced around Watson's face seeking intent and finding lots of it. The gun hand did not have a single tremor and the eyes were boring directly into Regan's.

'Shoot or ask me in, Englishman.' The voice was void of emotion and the eyes unwavering. Watson was at a loss and in that moment wished that Regan would attempt to draw a weapon, give him a reason to kill him and put the years of the hunt to an end. But he didn't. Instead, Regan walked into the mussel of the weapon until it was pushing against the bridge of his nose.

'Pull the trigger, Watson. Pull it now or listen to me.'

Watson was caught in a trance and the mellowing of the eyes to show that state of semi-trance was all Regan needed. He moved like a mongoose inwards onto Watson, his right hand shooting upwards clenching Watson's outstretched hand while his left came over the top, twisting the gun from Watson's grasp. In that single moment the tables had turned, for now Watson was at the end of the gun and Regan was staring him down. Watson's life began to flash before his eyes and a dreaded sense of defeat cut him more than the prospect of death. Then Regan knocked him with a clean punch to the lower jaw. Watson fell onto his backside onto the floor and sat there dazed and confused. Regan shut the door and walked past him into the spacious kitchen.

When Watson finally regained his senses and composure, he picked himself up and walked into the kitchen and found Regan sitting at the counter inspecting the pistol he had just taken from Watson.

'Make yourself at home.'

'Well, I wasn't going to stand at the door and wait for an invite. Your jaw ok?'

It was the fact that Regan asked about his jaw with an almost boyish grin that caused Watson to smile while rubbing the sore patch on his face.

'I have had worse.'

'Yeah, me too, Englishman. Me too.'

'So, you are Regan. You are the boy who became a man and have fucked up my life for so long. I thought you would be bigger. Well, to be honest, I didn't really know what to expect. I have allowed myself to hate you for so long that I have become immune to everything else.'

'Why do you hate me? I mean, we did what we had to do and I never killed anyone close to you. I never killed civilians.'

'You didn't have to kill the men you killed whether they were soldiers or not. You are a terrorist and I have pledged to bring you to justice.' The words shook as the came out of his mouth.

Regan slid the gun across the counter to Watson and challenged him.

'Kill me now then. Finish your game. I am not here to kill you but I will let you kill me now. Put me out of my misery and go home a contented man.'
Watson, again, was caught for words. Regan continued.

'I came here to ask for your assistance. If you help me, at the end of all that I have planned I shall go along with you to wherever you wish to bring me and face the charges you want to bring against me. I will not use any political clout that I now have, no diplomatic immunity as an American special services "Envoy." Nothing. However, if you do not wish to help then kill me now as I cannot do what I have to do with you on my back.'

Watson saw the sincerity in the young mans eyes and knew that he couldn't kill him. He knew that in that moment that he could never have killed him. All he really ever did was admire the man and knew he had to help him.

'For all that I have done to your countrymen, I apologise and I give you my word that I will face your courts once I finish what I have come to do. You have my word on that.' Regan extended his hand. Watson took it and shook it.

'Good.'

'Now what?' Watson asked as he stood and holstered his weapon.

'Let's go for a drink' Regan suggested as he too stood.

'Good idea, Regan. Just one thing, though.'

'Yeah?'

Watson caught him squarely on the chin with a right hook.

'Now we are even.'

Both men sat with pints of stout before them half way down the bar. Regan was visibly calmer than he had been in a long while and Watson sensed that. It was because he was home and felt no danger yet he was angled towards the door in case. Old habits die hard.

'I knew your sister quite well, Jack. I met her a couple of times when she used to visit your dad.'

Regan was staring into space yet it was clear that the words were registering in his head. It felt strange to speak of his sister in the past tense.

'I always thought that she would be listening to those words about me. I never expected to outlive her or my father. I mean, I never expected my life to go the way it did. I did some bad things but, I don't know, maybe what I do now makes up for it in some way.'

'Tell me about Dark-Eye.'

'Not much I can really say, Watson. It is a Hell of a unit. The men in it are really the best of the best. We have put a dent in Al Qaeda operations in the States. Not the kinda stuff anyone will see on telly but we get the job done. We hit them really hard recently but we suffered for it. We lost or first men in combat and the feeling really hits.'

'How many?'

'We lost four for their twenty-nine. One of our snipers and three really good guys in a support chopper that was downed by a technical fault on a fire run. It really went to shit but we held it together and wiped them out. We went to close out the deal on a house were we knew that an attack was being planned. However, the plan was more advanced than we expected and a bus full of the fuckers drove into the compound, as we were getting ready to raid the house. The chopper came in with its wing support; something went wrong and it fireballed into the ground giving away our position. All Hell broke loose and one of our snipers took a round to the head in the fire fight.'

'Christ, Jack, we didn't realise they had gotten more in there to stir the shit.'

'Remember the sleepers we had in London and throughout England, well I believe they have done pretty much the same.'

'How were you recruited, Jack. We lost all trace of you after the Legion. I mean, we never believed you died in action but you surely disappeared.'

'I spent three weeks training with some of our guys and a team from Delta. It seems one of the Delta guys was recruited into Eye and he mentioned me to the recruiters. Somehow they got to see me in action and then I disappeared.'

Watson stared into his drink mulling a million questions in his mind. He felt a strange sense of awe sitting with the young man beside him. It was as if nature had created a new entity and had not explained it to man. Regan was that entity, a chameleon of emotions and abilities, able to change in the blink of an eye.

'What now?'

Regan changed from emotional soldier to cold killer in order to answer the question.

'Now I go to Italy, find those who killed my sister and kill them.'

It was so matter of fact. Watson's answer surprised even himself.

'I want to go with you.'

13

A sister's face.

The President sat back into his chair angry at the report that was strewn on his desk before him. He knew that American policies were unpopular with his allies and with the people of the allied countries. America was a bad word in most peoples mind now and he was trying to change that. He had a war to fight and yet he had to fight it while trying to be diplomatic. The oil and water relationship between war and diplomacy was not lost on him. Nor was the ability to make tough and undesirable decisions. He had one to make now. He turned to his Sec Def and spoke calmly.

'Paul, this matter in Colombia,' he paused for a moment to rephrase his thoughts for the recorders that were ever listening, 'we must finalise it for the good of our relations with the Colombians. We must clean it away tidily. Have I made myself clear?

The intentional ambiguity was frustrating for Paul Borden. Regan was going to be a thorn in the Presidents side and he had to find a sudden cure for it. He would have to notify Petersen down at Dark-Eye's base of the President's intent.

Watson sat at his desk in the study of his spacious apartment. He was playing with the million thoughts that were now streaming through his mind. He knew that it was futile to try and grasp one at a time and to try to make sense of them. For all he understood of terror and counter-terror, this new step he was about to take with Regan disturbed him. The fact that he had dedicated a large portion of his life trying to find they young man played heavily on his decision to now try and help him. He had promised Jack's father that he would find him and make him seek revenge for what had happened to his friend's daughter but Jack was already on that trail and it was Jack who had found him. It was all head over ass! Yet it somehow felt right. Fulfilling a promise had always felt right to Watson and he knew that helping Jack was the right thing to do. He decided to call the Office in London. That was his first solid news.

The voice was cold and articulate, as was to be expected from one who held the lofty title of Head of the British Secret Intelligence Service, MI6, and the encrypted line was almost as secure as a prayer to God.

'Steve, how are things across the water?'

'Fine, Sir, very little happening over here except I am considering closing an old file of mine.'

The Chief was aware of everything that was on the table of his men and women and hit straight to the point.

'Your hunt for Regan is over?'

'In a sense, Sir, yes it is. The trail is dead and from all the information I have received, I can say with relative certainty that Regan himself, is dead.'

There was silence on the line for a brief moment and then The Chief spoke again.

'I think not.'

'Sir?'

'Steve, I have known you for too long. I don't believe that you think he is dead.'

'Sir, whether he is or isn't I don't want to spend the rest of my life chasing that shadow. There are other things I want to spend my time on. Dead Irish terrorists no longer interest me.'

'Your service to the Crown does not take note of your interests, Steve. You are employed to get the results that we request of your particular talents. No more and no less.'

'I don't think I can continue like this, Sir. With all due respect, I think I need a break. Some time to figure out where this is all leading. I think I have lost the edge and I want some time to reassess my position.

'Steve, we shall take the time to assess your position. Shall we say four weeks? Stay within Ireland or come home but for the next four weeks stay available. Go do some fishing or something like that.'

'Thank you, Sir, I think I need the break.'

'Very good, do that and we shall hear from you when you are done. Goodbye.'

The line went dead in Watson's hand.

The Chief punched a number into his phone and spoke to one of his senior operators.

'I want a tag on Steve Watson. I think he may be coming loose at the edges. Keep an eye on him.' His voice made it very clear that his intentions were to be adhered to.

Within an hour two agents were on their way to the airport with tickets in their pockets for Dublin.

Regan was sitting in his hotel room staring at the walls. He was trying to piece together all that had happened in the previous days and felt the speed of what was occuring needed to be slowed down. The pace was too fast for the carefulness that he always applied to his actions. Speed did not lean towards his meticulous nature and now he needed to depend on that nature more than ever before. This new hunt was going to test his skills to the maximum and he needed to draw on all his resources and his intelligence was his finest resource.

The triple knock on the door advised him that Watson was back and now it was time for them to put their plan of action into physical being. He opened the door to his newfound accomplice.

'How did it go with your Boss?'

'I really don't think that he bought my story but it might have given me enough time to get out of here and over to Italy before they start looking for me. He said I had four weeks to straighten out my head and see where I am going. Ha! I need more than four weeks to sort out where my fucking head is not to say where it is going.'

'Watson, are you sure you want to come in on this? I mean, it is not your problem and I have given you my word that I will come in after all this is over.'

'As much as you might not like it, your father was really my friend. I owe this to him and to your sister. I want to help.'

Regan looked up at him and a genuine smile crossed his face. 'Ok, Buddy, let's go to the land of pasta.'

'Less of the 'Buddy', pal.' Watson replied with a grin.

Izzo was sitting with head in his hands waiting for sleep to overcome him. It had been a long couple of days, made no easier by the fact that his wife had come forward to care for the young orphan that had been left by the dead Irish girl. Slowly, but surely, Izzo was being dragged further into the emotional quick sand of this investigation and the call that morning from Dublin had pulled him even further in. Her brother was coming to identify the remains and he wanted to meet Izzo in person. The man had spoken flawless Italian and Izzo had assumed that it was an Italian Diplomat from Dublin who was calling. He was shocked when he asked the man to identify himself. A cold voice answered, 'I am the dead girl's brother. Please be at the morgue.'

Now he was sitting there waiting.

The flight to Milan had been uneventful. Watson had read the papers while Regan just closed his eyes but did not seem to sleep. In fact, sleep was the furthest thing from his mind. The calculations that were running through his mind would have taken six months of confession with a patient priest to cleanse from the mind of any other man. The mathematical calculations of death were being expanded on the blackboard of Regan's mind. And the answers were coming quickly.... and vividly.

At the airport in Milan Watson could now see why he never got close to capturing Regan. The man just blended in, changed in a manner that was almost hard to believe for Watson. In gestures and spoken word, Regan had become an Italian before his very eyes. At the Hertz desk Regan even argued down the price of the car with the young lady at the desk. She fell straight for his charm and accepted his Italian ID card for copying without raising an eyebrow. He was an Italian and Watson could not help but admire the total professionalism of the young soldier. Indeed, so much so that Watson allowed himself to forget that Regan, in his mind, was the Crown's most wanted terrorist.

Regan finished up the transaction and walked away from the desk with Watson.

'Time to go to the morgue. The girl at the desk has sorted out the hotel for us. Something to do with a partnership that they have and our rooms will be ready for us later this afternoon. Let's go.'

Watson followed on without saying a word.

The battle against sleep was being lost when a doctor gently shook Izzo's shoulder. 'There are two men upstairs waiting asking for you. I believe you have been waiting for them.'

Izzo rubbed a course hand over his sleepy eyes, thanked the doctor and got to his feet. He was dreading this moment but he wanted to get it over with.

Walking through the swing doors Izzo's eyes were drawn to the taller of the two men instantly. Even from the distance that he was from them there was no mistaking that he was the brother of the girl who lay in the morgue fridge two floors below them. He was taller with broad shoulders and a straight back. The dark suit hid what Izzo knew, by experience, was a fit body and the dark glasses made him look like a fellow Italian. The man turned as Izzo drew closer.

'Signor Izzo?'

Izzo outstretched his hand in greeting and his hand was swallowed up by the firm grip of the man before him.

'Signor Regan, mi di...' his greeting was cut short by a polite interruption in English.

'Signor Izzo, please excuse my interruption but my lawyer does not speak your beautiful language and I feel it necessary that he understands all that we discuss. I believe that you speak fluent English.'

It never dawned on Izzo to ask how he knew that he could speak English and Regan was never going to tell him that Cinderella had done her job again by getting Izzo's file for him.

'Mr. Regan, I am sorry for the circumstances that have brought you here. I only wish that things were different'

'Signor Izzo, I thank you for the professionalism that you have shown and I know that these matters bring you no satisfaction. I feel, now, that I would like to see my sister. Only the slightest tremor when he said 'sister' belied the emotions of the man whose life had been torn apart.

'Immediately, Sir.'

Down in the basement a morgue attendant pushed the correct button for drawer 134 A to be released from the wall of similar drawer faces. The motor silently pushed outwards to the awaiting party. The attendant's job was done.

The body of Kathy Regan lay covered by an olive green medical sheet and the enormity of the task of uncovering her was left to Izzo. He did not relish the thought of seeing her broken body again.

'Regan, I can do this if you want,' offered Watson. 'You don't have to see her this way.'

'Thanks, Watson, but I have to do this. She is my sister no matter what anyone has done to her. Izzo, pull back the sheet please.'

Izzo did as requested and Watson could not stifle a gasp.

Her body was now a mottled blue grey but that did not hide the wounds that had been inflicted on her and Watson looked away, his eyes falling on Regan's face. He wished in that instant that he had kept his eyes on the body.

Regan's face had changed the instant the sheet was uncovered. For one moment a serene look of sadness and love and taken over his face, but not his eyes and the look that spread from his eyes to the rest of his face was that which Watson saw. It was a look that he had never seen and it chilled him with fear to see it now. And then it was gone.

'Are you alright?'

Regan didn't answer. He took his sister's cold hand and held it in his and squeezed it hard as he leaned over and kissed her forehead. His lips could not spread warmth into her cold skin nor bring her back to life. The blood began to chill in his veins as he realised that for all that he could do to bring death onto others he could never give life to those who he wished to bring back. A silent, solitary tear gently trickled down his face and fell onto her cheek. He wiped it away lovingly and leaned into her ear to whisper in silence. A silent promise of love and revenge. A silent promise of death.

He straightened up and walked away.

Watson nodded at Izzo and the body was covered once again and returned to the hollow wall.

Watson could not get the look on Regan's face out of his mind. He saw that which should never be in any man's mind. The look on Regan's face mirrored the workings of his mind, a mind full of death. Cold, manipulative, perfect death.

The story was now slipping back through the pages of the daily papers. It wasn't that people didn't care for the case to be solved but it was just another death in a world that was accepting terrible things as factually as breathing. The world offered so many instants of horrid death and in numbers so much more shocking than the death of a young Irish journalist. That was how life was and it wasn't really going to change much. At least, that was what the girls killers thought.

'Did we go too far with this one, Brother?'

'No, Marco, we did what we had to do. She was going to push further and further until she got a story that would have put us into the public domain. We are not quite ready for such fame yet.' He dropped the paper he was reading onto the marble coffee table and laid back into his chair. He looked over at his twin brother and with a lob-sided grin and threw an orange at him.

'You are an ugly fucker!'

They laughed a carefree laugh, a laugh of those who felt immune to the desires of others. Desires that were germinating in a fertile mind not one hundred miles away.

14
Understanding brothers.

Kathy had always known that Jack was different and yet she was the only one who really knew him and understood the anger that slept in his veins. His youth had visited sorrow on her family but she loved him none the less and it was when she was leaving Ireland that her heart was fully broken by the brother she loved.

She had been busying herself with the final rummaging associated with disorganised packing when she felt her phone buzz in her back pocket. It buzzed dozens of times each day and she answered a small percentage of them. Now, looking at a mountain of sweaters on her crumpled bed, trying to decide which ones would move to Italy with her, she figured than answering the call would be better than trying to decide between the wools and the cottons.

"Kathy speaking," her voice, even when she was happy, sounded formal. She was happy, especially today because she had finally achieved her goal of moving to Italy to pursue a career in investigative journalism. She figured the home of the Mafia would give her plenty to stick her curious nose into and, she assured herself, her bouncing red curls would open doors.

The silence on the other end of the line annoyed her and she was about to utter something abusive and hang up when a voice, clear and strong, broke through the silence.

'It's me, Katie.'

It was him, she knew it. Her heart leapt but her legs wobbled and she sat quickly onto the pile of sweaters before her legs went from under her.

'Jack?' she asked, knowing that it was him. Her little brother was alive and her heart nearly burst with joy. 'You are alive. My God, you are alive.'

'I am so sorry, Katie.' The voice was sombre, eager to explain but aware that small steps were required.

'Where are you? Are you near? Can we meet? Oh, Jack. I knew you were alive, I knew it.'

'I cannot come to see you at the moment, Katie. Not now, but I will. I am away, away doing what I do.'

The joy was swamped in a sudden realisation of anger and frustration that had been locked away under years of worry.

'No, Jack, where are you? You cannot do this to me,' she cried, tears streaking down her face and not for the first time over him. 'You have to tell me where you are. You are my brother and I care about you, I worry and I miss you.'

'Katie, listen to me. Stop crying now, please. I am fine.'

Kathy was the last person to see Jack Regan before he slipped out of the country and disappeared into the world where he felt comfortable and at one with himself. The Legion paid no heed to his past and recognised his talents quickly. All of this happened and he did not try to make contact with Kathy or his father.

The killings in Ireland were known to Kathy and then, of course, to her father. She tried to explain what it was that Jack had become but a man who saved lives found it hard to accept that his own flesh and blood took them remorselessly. Regan Sr. accepted that his son was lost, lost in a world of death but was happy, if he could use that word to describe losing his only son, that the killings would happen elsewhere. There were those in the papers who had fawned over the skill and ability of the IRA man who was, they said, haunting the hills and mountains of Northern Ireland. The doctor felt otherwise, his son was, it seemed, a talented soldier, but he was killing on those mountains, not haunting. There was a difference that was not subtle. He found it hard to consider young Jack a soldier, as he did not believe that there was a cause worthy of one man's life. His son was a terrorist.

'Where are you?' she screamed into the phone. The emotional tide ripped violently at her self-control, she wanted to see her brother but knew in her heart and soul that her brother, the killer of men, would not come to her. 'What if I need you, Jack? You are doing what you do to help others; at least that is what I figure. Maybe it is to help you control what ever it is within you that you are always fighting. But what if I need you? Me, your sister? If I need you, if I am in trouble and the only person that can help me is you, will you come to me?"

'Yes,' unmistakable honesty and then the line went dead.

Kathy sat on the bed and cried, her younger brother should still be at home but instead, he was somewhere, with someone else and not her. She could not accept that he was gone. She had tried to be a mother to him, and to an extent it had worked, but he had always had the angry side. As a boy, he chose his fights carefully, learning the trade from those who beat him. It was not long before those lessons became shorter and shorter until he won each fight he chose. With his father working the school could only speak to his big sister to pass the complaints home and so, in the end, only Kathy was available to try and wrestle his youthful exuberance from its self-destructive path.

By the age of thirteen, Jack was not so much picking fights but intervening in them. His sense of what was right and what was wrong, while admirable, was not open to discussion and he meted out punishing beatings to those who did not back down. His father tried to discipline him but it was impossible. Regan Sr. was not a violent man and could not raise his hand to his child but he did realise that discipline was a necessary requirement in order for his son to grow into a balanced man. He believed that boxing and martial arts were a path to discipline and, for Jack, they were. He did calm down for a period but it did seem, to Kathy at least, that he was knowingly building his arsenal of capability and waiting for a time to use it.

Tim Cloughesy was a quiet man and enjoyed the company of quiet people. It secured his need for silence. He did not like the rattle-tattle of those who voiced their opinions only when they had their fill of beer or whiskey and there were a lot of them about. No, he liked to sit and read, no matter where he was. At home it was books, in the pub it was newspapers, magazines when he was fishing. A cigarette, a cigar or a pipe accompanied each bundle of pages and each of those, in the same order, was twinned with a whiskey, a brandy or a pint of Guinness.

On the first evening that he had met Jack Regan, he was sitting in the back bar of Bull Ryan's pub drinking a pint and reading the daily paper. It was a late summer's evening and the heavy rain was keeping the bar empty of the regulars who did not fancy the walk to the pub in the typical weather. Cloughesy had been driven there by one of his men and would be collected by the same man. It would be a different man tomorrow night and to a different pub. Never the same place, never the same times. He didn't believe that the UVF or any other of those lads would come that far South down to kill him but he was not going to test that theory. Moving also tormented the Gardai and the Army Intelligence guys who had made their presence known on a couple of occasions. Tim Cloughesy was an IRA Quartermaster and, while it was well known, little was done about it. He was, after all, a quiet man.

Jack Regan didn't give a damn who Tim Cloughesy was, nor that he had two men with him at all times to cover his back. Tim Cloughesy's back was of no concern to him either as he was going to aim for the front - straight into the face. Regan was in a rage, one of those pure seams of anger that Kathy had seen before and was now incapable of controlling by any means. She had been sitting in the kitchen with her friend when Jack walked in smiling. She did not know why he was happy but the smile twisted when he saw Kathy's friend nursing a black eye and a split lip.

'What happened to her?' his voice was calm and so Kathy did not worry but she did not get the chance to respond. Her friend got her words in first.

'I was in Bulls' and one of Cloughesy's goons hit me,' she sniffed, trying to stop the tears from flowing in front of her friend's brother.

He did not even wait to ask why, it did not matter to him what the reason was. A young woman was assaulted and that bored into the core of his beliefs. He did not hear Kathy calling after him nor the questions of his father as he strode out through the door and into the rain.

The rain was still beating off the windows and the darkened skies caused the lamps to be lit in the bar. Cloughesy was laughing with two of his friends when his security tapped him on the shoulder and pointed to the figure standing in the shadows of the doorway to the main bar.

Regan was soaked through and that was not doing his temper any favours. He stood in the door looking at the men sitting at the counter and counting silently to himself.

'Do you need a towel, young fella?' Cloughesy asked.

'Not yet.' The answer was short and full of menace.

'I think you are too young to be in here, young fella. You should be home.' It was becoming obvious to Cloughesy that the young man had not wandered in by mistake.

'Call me "young fella" again.' Regan's voice did not seem to be coming from him, but floating out of one of the dark, dank corners.

While Cloughesy wanted to know that the young man's problem was, his security was not as patient. One sauntered over towards Regan; his right arm raised pointing the way to the door, and calmly told him to leave.

'Was it you?'

'What?' The man was confused by the question.

'I am not going to fucking repeat myself again, you thick fucker. Was it you?'

'That's enough, OUT!' The man made his move but it was too half-hearted. He did not expect the kid to attack, but that is what happened.

Regan went straight for the nose, flicking his fist from the short distance straight into the man's nose. Stinging pain, and blood, was the intention and he succeeded in spades. The nose did not break but the pain watered the man's eyes and the blood gushing down his face disorientated him. The blow to his neck, shocking his windpipe momentarily, dropped the man to the floor.

Regan looked over at Cloughesy, his eyes flaming in anger. 'Was it him?'

The second man supposed to be offering security to Cloughesy moved towards Regan picking an empty bottle off the bar before waving it menacingly into Regan's face.

'It was you, wasn't it?' his eyes boring into his prospective attacker. 'You smacked the girl, didn't you?'

'What of it? Is she your girlfriend?'

'Should that make a difference?'

'If she is, I should have smacked her harder.'

'Not exactly the Republican way, is it Cloughesy?' He had tilted his head in the direction of his final target, he was thinking that way already.

The man holding the bottle, the one who had hit Kathy's friend, was inching closer unsure how to deal with the kid who had just flattened his larger friend. He made his move, leading with the bottle.

Regan dipped to his right and deflected the bottle with a quick snap of his fist onto his attacker's closed hand. In the same instant, or so it seemed, he had assaulted the open rib cage with a powerful punch. At that stage the fight was over, in real terms the attacker had nothing left in his armoury but Regan was not ready to stop. Three sharp, powerful knee-kicks, as he pulled the man down by his shoulder, went into the sternum, outside leg and back into the sternum. A roundhouse knee connected with the jaw as the falling man went to the floor in an unconscious heap.

Cloughesy didn't move, even as one of his men's teeth skidded to a halt at his feet. He looked at it, slightly in disbelief, and then looked up at the kid who had taken his two men down. His response what glacier cold.

'Are you finished?'

'I don't know. I don't feel finished, if that is of any use to you in answering the question.'

'What is it that you want? You seem to have got the chap you came to see.' He did not flinch but, instead, reached for his pint and swallowed deeply from it. If it was a game of poker, Cloughesy had just scratched his nose.

'Why didn't you stop him? I smacked your dog, but you were responsible for him. Why did you not stop him?'

'She came in shouting about her brother. I needed her to shut up. She was drawing unwanted attention.'

'And so you let that shithead smack her around?'

'Her brother is a drug dealer, he got smacked and she didn't like it. These things happen in times of war. Go read your history.' The condescending manner was an insult to Regan.

'War is it, Cloughesy? What the fuck do you know about war? The war is up at the border, miles from this pub and your fawning friends. The war is where there are kids my age shooting the shit out of each other. You know nothing of war, you shit. You just want to bask in the aura of fear that your title gives you but it does not frighten me. You kicked the shit out of the kid for selling a bit of weed? How is that to progress the path to Irish Unity? Get off your arse, go up to the boys in Cross and see how you get on with them?'

'And what makes you a fucking expert on all of this, Regan?' He was angry now, not because of what the young man in front of him was saying but because it was true. He knew of the reputation of the young man and that was another reason to be worried. He was a much better fighter than anyone he knew. The two men on the floor were evidence of that.

Regan walked up to Cloughesy, who seemed to shrink back into his chair, and grabbed him by the collar of his sweater, "I am the expert who shot the fucking shit out of the helicopter last month when the SAS boys shot your "fellas" to pieces. That is what makes me an expert."

'So what?! You didn't kill anyone,' the voice had lost its composure as fear regained the ground lost to the beer.

Regan let go of the collar and turned to walk away. He stopped at the archway once again and turned back to face Cloughesy.

'That was last month,' four words, gestating with violent reasoning, that had announced the birth of the IRA's latest recruit.

15

How Brothers Respond.

Regan just walked. Up the stairs and out through the main doors and just kept walking. Watson and Izzo decided to follow, but at a distance. They followed because both knew what sadness could do to a man and they kept a distance because sometimes it was just better like that.

'Will he be ok, Mr Watson?'

'Please, call me Steve and, yes he will be fine. He needs to get his mind together. He might just need to find an outlet for his emotions but he will be fine.'

Regan walked for an hour before he realised that he was now walking through a large park. He mind was now starting to ease down from the frantic thoughts that had been racing through his mind like a bolting horse. It was time to reign in that particular horse and break it. It was time to regain composure.

As he walked around a slight bend in the wooded path his ear caught the unmistakable sound of a muffled scream. He came to a sudden stop and commanded himself to listen. His mind blocked out the background noise of traffic, birds and children playing and sought the source of the muffled scream. He stood trance like for seconds that seemed like hours and then, hearing both a slight struggle and pained cry, he darted left and into the bushes. Noiselessly.

Once past the bushes he moved quickly. He watched his step as went hoping to find something other than that which his mind was telling him he was going to find. His mind was right.

Just a hundred meters from the path a group of four young thugs were contemplating what they were going to do with the young girl they had dragged into the wooded area. High on drugs they were goading each other to be the first to have their way with their young victim. They had never gone this far before but that was going to change, and that sense of change was hanging menacingly in the air. Their leader was a massively built individual and he was holding the girl down, a knife prodding the skin of her neck. He had already ripped her clothing off and had used the strap of her handbag to tie her arms at the elbows. She was completely at their will and had now stopped struggling. This had increased the attackers sense of power and they felt the world was theirs not knowing that today was a bad day to be adding rape to their list of crimes.

Regan just appeared. The four attackers looked disbelievingly at him as though he was a ghost but they recovered their composure quickly. After all, there were four of them to deal with the stranger.

'Take a fucking walk. Turn around and walk away and we will leave you alone.' It was the voice of the leader and it was spoken with the authority of one high on drugs and empowered by the knife in his hand. 'Walk away or my three friends will cut you to pieces.'

'No.' It came out easily and politely as though he was regretfully informing a passer-by that he did not know the time. Just a simple 'No'.

'What the fuck do you mean 'No'. I am telling you to turn around and walk away.' He was becoming agitated and took the knife away from the girl's neck and stood up.

'I will walk away from here but only with the girl. That is the deal.'

The leader smiled and sauntered up to Regan. He was a good three inches taller than Regan and out-weighed him by at least ten kilos. He felt confident of his ability to take the stranger down. Unsurprisingly, Regan felt the same.

The leader lunged at Regan swinging his right fist in the direction of Regan's face. It never got near.

Regan stepped to the left and deflected the oncoming blow with a sweeping left parry of his own while delivering a powerful straight arm punch to the lower rib cage on his attackers left side. That blow alone was enough to break the lower floating ribs and put the attacker out of the fight but it was not enough for Regan. His right arm swept up and right back down onto the outstretched attacking arm clamping down on the wrist while a sharp flick kick to the left knee shattered the unfortunate joint. It was a blur of movement and the other three had no time to react. Their leader was now crumpled on the ground writhing in agony. Regan grabbed the knife that had been dropped and rolled to his left and jabbed the knife into the ankle of the closest target who screamed in agony. Pulling the knife out he quickly rolled upright while slashing the next target just behind the knee. He too went down.

The young girl was staring wide eyed at the events that were unfolding but did not look away. She saw Regan stand and face the fourth and final attacker. He stared at the young man without saying a word or making a move. The knife slid silently out of the hand of the fourth attacker and fell softly onto the leafy ground. He didn't want to be cut but that made no difference to Regan. He was now on a roll and was going to finish the job that he didn't ask for. He was going to punish the four men. Punish them for the attack on the girl. Punish them for being a release for his anger but most importantly, to him, punish them for reminding him how Kathy had died. He set to work.

It was Izzo who stopped when he heard the scream. It was the scream of pain from the second of Regan's targets and Izzo knew instinctively that trouble lay ahead. He just didn't know that it was going to be his first real step into the shadowy world of Regan's mind.

He grabbed Watson's arm and they ran through the bushes towards the sound. Izzo had drawn his weapon in anticipation of action and silently prayed that he would not need it.

In a matter of a few short seconds the came onto the sight of Regan holding the young girl, wrapped in his Jacket. Her head was buried into his chest and she was crying fitfully. Regan was sitting there holding her trying to comfort her, his large arms holding her gently. His eyes were fixed onto his handy work and it was a sight that made Izzo step back in horror.

Before he had untied and covered the girl, Regan had retrieved all four knives and put them to use. Each attacker had been tied up with their laces and then clubbed into submission. He then placed each against a separate tree and had secured them to the trees by driving the blade of each knife through the mouth cavity and out through the soft flesh of the cheek and into the tree trunk. It was a crude crucifixion of the attackers, a penance, in Regan's mind, almost equal to the crime. Almost equal, because he would have preferred to have killed them.

Izzo didn't know where to look or what to do. He turned to look at the girl but Regan was holding her like a mother bear and looked just as dangerous.

'What happened? What the Hell happened here?' His words were not aimed at anyone in particular but Watson answered.

'You better call assistance for the young girl, Mr Izzo.'

'And for those,' he replied pointing at the four young men impaled on the trees. 'I better call more than one ambulance.'

'You had better ask Mr. Regan for permission before you think of doing that.'

Izzo turned angrily and faced Watson. 'Sir, you would do well to remember that this is my country and my law applies.'

Watson placed his hand on Izzo's shoulder while surveying the carnage then looked straight into Izzo's eyes. 'Not anymore.'

As angry as he was Izzo stayed with the girl when the police and ambulances arrived. He sent Regan and Watson to their hotel with the request, an order did not seem like the proper thing to issue at that moment, to stay their until he sorted things out in the park. Watson led Regan away and left the explaining to Izzo. Just before parting ways Izzo suggested that he might offer the two men dinner later that evening as he was sure that Regan had questions that needed answering. He knew for a fact that he needed questions answered himself and needed the intervening time to put those questions in relevant order inside his own head. The day could only get more interesting.

At seven that evening Izzo parked his second-hand Alfa Romeo in the underground car park of the hotel where Regan and Watson were staying. It was his pride and joy and he maintained it as well as any DIY mechanic could. The door closed with a reassuring clunk as he shut it behind him and he walked to the lift that would bring him to the foyer. His temper had eased somewhat as he realised that he was dealing with a man who had lost his sister in the most brutal way imaginable. He was now going to have to go through the details of her death with Regan and hoped that nothing would set him off again.

On reaching the foyer he saw Regan waiting by the check in desk with Watson. He noted that the young man was now much more visibly relaxed and the palpable sense of tension that had surrounded him like a cloak of anger was no longer present. He seemed at ease again.

'Good evening, Gentlemen,' he offered.

Regan turned easily and extended this hand in welcome. Izzo shook it cordially and felt warmth in the handshake and that was comforting.

'We booked a table for three in the main restaurant here if that is alright with you?'

'Well,' Izzo smiled, 'let's eat.'

'And talk.' Regan added.

Small talk was not Izzo's forte and he wanted to get straight to the point regardless of table etiquette. He dove straight in with out checking the depth of the water but knew it was going to be deep.

'What are you, Mr. Regan?'

Regan looked up slowly at the policeman sitting opposite him and placed his knife and fork back in their places and gently pushed his meal away. He then sipped from his glass of wine, took a deep breath and sat back into the leather chair in which he was sitting.

'I am a lot of things, Mr. Izzo. Mr. Watson, Steve, can tell you a lot about me at some other time but I will give you the bare necessities for the moment. But let me start with this, everything I tell you is not for other ears. If you divulge information to others then I will cease to be,' he paused to think for a moment then finished, 'co-operative.'

Izzo nodded in silent agreement feeling the doors to Hell starting to creep open and not knowing how he was standing before them in the first place.

'I am a soldier. I am part of a unit that hunts and kills terrorists. We do not capture them, we do not interrogate them, and we do not try to convince them to change their ways. We simply kill them. We receive orders with relevant information and we go and kill them. In any country at any time. That is what I do. I do not consider the right or the wrong of the order I just kill. I take no pleasure in what I do and suffer no pain. I exist for one reason and one reason only and that is the termination of those who threaten the United States and any other country for that matter.'

Izzo was lost for words and even Watson was silent as he too was taking in what Regan was saying. Then Regan continued.

'And it is my intention to find and kill those who killed my sister. No judge, no jury and no prison. I shall suffice for those legal aspects of this trial.'

Izzo sat in silence for a moment before speaking.

'No. No, Mr. Regan, you shall not interfere in that way. You will let me do my job and bring those involved to justice. The incident in the park will not be expanded upon. You do not have a hunting licence in my country.'

'I am not asking for one, Mr. Izzo. I am not going hunting...I am going to war.'

Watson felt it was time to intervene.

'Jack, you cannot honestly expect Mr. Izzo to comply with your wishes. He cannot just break the law and allow you to run free and kill whom you wish. Be reasonable, man.'

Regan then dropped the bombshell that would change Izzo's mind and did it with the subtlety of a snake.

'Mr. Izzo, when I say that I will kill all involved, I mean all. I mean the Gasco brothers, their assistants, their support facilities and finally,' this was aimed directly at Izzo 'anyone who failed to assist my sister when she sought help.' Cinderella had been put to use again and the file that was in the police station computer system had divulged its contents to Cinderella's charms and she had returned that information to her master not two hours before dinner. Izzo felt fear build in the pit of his stomach and he felt weak.

'I didn't know what to do. I,' the words were not coming out the way he wanted them to, 'didn't think the file she gave me was enough to work, to investigate. I wanted to chase the big boys and didn't see any threat in the Gasco brothers. I just thought they were small time.' His voice began to tremor slightly as he tried to explain further but it made no difference. He could see the look in Regan's face and understood the implied threat. If he didn't assist then he too would become a target for the fury that was to be unleashed. He didn't need to be convinced of that fact. He knew enough already to know that the young man sitting before him had no qualms about killing and if Regan thought that he was in some way culpable then he too would suffer the fate that the Gasco brothers would soon endure. There was nothing for it but to accept the terms that Regan was going to put to him.

'I owe your sister the right to rest in peace. I promised her that when we found her and so I pass that promise onto you. I will assist in anyway I can. God help me.'

Regan sat in silence and in thought. He needed Izzo more than Izzo knew and was glad that his threat had worked even if it was only a threat and he had no intention of hurting the detective. Izzo would be able to get him close to those who were close to the Gasco brothers. The soon to be dead Gasco brothers.

'Thank you, Mr. Izzo. I believe with your assistance things will move quicker than I originally thought. In fact,' and he paused to mull the offer over in his mind, 'if you provide the assistance I require then I will not carry through on the full extent of that which I wish to achieve. It will suffice if I can take out the brothers and their top men. The rest I can leave to you and your men.'

'What kind of numbers are we talking about?'

'Ten. At the most fifteen if things go to Hell but let's say ten. The two brothers and their top lieutenants.'

'Alright.'

The deal had been struck and men were going to die both from the ranks of the Gasco brothers and from the alliance that had just been created at the dinner table. Such was war.

16

Taking sides.

The journey home was a mix of emotions for Izzo. The passing traffic was a blur of nothingness as he drove and he was ushered onto the correct side of the rode on a number of occasions by flashing lights and angry horns. It had nothing to do with the glass of wine he had had with his dinner but more so with the promise he had made to Regan. His mind would not allow the images of the park to leave and let him be. Instead it rolled the images over and over in his mind's eye until he saw nothing but the bloodied faces of those who had attacked the young girl. His hands were clammy on the steering wheel and his foot too heavy on the accelerator and in the back of his mind a voice was telling him to slow down. He stopped the car, suddenly wanting fresh air and space, and stepped out into the warm air.

He walked. The thoughts were not freed by the space nor calmed by the clean, warm air. Instead they seemed to be fuelled by the fire of freedom and burst forth out of his mind and into his body causing him to shake uncontrollably. He seemed to know that his promise was going to be the death of him one way or the other. He would either die helping Regan or his mind would be destroyed by the weight of what he was going to do. He stopped walking as he noticed the first drops and heavy air of a pending thunderstorm. He looked up into the sky at the heavy clouds in time to feel the rush of heavy rain topple onto his face and he closed his eyes, opened his mouth and screamed as the first clap of thunder roared in the sky. He felt as tight and as tension-filled as the air that filled his lungs and another guttural scream surged from his soul and attacked the night sky.

The rain continued to fall and had that fresh feel as it splattered on the back of Regan's neck. He wondered if it would wash the paint off the back of his neck but remembered that it was oil-based paint that he had applied to his skin.

Black all around his neck and mixed with olive green on his face. Dark paint on the brighter parts of his face such as the nose, brow, cheeks and chin and lighter paint on the darker areas under his eyes, mouth and nose. It camouflaged his face as the colour mix confused what the human eye was accustomed to seeing. There would be no human eyes looking for him where he was at that moment and the two sets of eyes twenty feet away were not what he would consider human. The were the all seeing eyes of two SAS soldiers who were staking out a cottage two hundred meters away from where they were perched on a tree covered hill. This was as close as Regan ever wanted to be to those whom he considered the ultimate soldiers. They were targeting a meeting of five senior IRA members and they were to call the shots on an assault on the cottage that would inflict a severe punishment on the main unit of South Armagh, Bandit Country, as it was known as to the British Army.

The two soldiers were as cool and calm as anybody Regan had ever seen. They had been in position for three hours and had barely said more than twenty words between them. They were patient men. Regan was equal in his patience if not more so. He had been dug into his culvert since the previous evening and had not eaten, urinated or sneezed in the time that he had been there. He was part of his surroundings and could not be seen or heard.

Three years previously it had been an SAS soldier who had thrown Regan to the ground when he and his friend had driven into the end of an ambush. The accidental encounter had been the catalyst that had created Regan and pushed him into the world of IRA activity. He took to his new place in that world with a stunning ability and became a killer of soldiers not seen since the early days of the conflict. Yet the peace process was rumoured to be in motion and some offer was going to come to the table in the coming months. It was because of that rumour that Regan now found himself a few short feet from his sworn enemy. He was going to give the SAS a lesson in revenge and do it before the peace process would begin. It would be good to have the British at the negotiation table, licking their wounds from the loss of some of their finest soldiers, a loss inflicted by the IRA's finest killer, poetic justice for the ambush that had drawn him into war. An ambush had drawn him in and an ambush was going to release him. This was to be Regan's last mission. He had killed enough.

The two SAS men before Regan had been attempting to listen in on the meeting but the laser that they had aimed onto the kitchen window of the cottage could only pick up the noise of the washing machine that was running. No words were vibrating the glass in the window that could be picked up by the laser and recorded by the two soldiers. This did not really frustrate them, as the information they were hoping to pick up was secondary to their mission. They were going to kill the five men who had entered the cottage an hour earlier and that was the mission. Taking out those five individuals would soften the negotiations, as they were hardliners, men who only knew war and nothing outside of it. They would never discuss peace and so peace would be discussed without them.

'How do you feel about this?' The question came from the soldier on the left whose Scottish brogue was unmistakable.

'Huh?'

'Being Irish, how do you feel about killing your own people?' Regan nearly coughed as the words sunk in. A strong Dublin accent answered the Scot.

'I hate terrorists. They are terrorists. Full stop!'

'Well, lets do it.'

Regan had forgotten that it was not unheard of to have Irishmen in the SAS. It never dawned on him that it would actually come into the equation of this mission. He didn't want to kill a fellow countryman yet he wanted to hit the SAS. His mind raced with confusion but the mission was about to begin.

'Hide 1 to Air 1. Do you copy?' The Dubliner was calling in a helicopter. Regan knew the plan. A chopper was going to come in and drop a unit from ropes and they would enter the cottage by force. The two soldiers on the hill were watchers until the unit landed. Once the assault commenced they two men were to become the snipers, hitting anything that tried to escape.

'Air 1, you are green light, repeat, green light.'

Regan had been flexing his trigger finger and gently rolling his right shoulder. He planned two shots to each head once the unit in the air began to rope out of the chopper. It would be over in seconds and then part two would begin.

Regan had devised the plan some months previously when he had identified a mole in another IRA unit. He had discovered it by accident yet he knew it to be true. A senior commander had wanted to kill the mole but Regan had convinced him that his plan would require the mole and after the operation, the mole could be killed. It would be worth the wait.

Now, a Lynx chopper was flying towards an empty cottage. The five senior IRA men had entered the cottage, turned on the kitchen appliances and exited through a tunnel that had been dug many years ago. By now they would had trekked the two miles to the pick up van and were safely away from the SAS operation. The plan was working out as the information gleaned from the mole was now useless to the SAS but incredibly valuable to the IRA. The table had now been well and truly turned.

The chopper roared low over the hilltop where SAS and IRA waited in a silent game and eased in over the cottage. Four ropes dropped from the doors of the chopper and the assault began...at the cottage and on the hill.

Regan gently squeezed the trigger on his silenced MP5 and two bullets bored through the back of the Scot's head. The dead soldier's head had barely slumped forward when the other soldier rolled onto his back and to the left drawing his pistol and firing towards his rear. He shot at waist height and in a flowing arc, well above Regan's head and expended the magazine in an instant. Regan didn't fire. He was drawn to the spectacle of a highly trained soldier under fire and was frozen to the spot. The empty magazine was replaced in an instant and the soldier rolled away further continuing to fire as he rolled. The second magazine emptied as quickly as the first and was replaced with the same fluid professionalism. Regan snapped out of his trance as bullets whizzed closer and thanked his lucky stars that the SAS man had not applied his night goggles. It was time to end the game. Regan had night goggles on and so his aim was not going to be blind. The head of his target rose clearly in his sights and Regan fired twice. The bright mottled green flash from the head of the SAS soldier confirmed the kill. Two down.

The assault on the cottage was over before the second soldier on the hill had died. The men who had entered the cottage knew instantly that it was a set up and had to decide how to react. Their first thought was to radio the hill and call the two watchers down to the chopper, which had now settled down between the cottage and the hill. The team leader radioed his men on the hill but got no reply. A second soldier called from his radio to ensure that it was not a malfunction issue and got the same silent reply. Then they got a reply.

'Air 1, this is Ground 2. Do you copy?'

The soldiers in the cottage looked at each other silently asking the question. Who was Ground 2? They got the answer quickly.

Regan was speaking into the radio of the dead Scot directly to the soldiers in the cottage. 'Your time is up.'

The soldiers had no time to move. Twenty kilos of Semtex high explosives ripped the cottage apart and blew up into the night sky with a horrific roar. The helicopter was toppled over by the blast; it's fuel tank erupting adding to the fireball and engulfing the already dead crew. Mission accomplished.

Regan looked down onto the chaos he had created at the bottom of the hill and then looked at the bodies of the two soldiers he had killed. He felt nothing. He thought there should be some feeling of elation but he just felt nothing. The eyes of the dead Dubliner were staring up at him and he bent down and gently closed them with his gloved hand. He walked over to the Scot and did the same thing. Two fine men had been killed on that hill and seven more at the foot of the same hill and Regan felt nothing. Then it started in the pit of his stomach, scratching up his spine and into his head. Frustration. He screamed up into the rain and the dark sky. Screamed until his throat was raw and then screamed some more.

Then he woke.

He was breathing heavily and covered in sweat, the sheets were crumpled on the floor and a pillow was clenched in his fists. It took a moment for him to realise were he was and he regained his composure quickly. The dream still held his nights to ransom and he could never pay off such a ransom. He would never clean his conscience of the image of the dead Dubliner whose eyes stare through him. He could not silence the roar of the exploding cottage or the screams of the mole as she was being tortured for her actions. The death that he had caused filled his dreams when he slept and his thoughts when he didn't sleep. Petersen had once said that Regan was the ultimate soldier yet he knew now what it meant to be such. He had lost his humanity. He didn't feel what other people could feel and there was no way to ease away from it. All he could do was kill and kill and keep killing. There would always be reasons and targets and so he would always kill. The reasons may differ but the results would be the same. Killing kept him alive.

It was that final thought that awoke him fully and in a single motion he reached out and grabbed the pistol on the shelf beside his bed and put the mussel to his temple. It was the only way to stop it and he needed freedom. It was all becoming clear to him now. He was addicted to killing and his mind had become numb to death. Well maybe now it would be numbed completely enough for him to pull the trigger. He urged his finger into action but for once it did not comply with the order. Another voice in the back of his mind urged him to stop. His sister's dead body floated in his mind's eye and he could nearly feel the wounds on her neck and chest. The sight of those wounds opened up wounds of his own and he shook with anger and frustration. The urge to kill raced back into his veins and his hand lowered the gun from his head.

It was clear to him again. He had not yet killed enough.

Izzo too was having trouble sleeping. He lay on his back and listened to the gentle breathing of his wife who was sound asleep beside him. On the far side of the room he could see the tiny bundle that lay in the cot that he had bought the previous week. The sleeping figure of Regan's nephew was worlds apart from the man he had met a few short hours earlier. Jack the toddler was sound asleep and safe in his world while across the city, in a non-descript hotel uncle Jack lay awake in a pool of sweat contemplating suicide. Izzo didn't know what was racing through the mind of Regan at that moment but he still felt it strange that at home or at work he was not going to escape from the world of one of the Jacks that now existed in his life. One was only beginning to be a part of the world around him while the other was trying to destroy parts of it.

Izzo turned and wrapped his arms around the warm body of his wife and tried to sleep.

Regan woke at six and rubbed the sleep out of his eyes as he stepped out of the bed and moved to the shower. The cold water washed the night off his body and he relaxed a little as the water poured over him. The night had passed and he was still alive and that was a success in itself. It had been the first time in quite some months that he had considered killing himself and was glad the feeling had passed once again. Night was a minor enemy to him as it was the only time that he relaxed a little and relaxing caused the images and dreams to come flooding back to torment him.

He stepped out of the shower and stared into the large mirror over the sink. It was time to take a step back and see the whole picture. He was moving too fast and working on instinct instead of using his brain. If he continued that way things would be missed and errors made. That was something he wanted to avoid if he wanted to get back to Dark-Eye. That was going to be his new goal. Finish the mission at hand and get back to his unit and put the past behind him. He might even consider asking Petersen to take him off active duty and put him into a trainer role. Yes, he thought to himself, that was a plan.

There was a knock on the door and he knew it was Watson by the rhythm of the knock. He was really beginning to accept the Englishman as, he tried to think how to describe his new partner and decided that partner was good enough. He wrapped a towel around his waist and went to open the door.

Watson had a concerned look on his face when the door was opened to him. Regan felt that Watson was only happy when he had something to be concerned about and decided not to add a smart ass greeting.

'You are up early.'

'Not too pushed about sleep. How are you getting along?'

'I have been thinking about the task in hand. I have a few more bits to add to it but I have the foundation of a plan in my head at the moment.'

'Where do I fit in, Jack?' Watson had used Regan's name for the first time and both men felt a strange moment hang in the air.

'Are we becoming friends, Steve?'

'I suppose in some way we are. Things are different now than they were even just a week ago.' Watson walked over to the bed and sat down and continued to speak. 'When this is over, Jack, I want to help you get back to where ever it is you want to go. I mean, I don't think you can carry on like this forever until you die of old age. You are not James Bond. You cannot just keep changing actors to stay young.'

'Steve, do you remember the ambush outside of Castlejamestown?'

'When that IRA unit hit the SAS for six? Yeah, I remember it. I trained with the squad leader a year before it happened. I knew one of the snipers too. An Irish lad from Dublin. Well, he was born there and moved to England when he was sixteen. What about it?'

'I was the IRA unit.'

'Jesus, Jack, all that was you?'

'My plan and my ambush, I didn't want anyone else in on it except the senior men who were to be ambushed by the SAS team.'

'It never hit the news as you expected in the end. They said it was a helicopter crash that killed a bunch of Marines and the crew. I saw the report and figured that it was an active service unit that had carried out the ambush. It was just you?'

'It was my swan song out of the IRA before the peace process was put on the table. I was going to walk away but then I got word that the SAS had a green light, along with you guys, to find and kill me. The Prime Minister had given the go ahead even as the peace process was under way. I understand why, I mean, I would have done the same thing myself. In fact, the ambush was my own revenge for an ambush the SAS had carried out a couple of years before. A full circle of shit!'

'Why are you telling me this, Jack?'

'I am telling you so you might try to understand me. I started killing because I saw what they did at that ambush. I became what they were and I know that they will still love to get their hands on me and I can't blame them for that. There are two SAS men in Dark-Eye. I have worked with them and they are two fine men, real specialists in their field. Yet they have no idea who I am. I trust

158

my life with those two and if they knew who I am they would kill me. It is a funny world.'

'Hilarious, Jack, fucking hilarious!'

'Yeah, fucking hilarious.'

The two men continued to talk well into the afternoon until Watson put a halt to the proceedings by raising his hand and announcing his hunger. Regan laughed and suggested that they could fit breakfast and lunch in together downstairs in the dining hall. They went down to eat while still talking.

At the table Regan listened as Watson described how he entered the world of British Intelligence. It was not as horrific as Regan's life but there were quite a few shocking stories. Watson was no angel and in fact, was probably booked on the same afterlife trip as Regan.

A large manila envelope landed unceremoniously with a thud on the table and both men looked up to see Izzo grinning down at them with a devious look in his eyes.

'Here is all you need to know about the Gasco brothers, Mr Regan. It is a full copy of the file that your sister had created. I couldn't sleep last night and so I went in early and made the copy for you. I read over it again and I must say that your sister had an ability to get information in a manner that would have made the CIA wish to have her in their ranks. It will be a good map for your war.'

Regan took the heavy envelope into his hand and felt the weight of it. It felt strange in his hand knowing that it was a link to his sister and to her killers.

'Sit down and join us, Izzo.'

Izzo sat down and beckoned the waiter over to order a coffee. 'I believe everything you need is in there. It is still in hard copy back in the station, as it has not been put onto the computer system yet. In effect, you will have a head start on those who will be involved in the investigation of your sister's death. You will see that your sister managed to get photos of the Gasco twins and most of their senior aides. The group is quite unique in the sense that they have no Mafia links. They operate by themselves without interference from others. All that they gain is their own. I am not quite sure how they managed to achieve that independence but it is a rare thing in this country.'

Regan opened the envelope after the waiter had dropped over Izzo's coffee, and spilled the contents out onto the table. The first thing to catch his eye was the picture of the two twins together sitting outside a café drinking together. His eyes stared at the crisp image as his fingers ran smoothly over their faces. His eyes and fingers, as usual, were working in unison though for the moment a trigger and telescopic sights were not the tools of the trade.

'Let's finish up here and retreat back to my room. We can set out the plans from there.'

They all agreed and paid their bill and left the dining hall.

17
Credibility

The three men sat around the large oak table in the middle of the living area of the hotel room. Izzo and Watson were pouring over the information that had come from the envelope and had started to create a structure to the organisation headed by the Gasco brothers. Regan was inserting a little red disk into his laptop and going on-line. The others looked questioningly at him as he muttered to himself with a frown.

'What's up, Regan?' asked Izzo.

Regan looked at him with a grin and replied, 'never much good at typing. This disk is my connection here in Italy. We couldn't carry the weapons I require and so this contact will be able to assist. Well, I hope he will or I will have to raid your station.'

Izzo did not know whether to laugh or cry.

The information passed from the red disk into the hands of Cinderella and she went to work quickly. A multi-layered encrypted message when seeking a match that floated in cyber space. The unique match was found in an instant and the decloaking of the multi-layers began. Each layer had to match its partner in a string of codes before the core message of each was joined. The message could only be sent once before it became inactive but when it matched it created a link between the sender and one of three devices held by the receiver. In this case, a small hand-held computer, in the pocket of an agent in Rome, vibrated. An e-mail address was created and would be active for five minutes before it too would disappear with the outside help of Cinderella. The agent in question memorised the e-mail address and walked to an Internet café just around the corner. Eight minutes were left on the invisible clock when the agent mailed the address.

Sender: Credibility.
Activated. Advise requirements and location.

Sender: D-E 1

Assault compliment x 3. Regina Elena Hotel, Milan. Top priority. Wednesday, 1900,
UPS DELL.

Sender: Credibility.
Acknowledged. Over.

And the link disappeared.

'That's it. We will have the hardware in two days time. By then we shall have a plan and things can get moving. For the moment we just have to advise the manager here that we will need the exclusive use of a meeting room for the set up of a company or some reasonable excuse like that. We can put the systems working there and store the weapons elsewhere if required.

'What are we getting?' asked Watson.

'All we require will be delivered by an UPS van in Dell computer boxes. Small arms, grenades, C-4, detonators and two sniper rifles.'

'How about a tank or a rocket launcher?' Izzo had a deadpan expression on his face but his eyes were twinkling.

'Those will come in the next delivery,' came the grinning reply from Regan.

Getting weapons was always just one step in special operations. Getting them, using them and then getting rid of them were steps in a very convoluted mechanism of mind and body and, unfortunately, when a special operation was a failure it made the news in spectacular fashion. When such actions were successful, as they often were, nothing hit the news desk. That was how it worked, you entered special operations for many reasons, the excitement, the danger and the belief that something was being achieved. You never entered for money, fame or women.

Weapons were always a major part of any operation but, when it came down to the nitty gritty of spec-ops, it was intelligence that was the weapon of choice. It was information, secret or public, that ruled the flow of conflict.

Conflict directed policy, policy directed politics and politics ruled the world. It was true, therefore, that information was power.

Right now, the men sitting at the desk in the sparse hotel room had a brown envelope. That was the limit of the information at that moment. The next step was to identify the content, place that information into a stream of knowledge and then to act on that flow.

To hit a target you have to know where it is, or, at worst, where it was going to be at a given time. For Regan it was just necessary to have an idea of location and that was possible using pictures. The pictures of the Twins and their cohorts were scanned and uploaded and then sent to Credibility. Patience was then added to the mix. Target positions, following intel sightings, if any were available on the database, would then be matched to mobile phone usage, internet log-ins and bank addresses, just to name a few of data strings required to create the targeting permutations.

Concurrently, Izzo and Watson were pouring over the hand-written notes that Kathy had left behind. Within the notes, times and dates were flagged; what restaurants were used, favoured drinking holes, whore-houses and so on. When Credibility answered, as they were certain it would, that information would be matched to the flags in the hand-written notes and a target map would be developed.

Slowly, carefully and with the precision that only revenge can encourage, the target map was taking shape and the Twins' mystique was beginning to fade and as clarity rose from the horizon of doubt, Regan saw a pattern emerging. One of the twins dominated the other. The first chink in their armour had been identified and a chink was all that was needed.

Piece by piece, the picture was forming and, combined with the information coming from Credibility, focus was being achieved. The list of targets was firming up and each one given a rating. Marco Gasco was the point of the pyramid, the closing of this operation once he was dead. His brother was secondary, but only slightly. Both had to be killed. The next line of targets took a little longer to formalise and contained six targets of equal importance. Six who would be added to the list of those who were now wore an invisible mark of death. However, the information, while building, was still very sparse and needed some real-time, real personal input. At that point, Regan decided that a "lift" was required and the target of that lift was to be Silvio Fanetti, the bullish 300lb enforcer of the Twins' organisation. He would be able to put the final pieces of the target map into place, whether he liked it or not. In realty, whatever Fanetti liked or disliked made no more difference to the outcome of his life that the meal he had eaten that afternoon.

18

Starter & Main Course.

Silvio Fanetti wiped the sweat from his brow with the arm of his expensive suit. He was a huge man, a man to whom food was not just his fuel but also his passion and he ate as often and as much as he could.

Born into poverty in New York thirty-five years earlier, he was repatriated to Italy when his family were killed during a botched kidnapping. His mother, father and two sisters had died in a hail of bullets as police and gang members shot it out at a check-point. He had been put into the footwell of the car and had, miraculously, avoided being hit by any of the sixty-two bullets that had entered the family car. His father had been driving the family home from visiting friends when the family car got caught between a police car and one of the vans carrying a kidnapped investment banker. The family car, a Ford, was the same colour and size of the car reported to the police as being part of the kidnapping and it was just in the wrong place, at the wrong time when the shooting started. Silvio, the only survivor and without family members in New York, was collected by his paternal grandmother two weeks later and flew to Italy. New York never beckoned again.

Now, a grown man and free from the control of his grandmother since her death 12 years earlier, Silvio dominated where ever he went. It was not just his size, which in itself was generally a large portion of any room, but it was also his personality and the effect his personality had on those near him. His size drew people to him, a gravity of its own, and his personality repelled people. He was two magnetic poles working against all those who knew him and he didn't care. He cared nothing for the law or those who tried to enforce it. In fact, he wore with pride a large tattoo on his chest, the figure "62" that represented the number of bullets that had entered his parents car. Some thought that it also represented the number of people he had killed, but it did not. He was a long way from sixty-two but, in human terms, twent-eight was a horrific number to have as a personal record, whether it was tattooed to the chest or not. Each life taken had been done in the bluntest of fashion, usually with his bare hands. On occasion, he was known to have tried to pull men apart, limb from limb. Some said he had succeeded, others just didn't want to talk about it for fear that such an end would visit them, and then they would know if the stories were true.

Silvio met the Twins five years earlier and was in awe of them immediately. Marco treated him with such respect that he felt cleansed of all his sins, an absolution from the Devil himself. The fact that Marco showed no fear of him frightened Silvio, a common trait of bullies. Marco spoke to him with his hand around his vast shoulder, and seemed oblivious of the body odor that assaulted the noses of others. Marco was a man to respect, maybe a man that he could follow. He watched as Marco's twin circled the room talking to others, ignorant of Silvio's presence. Marco, on the other hand, made him feel that he was the centre of the room and that every word he spoke was heard and, more importantly for Silvio's ego, listened to. Marco had that way with people, he spoke to people for an instant and they felt that they had his ear for the night. He never refused contact and welcomed peoples problems, solving them when he could, which often was just money, or gently letting them down, with a refusal, but in such a way that they felt the refusal was beneficial. He refused always when the request included some interaction with the Mafia and if the request was pushed too hard, he would direct it to Silvio with a nod. A single nod meant to remove the offending person from this room. A nod while adjusting his glasses meant remove the person from the room, the house and life. Only Silvio knew this signal, the only signal that his Boss gave to kill .

Five years now under the umbrella of the Gasco twins and he felt sure that he was due a promotion through the ranks. In fact, he felt sure that now was the time that he should demand it. Why not, he asked himself. Had he not shown them loyalty, respect and courage under fire?

In reality, and more so, in the minds of the Twins, he had shown none of those attributes at all during the three years, but he had shown an ability to get money from those who where holding back on their monthly protecting and racket payments. For that reason, they kept him on their books but he would never rise. He lacked courage and creativity and that is what Marco looked for in those he promoted. He also sought those who would die for him.

Men never say, very rarely if they ever do, that they will die for another man. Instead, their presence and action in times of need whispered that loyalty silently and without fanfare. It was a quality found in so few men because it was tied to the need for, and use of, violence. Silvio Fanetti was a violent man, but he used violence when his security men were with him, and never by himself. He was, in reality, a coward. And cowards don't fight. That, in the scheme of things, was going to work out well for Jack Regan. He hated cowards.

19

Chasing spirits.

The flight from Dublin had been uneventful for the two intelligence agents. It was a relief to get onto the plane with some kind of a plan in their minds as they had spent days in Dublin chasing blind leads. Now, having received friendly intel from their American counterparts, they were on their way to Rome to find the legendary Watson and, as they now suspected, once they found him they would find, and terminate with extreme prejudice, the demon-like Regan.

The two agents were skilled operators and had chased the uncatchable in the past. Niles Carter, the youngest of the two, was the consummate professional, applying the rule of law to all of their activities. His partner, Tom Fields, twenty years older, was old-school. He did not subscribe to the view that gentle persuasion bested a waterboarding or a good beating. Anyway, there is no frustration vented during gentle persuasion. Kicking gives good relief, rids the interrogator on pent-up anger and frustration. He tried to explain this to Carter in a way that would not offend the politically correct sensibilities of the young agent. Carter had his hands full.

The flight landed on time and both men alighted and passed through the diplomatic gates without issue. They were met by a driver from the Embassy and delivered to via XX Settembre in under an hour for their briefing. Neither, regardless of their character, enjoyed the process of the brief, Fields just wanted to get out there and get into the action. Carter was different, he felt he already knew what was required. He was an intelligence guru, a fact not lost on Fields and no small matter of concern. Carter was all about reports and intel intercepts, Fields was a boots and blood man. How they were put together was still beyond him.

There was little unexpected in the briefing, a couple of photos of Regan that had been computer-aged to match what they thought he looked like now. As Watson was well known to the two agents no picture was issued to them. The briefing agent continued with a number of other points for no more than thirty minutes, answering the two men's questions, until it came to the time that the "excess" orders were issued in sealed envelopes. The briefing agent thanked the two men for their time, excused herself and closed the heavy door behind her as she left the room.

Carter slid his pen under the flap of the envelope and opened his instructions. Fields did the same, but not with the same finesse. Either way, the result was the same and so too was the reaction of each agent. They knew that Regan was to be killed, they did not expect Watson to be added to the list.

Regan was looking at the pictures and building a plan in his already library-like mind of the actions that were to happen. It was a plan that he would share with the others when it needed to be shared but it was never going to be anything that existed on paper. In fact, once the images of the targets, their names and, where it was available, their addresses and work/play hang-outs, were committed to memory, Regan was going to destroy the file that Izzo had made for them. He would not need it again, not least as a piece of reference material, once he started to kill.

Watson and Izzo were busy talking amongst themselves when Regan chose his first target. It was an easy one to begin with because he wanted to start not with a flash of "Shock-and-awe" but with one who was detestable but, at the same time, one whose disappearance for a number of days, would not rattle the Gasco cages too much. Patience was required and it was something that he had to develop over the years for, considering all the abilities that he had been born with, patience was not one of them and it was, in his own mind, his Achilles heel. Getting weapons was always just one step in special operations.

Regan fingered the picture of Fanetti, twisting and turning it through his fingers, a diligent card-sharp would have been impressed, and then flicked it across the table to Izzo and Watson.

"This is the one. This is who I want to start with."

The two men looked down and the picture and Izzo smiled. "The scenery around can only improve with his absence."

"Who is he?" Watson asked, a little curious as to why the picture of the man now lying on the table would soon be a picture of a man lying in a morgue.

"Silvio Fanetti. He is a bag-man for the twins and I want to start with him. Not to low down as to draw no attention, not so high up as to draw too much attention. I just want to leave a message, an ambiguous message that will not alert them just yet."

Izzo stared at the photo for a second and then asked, "Is he enough to get the ball rolling?"

Regan sat back in his chair and took a sip from the glass of chilled water. Izzo was right, maybe the target in question was not enough to be the ripple in the Gasco pond. He needed the ripples to enlargen. "We take him, and whoever he is with. He is a bag-man so we take the bodyguards too. They are all part of the same pile of shit."

"Are we going to kill them all?" Izzo was beginning to worry again. Fanetti was a prize ass-hole, he wouldn't mind pulling the trigger himself on this one and he would be just as happy to explain it away to his bosses. However, the killing of the body-guards was going, in his opinion, a step too far.

"We won't kill them unless they want to be killed." The reply was short and very clear. He didn't care if they lived or died and Izzo could see that. As far as Regan was concerned, they were all responsible for his sister's death, and they would all pay. This was what was un-nerving for Izzo. Death begets death begets death.

Regan looked up at the two men again, his face not reflective of the buzz that was beginning in the middle of his brain, the buzz he associated with getting back into the game. "I need to contact *Credibility*. I need his whereabouts so we can hit quickly."

The short-burst transmission to Credibility, like to any member or associate of Dark-Eye, contained the bones of information only. In this case, Regan had sent the name, "Finetti, Silvio, location +/- 2hrs, number of assoc." It was a simple request. Find the location of the target with a window of two hours either side of an appointment that he would be known to attend and who he would attend it with. Regan didn't need anymore information and didn't seek it. He did not want to over-use Credibility. A resource like that was invaluable and, of course, he didn't know when he would be back in Italy in the future. So far the weapons he had requested had been supplied, all he wanted now was the target position. After that, he would decide if he needed the contact again. If it was possible to get information out of Finetti, then he would do so. Torture was not something he had planned to do but, then again, he did not define "*information retrieval*" as torture. "*Refined interrogation techniques*" was a better way of putting it, a way that would probably be more acceptable to Izzo.

Carter and Fields did have access to good intelligence but they did not have access to Cinderella or Credibility. In fact, in comparison to the systems and intel that Regan and his "team" had access to, the two M15 agents were operation in the dark. They were, however, two very talented hunters even if they knew that they were starting the hunt from cold.

'What have we got, lad?" Fields was staring at his picture of Regan while sipping his coffee. He did not expect an answer to his question, except one that maybe contained the words "fuck" and "all."

"Watson attended a funeral in Dublin a short while ago. It was an old friend who had passed away, so that got me thinking. An M15/ex-SAS guy with buddies in the Republic. Either he had balls the size of pumpkins or he played for the other side. Playing the other side for a guy like Watson was not going to happen." Carter was repeating from memory, he was good at that.

"Your point?" Fields' memory was not as good, nor did he care too much for detail. He liked targets and a good supply of bullets. A getaway car was always optional, just like clean passports.

"My point, old man, if you would let me continue, is this. His friend was a doctor, one Dr. Jack Regan Senior, father to Jack Regan Junior and his sister Kathy Regan. Kathy Regan was a journalist, here in Italy. She was killed, still waiting for an update on that, shortly before Senior died."

"So we have no fuckin' connection to Regan and therefore no connection to Watson." Fields was not impressed.

"We have a fucking connection to them all," an exasperated Carter sighed. "Soon after the death of the girl and, subsequently, the father, there was a lot of electronic chatter regarding the possibility that the son was still alive. Watson ended up in Dublin and then decided to come to Italy "for a break." The Legend that is Watson is starting to slip if he thinks we are not connecting the dots."

Fields looked at Carter with a cocked eyebrow. "I think I am beginning to slip as I have no idea what you are talking about. Get to the fucking point, Carter."

"I feel, I think, that Watson finally found Regan. Junior that is. Because of his relationship with Senior, it was supposed to be a genuine friendship at the end, he feels tied to something, I don't know, a promise to the dead man maybe."

"You are grasping at straws. Do you really think that a series of events, unfortunate ones admitedly, combined to bring back that chap from the dead?" Fields was beginning to think that his partner was losing his grip on reality, notwithstanding the fact that reality and fiction, in this case especially, was separated by a very thin membrane. He had heard some of the stories about Regan from the time in Ireland through actions in Africa. After that, especially now that the hunt was back on, further stories floated around like balloons caught in a storm. The best story he had heard recently was that Regan had been captured by rebels in Somalia and sold on between interested parties. He had been wounded in the chest by a ricocheting bullet and was suffering an infection by the time the third rebel band had "purchased" him and between being sold around like and unwanted puppy and the delerium of the infection related to the gun-shot wound, he seemingly lost his temper when they band tried to sell him on again. Once subdued, he calmly asked for permission to speak to those who wished to sell him in privacy while the new buyers waited in a separate room.

The story continued that when he was thrown onto an old bed, it snapped under the pressure of his weight, in comparison to the others in the room he was a giant, and, in a brief moment of fluid anger, he killed all four of his captors with a large piece of jagged wood that had come to hand.

Unsure of what was happening in the other room the new buyers were not too concerned with the screams that were coming from the room, thinking that the white giant was getting a well deserved kicking.
Regan walked out of the room with four heads gripped by the hair in one hand and a blood-covered AK-47 in the other. When he asked for keys to a car, jeep or some kind of motorised method of escaping the town he was offered four sets. He took all four in exchange for the heads and left.

Fields laughed to himself at the thought of a guy, mad with fever, exchanging the heads of four kidnappers for the keys to a car. Regan was his kind of man, even if there was a large degree of exageration to the story, and under different circumstances, he would surely like to sit with the man and swap stories over a couple of beers. He so admired Regan that he had memorised the poem that he had written on the wall of his cell. It was an insight into the man that they were trying to catch and it reminded Fields, each time that he would recite it, what it was that he and Carter was chasing. Once again, he worded it softly to himself.

Hear who I am.

I do not beg nor cry for your morning light
Daybreak can keep its natural calls
I prefer the scream of man as I strike in darkness
And blood bellows its silent fear

I do not beg nor cry for your hope
Fervour springs lighter in darkened hate of cloudy skies
I prefer the feel of death on my blood-wet hands
Drier than my soul can ever be

I do not beg nor cry for your joy
None such sentiment lives now in your blood
I prefer salted tears on weathered cheeks
Proclaiming fear has danced nearby

I do not beg nor cry for your honour
It flowed freely with your blood and sacrifice
I prefer your soul for I am Death
And I beg nor cry for no man.

There was nothing in those lines that left Fields in any doubt what Regan was, or what he believed himself to be, and it frightened him. Instead of trying to avoid the man, he was now tasked with killing him, and his cohort Watson, on behest of the United States Government. He wondered how reasonable the tasking was, how much thought had gone into it and why the Americans were not going after him, or why they were going after him through other means. Something did not sit well with him and he felt, for the first time in years, a gentle pull in his stomach that told him that something was wrong. Something was very wrong with the mission and when he had feelings like that it was best pay attention to them.

Carter noticed that Fields had gone quiet and he pushed the topic. "What's up, you thinking this through already?"

Fields pulled out his pack of cigarettes and offered one to Carter who, as ever, declined. He slipped one between his lips and lit it, dragging heavily on it before turning back to Carter. "This Regan thing, I am not so sure how it is going to go. We got tasked with it pretty quickly and we are not sure what the Hell it is we have gotten ourselves into."

"Oh, come on, Fields," Carter chided "we find him and his buddy Watson and quietly end their activity in Italy."

"Simple as that?" Fields brow had furrowed deeply. Hits never work out easily. "We are talking about tracking a guy down, a guy who, if we are to believe the stories, took out an SAS unit is South Armagh, escaped a band of rebels in Somalia and then, under the eyes of British Intelligence, us Carter, disappeared never to be found. Now, we get sent to Italy to find one of our own who may or may not be with this guy, kill them both and them come home for gin and tonics? This ain't for shits and giggles, Carter. We are not the right team for this. Believe me, this is not the first time the Services have gone looking for guys like Regan. When they find them, if they find them, a world of hurt is usually unleashed and people get killed. Not guys like you and me, just normal fuckers going out for a bag of lettuce or bringing their kids to the park. Guys like Regan do not like to be surrounded and they kill, indiscriminately, to get away. That is my problem with the whole plan, there just isn't one!"

"Come on, Fields. All we have to do is kill them."

"Fuck it, Carter, you don't get it. We are out of our league with Watson, not to mention Regan. We are not coming back from this, neither of us. Do you get it yet, this is a fucking suicide mission." He stubbed his cigarette under foot and walked over to the edge of the path where he stood for a moment before turning around to Carter. "We are not coming back from this, Carter. We don't know the half of what is happening and without the knowledge, we are dead. Kids like Regan, you have heard the stories too, they don't take prisoners. They take exception."

20

Pawn to….

Credibility was quick, very quick. So much so that Regan decided to act on the information immediately and not wait. He would need to pull Gasco and Watson into the frame as the target had two body-guards and it was not a kill mission. The photos they had browsed earlier had shown body-guards but it was necessary to have the information precise for what he had in mind.

Between *Cinderella* and *Credibility* a number of important items were quicky, but efficiently, put into place. Working backwards, a warehouse, on lease to an import-export company that had been in operation for eight years. It had been worked previously by the CIA before being passing over to special operations. It was empty but constantly "earning" enough to keep the owner happy and not enough to interest the taxman. In essense, nobody was going to snoop around.

Two miles outside of the city limits a black Ford Transit, keys in a magnetised box under the front left wing, was just cooling down after a hundred kilometer journey. The driver, an Italian/American retired US Marine, had parked the van away from cameras so those entering it later would not be recorded. It was also loaded with light arms and munitions and a selection of uniforms and protective gear. It also was rigged with ten pounds of C-4, linked by a very intelligent little detonator to the ignition so that the van and content would leap enthusiastically from the ground and spread itself over a large distance if someone unorthorised were to attempt to break into the vehicle. Nobody was going to do that as the van had been parked in a quiet residential area where joy-riding was unheard of so the van and its Aladin's cave of weaponary was going to sit, in the shade of a line of popular trees, until the new owner came to drive it away.

The weapons in the back of the Transit were untraceable, manufactured specifically for special operations and without stamped serial numbers. They were going to be wiped off anyway so why bother. Each had been test fired and calibrated by the retired Marine who now was walking down the street whistling the Marine Hymn. His first mission in five years had gone well.

Piero Bassi was a third generation Italian/American who, after years of loyal service to the Corp, had taken early leave, honourable discharge in fact, once the remnants of his face had been carfully put back together by surgeons in Bethesda. His once handsome Italian features had been denigrated by a thumb-nails sized piece of steel, probably a small bolt according to one of the surgeons who had performed the reconstruction, that had passed without hindrance through his lower cheekbone, through the front of his left eye and out through his skull just above the eyebrow. He had not even fallen, nor had he felt pain. He had been in a fire-fight for his life, and the life of his fellow Marines, as they tried to shoot their way out of a back-street in the Hell that was the Second Battle of Fallujah. He and four others like him from 2nd Recon had battled for an hour before they finally managed to evade their persuers. They ran straight into another company of Marines who had appeared like a God-sent angel into the square that they were trying to traverse. Their persuers met with a hail of lead from 1st Battalion, 4th Marines that ended their activity in Operation *Al-Fajr*. It had also ended Piero's involvement not only in Operation Phantom Fury but also in the rest of the war. He had been hit in the face by shrapnel from an improvised explosive device that they had believed they had avoided. Rodrigo, their Squad Automatic Weapon guy, SAW for short, had light bleeding from his shoulder and the other two had scrapes and cuts. Piero had figured that he could not see from his left eye because of the blood that he knew was coming from the cut over his eyebrow. His heart rate was probably touching one-twenty and his breathing was shallow and fitful, yet he did not feel as though he had been hit by anything. Yet, as soon as his heart rate eased and his breathing began to return to normal, he collapsed into the arms of a medic who could see, from first glance, that the injury was serious.

It took four operations for most of the visible damage to be repaired, operations that caused so much pain. Yet, he never complained. He knew that Marines had gone back to the front with prosthetic legs so he figured that his one eye and crooked smile would suffice now too. It didn't. A one-legged Marine can see the enemy while a one-eyed Marine, still better than most fighting men according to the surgeon, and every Marine for that matter, would not see enough to protect his fellow Marines. That was what hit him, he could not go back because he would be unable to protect his brothers-in-arms and that, just above the defence of his country, was what Piero Bassi lived for.

He had been a street thug in New York with no direction in his life except for crime and he was, it seemed, no good at that either. He had been chasing a young girl for months, Maria Bartolo, who had no interest in him, none whatsoever. She did not care for his way of life and he was not going to impress her with a worn leather jacket, cigarette hanging from his lips and long hair raggedly draped over his shoulders.

He waited for her one evening, knowing that she attended night classes in the high school, and standing in a Dean-like pose smoking against a lamppost he waited for an hour. Just opposite, ramrod straight and not smoking, another guy was waiting, his service uniform displaying him as a Marine. Bassi had not noticed, had not cared nor, he thought, never would.

Maria skipped down the steps of the school, books held tightly to her chest in case they escaped. As she reached the bottom she began to wave at someone when her left hand was grabbed from the side and she was whirled around. The action was not aggressive, not to Bassi at least, but she lost her grip on her books and they scattered across the pavement in front of her.
Bassi had just wanted to talk but his method had frightened her. She screamed in fright and pulled her had away from him in anger.

"I just wanted to speak..." his words had no chance of exiting from deflated lungs.

The Marine had covered the distance from one side of the street to the other, to aid his sister, in the blink of an eye, which, unknown to Bassi, was about as much time as you have to apologise to a Marine before he gets physical.

Mike Bartolo was a Marine Sergeant modelled on John Basilano, intelligent, tough and incapable of backing down. He had Piero Bassi caught by the neck and pinned to the wrought-iron fence of the school and would have put Bassi through the five inch space between the bars had his little sister not intervened. Still, he intended to frighten the suitor enough to make him wet himself.

Looking straight into Bassi eyes, a bare inch from his nose he roared at the trembling street thug. "You try to fuck with my sister you fuck with me. You fuck with me, you fuck with my unit. You fuck with my unit, you fuck with the Corp. Do you want to fuck with the Corp, shit-head?"

The question was not required twice and the big Marine dropped the weeping kid to the ground and left it at that. He knew when the enemy was beaten.

Bassi had waited long enough to be sure that the Marine was not coming back when he finally stood up, brushed himself down and pulled a cigarette from the crushed pack that had been in his back pocket. He was still shaking when he tried to light his smoke, the Zippo not reacting to his frightened fingers. He managed to light it while, in the same moment, deciding it was time to quit. He stubbed it under foot and walked home. He knew he had something better to do with his life.

The following year, closer to Christmas and while home on leave, Mike Bartolo answered the knock on the door and was surprised by the young man who was standing there. It was the same kid he had almost choked to death over a year ago but now he was in a Marine service uniform, filled it well, cropped hair and a look of confidence that was not surprising, though maybe a little to the Sergeant.

Bassi had removed his hat once the door was opening and stood at ease in front of the man he had hoped would open the door. "Sir, with your permission, I would like to ask your sister if she would be free to attend the Marine Ball. With me, I mean."

That's how quickly life can change. Now, more years later than he cared to count, Maria was gone, the innocent victim of Bin Laden's desires, his brother-in-law died in Afghanistan, avenging his sister, and he lost his new life in Iraq. Yet, he lived on, once a Marine, always a Marine. Like they said, leaving the Marines didn't mean you were no longer a Marine, you just had a different uniform.

Now, he had his stride back, and back with a purpose. He had moved to Italy after his recovery was completed and had travelled round the country trying to re-engage with his history. Bit by bit the language that he learned from his mother and grandmother began to fit more and more with his surroundings and his desire to return to New York dimmed. It was not long before he was re-growing from the roots of his past and it was only when he spoke English, something that was becoming a rare occurrence, that he sounded American. He was now a pure Italian-American, meaning that he could be one as equally good as he could be the other. People notice that, people who need that skill, and it was not long before he was headhunted by those representing the "other government agency." When they came looking he was ready to listen and he knew that whatever they asked, he would do it. He wanted a reason to continue to be a Marine and serving his country, in any way at all, was what a Marine did. Of course, the agent who spoke to him already knew that. Piero Bassi was immune to the looks that his scared face and patched eye drew. He was not immune to the draw that his country had on him. No Marine was.

Regan, to the others watching from a distance, was almost comical in his new attire. Walking down the street in an affluent neighbourhood required one to dress appropriately and not in black Nomex assault coveralls. Instead, he was wearing beige cargo pants, a plain white shirt and, funniest of all to Izzo and Watson, open-toes sandals. However, he wore it all easily and fit into the street like a homeowner out for an evening stroll. It was a stroll with a difference, but a stroll nonetheless.

Watching from down the street, Izzo and Watson admired the street-craft. Sauntering along the street, not a care in the world, Regan hobbled a little and then hopped. He leaned against the parked Transit and lifted his right foot to free the pebble, or so it looked to anyone who cared to see what he was doing, from his open sandal. He hopped again, this time awkwardly, and fell against the side of the Transit before falling to the ground. He jumped up quickly, a sheepish grin spreading across his face, put his hand in his pocket and took out the keys to unlock the door with a familiar *beep* of a disabling alarm. In the course of falling and getting himself up from the ground, Regan has snatched the magnetised box holding the key from the wheel-arch and popped it into his pocked while raising himself up.

Izzo and Watson grinned at each other thinking that he had messed up with the fall but their mocking smiles were short lived when he opened the door of the van and stepped in. Moments later he pulled up outside the bar where the two were sitting sipping coffees and he beeped the horn to beckon them in.

It was, as Izzo and Watson had admitted to each other, perfect field-craft. Anyone watching what had happened had seen a local fall over while adjusting his sandal before driving off.

Piero Bassi, sitting at the back of the bar, patch removed from his eye yet seeing everything, was in agreement with Izzo and Watson. He did not know who they were but the big one driving the van looked, if anything, familiar. He had stayed to watch what would happen with the van, contrary to the orders that he had received from *Credibility* as the draw to action was too much for him. You never know, he thought to himself, there might yet be a place for you in the world of action.

21

Of Evil Titans

Silvio Fanetti sat back in the wicker chair that was creaking under his excessive weight. He could hear the creaks as he nestled his ample frame into the surrounds of the chair and cared little for the hidden smiles of the security guards who were with him. He was a fat man, he would say it himself, and so what? There were few enough physical pleasures for a man of his size and irretrievably lost looks so he went with the obvious, food. Today, outside under the shade of the large sun umbrellas and nestled comfortably into the wicker chair, he was just about to order a large plate of fried vegetables to start and would then decide on the pasta dish that would follow. He sweated like a pig in a slaughterhouse so it made no difference to him if he ate light or like a pig, he was going to sweat anyway.

The young waitress floated between the tables with his starter and landed it gently on the place mat in front of him. Her short skirt and one-button-too-much opened top went totally unnoticed, much to her displeasure, as her efforts were the main source of her daily tips. Instead, Fanetti barely grunted a thank you as his head dropped towards the plate at the same time as his right hand began to shovel the food towards the mass of flesh and lips that was his mouth. The bodyguards knew not to watch, not because Fanetti did not allow for them to do so but because it was not a sight to behold if one was about to eat also.

Credibility had identified Trippini's as the singularly most likely spot that Silvio Fanetti would stop at that evening with two bodyguards and all after a day of collecting money. Taking him would look like a robbery with the exception that money and bodies would have to be taken. All of this was considered in the response that had been sent to Regan and his team. It was also the same information that Bassi had seen as he had been "looped" in order that he knew what was to be expected of the Transit van, its content and where it was to go. "Looped" was simply keeping those who needed to be in the know of what was happening in the loop. Now, having taken the shortest route to the restaurant that the hit team could not take, due to the avoidance of cameras, Bassi was sitting at a small table, on the leftmost side of the outdoor dining area, sipping a glass of white wine and poking his salad with the chilled fork. He had not really wanted to eat but he decided to try and fit into his surrounding as much as possible. He had parked his scooter a hundred yards further down the street so that he looked casual walking in off the street. As much as he would have liked, he looked anything but casual as he walked though the tables. He still walked like a marine, chest out and shoulders straight, nothing like his fellow diners who walked with the swagger associated with those of a fashionable lean. Bassi, patch over one eye and walking with a military bearing attracted the attention of all in the restaurant. All including Silvio Fanetti's bodyguards.

The black Transit van slowed, ever so slightly, while passing the restaurant but on a street where there was little or no traffic, the slowing engine, diesel engine too so all the more audible, raised a number of eyebrows. Having just put Piero Bassi's image into their memory banks, the two bodyguards now exchanged glances. Something was up.

Bassi had caught that he had been noticed and tried to re-work his plan. He was good at thinking on his feet and in that moment decided to revert to being a loud American. What ever the two bodyguards had picked-up on, following him with their eyes as he crossed through the tables, he thought being American would ease their concerns. True to form, he clicked his fingers for service and spoke in loud, slow tones to the waitress when she arrived at his table. He could see that the bodyguards lost interest immediately. They were good, though. He gave them that much.

Now, sipping still on the same glass of wine, he saw the van pass for a second time. Back in Baghdad, he would have already put rounds into the engine or the tyres of a vehicle that would have passed slowly by a patrol, fixed or mobile, and then returned for a second run. What the Hell were these guys up to? He could see the bodyguards glance at each other for a second time and then, in swift and violent efficiency, they both moved to protect their client.

Regan's plan was out the window. He had stopped the van down the road, about a kilometre from the restaurant, and had gone through what was happening with the other two. Izzo had offered to drive as he knew the area and in the unlikely event that a roaming anti-mafia patrol or Carabinieri unit stopped them, he would produce his police badge to allow for their passage. They had changed into the black Nomex assault coveralls and they had each attached "*Polizia*" front and back onto the Velcro patches. Such deception, they believed, was going to be enough for the pick-up once the bodyguards were quick enough to understand the situation as it was developing and not draw their weapons. The mouse had just been introduced to the well-laid plan.

"Fuck it, break now, break now, break now," Regan shouted to Izzo. He had seen the bodyguards react and he needed to react just as fluidly as they had but the element of surprise had been lost and it was going to fall to the element of deception to make this move work.

The two bodyguards were earning their money. Grabbing Fanetti from a table of food, notwithstanding his weight, was not a simple task. However, as difficult a man that he was, Fanetti knew that when his "boys" moved, they were moving for a reason and that compliance with their requirements would mean that he would survive.

Regan was out of the van and running in a crouched motion towards the two bodyguards as they were trying to lift Fanetti out of the chair. One of them, the taller of the two, let go of Fanetti's huge arm and moved to draw his pistol.

Watson was just behind Regan and to his left, which allowed him an arc of coverage to the left while Regan had the right. The table where their target was now being wrestled from his chair was in the convergence of those two arcs and, while the arcs where theoretical, they would quickly become physical arcs of lead if the weapon being drawn were to be aimed at the two men.

The bodyguard was reacting as trained by swiftly drawing his weapon from under his light cotton jacket where it was held in an unclipped holster on his belt. A former serving member of the "Col Moschin", the 9th Parachute Assault Regiment, the young bodyguard never clipped his holster. He also knew that he was defending a thug but, having left the Special Forces under a cloud for drug use, he was willing to guard anyone for a few Euro and this guy, well his boss, paid well. Did he pay well enough to die was the question that was racing though his mind and he did not know that his actions were to play no part in the answer to that question.

Regan and Watson both saw the weapon being drawn and Regan shouted a warning in Italian, something that Watson was not going to do with pidgin Italian.

"Drop it, now!" The warning was sharp, direct and left no doubt of the intention of the man shouting the warning yet the gun was raised to chest level, but didn't fire.

Regan needed all three alive and uninjured so he fired three shots into the air, the one and only warning that he was going to give. He knew Watson had the bodyguard covered so he was not concerned about taking his gun off target.

The bodyguard registered the treble clatter of bullets and the "*Polizia*" on the cover-alls of the approaching men and froze, then, as commanded he dropped his weapon.

Watson covered the men as Regan cuffed and hooded all three. To the on-looking customers at, and in many cases under, the tables, the police had just arrested three criminals and it was best to keep out of their way until the operation was completed to the required demands of the police. It was not an unusual sight to see armed police "bag" a number of Mafiosi or Eastern European criminals and so, thankfully, nobody thought of calling the police. The believed that they were already there and dealing with the criminals so it was best to leave them to their work and, when they were done, they would be able, for those still with an appetite, to return to their meals.

Bassi had the same idea, but for different reasons. He saw the skill in the manoeuvres of the taller of the two men, he must have been the guy who picked up the van, but he also saw the errors. The passing by the restaurant twice was the first, that had actually been Izzo's fault, and the second was the firing of the weapon into the air without the consideration of where the brass casings would fall. He was thinking like a soldier while the others were thinking like, he did not really know, but they were not acting like soldiers who had planned and trained. They were reacting to scenarios and not so much to plans so that was good and bad. Good, because they were unlikely to really make mistakes and take civilians out and bad because they were so intent on the target that they were acting like they were in a combat zone and not a civilian restaurant. However, from where he was sitting, as the taller of the two gunmen was bounding the three targets,

Bassi could see the evening sun glinting off two of the casings and where there were two, there had to be a third.

It seemed to last forever but the actions only lasted slightly over a minute. Watson covered Fanetti while Regan bundled the two bodyguards into the back of the van and onto the floor. Izzo now had the engine on high revs waiting for the back door to slam and the wheels to spin.

Regan ran over to Watson and directed him to return to the van, leaving Fanetti in his capable hands. "Keep an eye on the other two, I have their guns but our friend who raised his weapon may be a little more experienced that we are giving him credit for. Keep your eyes on both."

The seconds were ticking when Fanetti intervened. "What in the fucking name of Holy Mary is this about?" His bluster matched his size but his size did not match Regan's. He felt the large hand grip his neck before he knew it had moved and he was choking as he tried to continue with his bluster. Looking up at the balaclava-surrounded eyes, he saw hate peering out at him. The police never looked like that at him and he suddenly knew that he was dealing with a different enemy.

Still holding Fanetti by the fleshy mass that was his neck, Regan ran him at the door of the van and, just at the last instant, he directed Fanetti's head into the upright where the door hinged, knocking him out cold. That was the limit of what he was going to allow himself to do in that moment though he wished that he could just unleash his anger on the first target that would, he felt, begin the war against those who had killed his sister.

Izzo heard the bang of the head on the door and nearly mistook it for the door shutting; seconds later Regan's barked command confirmed that he needed to drive. He did.

Bassi moved quickly as soon as the van had screeched away and around a corner. He stood up, the first of the customers to do so, pulled out his wallet and left two twenties on the table. It was enough to cover the bill twice over which was a very generous tip. He stood for a second to see how the others at the tables would react and saw what he had seen too many times in Iraq. Shock slowed people down to a level of treacle and incidents like what had just occurred resulted in an eerie silence that settled around the tables like a summer morning's mist. It was in those seconds of insecurity and confusion that the mist masked those who could react and anything seen or heard could not be counted on for reliability.

Bassi walked slowly from table to table, crouching down to check if everyone was ok. At the fourth table he crouched down to check on the elderly man who still had his fork of salad in his fear-clenched hand. "Sir, sir?" he gently asked, trying to pry the man's mind away from the fear that had risen within his mind. "Sir, they are gone. Are you ok? It was just the police, ignorant dogs that they are."

The old man looked up at Bassi and a smile crept across his wrinkled face. "Ha, I thought they were coming after me!" Bassi smiled back, but for two reasons. He smiled at the courage of the old man and his sense of humour but also because by crouching down to speak to him he managed to collect the third and final brass casing that had ejected from the soldier's weapon. The physical evidence was gone and now he worked on the memories. At each table were he spoke to people he changed the colour of the van from black to blue, from blue to grey and from grey to dark green. Then he changed the number of men so that at the first table he mentioned three, the second table two and the other tables five. He also mentioned the black man on the motorbike and the Asian waiting by the door of the van. By the time the real police would get around to interviewing the clientele, they would be chasing a white van that was full of motorbikes and Chinese men. Memory distortion was a skill that Bassi did not know he had but he had picked it up very quickly; he had seen and experienced it first hand in combat and figured it a useful tool.

Izzo had floored the accelerator to get away from the restaurant and covered ample distance before Watson told him to slow it down. Having been dressed as police, the likelihood that any of the customers at the restaurant would have called the police was going to be pretty slim. So, with that consideration, there was no need to drive like Schumacher through the busy streets.

In the back, Regan sat looking down at Fanetti's slumped mass lying between the two bodyguards. He was breathing heavily and bleeding from a gash on the crown of his head. The blood mixed with the heavy sweat, matting the hair to his forehead before dripping slowly down the side of his face and into his open mouth. The build-up of blood was bubbling out from between his lips as he breathed and the sight, as a whole, was not pleasant. It was not meant to be, however. It was the first act of anger that Regan had allowed himself to feel and it was the first whiff of blood to an angry white shark. He was read to kill.

Watson looked over at Regan and watch the carefully hidden emotions sneak to the surface then melt away. He was a strange one Watson though. He had also picked up on the minor errors and wondered if Regan was too attached to the mission, understandably, or was there something else. Maybe he was just a good soldier and not devious, that would explain the perfect actions that disarmed the two bodyguards but also the fact that he forgot to pick up the casings. Maybe he was so used to using caseless munitions that the thought never occurred to him. Unlikely, he seemed much too professional when it came to soldiering. Yes, he thought to himself, it is the tie to the victim; this was what he was going to have to watch. Regan was hunting the killers of his little sister and so he was driven to follow instinct, to find and catch the killers, and desire, to maim and to kill them. This was not going to be like working with Special Forces in the past, this was a muddled mix of professionalism and anger. It was going to be different.

Bassi pocketed the three brass casings and walked down the street to where his moped was parked. He had left behind a mass of confusion, some caused by the "pick-up" and more caused by him as he poured misinformation into the ears of those willing to hear it and, most importantly, remember the amended version. He was not noticed as he walked away and he felt confident that even if people did remember his patch and physique, the police would not be too interested. He didn't want to wait around to see if the police were going to be called, it would be strange if they were seeing as "they" had picked up the suspects. It would be days before the news of the pick-up got back to the police and maybe even longer before someone at a police station asked, "Did we pick someone up?"

Sitting now on his moped, he decided to contact *Credibility* and let the contact know what had happened and whether or not his services were required. Then it occurred to him that he did not need to call, he knew where the holding point was because he was the guy who had arranged it. His mind started ticking overtime. He wanted to be back in the field more than anything else and maybe this was a way to make it happen. If he went back to the warehouse and introduced himself to the team, one of a number of things was going to happen. He was either going to be shot, interrogated, shunned or accepted and none of the first three were extreme results. He decided to go and try. He had died twice in the last number of years; maybe it would be a case of third time lucky.

It was not a dramatic screech of tires on asphalt when Izzo stopped the van outside the warehouse. He had driven carefully, not so carefully as to draw attention, but carefully enough not to excite a policeman with a speed radar gun or to activate the memory of a dog walker. They had made their way to the warehouse unimpeded and were now sitting in the back of the van waiting for instructions from Regan.

"Emilio, please pop the hood, get out and muse about the engine and let us know if there is anything out of the normal in and about the car park. Lift your cap and scratch your head if you think the coast is clear."

Izzo jumped out and walked to the front of the van, hood already popped. He lifted the hood and hooked it into place, pulled a cloth from his pocked and started rubbing bits and pieces. In the van, Regan smiled at Watson as the both looked at the Oscar winning performance that was being played out for them.

Izzo was swearing loudly at the engine, took three steps back from the front of the van spun on his heels and three the oily cloth at the ground in anger at some perceived fault with the two-month old engine. He then calmed himself, bent down to retrieve the cloth turned back to the engine for another look and stopped. He pulled back his cap and scratched his head while trying to figure out, it seemed, how to fix the fault. The others saw the scratch and went to move quickly, Regan sliding open the door, one hand on Fanetti's collar already. Then

Izzo slapped the hood three times in warning. They had not planned a warning signal but his actions relayed the message nonetheless, someone was coming.

Regan heard the sound of the moped and picked-up, as Izzo did, that there were no lights visible, a sign of trouble whichever way you looked at it.

Bassi had pushed the moped to the limit of its small engine capacity and would have caught the van if the warehouse had been another two miles away. He had, on entering the initial road to the industrial area, dimmed his lights. In keeping with his desire to remain stealthy until he fully knew what he was doing, half a kilometre from the warehouse, he switched them off completely. It was edging from dusk to darkness so he still had just enough light to see where he was going but, as it turned out, not enough to see that the van had parked and that a large figure with a gun aimed at him as he drove through the gate.

Regan was as visually impaired as Bassi but he was going to be able to direct lead into the target if he needed to. However, his instinct told him to hold fire. The noise told him it was a moped, a single moped, and that was the sum of those coming at this moment. Something was not right and so he held fire because anyone intending to sneak up on a warehouse lights on or off, would not have chosen a moped as a means of transport.

Bassi realised his own schoolboy error when he entered through the gate and saw what he believed was the brief silhouette of a prone figure standing to the left of the van, his outline barely visible by the light being cast by the light emitting from the open door of the van. He braked hard, too hard, because he was sure that the figure would have a weapon raised, and the back wheel of his moped lost traction and slipped from under him causing him to lose control and wobble uncontrollably for ten meters before he fell off.

Regan didn't know whether to laugh or shoot. He decided to laugh first and shoot later, if required. For a moment he waited to see what the man would do, would he get up and try to mount his moped again, would he make a move at the van and the men in it or would he just pick himself up, dust off and stand and wait to see what was happening. Luckily for him, with a Walther P99 aimed at his head, he chose the later of the three actions and so his life was spared.

Regan watched the man rise from the ground and dust himself off and he turned to Izzo, now back in the van, and quietly told him to hit the headlights on the van. Izzo did so immediately.

Bassi was initially blinded by the lights but took to the blinding better than he would take to bullets. He stood for a moment before deciding on his next move, but raised his hands just in case.

"I have your casings," were the words that finally came out. He could have said so many other things to ease himself into the trust of the others but he decided on the casings as his means of entering into conversation.

Regan walked slowly towards the man with his gun still aimed at his now more visible head. "What do you want?"

"I figured that you wanted the casings of the warning shots you fired at the restaurant. I didn't think it was a good idea to leave them there."

"You think following us and then sneaking up on a team of armed men is a good idea, in comparison?" Regan asked as he reached the man and placed the mouth of the pistol onto the patch covering the remains of Bassi's eye."

"I may not be armed and I may have only one eye but if you do not remove your fucking gun from my fucking eye-patch the last thing I am going to remember before you pull the trigger is my foot connecting with your balls." Bassi was angry now and he knew that he was screwing things up.

"I am figuring that a man with one eye, an American accent and that kind of tone means one of a few things," Regan said while pulling the muzzle of the gun one inch from the man's patch and resting it on the bridge of his nose. "Now, I have removed the offending weapon from your patch. Who are you, why are you here and what the fuck do you want with us. You better be in, or have been in, one of the US services because your time is ticking, Patch, and I need to move."

"I was a Marine."

Regan lowered his weapon; he didn't see any reason to kill a Marine.

"I am the guy who got you all of this via *Credibility*, the van, the weapons and the warehouse. I ought to have left it at that but, being one-eyed, I am a little short-sighted when it comes to making good decisions." His good eye glinted with camaraderie. "My name is Piero Bassi and if you are killing terrorists, I want to be part of the action."

Regan did not move the weapon from Bassi's nose until he had send a message to *Credibility* asking for confirmation that the man at the end of his gun was who he said he was. He also added the he was not entirely pleases that they had been followed by the man hired by Credibility to assist them. The response from *Credibility* was terse.

"PB on our side. Get over it. C."

Regan allowed a brief smile to crack across his lips while reading the answer. "I'd nearly swear that Credibility is a woman." Bassi continued to stare at him from the one good eye, waiting for the gun to be removed from his nose. Regan was not ready to open up and trust the man who had managed to follow them. "Why?" he asked, gun still sitting on a now sweaty nose.

"Maria Bartolo," the reply was short and followed by a fertile silence that floated around the two men, each one sizing the other. Both had danced this waltz before.

"I am doing this for Kathy Regan, my sister. The men who run the fucker who is unconscious in my van killed her. I am going to find them, I am going to hurt them and then I am going to kill them. I am not hunting terrorists, Marine. I am hunting the men who killed my sister. This is not your war."

"Is it a just war?" The question came from the heart and mind of the Marine. He was not going to raise his flag with Regan if the fight was not justified. Regan was silenced for a moment. The question was simple and in its simplicity lay the crux of the matter; was what he was doing justified? It was to him yet he had now dragged others into his war and it looked like this Marine was going to want to join in too. Well, he was a grown man capable of his own decisions so if he wanted to join, if he thought the cause just, then it was of his own free will. "My sister is dead. Tortured, maimed then killed by those who feel that they live and work in an untouchable world. Her body was cast onto a broken gate and she was left hanging there for nature to have her own way with the body. I am going killing, the men behind me, for their own reasons, have joined me. I am going to show my sister's killers that their world is touchable."

Bassi kept his stare steady while Regan spoke. He wanted action, he wanted to be part of something that would keep him away from the chair in his apartment where he would sit and remember his wife and then drink to ease the pain of those memories. "My wife died on a trip to London. She was on the underground when the suicide bombers hit. I was in Iraq at the time fighting people of the same mind-set who planted the bombs. This happened to me when I went back to Iraq after my leave of absence for her funeral," he was pointing to his face and eye, "I am a mixed-up Marine, all I know is combat, so I need to get back to it somehow.

"Different people killed the women in our lives, Bassi. Are you sure fighting my war is going to the slake your thirst for revenge?"

"I am already involved, why not?" The answer was almost tired.

Regan was between two minds. When it came to a fight, it was always good to have Marines around. This Marine may have only one eye but he didn't think that it was going to slow him down. *Credibility* saw something in him, that counted for a lot but he sounded tired of life, and Regan didn't want his death on his conscience. "Are you sure?"

"I am sure, I want in. I know you cannot give assurances that there is an "out" or that we will survive your war, but that was the way I lived before. It is what I am." It wasn't a cry for help, he was asking to be a Marine again and Regan was not going to deny the man that opportunity.

"It is going to be rough, Patch."

"Don't worry, I'll keep an eye on you," his eye smiled.

22
On Speaking Terms.

The introductions were quick and they would have to wait before stories could be swapped. Bassi and Izzo worked swiftly together to move the two bodyguards into the warehouse. They took them in one at a time and tied them securely to the chairs that were already there. The two bodyguards were coming around when the last of the knots were being tightened and looped, the excess rope, on each man into a gag around their heads. Neither man made a move or complained, they were professional enough to wait and see what was happening, to wait and see what their collective fates were.

It was a different story with Fanetti. Both Regan and Watson struggled getting the huge man out of the van and into the warehouse. It was like dragging a large couch, one that had trouble fitting through the door. Watson had Fanetti held under the arms and was not enjoying having his hands heated in pools of stinking sweat. He was envious of Regan, who had the feet, not a garden of lavendar either, and was struggling to get thebroad shoulders through the door.

"Fuck this, Jack, can we not cut him in two? I can't get his shoulders through the door!" Watson exclaimed with a hint of humour wafting from his frustrations.

Regan dropped the two feet with a thud and then stepped back to review the situation. "Leave him down for a second." Watson complied with the request and then did not know whether to laugh or cry at the actions of Regan who kicked Fanetti squarely in the chest and the body popped through the door. "*Lay on, MacDuff, and damned be he that first cries 'Hold, enough!'*" Regan said, grinning at Watson.

They resumed their positions at each end of the big man and got him to the chair, in between his two bodyguards. Izzo came back in from the van with Bassi carrying a hold-all. He showed it to Regan and figured it contained at least two-hundred thousand in bunches of used notes. "What shall we do with this?"

Regan looked into the bag and whistled. He had seen more but only in pay-offs to tribal chiefs and hostage takers. "Well, let me see. Watson and I are rich beyond our wildest dreams so you and Bassi can keep that as a down payment."

Watson nearly choked laughing at his "richness" but also at the look on Izzo's face.

"I am still a police officer, Jack. I cannot take this money." Izzo sounded both exasparated and sorrowful at the same time.

"Donato, you are party to a kidnapping, assault and, in a few minutes, torture and soon after that death. Bloody murder, if you wish. I would suggest that the money goes to your wife if anything goes wrong here. If you wish, I can give it to some people who will turn it into an investment plan for your wife. As for being a policeman, I thing you may want to consider a new career if we all make it out of this."

Izzo frowned a little then perked up. "It could be worse, couldn't it!"

"Who the fuck are you lot?" The words sounded heavy and course and all four men turned to see that Fanetti had regained conscienceness. The air changed in the vast warehouse. To Watson, Izzo and Bassi, a chill decended and surrounded them all. Regan stood before Fanetti glowing in rage and fury. The mask had been removed, the face beneath no longer hiding feelings that had been tempered in the fire of anger in his chest. Watson breathed in deeply and then exhaled slowly. He turned to the other two and whispered "Here we go, brace yourselves."

Izzo, Bassi and Watson did not know what to expect even though Watson had a worrying feeling that it was going to bad. Regan had remained silent at Fanetti's question, a powerful calm that was lost on Fanetti but not on the others, including the two bodyguards who were by now fully awake. An eerie feeling hung in the room and they all felt it. All, that is, except Regan. His mind was switching to kill mode in a manner in which it had not been calibrated to in the past. This was the first of those who had been part of the killing of his sister and he was going to ensure that Fanetti, and his men, were going to know why they were now tied up.

Fanetti sensed that there was a weakness among the men facing him at that moment. He decided that being tough was the best way for him to deal with his captors. He saw them as his captors only because he could not think of another tag to mark them with. They surely were not professionals or they would have had killed him and his two bodyguards already. No, these men were after something else and were going to try to play it tough with him. Well, he though to himself, let them fucking try. He had not moved through the ranks of the Twin's organisation by being soft. He could handle these guys.

'Well, Stronzo, are you not going to tell me why we are here. I am a busy man and have many things to occupy my day without having to sit here and make pleasant conversation with you guys. What the fuck do you want?" The blurred vision was correcting itself and he saw that three of the men were in black police cover-alls. He turned to each of his bodyguards and laughed, "I see! We did not pay the police enough this month! Who's fault is this?"

Regan didn't flinch. He pulled his pistol from his belt and shot the bodyguard to Fanetti's left twice in the face. The large head exploded in a mist of blood and bone fragments, covering Fanetti in a warm splash of bright red. There was no change of expression on Regan's face as he walked to the body that was now slumped on the ground. Standing over the dead bodyguard, he started viciously kicking the crumpled body with well-placed kicks to the groin. "Speak to me you fat fuck. This is your last chance you piece of shit." A bemused look passed over Regan's face when he stopped and turned to his three colleagues.

"Boys, I think I got that back to front. Shit, lets try it again."
Fanetti felt a warm puddle spread between his legs. He had never experienced anyone like this before and knew that he now had a serious issue to deal with.

Regan turned his attention to the second bodyguard who now didn't look as menacing as he had been minutes before. Regan pulled a knife form his belt and leaned into the face of the bodyguard. His eyes bored into the man's head. The bodyguard saw lifeless, corpse-like eyes, but that meant no pity.

Regan pierced the skin just under the nose with the point of the blade and pushed it hard. The bodyguard screamed in pain and writhed against the ropes that held him in place. Regan pushed harder until he saw that the blade had penetrated by an inch. The screams were a gutteral representation of the horrific pain the man was being subjected to but it didn't prevent Regan from continuing with his work of horrific art. He stood back and kicked the knife upwards with the toe of the boot. The scream that exploded from the bodyguard's mouth shook Watson but had no effect on Regan. By kicking the blade upwards three front teeth were pushed out of the gum and were now bloody white pieces on the lap of the bodyguard. Regan reefed the knife out and slashed it rapidly across the bridge of the nose, both eyes the unwilling beneficiaries of the knifemaker's precision edging.

The bodyguard, though now blind, was horribly aware that the nightmare was far from over. Regan grabbed him by the hair and jerked his head forward so that the man's ear was brushing his whispering lips. "I am not going to kill you. You are going to kill you." The bodyguard was now whimpering, a chastised child before a cruel teacher, his spirit completely broken.

Regan, once again, pulled his pistol but did not fire it. To Fanetti's surprise, Regan unloaded the magazine and left one bullet in the chamber.

'Now, Sir, you are going to use this one bullet in any way you choose. You may try to kill one of us, but with no sight that will be difficult, or you may end your own misery. If you choose to waste the shot, I guarantee that what you have endured until now will seem like a trip to Disney." He paused for a moment ensuring the words were having the desired effect. "Kill yourself," he whispered. The words were almost gentle but chillingly matter of fact as he pushed the gun into the man's unclenched hand.

"I have a wife and child." Bloody tears and a desire to live accompanied the words. That was not enough.

"I had a sister." The words from Regan's mouth explained everything. The bodyguard knew now who was facing him and remembered the words of the girl that the Twins had tortured. "You are Jack." It was not a question.

Regan grabbed him by the neck and urged him to speak.

"She called out your name. She said you would come. She said that you were death, death that would visit us all. Oh, Jesus."

Watson had never seen such fear as that which contorted the face of the two Italians. Regan, in that moment, was an incarnation of death and the men before him shook with fear. But nothing was going to save them.

"Kill yourself," he whispered again, gently but with more rigid intent.

The bodyguard slowly raised the gun to his head and pushed the muzzle into the shallow flesh of his temple. "Will you hurt my wife and child?" It came as a plea.

'No.'

A look of serenity passed over the man's face as he heard the answer and he pulled the trigger.

Watson felt his stomach lurch violently but he managed, just barely, to restrain the function of his stomach's desire to empty itself. He fought the same battle with his bladder which all of a sudden, felt like it was going to bust. He had seen men tortured before. Tortured in ways that resulted in immediate responses to questions that required such action – peoples lives depended on it. Now he was watching the ultimate in information recovery and realised that the results would not save lives but, instead, snuff them out in the manner in which he had seen happen before his eyes. He knew that the man – could he really call him a man when such brutality could flow from every pore in his body – was a terrifying example of how man can kill his fellow kind, but this was different. It could hardly be believed that such efficiency was man-made and not the result of some pre-programmed machine. He began to dread what was going to happen to Fanetti. He was about to be surprised.

The cloak of calmness was once again draped across the muscular shoulders of the interrogator and the fire in his eyes, which moments before would have chilled the throne of Satan, smouldered with clever intent.

'You have seen what I am capable of. Do you now wish to speak? I can assure you that you will leave this place alive today but it is up to you to decide the level of that life which will still exist in your body.'

Fanetti was in a state of shock and words, while they were mounting an offensive to escape his terrified mind, were not capable of jumping the gap between his brain and his tongue. If he was to live, the words had to find a way.

Chapter 23
Silvio Speaks

The air in the room was deadened by the fear that had crept out of every pore in Fanetti's body. He had tried to convince himself that he had never felt fear before but, to that extent, he had been lying. He just didn't remember cowering in the car after his parents had been shot, but there had to be a mental image hidden in his soul, an image of his mother slumped over his father's bloodied chest, her brain matter mixed with the dyed blond hair. Maybe, in the deepest, darkest dreams, where memory failed to function, could the young boy that still existed in some state in his mind, recall the horrors that death had paid him that day.

Now, sitting with a dead bodyguard on each side of him, the images of that faithfull day flooded back into his mind in the most disruptive of manner, and damaged him more than the expected torture could. Silvio Fanetti, in that moment was pulled back to his childhood, as if hypnotised, and a sense of absolute dispair and helplessness permeated his being. Regan did not know it yet, but there would be no need for the use of "enhanced coercive interrogation techniques" on Fanetti.

Regan stood looking at the body of the man who had just taken his own life and wondered, silently, was it entirely necessary. The discussion going on his head seemed to be part of a conversation that his body was not engaged in and that concerned him. He slowly wiped his mouth, not sure if that action would cleanse the taste of distain, and then looked away from the corpse and back to the main target of this operation who was still alive, still breathing.

"Have I made myself clear?"

Fanetti's head was bowed over and he was mumbling to himself, unaware now that there was anyone else in the room. His words were frantic, one moment targeted and the next pointless. Regan recognised it for what it was and knew that he needed to work quickly before the breakdown was complete and no further, useful information would come from the man. He snapped his head around to Watson and spat at him to record the conversation, if one developed.

Watson knew better than to argue and pulled the digital recorder from his pocket and switched it on.

"Mammy was killed, so was Daddy and so was I." There was a brief pause, a fragment of confusion dislodging from the mountain of loss in his mind, "No I wasn't, I lived but I think I didn't, I am not sure. Why do you care? I care because I was there. Too much blood. Brains did not go well with Mammy's hair. That hair was blonde, the brains were not. Daddy's chest was red and he had no face. Not a good day for shopping. No presents for me that day. No cake either."

Regan took a step back from the drooling beast that was slumped before him. It was shocking, and had to be real. Fanetti was broken, more broken that what torture or a good interrogator could hope to achieve. There may be nothing else left to take from this man, but he would try and then he would kill him.

He pulled a chair up in front of the weeping Silvio, took a cloth from the table beside him and wiped the blood and spittle from the man's face. There was no reaction from the man except a gentle whimper, the sound a child makes once the crying storm has stopped and the pain has surrendered to a parent's hug.

"Ok, Silvio. I am not going to hurt you." The voice was gentle, caring and, surprisingly to the rest of the men in the room, it was convincing.

Silvio looked up at his tormentor and said nothing. His mind was a jumble of information from his past and near past. What had happened in the minutes just gone had been wiped by the protective nature of his mind, a mind under terrible pressure.

"I know you have had a bad day, Silvio. I know you are hurting at your loss. It is right that you are sad, that the loss of your parents is hurting. You are only a boy and you should not have to deal with this reality."

Watson picked up on what was happening first and he turned to the others, "Fanetti has lost it. Regan is interrogating the child that is left. Let's step back and see what come of this." He didn't need to mention that a ticket to Hell was the result he expected.

"My parents are dead too, Silvio. My father and mother died a couple of weeks ago so I know what you are going through. I know how you are feeling. "

"How did they die?" the question leaked from the blubbering lips, the face still contorted with sadness and anger. Silvio the child wanted answers to the questions and the thread of friendship to the man, now sitting in front of him, who had also lost his parents, was beginning, in his own mind at least, to strengthen. He was not aware that the thread was one of many in the web of lies that would move him towards giving up the names of his friends.

"They were shot, Silvio. They were coming home from Church and some men shot them. I was with them when it happened; it was a terrible thing to have seen. I don't know how I would have managed if my friends were not there for me." The seed was sown.

"My friends helped me too. They were there for me and they helped me."

"Have they always been there for you, Silvio? Through thick and thin? That is the sign of a good friend, isn't it?" The questions, while still easy for the man to answer, were building up in number and intensity.

"Yes, they have always been good to me. Good to people like me."

"Now, Silvio, what do you mean by "like you." You are a good boy, aren't you?"

The body of the man began to shake as the tears of the boy took hold of the mind. Regan felt confident that he could push further into the wounds of the mind and extract the information he needed. He cared little for the physical or mental impact that what he was doing would have on Silvio Fanetti. In fact, considering the lengths he was now going to in order to get him to speak, becoming his friend, his ally in the shadow of their parental death, he felt the fat bastard deserved the pain. Never one to turn the mirror onto himself, Regan believed that every man could change, or at least know when they are doing wrong and try to alter the path they travelled. He did not believe that the horrors of a destroyed childhood would impact the man who grew from those horrors. If he did understand, if he had the compassion and patience to see that what had happened to Silvio as a child made Silvio the man, then he would have to look into his own soul and see that Regan the soldier must have come from the night on the border. Or would he have to look deeper still, into a childhood he could not remember before that night. From that night onwards, or so he believed, he created the natural sanctuaries in his mind, the pond where his thoughts rippled, the field of corn that lived and died by his temper and other such compartments of his difficult psyche. If he did turn on himself, point the mirror of accusations and threats to his own soul, would he collapse as Silvio had done? It mattered not, he was going to continue.

"Come now, my friend, I am here to help you. I can get your friends and bring them here so that they can be with you. We can all be with you at the funeral, surround you and protect you from your fear and sorrow. Does that sound like a good idea?"

Silvio looked up, a sense of hope drying his eyes and stopping his tearful shakes. "Can you? Can you do that?"

"Of course. I will go myself and collect them at their homes. I will tell their parents that they are going to be staying with their friend Silvio and I can bring them home after the funeral. When you are a little less frightened."

"Thank you. Oh, God, thank you. I do not even know your name." Silvio was wringing his hands, trying to thing of a way to thank the man before him.

"My name? You know my name, don't you Silvio?"

"I do, I do. I am so sorry. I do."

"Now, not to worry, I am going to listen carefully to you, my friend Silvio, and you can tell me where to go and who to collect. Is that ok?"

"Marco." The first name to spill out was the first step.

"Marco, of course. Marco has to come. Who else?"

Silvio scrunched up his face, deep in thought, and pulled the names from the dark recesses of his mind. "You can collect Mauro too, he will be with Marco. They do everything together. He does not like me much but he is Marco's brother."

"Oh, Silvio, I am sure he likes you. He probably is a little shy, that's all. Is he shy around girls?"

Again, the face showed that the mind was being searched and then the answer, the jewel Regan was looking for tumbled out."

"He played with her, so he must not be shy. I played with her too. We had lots of fun."

Regan eased himself back into the seat and breathed out slowly. "Very good, Silvio. Should I collect Kathy too?"

"No, she won't play with us anymore."

Too fucking right she won't, you prick. But you can play with me again soon and then you can see who won't be coming to play again. "That is a pity, but I can get the others to come." *Just give me the names and I will play my games.*

"I think Santo would like to come. Can you collect him?"

"Did he play with Kathy?"

"Yes, he did. She didn't like him. He hurt her."

"Oh, that is not nice. Were all your friends mean to her?" *Give me the names, fucker, I am ready to hunt.*

"Ale was there too, I am not sure he played with her but he was there. And that boy who likes numbers. He was not nice to her at all, he hit her and Ale didn't like that. "

"What is his name, I will bring him too." *I am going to hurt him.*

"Erasmo, it is a funny name isn't it?" The tears had stopped and the names flowed, each one being recorded on the micro-recorder but also in the mind of Regan. His target list was expanding. And it would soon contract.

"Silvio, tell me again about Santo. I don't think I know him so I want to be sure that I go to the right house. "

"He lives out in the country and comes in to Marco's house every day. He always brings fruit. I don't know where he gets it."

Regan powered on his tablet and switched to the Maps application. "Is it somewhere near here?' he asked as he pushed the tablet under Silvio's nose."

"Oh, Santo has one of these too! I wanted one."

"Well, you can have this one to play with when we are finished speaking. How about that?"

Silvio reacted like any child would and grinned with happiness and became so eager to assist his new friend. Flag after flag was planted on all the locations were Regan could find Silvio's friends and the tablet quickly became the home of the plan of attack. Looking at the flag for Santo, Regan decided that he would be the second to be picked up. Of course, he would prefer to hit the Gascos immediately, but that would not do. Gently, gently.

Silvio spoke for another hour, answering questions that allowed Regan to paint a picture of what happened when his sister died. He fought a battle to suppress his natural instincts while listening and Watson and the others watched in awe as he played the friend card with such aplomb. Watson wondered where he had learned such skill, switching from killer to kind interrogator in the blink of an eye. Whatever he had thought of the young man in the past, when he wanted him dead, he knew know that he, and those like him, had been fortunate not to have cornered Regan. He was now seeing what he would have seen if they had caught him. He continued to watch in silent wonder.

"Silvio, are you still with me?"

"Yes, I am. Of course I am," he stuttered in reply. "I am trying to remember your name. I thought I knew it, but it is missing again. Missing from my tongue."

Regan leaned forward and lifted Silvio's head in his two large hands and cradled it while he spoke. "My name is Jack, Silvio. Jack Regan. Kathy was my sister."

"Ah, yes. Jack. That is your name, isn't it? You are here now, Jack. You came for Kathy, didn't you?"

"Yes, Silvio, I did."

"Where is she?"

"Safe."

"Oh." The eyes looked up to those staring intently down at him and Silvio's mind, after everything it had been through, began to fight its way through the fog of confusion. "Jack," he said once more but with a little more clarity. "Jack is death, and he will come for you. He will come for all of you."

"Yes."

"Are you here for me?"

"Yes." The game was over and Regan wanted to finish his work. He pulled his pistol from the holster as Silvio began to speak again.

"You said I could play with the tablet."

Regan did not raise the gun and his breath caught in his chest. *The fucker does not understand.* "Silvio, you know what is happening, don't you."

"Bedtime?"

Watson felt sick. This was tantamount to killing a child. He wanted to say something, to intervene to stop Regan but he knew the soul of the man. He knew what killing those who killed his sister meant.

"Silvio," Regan said gently, "you and your friends killed Kathy. You know that don't you?"

No, he does not understand, he is a kid, for fuck sake. Watson had seen enough and was not going to let Regan kill the man, the man who was now a child. He walked out of the shadows and over quietly to Regan as the gun was beginning its arc.

"No, Jack. You cannot kill him. He is a child, look at him," he whispered gently from behind Regan.

Regan turned, weapon still raised, and faced Watson. "He is not a child, he is broken. That is all. If he were a child, he would not be here. "

"Jack, you can't kill him. Not now."

"He killed her, Watson. As surely as the Twins did it, he did it too. So did the others whose names he gave me."

"That is fine, Jack. That is the soldier talking. Now, listen to the lawyer. The information you gained today cannot be depended on. You don't know who he has given to you and you cannot go and kill them all."

"I can't?" The look he gave Watson was quizzical amusement. "I think you will find that I can." He turned back to look Fanetti in the eyes.

In that moment, as Regan's finger applied the two pounds of pressure to the trigger, a slight sneer appeared on the lips of the accused man and Watson in that instant, lost his regret.

The two bullets, the quintessential double-tap, splattered into Fanetti's large head and brain tissue, hair, some skull fragments and not a small amount of blood painted the wall behind his head with a gruesome collage. The bloody mess began to crawl down the wall just as the dead weight of the man slid from the chair and toppled to the ground. The sound of the wet thud, as the damaged head hit the ground without a bounce, would stay with Watson forever.

Regan looked down at the body on the floor and stood motionless for a moment before turning to Watson.

"There is nothing bad that can come of his death."

"Is there something good?" He had to ask.

"I feel better. A little."

"Great, good to fucking hear."

Regan didn't take the bait, probably a good idea then Watson thought to himself. Instead, Regan looked back over to Fanetti's body, then back to Watson and said "What the fuck" and opened fire again into the bloodied remains on the floor. The massive frame took the lead without a ripple and, the heart having stopped after the first two penetrations, only the blood pushed out by gravity and the man's body weight stained the clothes and floor.

"I told you I was going to kill them all. You do understand that, Watson, don't you? I have to kill them. Doing so eases the sense of guilt that I feel for not being to help her. I should have been there, shouldn't I?"

"No, Jack. You could not have helped even if you were in the country. How do you think that would have worked out? Be reasonable, and if not, try to be sensible. There are limits to what you, anyone, can do in given situations and that situation just happened. It does just happen sometimes."

"What?"

"Shit, it just happens. People get in the way of falling trees, loose cattle, falling stars. They get hit, they die and nobody can stop it. A juggernaut, a juggernaut full of sick fuckers, but it was a juggernaut that hit Kathy. You could not have stopped it."

"True, but I could have responded." The frustration was gathering in his words, pooling from the sense of guilt flowing in his veins.

"How, Jack? How would you have responded? Who would you have lashed out against? The police? The ambulance men or doctors? Who, goddamnit?"

Regan's head drooped a fraction and his eyes returned to look at his work as it lay dead on the ground, silent in its stench of death. "Everyone, Steve. I would have lashed out at everyone."

"Jesus, Jack, if there is a reason to everything that happens to us all then there is a reason to what happened to Kathy, and a reason why you were not here when it happened. The distance gave you some time to consider what you were going to do, that distance also allowed the fuse to burn a little and you have now the chance to get them all, as you want to do, but not to get those who were not involved. You will not be targeting people out of anger, though there is anger, you will be targeting them out of a valid, tangible sense of revenge."

"And a need to kill, don't forget that," Regan added with a sigh.

"How can I?"

'Have things quieted down yet?' Marco was sitting out on the veranda staring up at the sky. He had a habit of doing that when he felt nervous or agitated. His brother felt that it relaxed Marco to be able to see large open spaces, as he was never comfortable when he felt closed in.

Marco turned his head, removed his sunglasses and stared at his brother. His eyes were jumpy and his fingers drummed lightly on the arm of his chair.

'The story is all but gone in the newspapers. I can't imagine the police putting much more effort into the investigation as too much is happening in Milan at this time.

Another terror cell had been broken up before it had had the chance to go active and the citizens of Milan were breathing a sigh of relief again. The plot that had been uncovered was an audacious plan to attack the Duomo in the centre of the city. A stunningly large cathedral, it was constantly full of tourists and made the perfect target, one which would, undoubtly, kill and maim many nationalities and strike a blow against Christianity. Marco was amazed at the mindset of the terrorists to the extent that he almost admired it. Being entirely honest with himself he did actually admire them. They were perfect killers. Strapped in explosives they would walk to their target and hit with precision and with deadly effect. The Americans thought that they had precision bombing down to a fine art but there was something more creative about a suicide bomber. It was more personal and had a more telling outcome. People do not try to rationalise a Tomahawk missile fired from two thousand kilometres away. It is a lifeless machine. The suicide bomber is a machine full of life and, tragically, full of death too.

'Well, brother, we can now start moving towards our goal. Our police contact will be in a position to furnish us with a list of the names we require and where they are at this time. When we have everything ready we will cut the head off our rival and move into their territory.

'Is it not too soon, Brother?'

'The more the terrorists keep the police busy the less time they have for dealing with the Mafia. It is then that we shall deal with them instead. Hell, the police may even thank us when it is all done.'

Marco smiled, replaced his sunglasses and resumed staring up at the sky. It was a peaceful day and the police would never thank them for what they were about to do so why should he give a flying fuck.

Regan sat under the same sun that shone down on Marco's face yet he felt no warmth. In fact, it had been years since he felt any warmth from the sun. To a soldier of the shadows the sun was always the enemy and yet, in times of despair, every soldier sought solace from the sun. People like Marco did not understand such sentiments and there, in that singular point, lay his greatest weakness. There was no connection with nature, as a true soldier has, and so he would never be able to deal with the effects that would bear down on him when a force of nature, a true soldier, would rain his wrath upon him.

Such thoughts fortified Regan's will and he was able to ferment the grapes of his wrath into the sweet tasting wine of revenge. He allowed his mind to float amongst the thoughts and plans that were there. The images were developing slowly even thought he was able to put faces to the men who had killed his sister.

Silvio Fanetti had given up four names and, of course, the Twins and now the process was starting to take shape. Not only did Silvio give the names, matching them to the pictures that had been taken from Kathy's file and shoved under the tortured man's nose, but he gave up the simple information that Regan needed to speed the inevitable. For their end was written in the stone of his heart and while those men, the targets of his untempered fury, might not fear death they would, on meeting Regan, fear the cause.

Umberto Cali was next on his list and Fanetti and seemed to regret giving him up to Regan. *"He is my friend, and I am going to his birthday party on Saturday."* Regan had teased the address and details from the troubled mind like a blackbird pulling a worm from the early morning soil, cleanly and efficiently. It was going to be a fortieth that Cali would not have the joy of remembering.

Cali would be followed on the Monday morning by Allesandro "Ale" Becca. Becca was a smooth operator, handsome and charming and was everything that one did not expect from a criminal. Silvio said that Ale would have made a good Bond except that he did not like violence. He preferred fine wines and beautiful women. Money was needed to fulfil those needs and he got his money from being a supplier for the Twins, whatever they wanted, he supplied. They had wanted Kathy and he had delivered. For that reason, for his special delivery to the Twins, Ali Becca would would die.

Of the four names dribbled from Fanetti's broken lips, it was that of Santo Rapposelli that had peaked Regan's desires and he struggled to prevent the mind's eye from flooding his thoughts with images of killing Rapposelli. He knew that killing him was not going to be enough and so he allowed himself the small pleasure of plotting the capture, torture and killing of Santo Rapposelli. There would be nothing saintly to the manner of death plotted. Everybody dies but only some are killed and Santo was going to be killed.

Regan left the table where he was sitting and returned to his room. It had been a day of action and disturbing scheming and both tired a man physically and mentally. His bed beckoned but whether sleep would follow was an unknown. Sleep brought dreams and the dreams were not his friend.

Morning crept silently through the window and gently eased the dawn's light onto the flickering eyelids that were just opening. One hand reached up and firmly rubbed the night from his eyes and face. The other hand's fingers feathered the trigger, gaining comfort that it was still warm. Not so long ago his pistol was a teddy bear and the window would have had a shine that only a mother could put on glass. Regan was awake.

While helpful in most combat scenarios, training and the finest weapons do not make the best soldiers. They are moulded by something much more simplistic than that, the ability to sleep. Without sleep neither training nor weapons will make a difference to the capabilities of a man. Regan never had trouble falling asleep. He just had troubled sleep.

The dream was the same again and now was pushing other, similarly violent, dreams from his head in a cuckoo-like move to dominate the nest of his mind. Except the egg being laid in his head was an image of his sister and the damage that had been inflicted onto her. Images that in the cold light of day he was able to control, to keep from searing themselves to the fragile lens of his mind's eye. While sleeping there are no such barriers and the images that plagued him during his sleep were of the pain and suffering that his sister had endured, and that he was incapable of stopping.

However, all considered, he had had a good night's sleep regardless of the dreams and was now ready to repay the violence visited upon his sister. Considering the equity of violence, Regan was wonderfully rich.

25

Lady Luck

For some lady luck was an expected and much loved guest in their lives. For Regan luck never was a part of the formula that he inserted into his plans. Luck was a stream without a bed that could flow and meander as it pleased. Bad luck, however, was something that could always be counted on. So many times in the past he had seen men die for nothing more than just sheer bad luck. It could be counted on but it could also be countered by training, repetition and the rub of the green. Contrary to popular opinion the rub was not just luck it was an Irish thing. It was that turning of the tide that followed large amounts of sheer drive and determination. The rub of the green was a payment for hard work. This was especially true for Regan. Tonight was the first payment.

The restaurant catered for private parties and only parties that could pay the price of the exclusivity offered. No price was ever spoken yet it was understood that it was high. The clients who ate there did so out of the glaring eyes of the public, the media and, most importantly, the police. It was not that so many illegal deals were fed at the solid oak tables within, just that not all of the patrons were equally bad. One semi-famous brother and sister ate their once a month, he a wealthy industrialist and she the wife of a known mafia underboss. Privacy always had a price and the Silk Princess was the restaurant silently famous for such privacy. For that reason it was why Umberto Cali chose to celebrate his birthday there. He had invited his five closest friends and their wives to celebrate with him and he was going to do it in style. A man turned forty only once after all. Cali did not realise, nor how could he, that his birthday celebration was to be his last.

Regan had learned quickly in his career that over-training can blunt the finest minds and bodies to the point that they will not respond in the way they should. It was the same for planning. Simplicity was the key to the success of most of Regan's plans and this was not going to be any different. He knew the security of the wall-enclosed restaurant was good and so in order to fulfil his wish to enter and exit the target area as quickly as possible he decided to just walk through the gates. In fact, he was going to swagger.

Umberto Cali leaned back in his chair and surveyed the table and all at it. It had been a wonderful meal and he felt content. His life was changing for the better and all because he had followed his school year's friends. The twins had liked his scrapping ability and pulled him into their world. Not too far into it however as they deemed him too dim witted to be anymore use than his present role and that was of a brutal enforcer. Cali didn't need to understand the mental agility required of those who wished to rule their own world. He was simply the physicality that they dreamed of, that they required to engage in their chosen fields while keeping their greedy hands clean.

Walking into a crowed restaurant with a loaded weapon is not a difficult task. The cut of a professional killer's jacket is such that there is a little more material over the area where the weapon sits. It give the illusion, to a glancing eye, that there is nothing under the Jacket. Those whose profession it is to stop such unwelcome guests in restaurants, or any other such gathering point for civilians, would note the subtle change in the cut of the material. They would also note the confident stride that was not too fast and not too slow, hair that was neither black nor brown, a face that was neither pale nor tanned. The professional killer would stick out only in the manner of his, or, increasingly, her, ability to be invisible. For such people, being unremarkable was the gift of invisibility, a cloak that they were required to wear constantly. Experienced policemen and soldiers could see such a cloak of invisibility but none were in the restaurant when Regan walked past the matre'd, dropping his head with a slight acknowledging smile that said *I don't need your assistance, I know what table I am going to.*

Umberto Cali was gently easing his lips from the wine glass that had just given up the slightest sip of the eight year old Amarone. He had held it gently on his tongue before allowing it to find its own path to his gums. Then, inhaling a modest breeze of air, he converted the taste to a scent. It was the briefest of moments before he knew the bitter taste of disappointment. He considered the vintage, eight years old, and remembered, as he remembered everything of importance to his life, that it had rained during harvest that year. The winemaker had not been diligent enough in removing the rotten bunches from his harvest and now the wine was, to his palate, ruined. And so too, therefore, was dinner. However, there was always a sliver of silver on the clouds that crossed over the countryside of his emotions. Ever the optimist, he was not going to let the wine ruin his evening. He would assist the digestion of his partial meal with a Hine Antique XO and allow his soul the slight impairment for choosing French over Italian.

Regan slipped his hand into his pocket in mid-step and removed a single Euro coin and held it between his thumb and index finger. To his left, and just beyond the nearest table to him, a waiter was floating between the tables with a tray of tall crystal champagne flutes. A simple target for a flicked coin.

Umberto raised his hand to click for the attention of a waiter to order his brandy just at the same instant that Regan flicked his coin at the tray of flutes. In that instant, three noises followed each other, the second louder than the first but only a tuned ear heard the third.

Umberto's thumb slid from his middle-finger to his index finger creating the much maligned *click* that all workers in the service industry detest. All eyes at the nearest tables looked in disgust at the hand that had revived the old, impolite call for service. An untimed second later, the Euro coin shot from the latex covered fingers of the soldier who was about to hit back at those who had, unknowingly, hit him, and careened through the first two flutes on the tray, shattering their lead-crystal into tiny shards of natural perfection. Eyes turned to see what the waiter had done and the deflection allowed the second latex-covered hand to draw the weapon and, in the sweep of motion to align the unseen path for the weapon's bullet passengers, the safety was depressed an instant before the trigger. *Tap, tap.*

The first bullet, free from its copper casing, spiraled out of the short barrel of the pistol. Its path was unhindered as it spun, in a perfect pirouette, leaving a minute tail of burnt gun powder in its wake. It impacted on the ring finger of the still raised hand and spread its lead weight against the large gold and diamond ring. In effect, it was a botched shot but the result, when considered in hindsight, was endearing. The expanded bloom of lead cut through the three digits that had, a split second previously, clicked for service. It then tumbled into Umberto's face just under his nose, piling through his upper front incisors. But this was irrelevant as the the second bullet impacted on the bridge of the nose, passing through a small childhood scar long forgotten by the child who had endured it. The adult was not going to remember anything either.

Regan the soldier was about to turn and walk out when Regan the brother took over. There was a conflict of interest in the one mind as the soldier needed to exit the fire zone and the brother wanted to drain his soul of anger, just for one moment. He could do that by unloading the weapon into the already shattered head. The soldier could leave and be forgotten but a man standing over a corpse firing into half a head would be remembered. He holstered his weapon and walked nonchalantly towards the door. The soldier, more professional than the angry, emotional brother, had won two battles that evening.

26
A Wave Goodbye

Sitting on the beach staring out to sea, Alessandro Becca began to ponder the reality of the organisation's situation. Things had changed and most definitely not for the best. The attack in the restaurant three nights earlier had left one of their main muscle men dead and had happened in front of almost sixty diners and nobody saw a thing. What did that mean? The police knew his man so that meant that everybody knew him. He didn't expect any amount of respect, they were not Mafiosi, but they were known as serious men. It was strange, therefore, that a level of fear had not prompted people to speak. Their man in the force had heard nothing and what he had released to them in a single, frantic, call made him wonder. And worry.

It was not so strange that men in their circumstances died violently. For Ale such a death was how he hoped to go to. What he feared was not the bullets of an enemy's gun but the prospect of a slow, prison-bound death. Life, he assured himself every day, was a once-off occurrence and he did not want to waste it in prison. When it was his time to go, he would go with a bang, either aimed at his enemies or, if the need arose, at his own head. Slow suffering was not on his agenda and he had the will, the character of a killer, to turn a weapon on himself if he feared his way of life was going to stop suddenly. He was, if nothing, the perfect image of selfishness. However, notwithstanding that, selfishness did not kill curiosity and he wondered was their a connection to the fact that Fanetti was missing too.

He was worried about the two incidents, if that is what they were, because, as Marco had gently intimated, Ale was the last to see Fanetti and, more telling, did not turn up at Cali's birthday party. As brazen a character that Ale was, he was not going to point out that the Gascos did not attend the party either and, more than anyone else, they were the two most likely to benefit from Fanetti's disappearance. Ale knew that Marco had used Fanetti to his limit and that the fun was now gone from having a cruel enforcer as a dead-weight. He laughed to himself as he thought he had it all figured out. The Gascos were clearing the ship for a new crew and he was pretty sure that there was no cabin space for Ale Becca.

That was Ale's way of thinking, his thought had the benefit of his vivid imagination, and he cared not for the conclusions his mind was offering. He would like to know what had happened to his colleagues. Not that he liked to think of them as colleagues but he was, by the criminal threads of DNA, related to them.

Italy likes to know and tell. It is a pass-time to know what is happening to who, when and where and, most often, it is those closest to the police who have the information first. Then it is spread through the coffee shops and then the bars, out into the streets and, in a mix of Chinese whispers, lands on the ears of those who are only partially interested, but interested enough to spread the tale. In this case, however, there were no whispers, no nods of agreement and no indication that what had happened in the restaurant was anything but a normal death and Ale knew that.

Ale needed to clear his head and thought a walk on the beach would help. He had stopped after a while to sit and watch the waves flow in, pushed by the strong onshore breeze. Too cold to swim for most people but one man was in the water. Ale admired those who braved the elements and watched the young man cut through the water, covering lengths of 100 meters quickly and efficiently before flipping and starting again. Ale stood and watched for half an hour before the swimmer eased his pace and slowed as he turned towards the beach to come ashore. As he neared the water's edge, the swimmer stood and began to stride through the water. The sun, reflecting off the rippling water, tiger-skinned his tanned form and then glinted off the tip of the diver's knife strapped to his leg. He walked with purpose, striding quickly and without seemingly wasting energy as he came further and further out of the water. He was fit, his chest expanding to fill his lungs, but it looked easy. His body was muscular, yet worn. The scars on the chest and stomach voiced untold tales.

Nobody saw Umberto being killed because it was done swiftly, like a magician's trick; illusion, delusion and distraction. Thugs are not magicians, nor are Mafiosi. Killers who behave like magicians are rare. They are either trained, or, on a very rare ocassion, they are born with the ability to kill, an unholy stigmata. Ale now knew who killed Umberto but he realised it, unsurprisingly, too late.

Regan had swam, knowing that Ale was on the beach, until he tired the fury in his chest. He knew that he needed, for the sake of his anger and its need to be sated, to make this killing a more personal one. The first was efficiency personified in the spin of a bullet. Yet, while there was satisfaction in the kill, there was no release of anger. The anger was only released, as in the park, when he could touch the target and feel the life and soul leave the body. Life left in blood and pulse, soul always left through the eyes. Now, he had to kill and feel the life and see the soul leave the body of this man on the beach. This man, now just Target B, watched his sister die. That was enough, he did not know if he had a hand in the physical abuse of Kathy, but that did not matter. He was going to pay. He was not going to die, he was going to be killed.

Regan walked up the beach towards his target and unclipped his knife in a simple swift motion and pulled it cleanly from the sheath and flicked the heavy blade at his target's leg.

Ale knew. He was a smart man and, though a thug, maybe because he was a thug, he could read people well. In this case, he saw the face of the young girl they had killed replicated in the face that was walking towards him. Connections came quick just as the pain pierced his leg and split itself up and down his leg instantaneously. He hoped that is was going to be quick. Hope does spring eternal.

A moment after the blade hit the target's thigh Regan had leaped forward and grabbed Ale by the mouth and back of the head. He drove his knee into Ale's solar plexus, twisted the head and pushed him into the sand. Ale did not fight back. There was a realisation that his life would end someday and the fact that he had been a bastard all his life allowed his mind to accept the reality of his current, and final, situation.

Regan turned the sandy body around until he faced Ale. He pulled the knife from the leg and rested the bloodied blade under Ale's chin, staring into eyes that were without fear. That was strange. Fear and submission cauterise anger and neither was present in Ale's eyes. This was not what Regan expected and it inhibited his flowing plan.

'Are you her brother?'

Rules of engagement futtered out the window as the possibility of learning about his sister's dying moments surrendered his anger to the will of Ale's pained words.

'Yes.'

'Ahhhhh, yes. She said you would come. That was you in the restaurant, wasn't it?' The pain in his blue eyes was highlighted by the paling skin on his cheeks. Regan glanced quickly down to the leg wound and saw the blood pulsing out of the wound and gathering in a sandy puddle beneath Ale's leg. He had hit the femoral artery. Time, tide and femoral artery waited for no man.

'Why?'

'Why what?'

'Why did you kill her?'

'She was looking into our dealings, into the dealings of the Twins. They were making moves in many directions and 9/11 allowed police focus to fall away from them. She became a threat.'

'And it was necessary to torture her? A young woman?' He felt his chest tighten as the rage began to rise.

'It was deemed necessary by the Twins, yes. '

'And you?'

'Did I think it was necessary to torture and kill her? Ha, I suppose I did. It is hard to admit it now with a knife to my throat but I figure that knife is going in at some stage so I may as well be honest. She was a danger because she was pushy. She didn't heed the warning, and we did warn her. It seemed to drive her, to push harder and then she published that story. A push too far. They operated in freedom, hidden by the shadow cast by the fall of the Towers, and she fell under their shadow.'

'Did you hurt her?'

'Others did. She was killed by Marco and Mauro but she had been,' he wanted to choose his words carefully because he was going to direct some of the man's attention to Erasmo Gentile, 'tormented by others, some you may know but one in particular you do no. His name is Erasmo Gentile.'

'The accountant?'

'Yes, our moneyman. He likes to hit women. He went to town on your sister but I stopped him.'

Regan laughed incredulously at the remark.

'I didn't touch her. I took her to the Twins but I did not touch her.'

The knife crackled gently through the cartilage of his windpipe. It wasn't necessary, the leg wound was suitable to the task, but the need to kill was seeking solace, and it found shelter in the slide of a knife.

Regan sat back on the sand and allowed his heart-rate to slow to normal, allowing a clearer thought process to function. It didn't take long. Sitting on a beach, even as deserted as this one, under the sun with a corpse was not, generally, a good idea. Sitting with a corpse who had a large diving knife, with his prints on it, sticking out of his throat, was an even worse idea.

He had followed Ale from early that morning and did not expect the whole beach scenario to develop but, when he saw Ale stop his car and go for a walk, it gave him the opportunity to improvise and, as he saw, to improvise in a secluded area. He had parked his car further down the road and had slipped, unseen, into the water with the diver's knife attached to his leg. What happened after that, as far as the attack was concerned, went as planned except, between drawing the knife and throwing it, he decided that he had questions that required answering. He threw the knife underhand to speed the shot and deepen the wound.

Now his question was answered. Now he not only knew why his sister died but he knew that the Twins were fully responsible and that knowledge, in itself, was enough to drive him to catch and kill them both. He had a clearly defined target with a valid, conscience calming rational, to carry out the next stages of his attack. And, he had another target to add to the list. The accountant.

27
How Devils Fall

His fingers stretched the final millimetre to reach the tiny outcrop that represented a grip. He was a skilled climber yet this little rock face challenged him every time. Not because it was so difficult, it really was not, but because he climbed it religiously once a month, without ropes.

His brother had died from the same face of rock twenty years ago and Franco Gaglio relived the accident once a month from that day and each time he did it without ropes. After his brother died, he visited the rock face each month and went through the same ritual each time. A small tent was raised, a small fire lit and the fine dust from the ground the only talc used on his hands. They had no talc as kids and used the dust to absorb the sweat that a vertical face always pumped from his pores.

Franco's brother was older, by ten months, and they were inseparable. Almost like twins, they took turns in deciding everything they did together until such time as they could not agree. On the rare occasion that agreement was not reached the brothers tossed a coin. The day that his brother died, it was Franco's turn to toss and call the fall of the coin. He chose heads and elected to lead the climb, his brother was to follow and both were without ropes.

Santo Giorgio's Back was a vertical sandstone rock face a little over two hundred feet high. The brothers were often seen to scamper up the face during the summer months, the sweat glistening on their backs as their chests scraped along the scared back of the holy saint. For two years now, as they grew stronger in their late teens, the boys increased the pace up the face and, being competitive, they tossed the coin to see who would lead the climb. Franco was six feet up the face before his brother's eyes left the WWII era 50 Centesimi piece, the fascist eagle glinting in the sun. He was immediately behind his brother on the rock and they were swiftly up to fifty feet when Franco felt the first stab of cramp in his thigh, but he pushed through the pain. He had to, his brother beat him on every climb and he promised himself that the defeats were going to stop on this climb. At sixty feet he was still a body length ahead of his brother and his arms felt good and his fingers strong. His right leg, however, was straining and the cramp was threatening again. At seventy five feet, with his brother now a length and a half behind and Franco reaching the part of the climb where he excelled, the cramp struck the back of his thigh again, up to his lower back and down to the back of his knee. He arched away from the rock face in agony, a moment of relief balanced on the panic of losing his grip on the right side. He slipped as the pain disappeared and he reacted, cat-like, to regain the grip. Everything slowed as his right hand reached for the grip that was three feet over his head, the grip that would maintain his lead. And then he slipped.

Climbing now he remembered the sensation of falling. It came at the same point at each climb and it was not at the point where he slipped. It was always at the point where he fell onto his brother, causing him to fall. It was also the exact same point where he, through luck, faith, hope or glory, reached out and caught an outcrop and saved himself from falling any further.

Four fingers held his weight for the seconds it took to watch his brother fall to his death. From his nails to the shoulder joint separating under the stress of the jolt and weight, his body, mind and lungs screamed. His brother fell, facing upwards, silently, blameless and without accusation.

Now he was there again, fingers holding on for life, not dear life, just life. He didn't need to climb to feel the anger that lived in his chest. It was there every day since his brother died, or, as he saw it in his own mind, since he killed him. Accident or not, he killed his own brother and every time he killed from that point onwards, he felt less and less about the value of his soul and even less about the date that fate had decided was his day to go. However, fate had not decided on his day. His actions two months ago had sealed his fate and the shadow abseiling down the cliff face towards him, speckling his face with grit and pebbles, was fate visiting.

Regan had been handed the file two days previously and had scanned it quickly to find a weak spot. It was his second read when the death of Franco's brother caught his attention and he felt that that was something that he would revisit if it had happened to him. The information in the file matched, to an extent, the intel extracted from Fanetti and Regan had cause to wink at Watson. The method had horrified his English ally but the results were efficient. That is all that mattered and Watson, begrudgingly, returned the wink with a crescent smile.

Regan's sense of how to approach this killing was a little different that the others because once you start killing, in the manner that he was utilising, the silence of the method become loud by its own accord. People, disappearing into thin air make noise by their absence and by now the Twins would have to be wondering where their men were. Fanetti was missing along with his two bodyguards. It was not enough that the money was missing too giving the Twins the seeds of doubt that their big man had betrayed them for a couple of hundred thousand, killed his bodyguards and left everything behind.

What of Ale Becca and Umberto Cali? Two loyal, if not honest, brokers of the currency of crime that the Twins traded and they would be missed. Cali was a public killing, and nothing really out of the ordinary for that ending, but Ale would be founded on the isolated beach, the blood washed clean by the waves, his flesh a tempting morsel for crabs and birds. If his body had not been dragged out to see by an enthusiastic tide, then it ought to have been found by now. Three down and now onto the one who could have intervened, could have stopped what the Twins were doing but did not. Alessandro Becca probably had had the ability to stop them as well but he did not like to interrupt the flow, another coward. Franco Gaglio, on the other hand, was the silent thought process behind all that the Twins did. The others were the physical prowess that the brothers exuded, the physical confidence to inflict pain and suffering onto others. Franco was the idea behind every action, every robbery and usually every killing. In some way, during the course of what had happened to Kathy, Franco Gaglio would have advised the Twins to continue with the course of torture and suffering. He would have estimated the costs, physically and emotionally to the men involved and would have considered the death of the young journalist in the same way an actuary would consider the costs of life benefits for a life assurance client.

He was not wrong. He had arrived three hours before the target and prepared his ropes and his knife. It was going to be a swift, bloody death.

Franco never, in all the years he had climbed the face, encountered another climber and so today was so different than the norm. Not only was the intruder to his silence on his mountain but he was also using ropes. Ropes were almost an insult to his brother's death and the intruder was abseiling down too close for comfort and, in his opinion, too quickly.

Regan paid the rope quickly through the descender and was moving rapidly. For those brief moments, he was a soldier again, abseiling down the face of rock to an unsuspecting target but he was doing this differently now. This action was not the method he would use for killing a true target. This was different, as he was not going for a direct kill; he had to add pain to this. He needed to inflict not just pain but also a sense of fear and understanding. That was the key to keeping his sanity. Once they knew why they were dying, and that he could see the understanding in their eyes before they died, then he was able to format the knowledge in his brain and put it where it caused him no harm.

Ten feet from the target, directly above him and causing concern to the climber, Regan planted both his feet squarely onto the rock-face and pushed off and to his right. It was a massive push and he swung outwards, paying the rope as he looped and descended outwardly towards the target. As the outward loop peaked, he drew his Ka-Bar knife and prepared for the in-swing.

Franco knew a professional move when he saw one; he had been on too many climbs not to know when someone was, if not talented, at least capable. The guy coming down the face now was talented. And he had a knife.

He had timed the swing perfectly and swooped in on Franco, slashing the blade across his lower back, opening his climbing top and skin in a flash of blood.

Franco arched his back but did not drop. His assailant, resembling Spiderman, perched on a higher outcrop, stared down at him through the eye-space of his balaclava. Franco did not know if he was dreaming or if his brother had come back to haunt him. It made no difference. He knew that today it would all end. Today he would die. He did not expect his swinging assailant that day, in fact he required no assailant to die that day as he had chosen the day himself. He was going to kill himself, whether Spiderman, a ghost of his brother or just damned stubborn bad luck would take him. He looked up at his Angel of Death perched above him and cheated the Angel of its desire. He let go of the finger grip that he had held to so tenuously.

Regan watched him fall, facing upwards, silent and fearless. Just as his brother had died, but he would not have known that. He wiped his knife clean on the thigh of his climbing skins and turned and scrambled up the rock-face.

It took less than a quarter of an hour to reach the top and it was a quarter of an hour that allowed his mind to attack his soul. He had not killed Franco, he had been cheated by his target's desire to die and now he stood on the top of the Saint's back and peered down to the body below. The anger, hate and frustration boiled in his stomach and he felt the bile rise in his throat. He had been cheated of justice again and it seared his soul. He spat down onto the body, surely missing, and then screamed at it. He screamed, a guttural cry into the evening sky, aimed at the setting sun, the dusty earth and everything else that had witnessed his failure that evening. And then he cried.

28

Kill only the Guilty.

The following morning he sat alone at the breakfast table, slowing running the experiences of the previous days through his mind. Every death is different, no matter how and to whom it happens. Even those killed en mass are separated in death by milliseconds, intensity and speed of death. So death is always different and the effects that it has on the survivors differ too. Guilt and shame, two polar opposites, though often thought as being of the one emotion. Not so, not ever. Guilt manifests itself after the survivor evaluates the behaviour of the self prior to the incident; shame tries to hide itself in silence. Staring into the mellow darkness of his coffee Regan could feel neither shame nor guilt. He was a soldier and, by being so, he was expected not to feel. Yet soldiers do feel and what he was feeling now was not what he had projected to feel. He expected some form of elation, a rush of justification allowing his heart to lighten and allowing his mind a chance to breathe and consider what he had done and why he had done it. And, more importantly, why he was going to continue to do it until he could feel the sweat of anger and remorse, at the loss of his sister, not the death of her attackers, evaporate from his skin.

These feelings were muddled and pouring, as they boiled, from one compartmentalized box in his mind to another. This was not how it was supposed to happen, not how he was trained to deal with killing. The connection between the training and the act of killing was so similar to the often derided formula for teaching people how to escape from a burning building; repetition, repetition, repetition until the task is an automated response – there is a fire, an alarm sounds, stand up from your desk and walk to the nearest exit. Over and over again - raise your weapon, aim at the head of the target subject, depress the trigger, twice, in swift, calm, singular motion, see the head snap as the bullets engage, aim for next target. Reach fresh air and safety.

Regan was not sure if he had air and safety now. He was emerging from the first stages of his hunt and had collected a number of kills already. However, there was a niggling concern in his head that not all of the targets supplied by

Silvio Faneti were true targets. It was possible that one or two may have been the ramblings of a confused man, and in that moment of silence, as he sat in his room preparing for the next hit, he tried to figure out whether Santo Rapposelli was, as they had termed during the conflict in Ireland, a "Legitimate Target."

What a terrible term, he thought to himself as he fingered the documents supplied by Cinderella. Who was he to call the death of someone "Legitimate" and to think that a stupid term would ease the pain of those left to bury the dead. It made sense when he was eighteen years old, it did not make sense now. When he looked back now, remembering what he had done for a cause that he did not truly understand, he feared that his soul was truly tainted. He knew in his heart that he had only killed those they had defined as "legitimate" but now, as an older killer of men, he was becoming used to the questions that would, in the silent moments post kill, bombard him silently. The effect, though silent, was often felt almost physically and indeed, on the edge of his mind, where he allowed himself to peek into the abyss of hate that scored his soul, he sometimes felt that the questions were a physical entity trying to push him over the edge.

Where was that edge and how would he fall was something that he knew, at least felt he knew. Falling into the abyss would only occur by giving into the questions, giving into their rummaging physicality. In effect, the questions of death would bully him, cause him to lash out against the genesis of the questions and then, ultimately, cause him to seek the source of his torment and kill it. In the end, he was sure, he would find that he was the source of the torment and dealing with that would have a finality that he could direct. Jack Regan was planning his own death.

29

Finding Numbers.

Erasmo Gentile was a gifted accountant. He made numbers dance to his tune and they glided seamlessly across spreadsheets and accounts, no questions asked. His secret was complex movement, like dancing, which involved a series of repeating intricate manoeuvres between balance sheets and trans-national accounts. If money moved constantly, it was never in anybody's jurisdiction long enough to cause concern. Once it moved, it rejoined the dance that only he knew the steps to. As only he knew the steps, he was invaluable and, being invaluable, he could make wonderfully extravagant demands of his paymasters. And they, invariably, danced to his tune too.

Erasmo was a very wealthy man and was not dependant on the Twins to bolster his finances. However, he was a very frustrated man, and his needs were hard for him to fulfil. Slightly built and lacking in any essence of courage or manhood, he spent his youth buried in numbers and books. His friendless youth, hampered even further by a demanding father and an ever-absent mother, caused him to drift further and further into his own world, into fantasies unsuitable for those losing sight of reality. However, he entertained them in his head, when he was alone, and they did not creep into the real world. Not until he met Marco Gasco.

To Marco Gasco, Erasmo was the perfect cleaner. He was able to move money is such convoluted ways that it was next to impossible for the authorities to find, follow or trace it. That was the beauty of what Erasmo did as a cleaner, he laundered money so quickly and smoothly that the authorities were never in a position to start looking for it, and, being honest, they didn't know that there was anything to look for.

Marco and Erasmo's relationship was based on greed, the most fluid of personal capital. Marco had spent eight months making small deposits and investments with over forty banks before he found what he was looking for. There is a type of person for every requirement in crime. The cold, calm ones can organise, kill and engage the enemy ruthlessly. They are loyal and command respect from their underlings and are respected by their seniors. The oafish ones are cannon fodder, expendable and renewable and lack impulse. Cheap and plentiful.

Then, you find the bookish ones, the ones that don't know that they can be criminal if the right buttons are pushed. They drip through their days, functioning and existing, seeing their talents ignored or underused and, therefore, they are susceptible to criminal influence. It can start gently, and with Erasmo it did, with simple compliments and gratitude. Two very simple sentiments that can have a wonderfully moulding effect on the minds of those open to change.

Marco had met Erasmo, his thirteenth investment banker, on Friday 13th of the thirteenth week of his search. Marco did not believe in such superstition, but it was an interesting combination of times and dates. For the fun of it, he invested thirteen thousand Euro with the impossibly slender banker and that was just the first step. Erasmo noticed all the figures.

"How strange, if you are into strange things, that the numbers fall in such a way."

"It is just money and dates."

"*It* is never 'just' money, Mr. Gasco. Money can be what ever you want it to be but it is never just money."

"Ahhhh, and what, Sir, can my money be."

Erasmo did not nibble the bait at first, though his senses told him that the bait was a mere morsel of what was to come. He could be patient and test the strength of the line while ensuring that there was no hook hidden in the bait.

"It can be a trust fund for your children, an endowment for your wife, an account for your girlfriend."

"Are they expensive?"

"Trust funds?" he asked tentatively.

"No, accounts for girlfriends."

"Depends on the girlfriends. Actually, it depends on the number of girlfriends and the silence between them and, shall we say, your wife." His nose had touched the bait.

"Mr. Gentile, I have many girlfriends and, it would seem, many wives. I am not sure how to keep them all separate, it is a nuisance that I so dearly want to….," he left the end of the sentence hang in the air, hoping that Gentile would nibble the tempting bait he was waving in front of his nose.

"Contain?"

"Yes."

Hooked.

Containment, in the terms expected by Marco Gasco, has a price. The price, in this instance, as in all instances of corruption, was higher than Erasmo Gentile could have imagined. By laundering his newfound friend's money, he had sold his soul to an earth-dwelling Devil and was oblivious to the fact that he had made such a transaction. It was strange, he could tangle money into such unbreakable flows and yet he could not see, at the beginning, that dealing with Gasco was going to, ultimately, get him killed. His view, of course, had been blurred by the promises of wealth and, more importantly for Erasmo, girls. Girls he could hit.

Erasmo Gentile was a hitter and he liked to hit women. That does not mean that he was able to satisfy his needs. His size, demeanour and general inability to talk to women, disallowed any contact with them and so he lived his life wishing. His real world was numbers and money, in his dreams he wanted to be bigger, stronger, handsome and talkative. Because he was none of these, he allowed his mind to lash out at his dreams and he blamed women for his social woe. In his mind, he made them pay.

Marco had picked up on this weakness in Gentile and played on it. The first time they went for a meal he noticed how his eyes danced from girl to girl, waitress to diner, but did not stay on any one girl. He was terrified of any interaction with women and Marco saw that. The more he watched, the more he figured that he now, from that very instant, had his man in his hand and would use him as he wished. Of course, he was going to pay Erasmo, but he may be more useful the more he found out about him.

Erasmo was happy with how things had progressed and he was, for once, happy with the fact that he had jumped at an opportunity instead of over-thinking it. He now felt part of something bigger and better than he was, something more tangible than the family that his boss spoke often of, the family of the bank. That was not a family; it was heartless, without warmth or tenderness and those were the sentiments, for whatever reason, Erasmo Gentile was looking for. With Marco he had found leadership, direction and a warmth of friendship that he had never encountered before and he could speak to Marco and he would listen. It was all new and exciting and he felt wanted and necessary for the first time in his life. He opened up to Marco, telling him everything about himself, and it never seemed to bore or annoy his new friend. He revealed a little more every time they met and he knew, he felt it in his chest, Marco was becoming a friend, a true friend that he could trust. He would tell him, he would tell him about his needs and desires and knew that Marco would understand. Marco would help.

Marco did. He had known that there was something dark about the little man and was awaiting its release from the binds of his shyness. When Erasmo finally told him, secretively, that he wanted to hit women, wanted to hurt them, he clasped his large hand on the bony shoulder of the small man, and confessed that he too felt such urges. Men of power, he told Erasmo, were prone to such desires, desires that were of a higher sentiment that regular men, men with feeble minds and futile lives, could not feel. Why, oh why, he asked Erasmo, had he kept such a secret from his friend knowing that Marco had access to women, women who would do as they are told. Erasmo was ecstatic and could barely contain himself. Not only did his new friend understand, he also felt the same. Years of self doubt and loathing evaporated in a haze of joy and the thrill of expectation fluttered in his chest. He was going to be released.

In the weeks and months that followed, Erasmo changed. In fact, it may be said that he grew, flourished and became that which he was not before, inhuman. He had known that he was selfish, to say the least, but he also knew that he had something inside him that needed to shine and he did not get that from figures. Now, however, he was slipping out of his cocoon and spreading his colourful wings. He now attended meeting with the Twins, not sitting at the main table during the meetings, but on a chair by the door, taking notes related to the monies being generated by those sitting at the table. To others, it may have seemed a lowly position, but to Erasmo it was within the walls of the inner-circle and he was part of the powerful connectivity that was palpable in the room.

The matters discussed at the table were, for the most part, double-Dutch to Erasmo but at each meeting he was asked is opinion on one or two financial matters and he gave them happily. Those at the table were happy too, the figures being discussed, rising from the activities of Marco's little lap dog, were impressive. The organisation had not pushed its expansion during the last year, as Marco did not want to attract too much attention. However, Erasmo's magic with the same amount of money that had been generated the year before had resulted in nearly twenty percent growth in their vastly diverse portfolios. All at the table, regardless of what they thought of Erasmo as a man, were impressed with Erasmo the financial wizard. Money and power were the Twin's goals and Erasmo was adding to the first and unwittingly adding to the second.

After the third such meeting, Marco took Erasmo to dinner, a thank you of sorts for the work that was being done. Dinner was followed by a trip to one of the houses that Marco owned, a house guarded by tall walls and equally imposing security men. It was where high-end call girls were supplied to those who had money and didn't want questions asked. It was illicit protection for illicit activity. It was where Marco was going to cement the secrecy of their financial dealings by providing Erasmo with the living form of his fantasies.

Elena Lendova was three years in the game when she met Erasmo Gentile. She had been warned what to expect and had been promised a grandiose bonus for playing with Marco's friend. Marco had taken her aside and asked that she take his friend to one of the outhouses on the property and entertain him. He warned her what to expect and not to let him go too far with the physicality that Erasmo yearned. The outhouse would provide privacy from the other clients and not disturb the other girls. It also allowed for the cameras in the out-house to be pre-set, rolling already when Elena entered with Erasmo.

Erasmo was out of his mind with excitement, his agitation, blinking eyes and tinges of spittle on the edges of his mouth began to disturb Marco. His accountant had changed physically over the months, through gym-work with Ale, into a being slightly more masculine than what he had been before. Slightly more masculine made him twice as big as Elena and Marco realised that the plan needed to change. The frantic movements of Erasmo were telltale, once he was let loose on the girl, he was not going to stop. So be it. Such was the cost of doing business with moneymen. Elena could be replaced. Whores were not rainforests, nobody cared and the supply was endless.

Bound, drugged and coming in and out of futile consciousness, Kathy felt helpless to the pressures she felt on her face and body. The pressure was not of the ropes that held her to the steel beam in the room but something different instead; the pressure represented the beating that Erasmo Gentile was giving her. He was pounding into her with all his might, releasing years of frustration and angst onto the helpless figure before him. He was enjoying every wonderful moment of it, even if she was drugged. She did seem to register some of the blows, especially those to her stomach, and that gave him such delight that he stopped for a moment to kiss her cheek, a gesture more frightening than the punches he was throwing. The sense of injustice crept from every pore in Erasmo's body, piggybacking on the sweat generated from his exertion. It was a weight that had been cast onto his shoulders, from where he did not know, and now his hatred of women was being calmed by the storms of fury that swept from the deep recesses of his soul onto the beaches of humanity that was the skin and flesh of Kathy Regan.

Of course, this was not his first release. Elena had survived for three hours during which time he had destroyed her physically, mentally and emotionally. She had been sacrificed, in Erasmo's mind, to the God of finance, the God that had been created by his own God, the all-giving Marco Gasco. Every hit, slap, kick and punch delivered to Elena was the slow, precisely calculated release of the anger that had been vaulted away for years. Still without explanation, the anger sown in his soul was now making itself known and, at the same time, destroying Erasmo. The damage he was inflicting on Elena was being replicated in his own conscience and the piper would need paying. He always needed paying.

Just as his fury was peaking, at the point where he would begin biting, the door opened and Ale, on his phone, strolled into the room, somewhat oblivious to what was happening to Kathy. When Erasmo screamed at him to leave, to let him finish his work, Ale looked at him poisonously. Erasmo screamed at him again and that was enough for Ale. He disliked the little shit and would have happily beaten him to death except that Marco had told him to protect Erasmo from himself and others. That level of protection did not extent to screamed abuse and, more troublingly, the abuse Erasmo was doling out to the girl tied to the pillar. Ale was not an evil man, he was not the nicest man in the world, not even in his own village, but he did not extend his badness to the level of assaulting women. Such actions were not the actions of men. He was lawless, not evil. Erasmo, on the other hand, was now evil and what he was doing to the young woman was wrong, as it had been wrong what he had done it to Elena. It was going to stop tonight and he was going to be the one to stop it.

Erasmo screamed at him one last time before he realised that the scream came from pain and not from an order barked at Ale. His neck was constricting, his head jerking; Ale was crushing his neck with one hand and pummelling his head with the other. The brutality of the assault was not intended to kill Erasmo but to teach him a lesson that had been lost on the man, that lesson being that he was not a power-broker in the organisation. He was just a moneyman. Then Marco walked in and that was enough to stop the beating.

30
Kill, capture, dream.

Streets are a soldier's friend and his worst enemy. Like fingerprints, no two streets are ever the same, they change in light and darkness, when it is wet or dry. Shadows cast by tall and short buildings alike give cover and solace to the soldier seeking refuge and hid the weapons and intentions of those who hunt. It all mixes in a mathematical and emotional equation to which no soldier had the definitive answer. Some thrive in street fighting, like the Marines, and some hate it, like those on the receiving end of a Marine's fighting capability. However, when it comes to a one-on-one battle streets allow for a levelling of talent and the quickest and most street smart will get to the other end of the street, no matter what he meets.

Erasmo had finished his meal and leaned back contentedly in the plush leather chair of the busy restaurant where he had just had dinner. He could do that now, eat out by himself without feeling odd, without the sense of being alone. His confidence, socially and physically, had never been so high and he had Marco and his steady stream of women, receptive to his needs, to thank for that. His once greasy hair, and equally greasy complexion were now merely vagrant wisps of unhappiness on a breeze of personal joy. He looked better than he had ever had and even the waitress had not found him repulsive. She actually had warmth in her smile and had touched his arm, in a light brushed stroke, when thanking him for the generous tip that he had left. Oh, how things were changing for Erasmo Gentile. He drained the last drop from his hand-warmed brandy glass, raised himself from the comfort of the chair, flicked a small number of errant crumbs from his perfectly ironed shirt and walked towards the door collecting his tweed coat on the way.

The walk to his apartment was never anything but a chore for Erasmo, but that was in the past. Now, sauntering up the street, stepping over each crack in the pavement to avoid the bad luck of his past, he drew gently on his cigarette and blew the smoke confidently skywards. He watched in admiration each swirl as it floated, twirling and meandering on the evening warmth towards the street-lamp above him. Gliding around the lamp, somewhat shaded by tree branches, fire-flies danced in twinkling unison around the central source of light and, higher still, and deep into the night sky, the stars shone in their own special way. Yes, he could now say it; his life was good. His past, fading further into the darkness, was no longer a threat to his happiness.

'May I trouble you for a light?' The voice was soft, unobtrusive and without malice and Erasmo turned his skyward gaze back to earth to answer the man who sought a light.

'Why, yes, of course, one moment, please.' He reached into his jacket pocket and pulled out the engraved gold lighter that Marco had given him as a present and, deciding not to hand it over to the fellow, flicked it to life in one confident sweep of his fingers. Sure that the flame had indeed ignited, he reached out to meet the cigarette that was leaning towards the light.

The young man before him seemed to be crouching, bent over with some form of spinal malady and reached up to take Erasmo's hand in his own, it seemed, to steady the flame.

Once lit, the young man drew deeply on the cigarette, contentedly. Yet, he did not let go of the Erasmo's hand.

'I quit ten years ago.'

'Oh, and what has you back on them?'

'I needed an excuse, of all things.'

'To smoke?' the alarm bells had not gone off but a feeling of discomfort was creeping up his spine and to the still-gripped hand that held the lighter, and the hand began to shake.

'To meet you, to hold this hand.' The voice was emotionless and, now that the lighter had been extinguished by a gentle puff of air from the young man, Erasmo could see his face. Not just his face, however, he could now see that the man had raised himself to full size, and he had no back malady. The man before him was fit, strong and now, worryingly, in total control of the situation. Erasmo was convinced that he was going to be mugged.

'I am a friend of Marco Gasco,' he blurted out. Fear pushed him to call on names to instil fear in the man who, he believed, was about to attack him.

'I know you are,' the hand began to clench around the upper wrist and consumed Erasmo's thumb in a crushing grip. 'I know him too, and I am going to meet him soon. Just cutting through the low grass first.' More pressure was applied to the grinding bones and Erasmo began to whimper. It never dawned on him to scream for help. It would not have made a difference and now the man walked him towards an alley just a few meters from the lamp where the fireflies continued their dance.

Two days later a young couple, on their second date, slipped out of the same restaurant and, hand in hand, walked down the same street. The evening was a little hotter and the air was thick with humidity and, again, fireflies. To the young girl holding her new boyfriend's arm, the evening was going wonderfully. The first date had been, even by her standards, slow. She was not sure how interested he was but that evening things were different. He was much more engaging and he had filled her evening with witty conversation mixed with intelligent comment, just as she liked and just as she had hoped. Now, with bellies full and wine in their blood, she was going to steal a kiss. She knew, from the second she had asked him out, that she was going to be the one who made the first moves.

Now, walking past the lampshade where Erasmo Gentile had been stopped for a light, she grabbed her new beau's arm and pulled him into the alleyway. He needed to be coaxed and he was unsure of what was happening, yet happy to play along. She skipped backwards down the alley, only a few meters, holding his hand and pulling him after her. The heel of her left shoe caught in something and she staggered momentarily before his hand caught her and, before she knew what to do, he had her drawn to his body and was kissing her. He stepped back to steady her eagerness and tripped over something, catching both feet, and fell backwards, still holding her in his arms.

They landed with a soft thud and, between the wine and the first-kiss nerves, they both broke into laughter. There was no shame, both were relieved to have landed on something that broke their fall and he, though laughter, expressed the hope that they did not fall on someone sleeping. He was not far wrong and her scream identified the error in his thoughts.

"So, Doc? What did it?"

The examiner had had a busy week and was pushed to the edge of her patience with the jolly comments coming from the detective questioning her about the death of Erasmo Gentile. There had been a bus crash earlier in the week and she had to complete a file for six young people whose remains were going to be shipped back to the Czech Republic in two days time. Then the police had pushed for a rapid response to the death of the banker found down by the nicer area of town. Maybe the request would not have been so urgent if the daughter of the Mayor had not fallen on the remains of the banker, but that was the way some things were done.

"The file is being sent to your Chief and to the office of the public prosecutor. Your friend was killed. Not, as you had so wholeheartedly suggested, fallen while drunk."

"On that street it is strange for someone to be mugged. I actually cannot remember when someone was last mugged in that part of town. God, nothing is sacred."

"Mugged? Did I say 'mugged' at any stage in this unwanted conversation?"

"Excuse me. I just thought that a mugging was a reasonable explanation as to what happened."

"If you want 'reasonable explanations' then you sent our friend to the wrong address. If you want facts look at this," she glared at him as she pulled back the green medical sheet covering the remains of Erasmo Gentile.

The young detective was taken aback momentarily but, much to the ME's surprise, regained his composure quickly and leaned in for a look.

"What am I looking for?"

"Look at the wrists, to start."

The detective saw that each wrist was mottled blue/black, an unnatural wristband created by what he supposed, were bindings of some sort. *A murder*, he thought to himself. On that street?

"He was bound before he was killed?" he questioned, more for confirmation.

"The victim was hit twenty-seven times to the chest and stomach. The post-mortem examination showed numerous bruises over the whole body, a haemoperitoneum, a fissuration of the spleen and a massive peripancreatic haemorrhage associated with a complete dilaceration of the pancreas head. Histological examination of the pancreas revealed a massive necrosis associated with a subtotal disappearance of the acini, numerous sites of cytosteatonecrosis and a large haemorrhagic suffusion of the peripancreatic tissue. "

"What? In layman's terms, Doc!"

"Somebody, someone really, really unhappy with our friend, systematically punched him to death. Each side of the body received a certain level of, shall I say focus, and this is evident by the bruising of both wrists. He held the arms up and punched the victim to death. Each punch measured and targeted."

"He?"

"You are looking for a male, about six two/three, two-seventy pounds. This man who did this is fit, strong, intelligent and patient."

"You can tell that by bruised wrists?" the detective asked incredulously.

"The shoulder muscles are stretched and torn. This tells me the victim was held vertically while this was happening. The size of the bruising on each wrist is the same, so are the impacts. It was one man who did this. I am sure of it."

"Oh, God. A murder and in that part of town."

"Murder is not a term I would use here, but that is off the record."

"What on earth do you mean, he was systematically beaten to death. The intention to kill was there in buckets."

"I know, yes he was murdered in the legal sense. However, look at the evidence. You said he was systematically beaten so, yes, the *mens rea* is there, but look deeper than that. This is beyond a murder. This is killing for a reason. This is anger, personified in a beating, against someone who did something to someone else. I know, I am not making sense here, but the more I look at it, the more I feel we are missing something. If you want to kill someone, and I mean kill them, you shoot or stab. But, and maybe I am reaching here, if you really want to kill them, kill them in a way that they know they are being killed for a reason, admitted or otherwise, you corner them in a quiet alley and you slowly, carefully, and with precision, punch them to death. The victim knew, as he was dying, that he was paying the price for something."

"So, we are dealing with a psycho. Fantastic. All I need is another nutter added to the wave of freaks walking the streets at the moment."

"Why do you say 'psycho'?"

"Jesus, Doc, what else would carry out a beating in that manner?"

"Not a 'psycho' as you so eloquently put it. The man who did this is, like I said, fit, strong and patient. Not, you will agree, the general make-up of what you are calling a 'psycho.' The guy who did this, well, he did it for a reason that only he knows about. He did it because he felt it was the right thing to do and he planned it so that Gentile, the victim, would know that. He wanted him to die slowly and in pain and that, I am afraid, is what happened."

"And now he is out there waiting for his next victim?"

"I would think so. However, I would look into the dealings of our victim here and see what his past holds. I cannot be sure, I am not a psychologist, but the man who is out there, waiting for his next victim, is on a mission. Like a soldier, he targeted this victim and there may be others. "

"Are you saying that we have a serial killer out there?"

"Oh, God no! Not in the least. What you have out there is much more dangerous. You have a young, angry man, who is confident enough in his abilities to kill a man feet from public view and to walk away unnoticed. He was able to find, follow and target his victim without being seen and he killed him in a way that showed that, far from being psychotic, he is capable and considered in his actions. A psychotic attack would have left some form of mutilation. You have a body that was simply beaten. You, Detective, have to catch a man who knows how to hide, how to be visible and invisible and who can kill at will. You are chasing a ghost."

"A ghost?"

"Maybe not a ghost, but definitely a man who is trained to kill, to hide and to disappear. Special forces, I'd say, a Special Forces soldier who is pissed-off with somebody in this country and is looking to hit back. If I were you, I would check the files and see who else has died in recent weeks. Of course, only check those who died with, how do they say it, ah yes," her thoughts and fears met with words, "with extreme prejudice."

It would have surprised the Medical Examiner that at the very moment that she was explaining to the young detective that he ought to be looking for an angry killer, the self same man, the killer, was in the centre of town shopping. In fact, he was discussing the qualities of silk versus cotton underware, the woman's variety, with a charming young lady who was so pleased to have such a discerning customer.

"Gentlemen are always so nervous when they come into this store," she smiled at Regan.

"Well, they should be. Being greeted by an angel such as you should fluster any man." The response was accompanied by a boyish grin and twinkling eyes and the girl could feel her pulse quickening. Instead of the man being flustered, her body language let Regan know that he had her in the palm of his hand and it did, in tribute to the natural beauty of the young girl, take an effort to keep his eyes from wandering from her eyes downwards.

"Are you looking for a present for your wife?" she asked coyly.

"No, I was looking for a present for you."

The young girl beamed a blushing smile at Regan and continued to fuss. Was he holding the underware she would soon be wearing? Her mind raced, forgetting herself in that moment of playful flirtation. "You are terrible! What is it you really want?" she asked hoping that it was her he wanted. His impact on her had been immediate.

"Well, if you would like to come for dinner tonight, and say yes immediately, then I can speak to your boss with regard an order I want to make for my company back home in London."

"Yes, yes. I mean, of course. You can speak to the boss."

"And dinner?"

She fingered the strand of hair floating over her left eye and could barely muster a "Yes, of course" before turning to run to get her boss, Santo Rapposelli.

Santo Rapposelli, the man who Silvio Fanetti fingered as having had the most "fun" with Kathy refused to go out to meet the buyer in his shop. Instead, he grabbed the young assistant by the neck and pushed her against the wall and began to squeeze her neck, cutting the air off. It was not the first time.

"Do I look like some kind of fucking goffer, you stupid bitch? If he wants to buy something from me he can bloody well come in here and ask me for it. I rise for no man."

Ariana, the pretty young assistant was, once again, in fear for her life. She knew that one day Santo would go as far as he wished and there would be nothing that she could do about it. He had her by the neck but, because of the debt her father owed to Rapposelli, by the balls too.

She tried to squeeze an apology through the tightening windpipe but he was not listening and threw her at the door.

"Go now, and hurry. My patience is running low with you and your fucking family."

Every ounce of courage was called upon to stop shaking as Ariana walked back into the shop front. She struggled to fight back the tears and knew that the buyer would not, should not, care about her problems but she wished he did. Wishes such as those, she had already learned, did not come through for her and her family. Poverty's chains weighed heavily on her glimpses of happiness and she knew that it was best to decline the invite for dinner that evening.

Regan was still standing in the shop examining the cotton underware when Ariana came back. Standing two feet from the shop till, he was able to see the last sales slip she had made and with it her name, Ariana. Her name matched her beauty.

His plan was simple, he was going to invite Santo into the back of the shop to discuss terms and then, having drugged him, he would be taken through the back door and into the waiting van. Five minutes would suffice to cover the back-room scenario. However, he had now noticed that there were at least three surveillance cameras in the store and he would have to deal with them. Maybe he would have a lucky break.

Ariana walked back into the shopfront and called gently to Regan. "Mr. Santo cannot come out now, Sir, but is happy to have you pop in for a moment."

Regan walked towards her and, even though she had her head turned away to avoid eye contact, he picked-up immediately that something was wrong.

"Ariana?" The voice was soft and full of empathy, no longer the flirtatious charm of minutes ago.

"Please, just go into him, Sir." Her voice was breaking and that was enough for the mask of civility to slip from Regan's demeanour.

He reached out and gently took her arm, her warm skin soft in his dry, course hand. "Hey, Ariana, look at me."

She looked up at him, eyes brimming with tears and her neck red with fingerprints.

"He did this, didn't he? I figure he does this a lot."

"Yes, but it is not your problem, Sir." She tried to tough it out but it was not working. His had moved from her shoulder up to her cheek and he tried to thumb away the single tear that had escaped. It felt hot as it touched his skin. He cradled her face in his hands and spoke gently but quickly to her.

"Ariana, this has to stop and it is going to stop. Do you know where the surveillance cameras' tape recordings are stored?"

Uncertain as to what was happening, yet fully back under Regan's spell, Ariana nodded, the tears now streaming down her face.

"When you hear the door shut in the office, please go to the room where they are stored, remove today's disk and destroy it. Then, and listen carefully to this, you must come back down and work away as though nothing has changed. When it comes to the time to close the shop, do so. Then head home. Continue for three days and when you think that the time is right, after calling his cell a few times and leaving messages, call his wife, or family or the police. You will have to sound worried and concerned. Make sure you sound distressed, but be clear in what is wrong. That will be that you are concerned as to where your boss is. You did not see him since today when he left for a bite to eat. Is that clear."

"What is happening? What are you going to do to him?"

"What he did to you today, what he has done to you in the past, he did to my sister. I cannot forgive that. "

"Is she ok? Your sister, is she ok?"

"No."

Ariana looked up at Regan and saw the pain living in his eyes. She understood, she thought, what he was going through but she had no idea that his mind was already functioning on a different plane. The mechanics of torture, running smoothly in his head, were not for display in his eyes or face. Ariana did not know what to say.

"This is the end for him, Ariana. He is not going to hurt you or any other girl again."

"I have no problem with that. You were never here."

Regan walked quietly to the office, each step taken with cat-like silence and care and, before he reached the office, he could hear Santo on the phone. Once again, he was threatening some poor soul at the end of the line. From where Regan stood in the hall he could see Raposelli's reflection in the glass of the picture on the wall. His back was turned while on the phone and that suited Regan.

Raposelli was still loudly berating the victim at the end of the line when Regan floated in, noiselessly and dangerous.

"I don't give a rat's ass whose fault it is, do you hear me? I want names, numbers and cash and I want them last week. You hear me?"

The pause, as brief as it was in the tornado of words, was shattered by the unmistakable click of a weapon being cocked. An excellent ear, trained in weapons, would have known it to represent the cocking of a Sig-Sauer SAS Gen2 as the muzzle eased gently into the nape of Santo's neck. Santo did not have such an ear but heard the unmistakable sound nonetheless.

The pause in the flow of words became almost permanent as Santo, not a stupid man, figured out that he had milliseconds to make his peace with God or, hopefully, someone was just going to take him away. Not the best of options either way but he did prefer to live. Without moving a muscle he spoke gently into the phone.

"I will call you back." Not another word was uttered.

"Stay very still, Santo Raposelli. I am taking you in for questioning and you are going to come in quietly. That is why the gun is pointed at your head because you are going to come with me to the station or my colleagues will come in and take pictures of the remains of your head as they peel it off the walls. Me, I really don't give a shit but there are questions we need to ask you and then, well then we may let you go. What do you think?

"I think…" Regan clubbed him squarely on the back of the head and the Raposelli crumpled to the ground. Regan decided that Santo did not have to look his best for the "interview" so he walked the face of the unconscience man into the tiled floor without too much care. *Soon, soon, soon. Breath, breath, breath. His clock is ticking so you can deal with his shit for now. It won't be long before I can release you.* His mind commanded him gently and he responded, as ever, efficiently.

Piero Bassi saw the side door open and then Regan's head peep out. He started the engine and rolled silently into place just outside the door. The back street was empty for that time of the evening but it would have made no difference either way. The package was going into the back of the van one way or the other and now, for the moment, it looked like Regan had decided on the "other."

"Want a hand?" he whispered out the window to Regan.

"No, he is as light as a feather. What the fuck do you think?"

Piero jumped out of the van still smiling, he seemed to relish Regan's temperment and took pleasure in poking the bear whenever possible. He slid the side door open, took the legs of Raposelli and together with Regan they swung the unconscience body into the back of the van.

"Do we still have Fanetti's bag of cash?"

"Under this guy's ass," came the reply with a nod of the head in the direction of Raposelli.

"Great. Izzo is too honest to take it so I am going to do something good with it. Wait here a moment."

Regan kicked Raposelli over and pulled out the hold-all that was stuffed with cash and walked back to the open door. He turned and winked at Piero.

Ariana was true to her promise and was clearing the hard drive of the security recorder when Regan stepped into the room. She was startled when she saw him but regained her composure quickly.

"I have cleared the last four days using his access code. If anyone needs to check, it will seem like he did it."

"You have got some guts, Ariana. Guts and brains." He smiled at her for a second before handing her the bag. "Guts and brains will help you figure out how best to spend this money. It comes from one of Raposelli's friends so it has no owner now." He did not need to explain why. "I think you can take it for granted that your Dad's debt has been paid off too."

Ariana took the bag and looked into it. She stifled the gasp of surprise when she saw how much was there. "I can't accept this. I really can't."

"I am going to dump it in the river if you don't take it so either you take it and use it well or the fish will be the best dressed fish in Italy,' he smiled.

Ariana looked into the bag and all she could see were dreams. She closed the bag, took Regan by the hand and kissed him on the cheek. "Thank you. Thank you so much."

Regan turned and walked out of the room, down the stairs and outside to where Piero was waiting. His steps, for the first time in a while, felt lighter. He had done something good. The good deed did not fade in the light of horror that was to follow.

31

Nail lifting.

Santo sat upright, both hands cuffed to the padded arms of the chair. In front of him, within reach if he so wished, was a tall glass of water with a red, bendy straw hanging over the lip of the glass. Beside the glass were three sections of orange and some olives. Not the kind of treatment he was expecting.

There was a knock on the door before it opened and the tall frame of the man coming into the room blocked the light outside in the hall for an instant. The mad, dressed in black Nomex, nodded at him and turned to close the door. It was neither an aggressive nor friendly look, just a simple acknowledgement of Santo's presence.

The tall man walked over to the table, placed his writing pad down before taking a seat in front of Santo. He rummaged for a pen in two pockets before finding one in the third, grinned meekly at Santo and then his face straightened and he began to speak. His voice, without malice or feeling, was of an even timbre, deep and clear.

"Are you hurt?"

Santo, expecting a barrage of questions, was taken a little off guard. He had prepared himself for a bit of rough questioning, as it was not the first time he was in front of the police.

"No, no. I am not hurt. Thank you." Empathy, so easy to exude and so quickly absorbed; the man in front of him nodded and took note before raising his head and asking the next question.

"I hope you don't mind if I raise, for a moment, your past so that I can offer my second question. Please, at any stage, if you do not feel like answering or if you feel the need to request the presence of your lawyer, tell me. That is why I am here."

Again, Santo was surprised at the path of the questions and he nodded his agreement to the request.

"You have been charged in the past with membership of various organisations. It is not my job to figure out the legalities of your past. To me only the recent past and present are important. Digging too far back is a nuisance that neither you nor I need. Don't you agree?"

"To which? The past or the membership of illegal organisations?" Santo felt that he had allowed himself to mellow too much and gravelled his tone.

The man exhaled and smiled. Even if he was annoyed by the response, he did not show it but, instead, he continued.

"You are right, sorry. To both, please."

"Yes, I have been a member of various organisations but I have never been convicted of such membership."

"Well, Santo, that is not going to change. Your memberships mean nothing to me. I just don't want to be sitting in this room with Joe Civilian."

It was as though he had pushed a button linked to the internal pride of the man and Santo smiled and answered frankly.

"I am no civilian."

"Good, good, good. We do not have much more to get through."

"What are we actually doing and why am I here?"

"All in good time." The answer was, for the first time, cold. "So you are a member of the organisation controlled by the Gasco Twins. That is my main question. You are not someone who just tags around with them and the other members. I need to clarify that. I am not accusing you of doing anything wrong, it is just that I need to establish the facts before I continue with a certain line of questioning.

"Yes, I am a member of their organisation and now I think it is time that I take you up on your offer to contact my lawyer."

"Go ahead."

Santo felt the air change in an instant in the room and thought that a window had been left open. Looking around, the bare dank walls, it dawned on him that the room was windowless.

"Can you bring me a phone?"

"No."

"You promised."

"No, I said you could request. That is it. You requested, and I said no."

"I am not sure what you are playing at."

"Of course you don't. I am a soldier, Santo, not a policeman. I have my methods of gaining information, methods that oblige me to adhere to rules made many years ago in Geneva. Your organisation, the one you have freely admitted to being a member of, is at war with mine. To be honest, more so at war with me that with the organisation I work for, but that is neither here nor there. That is why I checked with you first, to make sure that you were in good health before I decided to get to the real questioning.

Santo looked more closely at the man sitting in front of him, trying to see the danger that the hollow pain in his lower stomach told him was present. Again, he looked around at the blank, windowless wall. It was an interrogation room, no doubt about that, but not one that he expected. Maybe it was his dependence on Hollywood to fill in the large blanks in his knowledge of police activity but he saw no two-way mirror. He had expected to see one. He wanted to look tough to the people who would be watching from behind the smoked glass.

"What is your name?" He decided he would try to ease the situation, try to turn it at least back to a level playing field.

The man's demeanour changed, least he, Santo, thought it did, and he eased back into his chair and removed a pack of cigarettes from a side pocket on his right leg. He carefully opened the flip-top box and eased a cigarette out, placing it loosely between his lips. His right hand fingered a lighter from his breast pocket before twirling it baton-like between the same fingers. Yet, for all the fancy finger work captivating Santo at that moment, the man still needed two hands to open the lighter and to strike it to life.

"I figured you would have a trick for lighting it," Santo offered as a way of trying to instigate a conversation that he could direct.

"It is not my lighter, so I am not so handy with it. Actually, not my cigarettes either but that is a different story; I quit years ago when I joined the army." He was staring into the flame, watching is dance, a hot ballerina on a brass stage tempting him into her heart. He eased the cigarette towards the dancer and drew carefully from the flame.

Santo looked on enviously, wanting a cigarette but not wishing to show the weakness of having to ask for one. The first fine threads of the scented smoke wafted under his nostrils and reminded him of someone, somewhere. Now, in addition to the windowless walls, the scent of the burning tobacco began to tickle the senses of warning in his nose and up into the back of his head.

The man leaned back to exhale the smoke in a steady stream of blue-grey towards the ceiling. As he exhaled he twisted and twirled the cigarette through his fingers tracing an eerie glow of orange through the settling whispers of smoke. Again, within the smoky whispers, warnings were hanging from the curling smoke.

"Would you like one, Santo?" The voice was quiet, flowing gently from a mouth happy with smoke.

"Would you mind?"

The man raised himself from his chair, picked up the cigarettes from the table and smiled, "Not at all. I will even light it for you."

The man walked around the table while removing another cigarette from the pack and turned it in his fingers until the butt was aiming outwards. He reached Santo's chair and, standing mountain-like over his captive, slid the cigarette between the offered lips.

Santo, in feigned bravado, cocked his head, peaked an eyebrow and, Dean-like, said in an equally bad American accent, "Thanks, Buddy."

"My name is Jack Regan. Let me light that for you," he pulled the brass Zippo from his pocket again and lit it in one fluid motion of his nimble fingers. Again, the ballerina of flame danced on the brass stage and her mirror image flickered in the eyes of the man staring into Santo's eyes.

It didn't make sense to Santo, the name meant something to him but he could not get his brain to gear up to speed. An event was occurring before his eyes and he just was not up to speed.

Regan, cigarette still hanging from his lips, continued to stare through the flame into the eyes of the one of the men involved in the death of his sister. He didn't need to know the details anymore; the accountant had identified enough men whose bodies contained enough blood to slake his thirst for revenge. This one, Santo, was there, present when she died, had to have heard her agonised screams, and had done nothing about them. He would here those screams again, but this time not from the mouth of Regan's sister.

Santo's brain clicked into gear a moment before his eyes saw enough to warn him. Regan, in an instant, blew out the flame just as his left hand shot down and clasped Santo's right wrist to the arm of the chair, securing it against his sudden urge to try to draw it back. As Regan's left grip tightened on Santo's wrist his right hand, now gripping the Zippo as a tool, drove the hot tip of the lighter under the nail of the middle finger where it lodged, for an instant, before driving between the flesh and the nail, separating the nail and folding it back.

Santo was up to speed. This was the guy that girl said would come and now he was here, feigning concern until he decided that removing nails with the hot tip of a Zippo lighter was fun. But it was not for fun, it was necessary to remove the nail to speed the meeting of the torn and bleeding flesh and the red-hot tip of the cigarette.

Regan flipped the lighter onto the table and, before removing the cigarette from his lips, drew on it a number of times in quick succession to super-heat the tip. He then drove into into the soft flesh that moments earlier had been laid bare by the work of the Zippo nail tool.

Santo's scream started deep within his chest, gushing out as explosive air, noiseless before the torrent of sound splitting screeching.

There was nothing to learn from Santo. He was a release of anger, the venting of one level of fury before moving to the next.

An hour later, and the screams now muted and muffled by swollen lips and broken spirit, Regan decided that Santo had had enough. He had put the man through unimaginable horror so much so that Santo's mind had probably snapped. Regan had taken a bag of cent coins, forty in total and with the aid of small pliers, a hand-held blow torch and an imagination unhindered by fear or remorse he engaged in what they called in the Legion, Rhinoing; heating the cent coins to red-hot then inserting them under the skin where they left horrific burns and blisters. Of course, the pain was unimaginable, the smell the same, and the result was skin that resembled that of a rhino. Regan, of course, explained all of this to Santo as he was doing it, even pausing to remember if it was a rhino or an armadillo. He decided, with a little chuckle that served only to chill the heart, not his skin, of the man who was being tortured, that it really depended on who was being tortured and where. Rhino would do for Italy, as they had no armadillos.

The last two cents were inserted under the skin of each cheek, just below the eye-sockets. Every last ounce of fight came out of Santo in those few, horrible, skin-burning seconds, and he lost control internally and externally. The smell in the room was indescribable, not just of burning flesh and bodily waste, but also mixed into the stench was fear, loathing and, just hanging on the outside of the cloud of physical despair, a silver lining of victory. Nike was not a welcome guest to this party but she was there nonetheless in Regan's mind.

He stood back and looked at his work, a Picasso of hatred, and wiped the sweat and blood from his hands as though wiping paint. He was shaking a little but was too engrossed in what he had done to care about shaking. It was not the adrenaline in his blood, and there was a lot of that, but the creaking of his own mind as he edged closer and closer to the abyss with each act of vengeance.

As a younger man, when he first began to realise that he could control the demons within, he would guide his mind through what he termed the fields of black corn and down to the stream where he would meet his sister and their friends. That image, her smiling face and the shouts of joy from their friends washed his soul and cleansed his spirit so that when he retreated from the image, the corn was once again golden yellow and caressed by a gentle, warm breeze.

Visiting that place now, to seek solace, only showed his sister's face and, on turning to mentally rush from her, from the pain caused, he would turn back into a field pillaged and burnt, an angrier man than the man who had approached through the black corn. And with this anger now, he faced the remains of Santo.

Santo was moaning incoherently to himself while Regan looked on, finalising the man's end in his head. He pulled a small anti-personal charge from his bag and set the timer on it without letting Santo see what was being done. With his swollen cheeks pushing his eyes closed, it probably didn't matter.

Holding the charge of plastique under Santo's nose he asked the man to take a smell of the device. Somehow Santo heard and understood what was being asked of him and he tried to sniff the explosives under his nose. Whether they were scentless or his nose was damaged, he could not smell anything and he tried to mumble that to Regan. He was not being listened to, however.

"Strangely, what you cannot smell is the additive added to the explosives so that the sniffer dogs can find them. Not really useful information to you now because there will be no such dogs sniffing around here. I just thought I would let you know. I bet the uncertainty is a torment, isn't it?" Regan began to attach the device collar-like, just below Santo's chin and the knowledge of what it was seemed finally to have entered his conscience and he began to shake and writhe against his binds.

"You were there, in the room with her. You did nothing to stop them from killing her and you had your own fun at her expense. She did not know what was happening except that you pricks were assaulting her body and her mind. Well, Santo, I have given you a taste of what she endured and now I will give you the final serving. I have attached a small explosive device to your neck, the main charge hanging under your chin. It is a nasty bit of work in the wrong hands because I am using it for the purpose it was not intended for. When it blows, and it will blow, the area around the blast will be damaged, but not to the extent that you might think, or might want. It will not kill you instantly, but you will die. And, it might go off today, tomorrow or some other day. You see, I am giving you the same end, one with so much more uncertainty that you may go mad waiting for the device to do its job. Ingenious?"

Santo was unable to reply. His mind had pulled focus to the undetermined timescale that Regan had given it and the clock began to tick. Was it going to be soon, later that evening or tomorrow. Could he wait til tomorrow, suffering the physical pain of the inserted coins combined with the emotional torment of when the charge would detonate on his neck. He tried to muster the last ounces of defiance to face his tormenter, knowing too well that his defiance was futile.

"Just fucking kill me, you sick bastard. " The words did not flow as easily as his anger had hoped, yet there was some impact.

Regan leaned forward until his face was inches from Santo's. His eyes seemed to dance in tune to his thoughts, gently moving to an internal dance.

"Why, Santo? Why should I ease your suffering while mine continues? Whatever happens to you now, you will die in a matter of days. You are too far away to be found. Any electronic trace of you is miles away so you will not be found. Nobody knows where you are, so you will not be found. I could draw a fucking map of where you are, nail it to the church door in your shitty one-horse town and, you know what? You will still not be found. I have hidden you away so that I can torment you in peace. I want you to suffer like you made my sister suffer. I can see the fear in your eyes and smell it from every fucking pore in your piss-drenched skin. But it isn't enough. Not for me."

Santo whimpered in concession to the facts, knowing, admitting to himself that the man before him, torturing him physically and mentally was right. He deserved every coin that was burned into him.

"You are right." The words came out quietly and calmly, buoyed on the swell of the ocean of pain he was enduring.

"What?" Regan stepped back and raised himself to his full height, taken aback somewhat by the silent words of the man he was tormenting.

"You are right and I am sorry. It is worthless, I know, coming from me, but I am sorry. Not because of the pain I am feeling, or knowing that I am about to die. I am sorry because I was wrong. I should not have done what I did and...'

Men who train to be fit are strong; those who train to kill add a mental strength to their physicality. When that combined strength is mixed with uncontrolled fury a man can lift another with one hand. That is what Regan did, taking Santo, still tied to his chair, and lifted him cleanly from the ground and drove him with all his might and anger combined into the wall behind him.

"Do not take my anger away. Do not take my anger away. Do not take my anger away," the words flew from his mouth barely controlled. His right hand clenched so tightly around the neck of Santo that if he had an ounce more strength the fingers would surely meet. "You cannot apologise now. I have come too far on this hateful journey to allow an apology to stop me. Do not take my anger away. You were part of those who took my sister, leave me with the fucking anger."

Santo did not hear the plea; the explosion of fury negated the need for the device under is chin. He was dead and was not listening.

Seeing the end.

Regan walked into the room, a waft of anger and the unmistakable smell of the job just completed trailing after him. The others looked up from the table and could tell that Raposelli was now dead, another red line scratched through the list of targets. Watson was the first to break the silence as Regan poured a glass of water from the tap over the sink.

"Are we near the end, Jack?"

"Not as near as Raposelli or his friends." The answer was weighted with tangled anger but not anger aimed at Watson. "I have more to do."

"Did you get more names to add to the list?" Watson asked, hoping against hope that the answer would be a silent 'No.'

"I was not looking for any, Steve. I don't need to add to the list." Regan leaned over the sink to splash some water onto his face and he tried to wash the smell of burning flesh from his nose. "However," he added, looking up and facing the others in the room, " I want to move faster. I have sent enough messages to the Gascos and I want to now send a message that they will not misunderstand. I want to hit the compound that Fanetti spoke of."

Izzo looked up from his coffee and looked at Regan. "You look like shit, Regan. You need to slow this down a bit before tiredness causes you to make mistakes. I have no cause to regret the deaths of those you have killed to date, but I do not want your errors to make the difference between life and death for some poor soul out walking his dog near the compound."

Regan was surprised at the rebuke not because of the words but because of who said them. "What would you have me do, Donato?"

Izzo's response surprised him even more. "Let us do it. You have cleared a path through the key figures and all you need to get now is the Twins. We are so deep into this little war now that we may as well fight and I know the others are capable, much more so than I am, and willing."

Regan poured a coffee and leaned against the wall while sipping from the metal cup. He was considering what Izzo had said and it made sense.

"What would you do, Donato? What would be the plan? Do you have one? I am not trying to be funny, if you have a plan then I would be happy to hear it."

"Well, I am thinking that we can go through the gate, using my police badge, and clear the place out," he offered. It sounded feeble to him as he said it and he regretted opening his mouth.

"And I can do over-watch outside the compound, from a hill maybe, in case there is trouble. Sounds like a smart plan."

Izzo snorted a laugh. "I will make general yet!"

Regan smiled his agreement. "The compound is Mauro's. He uses it as a getaway from his brother and it is also there that they killed Kathy. Any objections to getting the remaining girls out of there and then level the place?"

Watson looked up, nodding his agreement. "That adds a new level of complexity to the assault. Without consideration of the girls, we could be in and out in minutes without concerns. What do we think is in there, ten or twelve low-level members of the gang and say, oh, about twenty girls?"

"Ten foot-soldiers and it would seem about fifteen girls. It will be an evening assault so we can consider that some, if not all, will be working and there will probably be a queue of Johns waiting. It could be messy," offered Regan.

"How about the Johns," Piero asked. "Are they targets?"

"No, they are not. However, if they are hit in the crossfire, then it is just the shit that happens. This is not a rescue mission, regardless if we are trying to free the girls as a part of the assault." Regan was back looking serious again. "Piero, can you clear the rooms in the out houses? Move the girls to one open area?"

"How long will I have? Will I have to remove clients too?"

"The Johns will have to take care of themselves. Any aggression from them, shoot them. I will be watching through the scope and assist when you need it."

Izzo got up from the table and walked over to the wall where the map of the compound was tacked to the wall. He looked at it for a moment and then whistled, "Six buildings, four of which are outhouses where the girls work. Two main buildings, one where the foot soldiers stay. What is the other one for?"

"That is where they killed Kathy. Anyone going in or out will be taken care of," Regan sounded angry.

"By you?" Watson looked concerned.

Regan nodded. "By me."

"I thought you were taking a break? Easing off a little." He didn't want to push the point but he dreaded what Regan with a sniper rifle would do if he decided to cut loose onto the compound just because he got angry.

"I have it under control, Watson. You guys clear the targets, get the girls into the clear and then leave the explosive packs in each building before you leave. When I see that you are clear of the area, and that there is little chance of injury to the girls, I will detonate the devices. I will shoot if necessary, covering you all as you move between buildings. How does that sound?"

Watson was satisfied.

Later that evening Watson was standing outside smoking a cigarette and sipping beer from a bottle that was already distastefully warm. The heavy, humid air weighed on him as much as the concerns about the raid on the compound. He figured that it would be successful, he was good, so was Piero and even if Izzo was a civilian, he did have the look of a guy who could well take care of himself in any kind of scenario. As well as that, they had the Dark Guardian Angel himself to watch over their assault on the compound and he knows that Regan would not let anything happen to them. Dark-Eye would be watching.

Regan interrupted his thinking, walking though the door and striding over to stand beside him. "How are you getting on, Watson?"

"You keep calling me 'Watson" and never 'Steve.' I find that strange," Watson offered a s a reply.

"I don't know, maybe it is a military thing."

"Maybe you don't like me or the way I think?"

"Nope, that isn't it. I just like the name Watson. Why would you think I don't like you? You have been such a support on this," he thought for a second before adding, "adventure."

"Thanks, it is good to know you are aware of what is happening around you. You had me worried a few times. You know that, don't you? I mean, what you did to those men, well, it takes a special sort of person to meat out that kind of punishment to a fellow man." Watson frankly expected an angry rebuke from Regan but none was forthcoming.

"I know. I mean, it was clear to me that I had to leave something behind once I saw Kathy's remains in the morgue. I could not just walk out of there, consider going to Izzo and seeking the arrests of those who killed her." He stared out into the evening as he spoke and it was not a little eerie to catch the glint of the setting sun in his eyes. It made him seem silently demonic and Watson could not help a shiver from rising through his spine.

"It just seemed to me that you were beginning to unhinge. You have been involved in some very personal killing in the last number of days and it is impossible to think that it would not impact on you."

"I know, Watson. I suppose it is not like shooting a guy in the head in a raid but that is the way it works out. Killing is an intimate thing when it comes down to it and, like everything in the world, even the intimate things, if you do not change the method, then it becomes hum-drum."

"You change the way you kill to keep it 'spicey.' Is that what you are saying to me?" Watson did not know whether to laugh or cry.

"It is not sex, Watson. The needs and desires are the same, but it is not sex. I change methods to keep on the edge, so not to become blunted or predictable. It makes sense if you think about it."

"When did all of this happen to you? I know something happened in Armagh when you were a kid but there is a lot of information not accounted for. How did you become so good at it? How did you become so good at killing?"

"It just happened, Watson. I was not a killer, and then I was. It sounds really simplistic but, honestly, that was the way it was. I never went through the whole process of my "virgin kill." When I killed first, it was like I had been doing it, and not doing it, forever. I had no remorse. I am not sure that it is really possible to understand or to explain."

"Come on, Jack. There has to be more to it than that. It is hard to accept that you were in school one day and a few days later you were firing shots into a soldier's head and that the transition was, while not easy I would imagine, you feel that is was fluid." Watson wanted to know because he felt that if there was one Regan out there, one man who was just a natural born killer, then the law of averages, as often wrong as it was, had to throw up another one. People in his position needed to know that Regan was a one-off anomaly or a rare phenomenon, something that would occur to haunt them once ever generation or maybe beyond. Ireland was not the only conflict zone that had thrown up children who knew how to kill. Africa, the Dark Continent, had some horrible little wars that had child-soldiers. But they were different, weren't they? The cruel bastards who used those kids, loaded them with alcohol and drugs, melted their minds with untruths and then sent them off to kill. Regan and his type, if there were in fact others, were not laced with drugs. They killed because they could and because, it seemed to Watson, they needed to. Watson realised with a shudder that his analogy with Africa was wrong. Regan was drugged, needed his fix. Except, it was hard to see who his pusher was but it was one of two sources, God or people like him.

"Have I suitably confused you, Steve?" His hands were holding the rail of the balcony and his head was slightly bowed when he asked.

"I don't know, Jack. I am finding it hard to figure you out. I mean, I think I understand why you do what you do, beyond, in my opinion, the perfectly valid reason that you are doing it because they killed Kathy. However, you were killing long before that. Were you always as," he tried to come up with the phrase that most suited the moment and failed miserably, "cruel?"

Regan paused for a moment, the need to answer almost punishing him. He was not cruel; at least he did not think so and did not want to be seen as such. What he did, the manner in which he did it, was to gain information or to punish the guilty. It was not for pleasure and he believed that cruelty was an evil that gave pleasure to some. He could not count himself in that genre, could he? It seems that Watson did and that disturbed him. "Am I cruel, Watson?"

"The screams from Raposelli give cause to my belief."

"The screams from him? Ah, yes." There was a pause for thought and reflection and then the considered answer. "If I were cruel, truly cruel, I would have killed his wife in front of him. I would have given him no chance to protect her and ensured that it was a dirty, loud and painful death. That, Watson, is what cruel is."

Watson realised that it was another battle that he was to lose against Regan and he nodded his agreement and stayed quiet.

Regan turned and walked back inside, another attempt to reason his existence snuffed out in the fear that he knowingly created when he tried to explain himself to others. He turned once more to Watson before going in and said, "Nothing happened to me, Watson. I just happened. Remember that."

33

The Compound.

The van slipped quietly along the back roads leading to the compound without a word being said by those inside it. Piero was driving and was the calmest of the three who were to storm the fortified buildings. He was quietly confident that it would be an assault that would be quick and painless for them. After all, unlike a lot of the encounters in Iraq, they would have a sniper on over-watch and that was always a comfort. He could not help but entertain a slight shudder thinking of his last tour, the tour that cost him his eye. This was to be his next mission and hopefully it would not have the same cost.

Watson sat it the back watching Regan check his weapon. He admired the fastidiousness of snipers; he had worked with them before. He felt it was not the right time to question Regan on his preferred role, whether being a sniper beat being the guy who rappelled through the window or blew the door in. Now just didn't seem like the time and, he was sure, Regan didn't care so long as he had a chance to kill. That was the main worry leaning on the ramshackle fence of his mind at that time. Regan just wanted to kill and yet he had decided to take a back seat on this raid. There had to be something to that decision and then it dawned on him. Snipers could have a field day. In close quarter combat, the door-to-door mayhem that he was imagining they might encounter on this mission, soldiers get confused. They could be so caught up in the action that it was often difficult to see the wood for the trees and often, everything got shot. Snipers, however, were far enough away to be able to see everything and, considering the skill of soldiers at this level, Regan was going to have his choice of kills.

Izzo was nervous. He was a policeman, a good one, but there is a difference between soldiering and being an officer in a police force. He knew he was tough and that if it came down to it he would pull his weapon and fire it at those who threatened him or his new colleagues, his brothers-in-arms. That, however, did not make him a soldier and he had no muscle memory, no instinct or experience of a fire-fight or a combat zone. He was not frightened of fighting, or, for that matter, dying. He was frightened of letting his newfound friends down.

Regan was busy checking his weapon but still managed to cast a considered glance at each of the men travelling in the van with him. He liked Piero, much more than he let on, and felt that in the absence of the injury to his eye, he would have eventually made it to the arms of Dark-Eye or one of the other Special Force units. He was sure that Piero would argue that the Corps was already such a unit and not many would disagree.

Watson, on the other hand, seemed distracted. He still didn't know enough about his new friend to know how much of the block he had been around already or if he had been around it more times than he let on. He was a cool customer; one not to be messed with but there was something gentlemanly about him that made Regan unsure. Maybe it was a sense of fair play, so inherent in the English, which just didn't sit well with the need to kill in the manner in which he saw Regan perform. Whatever it was, Regan did not think he was up for the battle that was to come unless he was missing something.

Then there was Izzo, sitting staring out the window. His eyes, while not giving anything away, were seeing nothing. Regan could tell that he was battling with his need to keep within the law but struggling with his promise to Regan to assist to the bitter end. Maybe he knew something, something that superstitious genes fed off. Don't break a promise but don't break the law. Whatever it was, Izzo was fighting a moral battle that was raging in his head and Regan was grateful that Izzo had come along.

He then reviewed his own position while returning focus to his weapon. Why had he accepted the role of sniper on this mission? The compound was where Kathy had been killed and he wanted to destroy it, brick by brick. Maybe that was it, maybe he would not stop at the bricks if that were the direction his destructive tendencies were to take him. He knew that to be true. On entering the compound he was sure that his fraternal instincts would take over and he would lose control of the actions of Regan the soldier. How bad would that be? He knew, in both his heart and mind, that letting it, the essence of what he was, loose, was not a good thing. The presence of the girls, he could not bring himself to call them prostitutes, and their Johns mixed into the equation where he had allowed his very mind to let loose would mean that they would somehow, legitimately, be targeted. He knew that and knew it when Izzo made the suggestion to raid the compound and for that reason he directed his mind and body to the role he was now taking. Seeing the inside of the building where Kathy was killed was not an option. It would be enough to see it through his telescopic sights.

Piero was ready, he just had to drop Regan to the hill and then get the van to the gate. He was almost looking forward to the action and berated himself for losing focus in his excitement. This Regan guy was something else. He had known guys just as tough as him in the Marines and through the odd encounter with Delta but this guy was different. He had an ungodly presence that made the air in the van feel sticky yet he knew that he would follow him to the end. It was hard to explain but it was what he felt and it made him feel positive about himself and the action he was about to take. He was back on mission and that was what he was born to do.

The van eased to a crawl on the hill overlooking the compound while Regan was scanning for a position that would give him cover. It was then he saw the small, rundown house that had suffered at the hands of nature and of man. It was perfect. The windows were long gone and it and the goat that was rummaging around what was once a vegetable patch would run once the first shot rang out. Then it dawned on him. A small piece of land overlooking the Gasco compound, now empty except for a goat and whatever other wildlife was in attendance up there. He could settle inside the ruin and fire, if necessary, from within the darkened window.

"This is good, Piero. Leave me off here."

Piero stopped the van and turned to look over his shoulder at Regan. "Right hand raised, fire. Left hand raised, cease-fire. My call on the ground unless I am clearly pinned down, ok?"

Regan winked at him, patted his rifle and smiled, "Sir, yes sir!"

"I mean it, Regan. I don't want to be dodging lead from down there and up here. That compound was built to stop people looking in and to keep those unfortunate girls from leaving. It was not built to stop the bullets that you will be firing. Those big, lead bastards will pass through the walls and get to Rome before they think of stopping. I do not want to be on the receiving end of one."

"Gotcha, Piero. You wave, I shoot."

"Good." Piero looked relieved.

A sniper without a spotter is an assassin, or so Regan thought. He was looking through the broken door of the dwelling ensuring that there was nothing nasty waiting for him within. It would not be unheard of for a wild boar to be sleeping in the cool shade of an old shed or ruin and he did not wish to engage with one at this stage of the evening, or ever if he could help it. He had almost suggested that Watson should stay with him to act as a spotter because he felt that the uncertainty that Watson struggled with would be a hindrance on the compound raid. Well, that was neither here nor there now as the van made its way down the hill and towards the compound gates. It was nearly time for action.

The dwelling was empty of all but the smallest of life forms. Regan stepped carefully through the detritus that had accumulated over the years of abandonment, toeing larger vessels carefully out of his way in case he disturbed a snake or some similar creature that would try to take a bite out of his ass. The injuries to good snipers came not from directed fire but from bites on the ass from snakes, rats, scorpions and whatever other ungodly creature was sharing the sniper's nest. Training kept the sniper calm but a bite was a bite and the mind played wonderfully complex games with those bitten by some of those sneaky creatures.

An old oak table lay on its side in the middle of the room and Regan tipped it back over onto its legs, giving it a shake to see how sturdy it was. It survived the shake test enough that Regan felt certain that it would take his weight. He positioned it, in line with the broken window that looked down onto the compound, and was satisfied that he had a good nest. It was only a matter of minutes before the van would reach the target gates and he had to be ready.

He settled his pack onto the front of the table as a rest for his rifle and then pulled the single ruined mattress from the bedroom and onto the table. He did not know how long he would be in position but it was best to have his hardpoints cushioned just in case. Elbows, knees and hips would survive long enough in a static position on the foul-smelling mattress though he was not sure how his nostrils would fare.

He settled onto the table and not a shake nor creak came from the aged leg joints. He carefully shouldered his rifle and began to work through his process. The covers at each end of the scope were clicked up, his right hand slid gently into place with his index finger leading the way onto the trigger. His left hand was positioned firmly under the stock, supported by his mattress-padded elbow and he began to intentionally slow his breathing. Memories of the rainforest in Colombia bundled their way into his head and he welcomed them. The manner in which he used the rifle there was equal to the requirements that he expected on this evening's hunt and he felt sure that they bag count was going to be similar too. Izzo and Watson had, in his mind, conspired to keep him away from the compound and that was fine, but they could not keep his MK211 Raufoss rounds from paying a visit. They would create over-kill and were more specifically designed for dealing with light-armour but he felt that if things did not go to plan, then the bullets would be welcomed equalisers.

He was ready and all he needed was a clear target of for Piero to raise his hand.

Treat plans as loose guidelines of action, that is what Regan had told them. Every plan should begin with "This is going to go to shit when you say 'Go'" and every soldier who has ever pulled a trigger or launched an attack is aware of that unfortunate reality. In the case of the assault on the compound, it was not the massive oak gates that caused the problem; it was the fact that Izzo tried to use his badge to get through them. The voice laughed at the other end of the receiver when he shouted "Open up, Police!"

Piero reacted immediately flooring the accelerator and driving at the centre of the gates. He would have achieved more spitting at the gates. They did not even flex. The weighted gates were supported by heavier beams behind the main gates. Silvio Fanetti probably forgot to mention the gates before Regan sent him to the gates of the otherworld. That was it; the plan was in tatters from the get-go.

Watson moved. "Let's go, side gate on the right." The three of them piled out of the van and, as yet, they were ahead of the thinking of whoever was behind the walls because nothing was happening to impede their progression. Moving to a side gate was progression because they were still moving, however, they had to get the van through the gate because the pack-charges where in there to be dropped at each building by Piero as soon as they were ready to leave.

Piero kicked at the gate to open it but it too was made from sterner stuff. A large old-fashioned lock kept the gate closed to all who were not welcome. Piero stepped back and looked at Izzo and Watson with a bemused look on his face and offered a solution, "Let's climb the wall..." His words vibrated with the shattering bang, like steel falling on steel, as the lock, and a good part of the door, blew inwards into the yard. A split moment later, before even the three could look around, they heard the bang; sound would never be as fast as a Raufoss.

The initial hit, that blew the lock from the door, was followed by a succession of small snap-bangs, in effect, a hail of the same bullets hitting the large oak gates and exploding as they exited the eight inch oak planks. Anything behind or approaching the rear of the gates would no longer be moving. Regan and commenced over-watch and his terrible efficiency shook the other three into action.

Izzo went through the small gate first, followed by Watson. Both went left to remove the barrier from the gate so that Piero, who had jumped back into the truck and gunned the engine into life, ready to deliver his destruction in packages around the compound.

Above in the cottage Regan almost chuckled at the reaction of the three men when he 'opened' the side gate. He thought that if he were protecting the compound then he would have men behind the gates on static patrol. For that reason he fired into the gate, certain that his over-kill action was justified to protect him men going through the smaller gate. Eight shots into the main gate left one in the box magazine and Regan switched to reload in an instant. He did not wait to find a home of the last round in the box.

Calmness spread for a moment as he saw that there was yet to be an engagement between the Gasco men and his own. That would change but, as the sun was setting behind him, he felt that the mission had a good probability of succeeding now that the inevitable had happened; the plan was back on track after the initial problem.

There were six buildings and three men to take them down with the assistance of Regan on sniper-watch. The enormity of the task was not lost on Watson but he did feel better about the assault now that it was ongoing. They had yet to encounter any of Gasco's men but that was to change now that they had entered the compound. They had agreed on the approach to the gates that instead of taking the two main buildings one at a time, Izzo would take the first and Watson the second. Piero would stick to the plan to clear the outhouses and lay the charges.

Watson figured that if he took the second building, the building where Kathy lost her life, and let Regan see him enter it, then it ought to negate Regan's desire to treat the building like an oak gate. Izzo had no problem with that, as he was happy to hit the first building. Piero just wanted to get going and would have been happy to hit all the buildings.

The power transformer was the next to be downgraded by Regan's shots. The sun was setting quickly and darkness was a soldier's friend. The exploding transformer did two things; it blew the lights and phones and alerted everyone else in the compound that they had visitors.

Piero got to the first outhouse in an instant and, leaving the engine of the van running, ran to the door and kicked it in. The muzzle of his silenced weapon followed the swinging door as it sniffed for trouble.

A man stood in the middle of the room, his Zippo lighter adding light to the fading sun that barely penetrated the room. On the bed, smoking, a young woman, naked from the waste up, was rising from the bed. A second man was rummaging in a drawer and Izzo was not sure if it was a candle or a gun he was looking for. It did not matter as the first man drew his weapon from his side holster but did not get to fire it. Piero, in action for the first time since his injury in Iraq, showed that Marines don't fade away. Two bullets danced their way through the man's head, coating the young girl in a splatter of blood and brain tissue. He decided not to wait and see what was coming from the drawer; he turned slightly to the left and introduced the second man to the same swift ending as the first.

The girl sat back onto the bed, her face covered in blood and her mouth opened in a silent scream. Piero pulled a sweater from the back of the chair nearest to him, it was one of the few items in the room untouched by the crimson splatter, and threw it gently to the girl. "Hey, Kid, cover up and let's get out of here."

She looked up and him, willing the scream of fear and shock to leave her body, but it did not.

"Come on, go. There is nothing to hold you here anymore and none of the men here will be touching woman ever again.

Her need to scream subsided and she seemed to deflate. Piero walked over to her, gun still in hand, and offered to help the girl.

"Really?" she asked quietly. "Am I really free?"

"Yes. We are putting an end to this place and letting you all go. There is more to life, you'll see."

"And the men who work here?" she asked, a Helsinki Syndrome concern at their future prospects.

"There is little prospect out in the real world for men like them. Who hires pimps and women abusers?"

"They are not all bad. Some of them are nice to us."

"We have no time to decide on that and it would seem unfair that the two on the floor be the only beneficiaries of our anger."

She looked across the floor at the two men, their deaths finally registering with her and she looked up to Piero while raising herself up, the sorrow in her eyes replaced now by angry realisation. "Kill them all."

34

Presidential Disapproval.

"Mr. Petersen, I am not in the habit of repeating myself." The voice was cold, hiding the fury that stabbed at his stomach. He was not used to people ignoring him and that was not a sense inherited when he became President. He was a pompous figure who enjoyed the fawning of others, a fact that began in his childhood. However, it was not just his wealth and power that drew people to him and made them bend to his will, he had a presence that balanced between the oppressive and the welcoming matching his size and sense of humour. The sense of humour, however, was part of his public persona and the spin-doctors worked very hard to ensure that the dark, angry side of the President, the side that flew off the handle when he did not get his own way, was well hidden from voters and donators.

Petersen was as calm as the President was angry. "Mr. President, I can understand your frustration with the speed of our asset recovery but, as you are sure to understand, these assets were made not to be recovered." It was not a lie, a lot of time and money was spent making the Dark-Eye members efficient, very efficient, at being able to avoid detection even in an empty room.

"Petersen, I believe that I made myself clear. I now believe that our friends across the water have discovered that the man they thought was dead is now alive and they want him. He owes them a debt, I believe."

"He owes them nothing, Mr. President. He paid that debt in full." Petersen's voice was still calm but his eyes were looking for a cigar to chomp on while taking abuse from a man he had little time or respect for.

"I believe he does. We have been informed of the numbers he killed during that dirty little war and I see that it is unbefitting our strong relationship with the English to allow the asset to continue to be a part of our unique operations. I believe that they have put two men into the field to find our Irish friend and..."

"And because of the British," hoping his subtle correction was picked up upon, "friends, we need to…"

"End the Envoy's association with Dark-Eye. The asset is now a liability and I want the account closed. We need to assist their men in the field if necessary; a mutual assistance. Do I make myself clear, Mr. Petersen?" The President had picked-up on the geographical correction and was not impressed with the man's impudence.

"Colonel," Petersen replied.

"What?"

"I am referred to as 'Colonel,' Mr. President. "I was at the rank of Colonel when I accepted this position. I worked hard for my rank, Sir. Please use it."

The President snapped. "Listen to me, you fucking Swedish immigrant. Get that Mick bastard back on a boat to England or you and your fucking Unit will be looking for work. Do I make myself clear?"

Petersen responded calmly. "I understand, Mr. President. Sometimes titles do not sit well on some men's shoulders. Someday you will not be President and maybe we can have a drink that day. I, for one, would welcome meeting you in the absence of those who protect you. " He did not wait for a reply and just put the phone down, with a little more weight than was warranted.

The President was furious and turned to vent to Paul Borden when two of his Secret Service agents entered the room. Having listened to the call, they understood the subtle threat and came to the President's assistance without being beckoned.

The President scowled at them when the entered but quickly changed his tune. A big man, his size did not prevent him from being what he was, a bully, and, unknown to most, a coward. He was afraid of his protection.

"When he is finished getting that asset back I want you to arrest him."

"Yes, Mr. President." The two men turned on their heels and left the office. Out of earshot one turned to the other and expressed what he really felt about the President. "Fuck him. Petersen deserves more than what that asshole said to him. Arrest him, my ass."

In London, a similar conversation was taking place, face to face, between the Prime Minister and her Head of Intelligence.

"I thought this story was dead, long dead, and now you are telling me that it is, once again, a new, and particularly thorny, development?" The Prime Minister hated the comparisons, the obvious ones because of her sex, to Lady Thatcher, the Iron Lady, but they happened nonetheless. However, she was a different woman and not the type afraid of confronting comparisons. "This young man, Regan. Where did he come from? I would like to know why he is still out there causing trouble." The information from from the Head of SIS had not been as forthcoming as it ought to have been and the Prime Minister was not impressed. She could smell a rat in a warehouse of cats.

"Yes, Ma'am. The whole incident is a bloody nuisance and we are moving to contain it as we speak." The disinterested air of superiority hung on every word.

The Prime Minister returned her half-empty cup to the fine china saucer and moved her hand to her face to dab her lips. A short woman, she did not take kindly to being looked down upon, and was especially fiery when she felt, as she was wont to say in her own lexicon, "fucked with."

"Listen to me, and listen very clearly. I want you to understand, without any cause of ambiguity, what I am about to say." She paused, breathed deeply and then began to hold a stare with her Intelligence Chief that she would not break until she had had her say.

"Some years ago, it seems, before you or I were in the positions that we are now in, somebody thought it was a good idea to hit an IRA unit on territory that can be defined as "not ours." That border crossing was on the Republic's side of the divide. What ever happened, and I do think I know a little more about it now, a young man saw something that made him angry and turned him into the open arms of the IRA. Now, all that aside, let's follow the steps. He attacked an SAS unit, the Cease Fire came into effect and he left Ireland and died in the Legion."

The Intelligence Chief nodded agreement.

"Now, it seems, that the young man is alive, working for the Americans and we have sent two officers to Italy to kill him. Do I pretty much have the facts in order, if not the complete facts?"

Another somber nod, the Chief now being to worry slightly.

"So, as my Intelligence Chief, can you please let me know where the intelligence is in this little story because it seems to me that we are sending agents to kill a solider of the US Government on the territory of our ally, Italy. It beggars belief. It really does."

"Ma'am, Jack Regan is a liability."

"To who?" she snapped. "We made peace, remember? Our relations with the Irish, on each side of that bloody border, have never been so good and now you are trying to kill a man who is already dead but, if we kill him again, we are sure to start another shit-storm on that island. Is that what you are trying to tell me, because if it is, somebody has truly underestimated my interest in keeping that island peaceful."

The Chief sipped from the cup of tea for the eight time, wishing for some interruption that was not going to come.

"To save your blushes, which ultimately saves mine, I have spoken to President Malcolm this evening and I understand more of what is happening. I am not happy to have been kept out of the loop but I can see the importance of closure on this, I think. I shall allow for your little expedition to continue but I want Regan caught, if possible, and I am going to put that in writing to you. If it happens that he dies, I will need to know the how's and why's so you better have your men informed immediately. This is not a hunt/kill operation, not anymore. If you have orders to," she thought for a moment, tilting her head to the left in thought, "amend, then do so immediately."

The Chief nodded silently in agreement, wishing again to be elsewhere.

"That is all."

The Intelligence Chief was a smart leader of men, one who knew how to press the right buttons in order to get the right results. That was the key, in the end it always comes down to the results. President Malcolm had made himself clear to the Prime Minister but, somehow, he had managed to get a message to his London Station Chief to him. Malcolm wanted Regan dead and he was not able to say that to the Prime Minister. Now, as Chief of Intelligence, he was, it would seem, working for the Americans because his own Prime Minister would not deal with Regan. She did not see how dangerous it was to leave such a creature alive, mixing with the general population and, as he already believed, reeking revenge on the scum who had killed his sister. He did not blame Regan in one bit for going after those who killed her, he actually very much admired the robotic sense of justice and morality that Regan had. It was just that the President wanted to brush the whole sorry story under the carpet and he was not gaining support from the Prime Minister. She would come around after the fact; she really would have no choice.

35

Room to room.

The second and third outhouses were easier than the first, practice does make perfect, and it was easier than the door-to-door "cleaning" he had done in Fallujah. In total, he had taken four girls from the three houses and sent them towards the centre of the compound so that they would not get caught in the effects of the blasts that were about to come. Of course, if Regan and the others started a firefight, then the girls would be in danger again. However, as Regan had advised, the mission was to destroy the compound's capability. If the girls were capable of being freed then well and good. Otherwise, stick to the plan. The compound was part of the money machine that the Twins enjoyed and a large spanner was to be thrown into the works.

Regan was watching the activity through his scope and he had a slight smile on his face watching Piero move from house to house. He was quick on his feet and very careful, a good sign, and he had saved four girls. He did not need to continue to focus on the outhouses now and felt that it was time to lay fire into the building where Kathy died. It was while pulling focus that he saw Watson break through the ground-floor door and step into the darkness. That was not part of the plan, not the plan he had at least, and the mission depended on adherence to the plan.

"Watson, I need you out of my line of fire."

There was no response and Regan fired off the same request for a second time. "Watson, do you copy? I need you clear of Building Two."

Again, there was silence until Izzo's voice, clear and crisp, entered the one-sided conversation. "Regan, do you want me to check Building Two to see is he ok?" Piero added his offer a second later.

"No, there has been no sign of gun-fire so he ought to be ok. Stick to the plan, I am coming down the hill and will cover Building Two. I am about five minutes out and moving now."

Watson was listening, he just was not responding. He did not want a hail of bullets going into Building Two without reason and he feared that if the Twins had tortured Kathy in there, then it was possible that there were other girls in there too. Having Regan unleash his anger through the walls was not sensible and put the innocent at risk. For that reason, but not just that reason, he broke rank and entered the building.

The second reason was the promise that he had made to Regan Sr. and the fact that he had, for the most part, broken it. He had promised to find Jack and to get him to fulfil his father's wish for revenge. Looking at how things had turned out over the past while, it was clear to him that he had succeeded. Jack had been cut-loose on the unsuspecting Italians. However, he needed to ensure that Jack survived so a Regan would raise Kathy's child. That part of the plan was coming apart. Maybe he could balance the promise in part by taking the building where Kathy had been killed, freeing any poor unfortunate that might be held in there and killing those who were running it. He was an accomplished agent, good in the field, and was capable of killing. He needed to avenge Kathy's death too as he had known her, had liked her a lot and he had promised her father. There was such emotional confusion to this bloody operation that Watson felt that he might as well wade into the pools of blood that Regan was causing. Maybe he would feel better for it. As he ducked through the opened door, he reminded himself that he never felt good about killing and would probably never would. He was not Jack Regan.

Regan was already moving at pace down the side of the hill. Something was not right, Watson was playing his own tune and the conductor was not happy. The ground underfoot was hard but stable and he moved quickly. He had dissembled the rifle and left it under a broken down old closet. Having removed the firing pin, bullets and scope the weapon was useless to anyone who found it and that was the best way to have it.

He stopped for a moment, both to catch his breath and to take stock of his situation. He could see the outline of the compound, the outbuildings gleaming in the moonlight with their white painted walls and the other buildings visible regardless of their stone facades. Piero had worked his end of the mission very well and by now would have planted all three charges and directed any "friendlies" towards the exit, more likely the side gate that Regan had blown open. Izzo, had not come back on the radio but he had the easier of the targets and ought to have been coming to the end of his clearance now. Watson, well he would deal with that when he got there but, regardless of changing tack, he would be professional in his methods and so Regan was not concerned.

He was just over two hundred meters from the compound so he removed his MP5 from the Velcro grab on his chest and pulled his night vision goggles from the pack on the side of his belt. He was going in ready for action.

In that instant all Hell broke loose in the compound and Regan, two hundred meters away and without his rifle or a good firing nest, was not in a position to assist his men.

Whether by accident or design the defenders of the compound, though they would never have seen themselves in that light before this night, rallied and fought back as one. They had no radios or means of communication except for their phones and it was too late to use them now that they were under attack. From the upper floor of Building Two, the windows were broken out and Piero could see at least three figures peeking out from behind the window frames before opening fire. The van was far enough into the compound and to the side of the shooter's vision for it to be in danger and he propped himself behind the engine mount and took stock of the situation. The plan had lasted longer than Piero had imagined it would and he was still confident of its success. In fact, the wild, untargeted shooting secured his belief in that theory until he saw what they were shooting at.

Across the large courtyard of the compound, the girls who had been freed were huddled together, in the watery moonlit sight of the shooters and it was no great marksmanship to kill them.

Piero could see the slaughter that was happening and took aim and laid lead into the line of windows. He was not sure of the efficiency of his one-man-assault but he had to try something. He had changed magazines twice before he decided to hold fire.

Watson was half way up the wooden stairs when the men upstairs started shooting out the windows and it was only a second later before fire was being returned into the building. Having unclipped his radio for a moment, it was of no use calling for the shooting to stop. He fumbled to re-set the communications when the fire stopped.

"Piero, is that you? I am on the stairs in Building Two. Cease Fire. Regan, if it is you, please try not to kill me."

"Watson, it was me. They started shooting the girls in the courtyard and I tried to lay down suppression fire." Piero was bouncing his sights from window to window, waiting for a muzzle or face to appear.

"Well, it is three to zero for the Marines, my friend. All targets are down. I am going to clear the upstairs and move to Building One. Any news from Izzo while I was off air?"

"I am still in Building One, gentlemen. There was a burst of gunfire down the hall by the main stairs. I returned fire and will check it out in a moment. That is the only contact I have encountered. There was a flurry of activity on the other side of the building and now there is silence." Izzo spoke like a soldier and Regan, listening in, smiled and jumped into the conversation.

"Gentlemen, we seem to have this under control. Izzo, the men who left your building went through the main gate and fucked with the fuse box before I could get them. The gate is closed again and three men are down."

Izzo felt a buzz of elation that the mission was almost over and a success. At least it was a success in the sense that none of the four men had taken a bullet or had been killed. The count, if Izzo figured it correctly, was three dead in Building Two, three outside the gates at the hands of Regan and one down the hall from him. Add the likes of Fanetti and the others and it was a good bag of kill. Surely now, Regan could concentrate on the Gasco Twins and this war would be over soon and he could go back, if his name stayed out of the reports that would follow all of the killings, to being a policeman. Maybe life could be that simple sometimes.

Watson stepped over the faceless body and looked out the window. He had told Piero that he was going to do so just so that Piero didn't raise his kill rate for that night's work to four. All three corpses in the room were hit from the chest upwards and had been hit multiple times. Once a Marine, always a Marine Watson chuckled to himself. Those boys were famous for their belief that they did not get paid for bringing bullets home. Now, looking out one of the shattered windows, he could see Piero making his way over to the bodies of the girls on the ground. It was a necessary task, having saved them Piero wanted to see could he do it once more. Watson could tell in the shadowy light that Piero's attempts were going to be in vain. The four girls were dead, lying in silver-black, moon-reflecting puddles of life.

A small door, one he had not seen in the darkness, opened and a torch, followed by a head, peaked out and illuminated the room. Watson did not wait to discuss the benefits of the hide-hole but switched his stance, raised his weapon and fired into the hole. The splatter of bullets off the door and those within was almost as loud as the suppressed sound of the gun firing and Watson had forgotten how quiet death could be sometimes.

He waited for an eternity, his heart booming steadily in his ears, before edging towards the small door. A hand, still clutching the torch but now covered in dark blood, pillowed the head of the man who was coming out. He was dead and his torch would be of no use to him so Watson relieved him of it and shone it through the door opening. He took a deep breath and tried to relax his breathing but he had killed men he did not know, who had done nothing to his country and he was struggling with the conscience that was murmuring in his head. Behind the torchless man lay three others and Watson fought the urge to vomit. The light from the torch showed them all to be dead. The numbers were getting higher that night than he had originally intended and now that he had successfully prevented Regan from going on a killing spree in Building Two he cursed himself for taking up the mantel instead. One more quick look into the room from where the men were trying to escape and, assured that it was empty, he quickly made his way to the stairs to rejoin the others. Piero would be returning to the van now and he could go and finish up with Izzo.

"Who are you?" The voice was rasping and bodiless. The hairs crept to vertical on the back of Watson's neck at the same time that his stomach tightened into an unbreakable knot. He turned slowly and saw, in the shadows the body of a man slumped against the wall. Piero had hit four but this one had survived and now had the drop on Watson.

"Nobody," came the short answer before he fired his weapon into the shadows. He was now as bad as Regan and could not condemn the man anymore. Five men dead in as many minutes.

He had to keep the momentum going and to push the thoughts of regret and anger from his mind. The killings would be over soon and he would be free of the compound but first he had to make sure the others were on the way out. Time had slowed to dreamlike improbability and Watson did not know if they had been there for minutes or hours. It had to be no more than twenty minutes and probably even less. Across the courtyard he could see Piero still checking the bodies of the girls. What a mess that good intention had turned out to be. He knew that it would bear heavily on the Marine's conscience, those guys, as tough as they were, had to deal with emotions that were fortified by their belief that their existence, in any given situation, means that there is safety nearby. It did not work for the four girls that evening and Watson knew to tread carefully with Piero in case his emotions, his true emotions, came flowing out.

Piero looked up as Watson jogged over to him. The look on his face said it all, to have done so much to help them and yet still fail the young girls. His eye burned angerly at Watson.

"You changed the plan. You changed the plan and the girls died. Is that what you wanted?"

Watson was shocked and was trying to formulate a plan when, from behind Piero's left shoulder, two men came out of the shadows with weapons raised. Watson was in the killing zone, not the area where kills occur, but mentally in a place where the previous killings that evening rekindled his ability and he raised his weapon and fired rapidly at the approaching threats.

Piero spun on his heels, weapon raised immediately, in time to see the two figures crumple onto the ground. He was not needed in that brief fight and turned quickly back to Watson.

"That is the sixth and seventh killing for me this evening. I did not kill those girls." The words hissed out, Watson's anger clear for Piero to see.

Piero looked at him and shook his head. "I am sorry, Watson. I am never going to get used to seeing shit like this. We had them saved and then we didn't. I am sorry. My frustrations got the better of me and now you go and save my life."

Watson turned to go towards Building 1 but stopped and turned back to Piero, a look of sadness in his darkened face. "Yes, Piero, I saved your life but after tonight, who is going to save our souls."

Piero nodded his agreement and turned to walk towards the van.

36

The Killing House.

Izzo moved silently, step by step, towards the muffled pants and groans of what he knew to be an injured man. The ceilings were high and the halls narrow but he knew the sound of an injured man and was intent on cornering him. Notwithstanding the wishes of Regan, Izzio wanted to bring in a lieutenant alive, it was the only chance that he would have to rescue the remnants of his police career and reputation.

Mano Fuzzo was crouched in the corner unaware of the true extent of his injuries, unaware that his panting, futile as it was in bringing oxygenated blood to his brain, was being heard. He did not know that the warmth, puddling around his his legs, was his blood, or his urine. He was frightened, alone and without hope. He was no longer a soldier in The Gasco gang, he was a twenty-year old kid whose life was slipping away before he had even the chance to really live it. He had not seen his girlfriend in three months and was unaware that she was waiting to tell him that she was pregnant. He was to be the father to a child that was to be father-less. As he had been. In that moment he knew the pain that mothers feel, and knew that he was the cause of the pain that his mother and the mother of his child was to feel. And yet, he thought he had it all worked out. He would earn enough money from the gang to be able to move away from his home-country, maybe to America or Australia. Somewhere where his past would not catch-up with him. Except now, that was not going to happen and his past, despite his hopes, dreams and wishes, had caught him in the shape of a tumbling ounce of lead that had entered his back, splintered through his ribs, ripped his liver asunder, shredded his large intestine and then blown out in unison from his stomach wall.

Izzo heard the pants and followed silently, intently listening to the muted struggle for life that slid along the painted walls. The sound was unmistakable, pain being masked by a need to stay hidden, and it gently eased its effect along the walls, up to the ceilings and around the corners. In the silence of the hunt, the muffled sound of impending death was deafening. Twenty feet from where Mano was lying in his pool of life Izzo was struggling to pin-point where the noise was

279

coming from. The darkness and the constrained breathing abused his senses and he was absorbing the information incorrectly. Each mental decision he made, believing he had identified the location of Mano, was out by a small distance but that small distance at twenty feet meant an error in judgement when Izzo finally turned the corner, aimed his gun and hit the button on his torch to illuminate what he thought would be the twenty-year old lying injured on the lower steps of the stairs. The beam of light high-lighted his error of judgement and the metallic click of a weapon's safety being turned off was, this time, an unmistakable beacon of noise that announced his prey was behind him. He froze to the spot .

Mano sighed heavily as he clicked the safety off on his weapon. He had held the pain in for as long as he could but now that his hunter was standing in front of him with his back turned all the regret that had penetrated his soul had evaporate in an instant. This was not the man who had shot him, but that would make no difference. If he was to go to Hell, then he was buying two tickets for the one-way journey.

"Turn,' he spat through bloodied lips. He was respirating blood so time and his life-span were equal partners.

Izzo turned slowly knowing that he was either going to be lectured by a dying boy or be shot. He hoped against hope for the lecture.

Mano's hands were slick with blood but he still had a good grip on his gun. He stared up at the figure of the man before him and his finger began to follow the orders commanded by his mind. Pull.

"I can help you." He had to say something and surely the kid needed help.

"How? Look at me. Look at what is left of me. How can you help me now?" It was more of a challenge than a request, he know he was all but dead.

"I can get you away from here, not just this place, I can get you out of the gang and out of the country. I can change things for you. Life does not have to be this, it can be changed by a second chance."

"And you?" The question was cutting as Mano knew that what had happened was illegal. "What happens to you? Who is going to save you?"

"My wife?"

"Naaaw, I don't think so." He had to pause to drag air into his dying lungs. "I'd be doing you a favour pulling this fucking trigger. Your life is as over as mine. We just will go to different places, probably."

"I have a wife, remember."

"Yeah, I remember. I was hoping to have one too," replied Mano. His voice was beginning to gargle on the blood filling his throat and he was shivering from the cold, the side-effect of blood loss. It was remarkable, he thought to himself, he was cold yet sitting in warm blood. Surely that should not be. Opposites became equals in his mind and equals made no sense. He ought not pull the trigger. He should leave the policeman go home to his wife. He should. He really should. The angel on his shoulder was gaining traction in the decision process bounding through the closing doors of his dying mind. Yet, the Devil had been a squatter in that mind for years.

Regan made it over the wall in an instant. It was built for privacy more than protection and, either way, it was not going to make a difference to someone like him. Spread over the top of the wall, his weapon slung onto his back and his NVGs activated, his attention was pulled to the left, a flash in a window. His mind raced to recall who was tasked to what building and knowing that both Watson and Izzo had suppressed weapons, he decided that whoever had fired in the building on the left had not been one of the good guys. His mind also recorded that there was no audible response. There was one shot and that had signified the end.

He dropped the ten feet and landed feet, hip, shoulder, a quick roll, and then back onto his feet, weapon shouldered and eyes following the muzzel in a solid sweep. He was moving towards the side door, it would bring him in close to the vicinity of the flash. There was no other noise and his ear-piece was silent . Whether it was working or otherwise it was not a concern. He moved in the dropped-crouch fashion that allowed him to move quickly but be a small target. Weapon and eyes scanning, he entered the side door.

Piero had moved himself to the van and quickly began to check his firing mechanisms for the explosive charges in each out house. Izzo would leave a charge in the main building and he could forget about Building 2, that was written off as Watson must have dropped the package at some stage during his killing spree. Enough of the compound would be destroyed.

Watson, before he made his way to Building 1, had to inspect the last two men he had killed and he crouched down and rolled the first body over. His shots had been clean "stoppers", straight to the chest, as he did not feel confident with head-shots, he had, after all, been out of the game for a while. His target had been a large man in his late forties and he had probably killed him before a heart-attack did. That was not an ease to his mind. His second target was the same as the first but his shots were better placed than expected. It still surprised him how little blood comes from a shot to the heart. It was relatively clean. Unlike the conscience that had been damaged by that evening's activities. He needed a shower but no water was going to clear his conscience. It was time to find Izzo and to leave the compound.

On entering the building, Regan's mind was matching calculations coming from his immediate environment with the numbers he had gathered previously. His entrance into the compound had been un-scheduled so he was working off instinct, a batch of number that were too old for the mission and, as ever, experience. The flash he has seen while straddled on the compound wall meant only one thing, a shot from an un-silenced gun. The hairs on his neck began their prickly rise, notifying his nerves that something was wrong. He knew that anyhow.

He moved quickly through the lower level, alert to every shadow and every noise, acutely aware that he was going too quick to be truly silent. There was no internal light except that which was coming through the windows. It was enough, and he powered-down his NVGs and reverted to normal vision. The view was to be the same and as he eased around the corner he noted that two bodies were ahead of him, neither moving. He halted his advance and studied what he saw for a moment. There was a glint off the belt of the body on the left and there was some movement. The glint was from an opened police badge and Regan felt a weight compress his chest. Not now, God, not now.

He dropped the night-goggles back into place and he sped down the hall to his, he had not considered their relationship until that moment but for all intents and purposes, considering Izzo had put his life of the line to assist Regan, he had to consider him a friend.

As he neared it was clear that it was Izzo and it was just as clear to see that he was gravely injured. He dropped the goggles down over his eyes once again, hoping that the clarity would not solidify his fears. His instincts, however, did not fail him and he took care of the other body first. He, in a fluid, simple motion, targeted the head of the body on the right, depressed the trigger twice and saw the head plume in bright green through is goggles. What ever had happened while he was on the wall, whether Mano was still alive moments ago, whether he knew of Mano's plans to marry and escape it all made not a note of difference. He was now well and truly dead.

Regan turned to Izzo and threw caution to the wind. Somewhere in the bowels of the building he heard the din of a diesel generator taking over from the damaged power poxes. He reached over to the wall and hit the light switch, best to see clearly what damage was done before he tried to figure out a solution. The generator was fulfilling its job and the lights illuminated the halls.

The shift from darkness to bright light barely registered in Izzo's eyes. There was a flicker, a murmur and then nothing for a moment.

Mano had pulled the trigger, succumbing to the gangster that was flowing out of his wounds. He pulled the trigger to spite the man before him, so that he too would lose all that he was losing too. Life was not fair but even a dying man could add his balance to whatever ill-conceived equation was applied to the scales of life. Mano did that by pulling the trigger and now Izzo lay, ironically, on the steps where he thought he would find Mano.

Regan pushed his gun around onto his back and he crouched down over the shaking body of Izzo. He had seen it too many times in his young life to discount the belief that life leaves through the eyes. Even eyes as dark as Izzo's were alive in those last few moments, fighting the impending end.

Izzo fought the urge to relax, fought the urge to allow the end to visit him. He willed every muscle and sinew to life and grabbed Regan by the shoulder and pulled him closer.

"Get me home, Regan. Don't leave me here. "

"Easy, big man. Let's check this out first before we decide what to do."

Izzo tightened his grip on Regan's shoulder and tried to speak, but life was evaporation through the gaping wound in his chest. "You need to know something that I have not been able to tell you. My wife and I, we have your nephew, Jack. We took him in when your sister died. Monica is minding him while I am away."

Regan was lost for words but knew he had to comfort the dying man.

"Tell her......."

Regan lifted Izzo's head to help clear the airways. "Tell her what, Donni."

"Tell her I died for something right. I died doing what I love and that if I were to live my life all over again, I would not change a thing. Do you hear me, Regan?" he was pulling Regan close to his face, "not a thing! Now, you have to finish this. You have to finish this so that you can tell my wife what happened. She will need to know and I do not want to die in vain, " his voice was fading but he pushed more words out, "Get them."

Regan felt hurt and sadness rush through his chest. He had strong-armed Izzo into this fight and now he was bleeding to death on the stairwell of a gangster's fortress brothel. He held Izzo's head in his hands while speaking softly to him. "She is going to be fine, Donni, we will be there for her. She will not want for anything and she will know that you died well. I will take you home to her, that I promise you. Monica and the child will be fine."

He had meant every word, his promise signed in blood. But he had been speaking to deaf ears, Donato Izzo was dead.

He needed to exit the compound, with Izzo's body. Whatever else was to happen that evening, the body of the man who had just dies in his arms was to be taken from this compound. He hoisted Izzo onto his shoulder, fireman fashion, and began moving down the hall he had previously sneaked through, out the door and into the main yard. It was not going to be a long trek, just about one hundred yards to the van parked, he hoped, by the main gates with the others waiting, but he needed to do it fast. The warm stain of blood seeping through the cloth on his back would stain more that the Nomex of his camouflage, it would stain his mind more so than many of those he had killed in the past. Those, more often than not, died because he decided that they were to die. Donnato Izzo died because of Regan's desire for revenge pulled another soul into the daily Hell that was his existance. That hit home to Regan as he jogged across the open yard to the main gate. His weapon was cocked but he was sure that there was no-one left to shoot at him. Izzo and Watson had performed the raid well, save the death of Izzo.

Watson had problems of his own but they were not related to the death of Izzo, though the silence on his radio told him that something was wrong. He was carrying the weight of conscience, and not that of a dead commrade, and it was becoming difficult to continue carrying that weight. The raid, almost a sop to Regan to ease his temper, had gone so right and so wrong. The killing was easy as they had only encountered the lower lieutenants of the organisation. They had been ill-prepared, not just for the para-military training that Izzo had had in his past, but for the onslaught that a trained intelligence operator could bring to the pitch. In all, Watson had dispatched seven men of which five, he believed, were armed. The other two, well, the likelihood was that they were not. And that, once upon a time, was acceptable to him. Actually, during his time fighting the men who would have been Regan's brothers-in-arms, it was more than acceptable. Now, it was not. He could not bring his conscience to walk in sync with his still functioning ability to kill. Maybe it was that he was getting older, wiser, probably not wiser, but the sense that he had a life away from that world was leaning on the weak structures of his conscience. The foundation was beginning to give and he wanted away from all of it, not just Regan's war, for that is what it had turned into, but away from all of the needs that would drive a man to kill for his career. When it came down to it, when one really thought about the reason for killing another man, the idea that one did it for Queen and country was obscene to Watson. He killed, in the past at least, so that the IRA did not detonate bombs on the streets where his wife was shopping, or where his brother was popping into a pub for a pint. It was that personal. If he had not the skill and mental fortitude to kill and if he thought that the actions of others would harm his family, then he would never consider killing for Queen or country. Those beliefs were too abstract and as arbitrary as killing for circus clowns and daisies. And he didn't want to kill for clowns.

The locks on the gates were basic but big and Regan did not have the time to deal with them with the finesse that one would expect from a specialist. He was considering his options when Watson made his presence known.

"Who is....', the words faded as realisation assaulted his eyes. "Oh, God. How?"

Regan turned and looked at him, his face and eyes for once giving away emotion.

"I happened, Watson. I happened to Donato, to you and to the others and this is what happens when I "happen."" He was standing holding Izzo's large frame with ease but his face carried the weight of the world. He eased Izzo off his shoulder and placed him against the wall. It was a blessing, if one could be counted, that it was a clean death and that his wife would see his body before it was to be interred. His head was cocked slightly to the left, one eye still partially opened and a speckling of blood around the mouth from where he had coughed his last words.

Watson looked at Izzo with sorrow. He had formed a bond with the young Scillian and it had been one that had, or would have, developed into a friendship. Now, he was slumped against the wall, his lifeless eye peering through the slit in his lids. It did not accuse, nor offer an insight into what happened. It just stared.

Not sure whether it was out of respect for the dead, or out of being spooked by the eye, Watson knelt down beside Izzo and gently closed his eye. Then, to Regan's surprise, Watson moved his head within inches of Izzo's ear and whispered an Act of Contrition.

"I never took you for a Catholic," he whispered.

"I am not, I just had to do this a couple of times and it has stuck in my head. It just makes sense, doesn't it. I mean, to say something a little more effective than "Gee, sorry we fucked up and now you are dead." Watson was angry.

Regan knew he had to say something but his emotions were getting the better of him and all he could do, in that moment, was surrender to the feeling, the need, to put an end to it all. "It can stop here. It can stop here and we can walk away. I cannot drag you further into this and what is the point anyway. There are always going to be more Gascos. They are a Medusa and I cannot keep killing her."

For the second time since they met, Watson launched himself at Regan so quickly that he really had no plan for when they connected. He shouldered Regan into the wall, briefly winding him and grabbed him by the drag-handle on the back of his camouflaged top until he had him doubled over the face of Izzo.

"Look at him. He is dead, Regan. It is over for him because he gave his all so that you could win this bloodly little war. And now, now, you want to stop?!"

Regan was taken aback but did not react. That made Watson angrier.

"We are not going to stop now. We are going to finish this, one way or another, and we are going to finish it together. You are going to rid your soul of revenge and then stop. It will have to stop, Regan, but not on your terms any longer. We have to make sure this kid's death was for something so that his wife and child, his son, will know that his dad died for something. They will never mark his grave defining the work he did with us so we have to let his son know what he did, that what he did was for the good of others. You owe Donnato that. You owe his kid that. This is the payment and you better fucking pay-up. He released the grip on Regan and stepped back, not knowing what to expect.

Regan stood there, shocked as before when Watson had hit him, but had no cheeky grin on his face now. He knew Watson was right, the end could not be a disjointed trail of death and distruction. He needed the end to be real, not just for Izzo and Watson, but so that he too could have choices. Once this ended, and he was now, almost by a blood oath, obliged to end it properly, he could decide the path he wanted to take. Whether that was to be back to the Unit or, as was the thought taking seed in his mind, a life without the thrill of the kill. He had to figure if that was something his mind and body could handle as, and he knew it to be true, the whole process of what he did was addictive – the hunt, the kill and then the escape. Leaving all of that behind might be as destructive as continuing with such a life.

He stood in thought for a moment and then looked once more at the body of Izzo slumped against the wall. He then turned to Watson and spoke. "You are right, sorry. I am coming apart, Watson, and I need to pull it together. This," he was pointing the muzzel of his weapon at Izzo, "was not meant to happen. He was meant to go home to his family when this ended."

"You didn't put a gun to his head, Jack," offered Watson.

"Might as well have. I threatened him, remember? At the table in the hotel after the incident in the park? I gave him no choice, Steve, and he fell into the trap."

"I think he felt he owed your sister, Jack. I don't think, at the beginning at least, that he felt that he owed you. There was a connection between them and he was being drawn into this even without you dropping, shall we say, hints."

Regan visibly eased and a look of relief spread over his face. "You are turning into my conscience, Watson."

"My arse, Jack. Remember, you are coming with me when this is over. You have a date with the judiciary back in England. How is that for conscience!?"

The smile flickered briefly on Regan's face but he stopped its progress because, as amusing as the comment was, it was not the place to be smiling now with Izzo's silent distain at his own death still hanging in the air.

"I will be allowed to choose my own legal defence, won't I? I know, I didn't mention it before, but will you ensure that I can choose my own? Forgive me if I do not trust your Government to appoint a balanced counsel to my cause." He was placing two small charges onto the locks on the door and setting the fuses short so that the could leave the compound quickly. He then gently hoisted Izzo back over his shoulders and turned to Watson, "Well, have we a deal?"

Watson felt that it was a fair request. Things had changed since the trials of the past that had so tarnished the concept of justice in the UK. It was different now.

"Sure, Jack. You can choose your own counsel. We can give you that much."

Regan knew that there were seconds left before the charges blew. "Get behind that pilar, these are about to go. Oh, and I choose you as my counsel."

"What the...,' the words were drowned out by the double blast followed by the shattering of the heavy wooden gates.

The black Mercedes CLS 350 glided off the motorway and down the slip-road towards the quiet village. The street lighting only went as far as the slip road and then there was darkness. The driver switched on the head-lights and did not spare the petrol as he drove through the village and down the valley towards the compound, the powerful engine purring its way through the rev counter.

Mauro had received a call while he was enroute to the compound, a brief call telling him that there was some breach of security and that, at that point during the call, the situation had not been resolved. His driver and personal guard's presence in the car, both big burly men, were a silent sense of security that he needed. His words to the compound worker were strong and reassurring only because of the two men sitting in front of him. Otherwise, he would not be so bravado heading towards the compound.

The driver was a good one, aided by the Germanic precision engineering that worked in conjunction with the thin strip of soft rubber compound that separated the car from the tarmac of the country road. When he saw the flash coming from the compound he did not have to wait for Mauro to bark the command to go faster. Something was wrong and he dropped his right hand down from the steering wheel to the safety-belt clip, releasing the clip in a smooth motion that allowed him to return his hand to the wheel in a split second before he needed to turn into the tight-left hair-pin bend. The belt slid across his torso and upwards towards its mount but ceased its automated recoil as it caught just under his left arm. It did not interfer with driving but it would still have a life-saving impact unbeknown to the driver.

Mauro saw his driver unclip his belt and mirrored the action, never being one to have an original thought and blind to the fact that a good grip on a steering wheel was, if your belt was unclipped, at least something to hold onto in crisis driving. Mauro now had nothing to keep him stabalised in the back of the speeding car and he was busy ejecting the magazine from his pistol. He had not fired it in over two years, Marco did not let him fire it, and there was really no need to check to see if there was a full metal jacket, it was always full. The car, reacting to the speed, pot-holed road and turbulent driving, lurched to the left before regaining traction, a split second before the driver would have, and bounced Mauro off the padded interior of the right-side door. The gun tumbled from his grip as he swore angrily, not at the driver, he was beyond being given out to, but at his sweaty hands.

The driver was now at one with his machine and the car roared down the dusty road at speeds touching 180 kph in places. It was only a matter of seconds before he would reach what he could now see, was the remains of the gate to the compound. For a moment, his lights, before disappearing into a dip in the road, showed what he thought was two men running out through the glow of flames. When the car exited the dip he saw nothing and was beginning to identify his entry into the compound, whether he should enter or break hard and enter with the body-guard on foot. The decision was made for him when the wind-screen shattered milliseconds before his right shoulder did too.

Regan and Watson were exiting the smoking ruins of the compound gates when they realised that a car was bearing down on them at speed. Regan forgot the niceties of dealing with the dead, dropped Izzo's body like a sack of potatoes and drew his weapon. Watson was not as quick to react but it made no difference as the bullets spat from Regan's weapon following a straight and true path to the windscreen of the approaching car. Watson found it strange that he was expecting the tap-dance of targeted fire usually expected from the cool-headed response from special-forces soldiers. *Tap-tap, tap-tap*, two bullets at a time, hitting the target every time. Not this time, the weapon in Regan's hands was, in the words of his old army buddy "cutting loose" on the target and, the marque now visible as it was near, the windscreen shattered as the stream of bullets walked up the bonnet.

The car came to a shuddering halt as the tyres gripped and lost grip on the sandy surface of the road, then caught a large dyke in the side of the road causing the car to lift off all four wheels before smashing down in a dead-stop.

Inside, Mauro had been flung against the window, by way of the headrest on the seat in front of him, and was unconscious before the car hit the ground and came to a halt. The driver and body guard were alert to the danger and burst out through the doors, the driver to the left and the body-guard to the right. The car was facing forward which, in the scheme of things made no real difference except if it had been facing the the other way, the targeting would have been different, causing a different man to die.

Regan shouted at Watson to drop and to take the man exiting from his right, he would deal with the passenger coming out on his side. The security guard was quick to react, but not quick enough and, while he had one foot planted firmly on the road and was driving himself out of the door with gun in hand, he was dispatched with two shots to the face as he raised his head out and over the level of the car door.

Watson, tasked with the driver, was about to have a similar experience except on leaping out of the car, the driver forgot that he had not fully released the seat-belt and he was wrenched to his left as he dove from the car. In doing so, his back was suddenly turned to the approaching Watson and he became less of a target. Watson had his weapon raised but he was not going to shoot the man in the back, regardless of who he was.

The driver swore loudly as his bulky frame, by momentum alone, wrenched his shoulder free from both the seat-belt and, much more painfully, his shoulder socket where it was moments before. The pain, screeching through his shoulder was matched quickly by the blinding pain at the back of his head before the instant darkness and crumpling legs.

Watson had clubbed the driver quickly to the back of the head having decided that enough men had been killed that evening. The brief chat with Regan having sowed the seeds of doubt about the policy of an unlimited kill bag.

Regan toed the head of the body-guard on the ground, knowing already that the man was dead, but best to make sure. Little things like kicking a corpse in the head quite often made the difference to a mission and sometimes, even though soldiers were not prone to admitting it, kicking the enemy in the head was just what the doctor ordered. It was not the kind of thing you wanted news crews seeing, or worse recording, but it was done. The enemy was the enemy after all and honour amongst soldiers did often prevail, it was most often seen in clean fights when officers were allowed to continue to bear their side-arms, where cigarettes were given to prisoners and wounds bandaged. However, dirty wars do not allow for such niceities on the battlefield. Dead enemy soldiers, if they were not dead enough, would receive more than a kick to the head. Anger, frustration, fear, loneliness – all of these emotions become focused on the search for reason and release and sometimes, just sometimes, the dead are insulted further, if that is possible, than the bloody, dirty death they had already endured.

Regan was once more in that mood as the guilt associated with Izzo's death now bled into the pool of anger that had replaced his soul so many years ago. He needed to unleash again.

Watson saw the look return to Regan's face again and knew that remorse in the heart of a man is different to the remorse in the mind of a soldier. He knew that Regan had, once again, compartamentalised his guilt and emotions and, ironically, for a man who was so adept at hiding his feelings, to Watson it was abundantly clear, Regan was hurting when he showed no pain.

Regan slid across the bonnet of the car and and landed with Watson between him and the prone figure of the driver on the ground.

"Done?" he asked quickly.

"No. He is out cold but I am not going to kill him."

Regan went to push Watson aside and to finish the target but Watson stopped him.

"Jack, there is no need. Think about it, he is a driver. He is unarmed. Ease off for the love of God."

Regan's body tensed and his eyes flashed a moment of anger then softened slightly.

"Sorry, you are right. I need to pull back and be more targeted. This is not a pigeon shoot. We should..," he was interrupted by a blast of profanities from the back of the Mercedes that would abuse the ears of those with religious sensitivities.

"What the fuck?" Watson shouted as he saw the figure rise in the back of the car. He raised his gun to fire, a response to danger as opposed to a desire to kill, and it was Regan this time who prevented the killing. He shouldered Watson to the ground and then, in a blur of speed pulled open the back door and dove into the seat and onto the dazed figure who was swearing.

Watson was shaken by the sudden jolt and was raising himself off the ground when he was bowled over again by Regan. Except this time Regan had more that his gun in his hand, he was pulling Mauro Gasco out of the car by the hair.

Lying on his back but raising himself up on his elbow, shaking his head to clear the effect of two sudden hits, Watson stared up at the image before him.

A breeze had picked up and turned gusty, pushing the scattered clouds from their shrouded moon. The light spilled onto the countryside lighting the greys and mottled hues of the surrounding area. Against that watery light, the silhouette of a man balancing on his toes as he was gripped by the neck was the first indication that the hunter had captured his prey.

Regan felt light headed as questions and emotions ransacked the order and balance of his mind. He had Mauro. The course of half the battle was now firmly in the grip of his right hand and, hidden in the silhouette, unseen to Watson, the muzzel of his MP5 was borrowing into his sister's killer's neck. The need to pull the trigger there and then filled his chest until he was sure that his heart would burst through ribs, muscle, skin and body-armour and cover his prey with bloody frustration. His mind raced on.

Watson saw that it was Mauro who was being slowly strangled and, in awe, he could not bring himself to move neither to help his friend or to attack Kathy's killer either. It was the evil that whispered through the air, both spoken, from Mauro, and unspoken from Regan.

Mauro was feeling pain and panic in equal measures. His neck was being crushed in a hand that was connected to an arm, connected to a shoulder, to a neck and eventually to those grey-blue eyes. Those eyes were frozen into position and that frightened him more as they were the eyes of a man who had made his mind up. Had he been considering what to do with his prey, the eyes would have danced about his face and body, checking the surrounding area for ideas – hiding places, weapons, threats. Not with this man, he had Mauro squarely in his sights and was strangling him to death with one powerful arm.

"What!" he choked through spittle and fear. No response was forthcoming.

Mauro began to struggle but he had left it too late. His powerful frame was fading with the lack of oxygen and his attempt to beat the arm of his aggressor was pitiful in its ineffectiveness. He was a child in the mouth of a lion, sad, horrifying and destined with one outcome. Mauro's body went limp and the strength in Regan's arm, as impressive to Watson as it was, would not hold a dead-weight the size of Mauro Gasco. The body crumpled to the dusty ground.

"That's one of them, isn't it," he asked incredulously.

"Stay quite," whispered the prone figure still silhouetted against the moon.

In the silence of the moment Watson could almost hear the battle being raged between the young soldier's heart and his brain. His heart screamed for revenge, to end the life of his sister's killer there and then. It would release a part of his soul back to his natural body but his mind screamed at him to cease such boyish need for revenge. His mind knew that Mauro was the weaker twin, the one who followed his brother like a lost lamb, and killing him, in that instant, would ruin the opportunity to kill Marco, the true target of his rage.

He pulled his knife from its sheath and crouched down over the body. Watson said nothing and fought the urge to intervene, it was, afterall, one of the two who had killed Kathy and he felt that, in this case at least, any retribution was fair.

Regan allowed the blade to glide over Mauro's pale face tracing a bloodless design onto a canvas he so dearly wished to apply his art to. The knife moved lightly, catching the odd glint of moonlight as it gently spun, an evil ballerina being directed by an angry composer onto a stage of an unfinished work. Yet, the tempered steel tip never penetrated the facial skin of the unconscious Mauro. Instead, Regan allowed the moments to pass and to ease the beast within, the beast that wanted to rip the face off its boney mount and consume it in anger. Maybe it was because Mauro was unconscious that the desires of Regan went unquenched. Something in his soul would not let him attack the prone figure and he was not sure if it was the remnants of his human being or the demon within wanting to wait to see the facial contortions as each wound was inflicted. He pulled the knife away from Mauro's face before he changed his mind, sheathed it silently and stood up.

Watson was already back on his feet and he could see Regan's chest expand, drawing in air to expel the sense of uncertainty that leaked from his very being. He approached Regan carefully and put his hand on his shoulder, gently turning him around.

"We had better get out of here. People will be coming soon and we need to go."

Just as the words left his mouth he turned at the noise of screeching tyres as Piero raced the van through the blown gates. In the minutes that had passed, with the death of Izzo and the capture of Gasco, they had forgotten about Piero and the van. Now he was here, things seemed to balance back in their favour.

Piero stopped the van feet from the smouldering Mercedes and jumped out. He did not flinch at the sight of Izzo's body but, instead, he opened the van and lifted the remains into the back, gently. There would be a time for mourning the dead and, unfortunately, Izzo was not the first brother-in-arms whose dead weight he had lifted. Once he had the body secured into place, he patted the shoulder and whispered "Sleep well, Donato." That was all he had to say.

Regan and Watson appeared with another body, this one not yet a corpse, and Piero helped bind and load him. He listened to Watson's explanation of who the new passenger was and, while loading him in through the door, accidently kneed Mauro into the ribs. Twice.

Piero saw that Regan had slipped into silence and decided not to push any buttons. He knew that the death of Izzo, however it had happened, would weigh heavily on his soul and so he remained silent.

All three loaded quickly into the van, Regan in the back both as a protector for the remains of Izzo and a guard of what would become remains in the near future. Piero gunned the engine and they were away at speed. They were little over half a mile away when the night sky lit up behind them. Piero's handiwork and detonated and leveled the buildings.

Marco Gasco was lying on his bed staring through the ceiling in thought. His mind was restless, moreso than usual, as it attempted to organise the tumbling thoughts scattering across his mind's eye. He had given orders that he was not to be disturbed for the rest of the evening and he fully had the intention to lie on his bed until sleep crept up and dulled his urges.

When everything is right it is a sure sign that something is going to go wrong. Not so much Murphy's law but an interpretation a little more severe as it taunted those who felt everything was going well, and that maybe they were untouchable, high in the ivory tower of success and power. Now, however, Marco knew that things had changed in the last number of weeks and he was finding it hard to identify the how and the why. Just a few short weeks ago all was in order; drugs, gambling, women and a number of other illicit activities were running at a very high profit versus the risks attached. His captains and lieutenants were beholden to him, though honor and through the lucrative nature of the business but now, it seems, they had abandoned him. Obviously, not by choice, as they had been, carefully and without doubt, picked-off one by one. Leaving the "business" without permission, even in death it seemed, was an act of betrayal in Marco's books.

Ale's death was possibly the result of a simple mugging on the beach but he was not convinced anymore because of the disappearances of the others. The death of Antonio, in clear view of more than fifty patrons in the restaurant that he owned, through various slights of his investor's financially magic fingers, was the first real shock he had endured. Antonio was a clear message that someone was after him. Maybe not him, but his organisation. For all the security he had and the thousands he spent getting the police interview details of all those who had been present in the restaurant at the time of the shooting, he was unable to get a description of the killer. If he were to chase the cumulative result of the interviews, he would be looking for a six-foot tall white man who may have been a woman with black hair and may have been about five feet five inches. How could a killer walk into the restaurant, kill Antonio, turn on his heels and walk out without anyone getting a clear look? It was nonsense.

Marco had not read the reports meticulously enough. If he had, he would have seen that nearly all the patrons had mentioned that there was a shattering of crystal a second before the shots were fired, drawing the attention away from the killer, and that the internal and external cameras, while untouched, had failed to record an hour each side of the killing. Credibility and Cinderella had worked together on that one and yet nobody, not the police nor the dead man's colleagues, had questioned why that had happened.

He was now wondering if something had happened at Mauro's compound and mentally flicked through the incidents of the past year in his mind to see did anything jump out. Each incident that did alert him involved Russians and Albanians, neither gang type a breed of lunatics to be picking a fight with. However, all of those incidents involved minor members of the respective crews, men who had money but no clout. Why would they start attacking the hand that fed them the women and drugs that they craved in the compound? No answers were forthcoming and nor was sleep. It was a frustrating attempt at sleep and so he rolled over onto his stomach to reach the figurine of the child ballerina on his bed-side desk. Within the base of the statuette, he kept a small number of powerful sleeping tablets and he know he needed one now. He needed to rest and to stop thinking about the cloud that was closing in on his organisation. Sipping from the glass of grappa he had taken to his room, he knocked back two of the tablets, lay back and awaited their welcomed numbness.

As he waited, coaxing the timid desire to relax, he felt his head and eyes become physically heavy. Sleep was coming but it was interrupted by a fading though that suddenly tried to fight through the blur. She had said that her brother would come. What if this was all to do with that journalist bitch that he and his brother had violated, in more ways than one. What was the name she had screamed as she died. His mind was numbing yet the answer was floating there in front of his eyes. Just before falling asleep it had all become clear to him. All the deaths, the misfortunes the business had encountered, could they possibly be attributed to one man, the brother of that foolish girl they had killed. What on earth was that name, his mind queried as he fell asleep. He saw the name as he fell asleep and in that moment, fifty miles away under the pallid light of a late moon, the self same brother of that girl was dancing a knife around the face of Mauro, his own brother.

Moving bodies is not as hard as people make it out to be. It is only a difficult task when care is required. When you have no feeling whatsoever for the state of the body, alive or dead, that you are moving, then a few bumps, bangs and bruises are the price one pays for the swift movement of an unconscience man from the ground to the van, out of the van and into a secure building. Mauro Gasco, if anyone cared to check, would have required fifteen stitched to his head alone, the rest of his body would require morphine.

Watson was wary of what was going to happen. The trip back in the van was tense, the air filled with a troubled silence as each mind screamed silently at the horror within the van. Donato's body was covered in a heavy tarpaulin while Mauro, bound and gagged, was tied to the read door in a way that would ease his removal from the van but ensure that he was unable to touch, accidently or otherwise, the remains of Donato Izzo. Regan was adamant about that, under no circumstances were the two to be in contact, the body of Izzo was damaged enough without soiling it by having it in physical contact with Mauro.

A man once said, "It's nothing personal, just business." Such sentiments are suitable for men of power and position in society, like the Godfather was, but it is different for mere mortals. Those who feel anger at injustice feel the desire for revenge but also feel the tangled knot of emotion that tightens around the neck of one's mind, cutting the flow of oxygen to the cortex of reason within the brain. Contrary to what the Italians say, revenge is a dish best served at any time of the day or night; a day after the incident or many years later. The release from the binds of revenge is mentally and emotionally orgasmic, shuddering the whole body to a point of climax that mirrors the cessation of life for the target of those vengeful urges. It is then, therefore, not only a most business-like activity to hunt your prey, but also the most personal and intimate of human relationships outside of lovemaking.

Jack Regan knew that the Godfather had it all wrong and that the son, Michael, had it right – everything is personal. Emotions flow like water in the soul that is light of spirit. In a body wracked by anger and desire for revenge, emotions trickle to the cracks and crevices of the mind, of the heart and of the spirit, slowly drowning them in sticky tar-like feelings of inhuman desire. The desire, at first, is planted seed-like by the very incident that becomes the focus of the vengeful. That seed can grow, or it can die of malnourishment. But, in the souls of men who have lost loved ones, the soil is fertile and the dark rains plentiful. The seed, unaware of what its existence means, spreads a filament of roots stretching into the physical being while the first green shoot of growth bursts forth to the source of its sun-like energy – the mind.

The nourishing rains of anger and desire feed the young shoot and make it stronger; the roots dig deeper giving themselves a true hold in the body and mind of the vengeful. Externally, the vengeful man's demeanour sours the air that he breaths with anger and frustration until that air is cleared by the fresh breeze of understanding. It is with understanding that the vengeful man knows what is to be done and sets his mind and body to task. The mind plots and the body prepares physically for what is to come. When the time comes for the prepared man, the results are physically challenging and mentally destructive.

In some men, the time to plant and grow the seed of revenge can take years. In Regan, the whole natural cycle had occurred when he pulled the sheet back and uncovered the face of his dead sister. As for the mental and physical demands, he had killed before. He was good at it.

Mauro awoke to the annoying buzz of the blue neon light above his head. He was face down on a wooden table and bolted upright with the realisation of the one thing that frightened him in this world. His brother was not with him.

Mauro was the weaker of the twins but nobody but his brother realised that. Mauro was the protected one and in that way he was his brother's weakest link. Now more than ever that was true to fact.

He settled back into his chair and tried to figure out what had happened but nothing would clear the fog of his mind. In the shallow blue light he could see a figure sitting before him but he did not recognise the face. He felt that it must be a police officer judging by the serious demeanour. He decided to talk.

'So?'

'What?' The reply seemed distracted and uninterested.

'Am I under arrest?'

'Why would that be?' Again, total disinterest.

'Well, this is a police station. Am I under arrest?'

'You are wrong.'

Marco's eyes began to focus more and he saw that behind the man was a video camera perched on a tripod. The red led light showed that it was recording the proceedings. Silently, he thought that this was a good sign as the police had to video each interrogation. That would give him time to stall before his lawyer arrived.

'I have nothing to say until my lawyer comes. I know my rights.'

'Yes, you have rights.' The voice sneered at him barely controlling a laugh.

'Yes, rights, I have rights like any other suspect. You cannot force me to speak.' The words sounded unconvincing even as he spoke them.

'You are going to speak, you are going to scream and you are going to die. All of that will happen in the next few minutes and your brother will see it all.' There was no emotion in the voice and no visible change to the face that now smirked at him.

'You are a police officer. You cannot speak to me like this!'

'Get tough with me then. Show me how fucking tough you really are. One on one if you wish. Actually, no, me on you and show me how tough you really are when you are tortured.'

Fear began to ferment in the pit of Mauro's stomach. The man in front of him had not moved a muscle except his mouth and that was enough to frighten Marco.

'What do you mean? What the hell have I ever done to you?'

'Physically? Nothing.'

'Well, what then? Why am I here?'

'To pay.' Still no physical reaction.

'For what?' The first strains of anger burst from Marco's mouth.

'A sister, a mother and a daughter.'

Marco looked into the eyes of his accuser and saw nothing yet he knew that he was staring at a dormant volcano of anger.

'I have no idea what you are talking about. I really don't.'

'No? OK, let me give you a hint.' Regan burst from his seat and buried his right fist below the left eye of the target of hate.

Outside, in another room, Watson watched the live footage with Izzo. He knew that he was never again going to see such cruelty yet his eyes would not move from the footage.

The effect of the punch was more than was expected as it caved in the cheekbone and snapped the lower structure of the eye socket. Such was the force of the blow that the eyeball was incapable of remaining in its natural position and instead it popped out and dangled on the shattered cheekbone. The scream of pain was muffled by incomprehension and flowing blood.

Regan fell back into his chair and heaved deeply in an attempt to draw air into his lungs and focus on the task at hand.

'Any idea yet?'

Mauro's head was spinning and the realisation that his left eye was no longer in his socket had not yet registered. He pain had not yet overcome the multitude of questions running through his mind.

Regan raised himself from his chair and walked over and gripped Marco's head with his right hand, holding it back by the ponytail. The dangling eye was a distraction but he made sure that it was seen on camera long enough for the effect to be recorded before he scooped it up with his left hand and pushed it back into its socket. The screaming began.

'Come on,' he teased, 'really, no idea yet?'

Mauro had no reply. Regan had more visual aids for his student.

'Let's try this. I know this will help.' The silk shirt, now drenched in sweat, was ripped open and the black matt of a beautifully sharpened combat knife swept through the air with a faint whistle and sliced easily through the muscular side of the writhing Mauro. In an instant a mound of flesh splattered onto the table in full view of the camera and the knife slid easily back into its sheath on Regan's hip.

'You have to have guessed by now, Mauro!'

He did. He had the answer to pass the exam.

'Jack?' The questioned answer hobbled from his broken face into the air and slid into the ears of his attacker.

'Yes. I am Jack.'

Now it all became clear to Mauro. The girl had said he would come and now he was here. She said that he was death and he felt that at least she had died telling the truth. He was replicating the wounds that he and Marco had inflicted onto the girl. He was exacting a perfect revenge and all that awaited him was a knife through the lower chin and into his brain. Oh, the relief of death was close. It wasn't.

Regan ripped off the rest of Mauro's shirt, threw it on the table and reached for his knife again. Now, standing behind Mauro and with his face to the camera, he spoke in a balanced and careful voice that belied the emotions that lurked beneath his skin.

'Marco, I am going to torment your brother just so you can see it. I will kill him but I will take pleasure in doing it slowly. You may not have felt anything when you killed my sister but you will feel this.'

In the next room Watson and Piero shared horrified looks. Piero had already vomited and Watson was not far away from the same gut reaction. Yet worse was to come, the anger was now off its leash and free to attack within the confines of the four walls. Death was not going to come easy for Mauro Gasco.

Taking a clump of hair in his left hand, Regan drew back Mauro's head and with swift pecking-lick movements, peppered the face with shallow stab wounds, around the cheeks, across the forehead and on the chin. Blood was dribbling gently out of the wounds and the effect on Mauro's features, and spirit, was horrifying. And yet worse was coming.

None of these actions were pre-meditated, Regan just let his anger flow and it flowed like torrents of water from a burst dam, powerfully and with only the direction that gravity would allow. Gravity, in this instance, was the weight of his mind balanced on the will of his heart and now, with nothing in his way to stop the excesses of anger, he reefed a clump of the once beautifully oiled hair and, with one precise glancing sweep of the blade, he removed the front portion of skin, little more than the size of a business card, hair included, from above Mauro's forehead.

Watson could not fathom what the young man had just done. He had scalped a man. *What is he? This is not right.*

Regan threw the bloody mass of scalp at the video camera and then, taking a deep breath, inserted the knife carefully into the skin that was stretched over the lower spine on Marco's back and began to pull it upwards, slicing a bloody trail the length of the spine until he reached the nape of his neck. The spine poked through the bloody musculature like a series of hatching chickens. Watson looked away from the screen.

'Half of my revenge has been realised. Your brother is about to die.' With those words Regan inserted his fingers under the flesh and through the muscles that protected the spine. The fingers and thumb met in a solid grip just as Marco began to writhe and scream and Regan jerked the spine to the left and then to the right. Marco's body began to convulse, a puppet whose string master had decided to give way to lunacy, his mouth shearing open in a noiseless scream, as a child informed of a parent's death. Then, with a swift jerk backwards, it was over. The spinal cord was broken and Mauro was dead.

Regan removed his hand from his puppet's back and grabbed the shirt from the table and wiped his hands with a look of disgust on his face.

'Marco, your brother just soiled himself. Did you not teach him how to hold it in?' There was no look of satisfaction, no joy or no hate. Just a plain, inquisitive look into the camera.

'Oh, one more thing.' Regan took the knife and pulled Marco's body back upright into the chair and, staring into the lens once more, drove the blade up through the chin and into the brain. There was no discernible increase in Regan's breathing, no flash of anger in the eyes staring into the camera, just calm, focused efficiency. Then his words, carried on a voice so commanding, penetrated the camera lens.

'I don't care about life. Not mine, not your brother's, not those of your fucking dead henchmen. But know this, I care about yours. I care about it because it is going to be my greatest prize, my most splendid death.'

Watson was now frightened. He was now assisting in something that had gone to far. He understood that killing Marco and Mauro were to be a part of what he had promised to help Jack Regan complete. What he did not sign-up for was the release of a demonic presence into Italian society. He ought to have figured it was going too far when he saw what Regan had done to the young men in the park. Alarm bells had rang but his hatred of rapists and, he figured, the numbness the image of the men speared to the trees caused, combined to subdue the need to question the actions of the man he had promised to protect.

Now, having seen the torture and slaughter of Mauro Gasco, and having heard Regan promise that the needless killings would stop, Watson began to feel that the young soldier had slipped to far from any level of humanity that would help him get past all of the killing that he had been involved in. There was no going back after what had been done to Mauro. No man could reconcile his mind, or his soul, to such actions, regardless of what was done to a family member. In those moments of madness, Jack Regan had turned from a professional soldier into a man who killed. In society, they are seen as two different breeds of men. One breed maintains the status of man amongst his peers, the other is a killer of men and treated as an outcast, a rabid dog that is to be feared.

Watson stood motionless when Regan came out of the room. Regan did not look at the two men who were waiting for some kind of comment. He walked to the sink and turned on the hot tap. Rolling up his bloodied sleeves, Regan picked up the unused block of scented soap and proceeded to wash the blood from his hands and arms.

38

Pass-the-parcel

Marco sipped gently from his glass of chilled grappa and stared thoughtlessly through the window. His eyes hovered over the flower-beds, drifting towards the gates where a small flock of doves had landed and we now picking needlessly at the gravel, endlessly foraging. He missed his brother. He was concerned that he had not heard from his brother and that worried him. He missed him and, with everything that had happed to his organisation over the recent days, was concerned that the dark shadow that had taken the other men had not visited his brother. The connection to his brother was a natural requirement even for the man who had, through his violence, lost his connection to society and now, like an injured lion, wished to to be alone with nature and leave the pride behind.

The heart-jolting screech of rubber fighting its connection with asphalt was matched by the the sudden, unified flight from danger of the flock of doves as the metal gates to the drive were forced into a tangled flight of their own. Time slowed to a treacle drip as Marco continued to stare, not having time to react but his eyes now recording what he was seeing.

Jack left the driving to Piero and he stayed in the back of the heavy, refrigerated van with the corpse. He was now in total control now that the demons of revenge had been somewhat sated. He was now a soldier again, a soldier primed for a short, sharp shock to the enemy - what remained of the enemy.

Piero opened the hatch between cabin and container and calmly said 'Thirty seconds.' With Piero driving, than meant twenty-eight seconds. Jack was ready.

The gates had just landed and the doves thirty feet off the ground when the van slowed to a halt on the gravel. It didn't skid, shake or jolt. It eased to a halt at the hands of an experienced driver who knew that he had to count to thirty and drive away, with or without a cargo. He engaged first gear, kept the clutch floored and revved the van's highly tuned engine to five thousands revs. His mind was already on twenty-eight.

Marco's mind had not found a gear capable of being engaged and his hands dropped to his side, the crystal glass of grappa splintering on the polished oak floor. He almost knew what he was going to see an instant before he saw it. The doors of the van sprang open and a body was kicked out onto the gravel. It was his brother. The distance was not too great for him not to recognise the shock of black hair but it was, thankfully, distance enough that he did not see the extent of his injuries. That illusion allowed him the drowning man's grip on the straw of hope sprouting from the bank of his mind.

Jack's mind was on twenty-five when he crouched over the body and it was not clear what he was doing. Piero was watching via the rear-view mirror waiting for all Hell to break loose and still counting down.

Two gang members came running from the right-hand side of the house to see what the commotion was. They were not soldiers so they did not automatically draw their weapons on the first inkling of danger. Even if they had, it would not have saved them. As they came into view they saw the van, the damaged gates and a black-clad figure crouching over a body. Their minds were not ready for what happened. They had been warned to keep alert, to watch for anything strange but they were not warned of a direct attack. Simple men follow simple orders to the letter. Soldiers improvise and look beyond the orders.

Regan knew they were coming. It wasn't a sixth sense, nor a gut feeling. It just made sense that someone would come and that whoever did come, they would not be friendlies. They would be targets and would be employed as such.

On eighteen seconds, Regan maintained his crouch position and pulled his MP5 around from the hanging position on his side. One fluid motion and the weapon was at eye level at which time it had alread relieved two rounds of their Jacketed boredom. The second pair followed quickly and it all sounded like a slippered toddler gingerly walking down a wooden stairs, tap, tap.....tap, tap. Two men dead. Sixteen seconds.

Marco felt his scream before he heard it. It welled in his belly before scalding his throat with the power of its release. Anger, shame, frustration and a peppering of fear all mingled in the tones of that scream and the security men in the house, more experienced than those outside, knew what the scream meant. They were, once again, under attack and it was time for them to change the wind of fortune which had been at the back of their attacker in recent weeks. They, numbering eight, burst out the main door, two going left, two right and four straight towards the van. Twelve seconds seemed like eons to Piero.

Jack's eyes tracked left and right in an instant and his mind made the decision to target the four. The others were moving to take position and that, in the seconds that Jack had, meant that they were not going to be in the fight. The toddler had mastered the steps, tap, tap..tap, tap..tap, tap..tap,tap. It was not time to show his shooting skills so all shots went to chest. All chests went to ground. Eight seconds left and Piero was rapidly casting is glances from right to left, ensuring the road was clear, and from wing mirror to wing mirror viewing the calm stream of death going on behind his concern.

Jack's mind gently urged him to go and he did. He lowered his weapon a fraction to see where the other four were. The two on the left were positioning themselves behind a glasshouse and the other two were clawing along the high garden wall. Neither were of concern as they were not going to have a drop on him within the next couple of seconds. Five to be precise.

He lowered his weapon and was about to turn and jump towards the van when he saw the figure standing at the window and five seconds turned to eternity. The figure was the surviving half and Regan's weapon was raised and fired in an instant. Two twisting, tumbling pieces of lead careened towards their target at 400 m/s just as two different pieces of lead, of similar parentage, cracked past Jack's head. Three seconds.

Marco did not even flinch when the bullets hit the reinforced glass panes. He just stood and stared in bleak shock and admiration. Six more of his men gone. Did that bastard think he was able to produce men like he produced money? The window panes cracked but held fast and Marco knew he was in no danger.

Regan heard the engine rev harder and knew it was seconds to go before they had to move. His muscles tensed, ready to spring at the tail-gate of the truck, but he took one last second to stand and stare at the man he needed to kill ensuring, despite the distance between them, that Marco knew who he was and could see his calmness of presence. In times of great turmoil those who hold their calm, keeping their own personal turmoil on a tight leash, ooze a sense of power and determination which is admirable to all, appealing to some and, for just a few, it is terrifying. In this instance, it was clear who the few were and Marco was one of that few.

Regan turned on his heels and leapt into the back of the truck just as Piero's mind said 'One' and his foot hit the floor. In an instant of screeching rubber and flying pebbles and dust, the truck fish-tailed away from the gates and hurtled down the road. Part one of the mission was complete and part two was just about to begin.

Marco stared out the window and, for the first time in his life, he did not know what to do. Worse still, he felt completely powerless and in need of guidance. He wanted to step away from the window and sit down, take a second to gather his thoughts. He needed to gather his thoughts but he also needed to go to his brother's corpse. That was the most important thing to do as it would steel his resolve and shake a bit of life back into his shaken spirit. He could see the surviving men of his crew approach the body, slowly as they were still in awe of him even though he was dead. One moved closer as the others eased their eagerness to see the body and Marco looked on. It should be him reaching down to check his brother, not one of the security.

Fabio wanted to show Marco that he was worthy of trust within the organisation and thought that by showing due respect to the corpse of the brother, he would be seen as an automatic choice for future easement up the chain of command. He kneeled down on the rough gravel and reached under the dead man's neck in order to raise the body. It seemed like the right thing to do, check the wounds, find a pulse, maybe hear him breathing. Raising the corpse a fraction released the pressure switch on the flat explosive back taped to the corpse.

Marco decided to move. Fabio was not the person he wanted to have comforting his dead brother. He knew he was dead even if Fabio seemed blind to that fact. Either way, Marco decided that he should be the one comforting his brother's corpse and not Fabio. He glanced out the window just as he was stepping away from it and had pulled focus from his brother, Fabio and the remaining bodyguards were engulfed in a hail of steel ball bearings.

The pressure patch on the device worked as expected. Only one in ten thousand would fail and this, as evidenced, was not one of them. Once the pressure was released, the small charge generated enough of a spark to assist the detonation process within the five pounds of C4 and ball-bearing mix. The scattering balls cared not for what they hit, cared not if the hit anything at all. Ball bearings just don't care, they kill.

The re-enforced windows flexed with the explosion and held against the barrage of metal that had cut a swath through man, vegetation and concrete. Fabio and the corpse would require gifted forensic technicians to separate the parts, the remaining three guards were most definitely dead but somewhat more intact than those closest to the detonation, but only somewhat. There would be no open coffins resulting from the afternoon's work.

Marco heard the dull, gentle thuds of the lead pieces falling from the shallow resting places in the glass down to the patio. His mind fought the physical desire to retch and, for the moment, he won that battle. Looking at the window, cracked and pitted by both bullets and ball-bearings, his eyes drifted to the patio outside where the rested on one, single ball-bearing roling to a gentle halt. It left a visible trail of blood. Marco vomited.

Piero braked hard half a kilometer down the road and pulled into a lay-by at the pre-determined point. There, breathing heavily, he sliped the gear stick to neurtal and took his feet away from the pedals. The engine purred contently. Jack was staring out the back of the truck and mentally preparing for round two when the police car skidded to a halt behind the truck, feet from the door. He smiled.

Watson jumped out and threw a uniform up to Jack who was already out of his Nomex suit and ready to change. Piero came around from the front and gathered his uniform from Watson, leaped into the back of the truck and changed quickly; his shaking hands were little hindrance to his actions. Once done, both jumped out and straightened themselves, checking each other's uniform for any major deficiencies. None were found.

'Time to roll,' Watson proclaimed.

Piero jumped into the back behind the driver's seat where Watson was settling in. Regan ran up the embankment to the right side of the truck and took a quick scan of the area. No one was visible. He slid down the embankment and sliped into the car beside Watson who was revving the engine ready to move.

'What was that about?'

'Checking for kids. You never know when and where they turn up?'

Watson floored the accelerator and the car sped off without fuss while beside him Regan flicked the safety switch on the detonator he had removed from his side-pocked. He depressed the red button.

Looking in the rear-view mirror, Watson saw the truck lift off the ground as the charge of C4 that had been limpeted to the fuel tank erupted in an impressive ball of flame. He looked over at the grinning Regan.

"See, no kids, Steve!"

Watson shook his head and continued to drive, not knowing whether to laugh or cry at Regan's concern for collaterals.

39

Aftermath

For the first time in his life, Marco Gasco felt that his back was firmly against the wall and that his options were disappearing at the hands of a murderous Houdini. It had all happened so quickly that he had not time to remove himself from his high horse of self-belief to deal with actions on the ground, actions that had now impacted his ivory tower and left him without family. Who was killing his men and why had they attacked his house? It was not a little disconcerting that it was so well planned and precisely carried out. He would not have had the control to walk away after a set time, but these men did and did it like soldiers. If that were so, if they were indeed soldiers, why were they attacking him? It did not make sense.

The chime of the doorbell interrupted his thought process and he lifted himself from his chair and walked to the door to see who was calling. He was not concerned about being attacked again as he had beefed up his security and only those checked at the gate would get through. He calmly opened the door and smiled at the young UPS deliver girls who was standing there waiting to complete her day's work.

"Package for you, Sir. Please sign here." She offered him the plastic stylus to mark the little screen on here electronic confirmation set.

"Thank you, young lady," he smiled, falsely, as he made his mark. "How do you know it is for me?"

"The client said that you would be tall, with a ponytail and that you would look..." her voice tailed off as though she did not want to finish the reply. She did not feel comfortable at the address and the size of the man and his lost demeanour troubled her.

"What? Tell me," he ordered, more gently that he intended.

"Sad. The man said you would be sad. I do not know why he said that, but it seems that he was right."

Marco opened his wallet and took two one hundred Euro notes out and held them up for the girl to see. "Did the man know that my brother was dead?"

"He didn't say. I have to go now." She felt unsafe and knew that she wanted to leave.

"Who was he? The man who sent this?"

"He said that if you asked, I was to say that he is a brother. I am not sure what that is supposed to mean."

Marco gave the girl the two notes and thanked her. She left quickly.

Marco sat for two hours looking at the package and sensing that he did not was to know what was within. He fingered the edge of the package, lifting it two inches off the table before twirling it around and looking at the address on the back. It said "J.R, Rome." Who was J.R and what was he sending to him. He had had enough of the game and he pulled a small pocketknife from his jeans and slid the small blade into the plastic wrapping. It was just to light to be a bomb, or so he believed.

It was an SD card. No note, no card, nothing but the small SD card. He picked it up, sniffed it, not knowing why he did, and rolled it between his fingers as he thought of what the content was. He was unable to think of anything but figured that the contents of the card were going to be some feeble attempt to extort money from him. Pictures with prostitutes? Who cared? He was not married and he had no boss to report to. He stood up and walked to his desk and slid the card into the side as he switched the laptop on. It took a few seconds for the software to run and then the video played. He watched, eyes fixed to the screen as his brother was slaughtered before him and then the words of his brother's killer;

"I don't care about life. Not mine, not your brother's, not those of your fucking dead henchmen. But know this, I care about yours. I care about it because it is going to be my greatest prize, my most splendid death."

Marco felt his chest tighten and his head felt light. That was the "Brother" the delivery girl spoke of. He sat back into his chair and tried to breath deeply but each breath was a struggle. He pulled the SD card from the side of the computer and snapped it in half. Nobody would ever need to see that again, and he did not was it in the hands of his enemies. Mauro's death was a personal event and not one that would be released to the ever curious public.

He stood up and walked to the drinks cabinet. It was early in the day but how many days start with the image of your brother beings slaughtered like a pig and, as well as that, he needed to ease his fear. It was a simple thing to admit, though he would not say it aloud, he was afraid. That man, Jack Regan, the man who's name was screamed by that fool of a girl they had killed had truly come to make him pay for her death. What had she said, while bleeding and dying at their hands? *"Death. Jack is death, and he will come for you. He will come for all of you."* Now he was here, in Italy, in his town, killing his family and friends and all he could do was to go to the drinks cabinet and pour himself a large brandy. Not the response he was hoping for but he hoped the brandy would calm his fears a little and allow him to think of a response to these events.

The second brandy allowed him, he believed, to consider his options in a much better light. Who was this Regan? One man cannot cause such damage so he had to have someone working with him. Obviously, there was a driver, the one who drove the van through his gates to deliver the body of his brother. There had to be others, hadn't there? The questions kept rising, bubbles in a pond of doubt, and Marco did not have all of the answers. He had very few answers if he disallowed the bravado the brandy was allowing him to feel. Jack Regan was a soldier, that he was sure of but that did not mean that he was going to be easy to catch. The attack on the compound showed that Regan was not acting by himself and that those working with him were skilled operators. And then, in that moment, the crux of his whole existance came crashing through the blur of brandy. Why would he even try to catch this man knowing that he would probably fail, and die, in the process. Why not retire, enjoy the wealth he had built up over the years? Disappear from Italy and set up a new home on some small island, so long as it was not Ireland. He allowed himself a small smile at that, acknowledging finally that dealing with Kathy Regan in the manner in which he and his brother had done, had been stupid. He was paying the price now and, knowing that Jack Regan was going to come after him, put his position into the headlights of a stark reality. It was time to retire from life in Italy. It would not be difficult, his key men and his brother were dead, his organisation, in effect, crippled. He would take the money and run and let Regan do what he wanted.

He woke on the couch three hours later, a dull thumping headache announcing the arrival of an early afternoon hangover. Drinking in the morning was not something the clean-living Marco would have been accustomed to and he angrily faced the inevitable because of his morning triste with brandy. However, his mood had changed and he no longer felt the need to leave Italy, nor to ignore that some fucker from Ireland had decided to attack all that he held dear. It was not the death of his brother that had steeled what had earlier been a willow-like spine. He was angry that his empire had been attacked and he wanted to fight back. It mattered not that he would be facing a man whose ability was multiples of his own but he had money and resources to call upon. He did not believe that Jack Regan had the same fortune.

Watson sat at the table with the others but his mind was elsewhere. He was disturbed in himself and did not like feeling as he did. It did not help that he could not contact his wife. She understood that his work meant that he travelled a lot and was not always contactable. She was a clever woman and knew some years ago that her husband was no more a lawyer than she was an astronought. It did trouble her, of course, but she had become quietly accepting of Watson's work knowing that it probably made the world a safer place. She did not like the nightmares and tried to be there for him when they visited him during the nights. She never spoke of them to him but was always hoping that he would open up and speak of them. Regardless of what happened, or what was contained in those dreams, she would be there for him. For that reason, Watson was never distracted while on duty. He knew his wife loved him and he loved her equally in return. Being married to an agent was not something a partner knowingly entered into but it did seem to Watson that his wife knew and accepted what he did for a living. It made dealing with Regan a little easier to face.

The reality was, however, that he could not deal with Regan. The man slid from sanity to something so terrifying that insanity was not a deep enough word to describe it. How he had killed Mauro was beyond comprehension and he did not want to deal with that Regan again. It seemed as though he was physically steaming when he came from the room having killed Mauro and few, if any, of the eyes in the room met his glare. Watching him calmly washing his hands unnerved Watson because torture, in his mind, was an action of last resort. He agreed with its necessity, it was a practical need when time was of the essence but in Regan's dealing with Mauro Gasco, there was no need for it. Or was there? It was not his sister who had been raped, tortured and killed, was it? It was not possible for him to understand the feeling of loss that Regan must be feeling but was that a good enough reason for a man to lose his sense of humanity? Breaking a man's spine with a bare, bloodied hand was just wrong. It just seemed that each level, as it was passed, brought new and more evil ways of dealing with his enemies that even the most imaginative mind could possibly hope to create.

He looked around the rest of the room and saw discomfort in the eyes of the others, all except Piero Bassi. He was a good man but Watson felt that life had dealt him similar cards as Regan had received and that his mind was, to say the very least, a little unhinged. He seemed to revel in poking the bear that was Regan and did so without a response. Regan liked him, it was obvious, but he could not tell whether it was because Piero was a Marine or because his life had been ruined by horror too. Those whose lives had been impacted by the evils of others were bound by a thin thread of reality and linked by a ferous chain of rage. Watson could not help thinking that without the influence of Izzo and Watson, the other two may have already gone on a bigger killing spree.

It was hard to describe the feeling but a weight had been lifted from his troubled mind. He thought the feeling must be similar to that the wives of fishermen, who have gone missing at sea, feel when a body is finally found. There is relief, a body to give a burial to and sadness that a life has been given to the sea. That was the strange cocktail of emotions that Regan now felt. Of course, his sister was still dead but there was a true sense of physical relief that he had killed Mauro.

He thought about it for a moment and allowed his soul to chastise his inner thoughts. He had not killed Mauro, he had brutally slaughtered him in a manner which was inhuman, animalistic in its savagery and an affront to any sense of socially contrived justice. That was it, wasn't it? He was expected to live within the norms of a society that had blended itself into an muddied pond of social inequality, and from inequality came injustice. He was not considering the injustice of hungry and sick children, no, that was not something he felt he could fix. He considered it an injustice that the society had removed the right of man, him, to impose his Darwinian justice onto those who attacked him or his family. It was how he considered it, adapt and develop to the surroundings and improve to survive, even if it is to the detriment of others. What he had done to Mauro was his natural response, but not something that he could argue in a court of law. That was why he had fit so well into the Legion and into Dark Eye. Politics, and its practitioners, did not have a say on how the Unit responded to terrorism. If terrorists wanted to blow people up because of their beliefs, then they had to expect that good men, with beliefs equally intense, would come looking for them. Society gave terrorists the chance to hide behind a structured set of human rights that disallowed the rights of those who were attacked. Dark-Eye was tasked to kill the monster and it worked very well. However, in killing monsters, we have to become monsters ourselves. There were no answers for Regan except when he went back to basics. Hurt me and I will hurt you, except my hurt is final.

"This might work in our favour," said Piero as he threw a newspaper onto the breakfast table. Regan looked at it and smiled back up at the Marine. The front page picture showed the smoking ruins of the Gasco compound under the headline "Who did it?" Regan glanced through the paragraphs and smiled easily as the journalist stomped through swamps of conjecture in an attempt to carry off a true journalistic scoop. In Regan's opinion, the journalist failed miserably, stating that the killings were the work of the Mafia.

"This will make the police look deeper into what is happening. If they do, then we will have more intelligence available to us."

"Fanetti did not cough-up Marco's back-up address. I didn't get it from the accountant either. Can we get it?" Regan was speaking while reading and did not see Izzo roll his eyes to Heaven.

"Sure, anything else?"

"Coffee?"

"Go fuck!"

40

The last three sips.

The intensity of the last few days had finally eased into an emotional coma for all of the men. Izzo's death had finally caught up with them, an added straw to the emotional back of an already tired camel. The U.S Army's creed of 'leave no man behind' was an honourable belief, a standard that soldiers have always sought to be true to. However, when the soldier is a policeman and his comrades are in-country killing people, and not themselves policemen, then bringing the body home is one thing, doing something Christian with the remains is a totally different problem.

Regan dealt with death on a different emotional plane to the others. He began to over-think the operation on the compound and measured the success of finally killing Mauro against losing Izzo. The loss, in real terms, was acceptable. The compound was flattened, a good number of the lieutenants were killed and the one of the Key Targets was taken. All of this for the loss of one man but that man represented an operational loss of twenty-five percent. That was not acceptable to Regan.

The union between the three didn't end as expected, not in any way that they thought it would end. Izzo was dead, and that was end enough for Watson and Piero. For Regan, however, the end was just a word, a beginning of one end and the start of another. Everything that culminated in death was an end and such instants never had beginnings. If he sat and considered how he was feeling and thinking, then he would realise that his thought process was flawed, and not the least bit confusing.

They sat at a table, three men in black suits under a warm sun and not a bead of heated sweat formed on either man. Yet, two of the faces had been streaked with salty tears not two hours before. Izzo's funeral was, in its honest intensity, a difficult thing for Piero and Watson to bear. They had stood well back in the crowd watching the procession of tears as the body of their fallen comrade was interred. The man's wife, family and friends shared their grief in a sumptuous meal of disbelief and sorrow. Piero, the scar-covered Marine who had seen, and felt it all, shrank as Izzo's uniformed colleagues fired over the coffin. Each crack of gunfire caused him to jolt, and each jolt pushed another tear down his scarred cheek, both eyes crying, only one producing tears. Watson stood behind and to Piero's left and had placed his hand firmly on the young man's shoulder and it was accepted. Some form of human touch always was at such times.

Regan behaved differently to the others. Again, as ever, he just blended into his surroundings and he was seen by Piero and Watson walking over to Izzo's wife and comforting her with words only she would hear. She stood back, removed her darkened glasses to look clearly at the man before her, nodded silently and then hugged him. A silent pact, the calling card of Jack Regan, had once again been created.

The table was silent, all three minds wandering in different directions and it was finally Piero who broke the silence.

"You have to tell me what you said to her?"

Regan looked up from his coffee and stared at Piero. The silence was taking the ghostly form of Izzo, the fourth seat at the table, and Regan needed to banish it and banish it quickly. He drew a deep breath and answered slowly.

"My sister had a child, Jack Regan. When her body was found Donato went to her appartment and found a frantic childminder there, worried out of her wits as to the whereabouts of the child's mother. Well, he took the child to social services, they had no where to put him and so he took him home to his wife. That is a very shortened version of what has happened. Now, with no husband and someone else's child to mind, I felt it necessary to tell her who I was and what I was doing."

"And you bloody told her that you were here killing her countrymen, resulting in the death of her husband and now she has to mind your nephew because you have a few more people to kill?" Watson's words were spat at Regan from grappa-moistened emotions.

Regan, in a exaggerated slow move of his hand, raised his cup to his lips once more and sipped gently. It was not clear to either of the two men at the table that he had made a significan advance in the management of his fury, for the first time in his life. Instead of launching himself at Watson, as every fiber in his muscles wanted to do, he sipped three times, two seconds between each sip, and then lowered the cup back onto the saucer. "Let me say this, and I shall say it once. Donato's death was real to me. That may mean nothing to the two of you, and I mean the reality of it to me not the death. I know you are hurting too. His death ranks only second to Kathy's death. It is ripping me apart because I know I am the cause and reason for it."

Watson did not let him finish what he felt was a prepared speech. "Enough," he whispered, the words as meek and beaten as he felt. "Enough, Jack." He drank the silence instead of the remnants of grappa in his glass and then continued, "I am not going to kill again. Not for you, for me, the Queen or anyone-fucking-else. I can't do it anymore and I don't know why I didn't stop before now. I owe you nothing, do I? I mean, how in God's name did I allow myself to get caught up in this except that I promised your Dad that I would find you and make you responsible for the future of that child. I can't remember signing-up for a killing spree, but I did, didn't I. And Piero and Izzo did the bloody same. What the fuck is wrong with us all?" Regan held the stare that Watson's emotions were balancing on and he did not speak. He knew that ranting was Watson's release and he let it run.

"I don't mind the killing," Piero waded into the mire.

"Well, that is your fucking problem then." Watson was deflating with every word and had hoped for some form of support from Piero.

"I don't mind the killing, Watson, because it is being done for something bigger that we are." Piero was measured in his response, knowing that Watson was angry and frustrated.

"You are, and always will be, a Marine, Piero. You do not have to keep killing in order to keep the uniform."

Piero wiped his hand wearily across his eyes and nodded in silent agreement. Watson had hit the nail on the head and the truth had splintered out.

Now, sitting at the table were three men, divided in their wishes and intentions but, of the three only one could continue with the killing.

"I have to go on." Regan was now sitting back in his chair, a look of tired understanding on his youthful face. "I have to go on because it is what I am. I need to finish this and then find my next war. I cannot ask you to continue and I do not want you to. Marco Gasco is the final target that I need to kill here and then I am gone."

"Where?" Watson asked with an expectant tilt of his head.

"I have a promise to fulfill in London. A promise I made to a man who wanted to kill me once."

A tired smile crossed Watson's face and a laugh almost bubbled out. "I cannot hold you to that promise, Jack. You would be killed before you got to the courthouse. What is worse, if they didn't succeed, then you would go on a killing spree in London to seek revenge and you would turn to me to help." He paused in thought for a moment and then continued, "And I would say yes, wouldn't I?"

Regan smiled at Watson and Piero and then eased himself from the chair. He stood for a moment, looking at each man, and then extended his hand to both. The both shook hands, firmly, with him understanding that he was walking away and did not want them to walk with him on the final battle of the Italian war.

"I am forever in your debt, gentlemen. The next time we meet, and I hope we do, it will be under different circumstances and maybe, I hope, I will be a better man." He turned and walked quietly away.

Watson looked at Piero and they both smiled a smile of relief. In essence, the hard part was over, they had ended the fellowship of death easier than they had figured. Watson had not expected to survive Italy but now he would be able to go home to his wife and what he hope was retirement from the Services. There could be no other outcome, really, because he had failed in his mission and did not want to be a spy anymore. Maybe it was time to go back and practice law. That idea made him laugh but at least he was laughing, and had an option. In some way, he knew that he was tied to Italy for the rest of his life and the hope of retiring in Tuscany, as his wife had hoped to do, was now a most definite no. Maybe France.

Piero sat back and watched the thought process working through Watson's head. He could see the first signs of relief on the man's face, a face so often laden with worry. He would be the only one left in Italy and he was not sure that it was a good idea for the time being. He had his handlers to answer to, and he was sure they would have questions as to why he disappeared for a while. A lot of people died while he was "missing" and the papers were already shouting about it. The handlers were smart folk, they could put two and two together. Whatever answer the came to, they would probably see fit to pull him in for questioning. Maybe a trip abroad was something he should give consideration to. He stood up too and stretched out his hand to Watson.

"You are a good man, Sir. You saved my life twice and I am grateful to you."

"Twice?" Watson asked confused.

"Jack Regan has gone to complete his mission without me. I think that counts as the second time."

Watson stood up and embraced the man. Their war was over and the parted as soldiers do when war ends, thankful to be alive and happy to be going home. The wounds would or would not heal, that was up to them.

41

How the end begins.

It was probably because he was so close to the finish that he finally allowed himself a second to breath. He was sitting in his room staring into the fireplace where a pile of documents was smoldering after the initial enthusiastic flame. Intent on leaving no further trace of their activities he had set about busying himself destroying the Gasco file and the copies of his plans from which they had worked. Everything else he needed to commit to memory was already stored, he was now like an athlete who had finished his final training session before the big race. He was ready.

Three days had passed since he had said goodbye to the others and there was a sense of loneliness that he was not accustomed to. It felt like a stranger in the room, a stranger that he did not feel comfortable with, nor to whom he wished to make an acquaintance. The connection to Watson, Piero and, of course, Izzo had become strong through the violent necessity of their fellowship and he missed the camaraderie. Watson, his very British wish to stick to the rules, Piero, the mirror opposite as he was Italian and Izzo, the Sicilian bull who could have, should have, become a staunch friend. Life had been taken in buckets in the recent days and there was nothing he could do to change that. However, he did intend, promise himself was a better way of putting it, to change. He was that one step away from the internal summit of hate that he was climbing and could almost taste the fresh air of freedom that killing Marco Gasco would bring. At least, that is what he tried to convince himself. He knew that once this was over, if he survived it, then he would probably find another war.

During the course of the previous three days, Regan had been busy organizing himself for the final kill. Finding Marco was not difficult, he knew where the back-up residence was, that was the last piece of information that Watson had gotten for him. However, getting to Gasco was going to be a different problem. Since Mauro had been killed Marco took to moving in a convoy of security and the number of men protecting his home had been visibly doubled. What he did not see worried him too as it was possible that Gasco had men protecting him and looking for Regan. As close to the summit as he was, he had to be ever more vigilant to stay alive. There was a precarious balance between success and failure at this stage, one that would be weighed in favor of Gasco's success if Regan dropped his guard.

Of course, Regan did not drop his guard. On the night that followed his goodbyes to the others, he managed to get within fifty feet of Marco's house and stayed there overnight, watching and listening to what was happening. On a number of occasions he saw Marco stand by the window with a drink in his hand. The warm light coming from his study adding a friendly aura to the image that Regan was looking at. He no longer had his sniper rifle and so the shot, as simple as it was, was not on. Would the bullet penetrate the glass? He was in no doubt that it would, but he wanted to kill Marco, not let a few ounces of hyper-fast lead do his work for him. He needed to get in close for the personal kill that he craved, one that let Marco know who was killing him and why. In addition, he just needed to kill him and had no more desire to torture anyone. It would be clean, simple kill.

The second night was no different. The security team had changed the patrol patterns from the night before and they had probably changed them from the previous night too. To that extent, they were good. He also noted that none of them smoked, or, if they did, they did not do it while on duty. Gasco was spending his security budget well. Regan knew that he needed something more than luck to get past the security men and figured that the on-site assault would be futile. He would watch some more and see if Gasco moved.

Gianni Vacarra had been driving for Marco Gasco for nearly five years and it was no lie that he loved his job. The hours were good, the money was better than he ever earned and generally the people he drove about were visitors collected from the airport and taken to the house or the compound. He did not like, however, his boss and detested his brother even more. For that reason, he was smiling at the moment because Mauro was dead and that Godforsaken compound was blown to smithereens. Of course he smiled internally and did not let anyone see that he was happy that the tide was turning against the Gascos. To be seen to be disloyal, well, it did not take much for one of the Twins to attack a worker for little more that spilling a coffee or speaking out of place. Gianni had no direct reason to hate the twins, nothing like some of the other men had, but he hated them nonetheless for what they represented. He should have walked away from the job but he had a wife and children who enjoyed the benefits that he took home. Yet, he felt troubled. Delivering people to that bloody compound meant that he was assisting in the Twin's misuse of young women. He was a father to two young girls and dreaded the time that they would begin dating, not to mention allowing his mind to consider what would happen to his girls if the Twins had their way with them. It made his conscience rest a little easier that Mauro was dead and that the compound was a smoking ruin. His conscience may have been eased, but his sense of manliness, of being a father, was impaired.

Gianni checked the schedule with the chief of security once more before leaving. He did not want to go home without being sure that Marco didn't need his services anymore that night. The schedule was checked, and then Marco was called and, as expected, he was free to go for the night but would be back for eight in the morning.

He replaced the set of keys on the board by the security desk and bid goodnight to the security men he could see. There were probably more of them than he could see, but that did not worry him. They seemed professional and did not treat him like dirt. He walked out the opened gates, they were due to be closed in twenty minutes, and began to walk down the road to where his car was parked with the others. He never liked to let his employer see him smoke so he waited until he walked a few more meters, just past the line of trees, before stopping to light his cigarette.

He drew deeply from the first spark from the tobacco and coughed his surprise when he was asked for one. One of the security staff had been walking on patrol behind him and took advantage of the slight cover given by the trees to sneak a smoke without the head of security seeing him.

"Thanks, I am on a double shift today and have not had a chance to smoke or take a piss." The guard took the offered cigarette, closed one eye before Gianni lit it, and then drew as deeply as Gianni did.

"Why did you wink at the lighter?" Gianni thought it looked funny and couldn't help himself from asking.

"Wink? Oh, no." The large man laughed quietly for a second before responding. "I closed one eye so that my night vision would not be totally ruined by the flame of the lighter. An old trick from the army and my officer there would have been just as unimpressed with my smoking on duty as the Big Man inside."

Gianni smiled and continued to smoke. "Are you all soldiers? Sorry, maybe I should not be asking."

"Hey, it is ok. We had you checked ages ago so you are not a problem. Yeah, most of us have a military background. At the moment, the closer you are to Marco, the further you are from the Italian military. Two of the guys are French. He really trusts nobody."

"After what happened at the compound, who would blame him!"

The guard turned slightly away from Gianni and unzipped himself. "Like I said, no time to smoke or piss, so I better take advantage of the situation."

Gianni laughed quietly as the guard relieved himself quietly into the bushes.

Regan closed his eyes as the urine splattered off the ground and then across his head and right shoulder. He did not breath, move or complain. He was in sniper mode and would not move for love nor money. Of course, in this situation neither love nor money included some big guy pissing on his head. Every cloud had a silver lining and he now knew, completely by accident, that the house was more protected that he had anticipated. Getting soaked in urine for that information, was worth it.

"Thank God for small mercies, Gianni, and thank you for the smoke." The guard zipped himself up and turned back to face Gianni. "I best get back on patrol before someone gets in and shoots Marco." He winked at Gianni, turned and walked back up the path.

"Prick," muttered Gianni as he pulled again on the cigarette. "Pity your boss wasn't in the compound with his fucking brother."

"What if he was?" The bodiless voice whispered carefully into Gianni's ear, just as a firm hand covered his mouth. He felt a knife slide gently into place under his right ear. "What if the brother was to die too, Gianni? Would that be a bad thing?"

Gianni did not know if the smell of urine had come from him. He was terrified in that moment and did not know what to say. He figured staying silent was a bad idea.

"I have two little girls. What the Twins do to women is wrong but I have never used violence against another human being before. I do not have it in me."

"I do." The words were softly spoken, whispering threads floating on the warm evening air.

"Are you the one who attacked the compound?"

"Don't worry about the compound. I want Marco."

"What's in it for me."

"Your daughters."

"You are not going to fucking touch my girls, do you understand?" He sounded almost believable.

"I have no intention of touching them, you fool. We took Intel from the compound. The Twins have your girls lined up for future use. It looks like you will be collecting men at the airport and delivering them to your daughters." Gianni nearly vomited at the news. "But I work for them. Why would they," he corrected himself mid-sentence, "he, do such a thing?"

"Why did Hilary climb Everest? Because it was there. Marco sees everything as a challenge. Your two little girls are one of his future challenges."

"Can you stop him?"

"With your help."

"I am yours. Tell me what to do." The intent in the voice made it clear to Regan that he had turned Gasco's man, even though he has used a white lie. No Intel had been taken from the compound but the story was believable. The only information that Regan had on the driver was very basic, his address, how big his family was and that was it. He was not on the target list.

"Show me your phone."

Gianni slid his hand carefully down to his left pocket and removed his phone and handed it carefully to his captor.

It took Regan seconds to add a number and to title it "Wife." He slid it back into the pocket and turned Gianni around to face him. Gianni did not like what he saw, the little of Regan that was visible. He stood before Gianni in the darkness, a menacing shadow of a large man.

"When you think he is moving to an area where I can hit him, and hit him close up, text the number under 'Wife' and let me know. After that, I suggest that you lose your phone."

"What will you do with the information?"

"What do you think I am going to do with it, Gianni. I am going to save you and your wife the expense of burying your children."

Gianni was visibly shaken and Regan needed him to be strong.

"Don't over think it, Gianni. I am going to kill him. It is as simple as that." He slid the knife away from Gianni's neck and slipped away into the darkness.

Gianni could not tell if the smell of urine was off the man who had just frightened him half to death or whether his bladder had loosened from fear. Either way, he had made a pact with the devil to kill a devil. Such, he thought to himself shakily taking another cigarette from the box and lighting it, was life.

Marco sat back into the plush comfort of the seat and toyed with a cigarette between his fingers before laying it on his bottom lip. The driver was waiting, with the Mayback's engine running silently, for his boss to direct him. He never knew where he was going, a fact detrimental to his young marraige, and need to respond at a moment's notice to Marco's beck and call. Now, he hoped, having had a couple of weeks of turmoil within the ranks of the organisation plus the funeral of what was left of his brother, Marco would just want to go for a quiet meal.

"Teatro San Giovanno, Gianni. Please."

Gianni was taken-aback by the manners. Not that Marco was ill-mannered, in fact he was quite the opposite. It was that he never had time for "little people", drivers, gardeners and those who served in the shadows, and now he had used his name for the first time. Gianni had been sure that Marco did not even know his name but that was an error of judgement. Running the business the way he did, Marco knew the name of every employee. In fact, not only did he know the name, he had a complete file on each member of staff that was not directly involved with the criminal aspect of the operations and in that file he had detailed accounts of family members. Marco knew not just his driver's name, but he also knew that of his wife, children, surving in-laws and so much more. He was that precise.

"Il Trovatore is playing tonight and I managed to get a box to myself. I need the privacy, it has been a tough couple of weeks."

"Yes, Sir" replied Gianni as he checked the rear-view mirror for signs of emotion on Marco's face. Marco was staring out the window, lost in a world of worry and pain and Gianni felt sorry for him. He was under no illusion that his boss was a dangerous man, but he held him in esteem and, notwithstanding his business, he had lost a brother, a twin, and that, for any man, was a difficult loss. "I am truely sorry for your loss, Sir. It is a terrible time for you."

Marco's voice, for once, softened and even sounded somewhat feeble, "Thank you, Gianni. I will remember your kind words."

"Shall I collect you after the performance, Sir? Or do you wish to go for something to eat?"

Marco thought for a moment, then replied "Drop me off, Gianni, then head home to your wife. Please take the rest of the evening off and I can call a cab or one of the security team."

"Thank you, Sir. That is very kind. Do you mind if I text my wife to let her know?"

"Please, do. Though women should never be shocked by their husbands coming home."

Gianni checked the rear-view mirror again and saw a half-smile on Marco's face. He fingered the buttons on his phone while pulling away and sent the message. He then eased the car out of the drive and accelerated down the hill towards the city. He could see the security cars falling in behind and knew, also, that there would be a car some distance ahead, just in case.

Teatro San Giovanni, in ruin for many years since the War, had enjoyed a revival in recent years. Years of promises from politician after politician had fallen through and the burnt out remains of the teatro was all but set to crumble when a private benefactor, often thought to be the internationally renowned operatic tenor, Giuseppi Patrone, quietly approched the town council with a plan to resurect the teatro from the ashes of the war and public apathy. Patrone, who's grandparents came from a nearby village and himself was born, raised and educated in New York, was known to have an interest in reviving the wonder of opera in the town of his ancestors and so it became rumoured fact that he was the financial fountain of hope that was rebuilding the teatro.

It had taken nearly eight years, but it was a sight to behold when it was complete. Each step of the reconstruction was well documented on a website that showed the slow progress and all wondered at the workmanship that went into the job. Now, it was once again open and, true to the hopes of the locals, it was a wonderful success. Not only had it become the new focal point for the great and the good of the surrounding areas, it was drawing performers from all four corners of the world to perform there and the beauty of the theatre was not lost on the performers nor those enchanted by their art.

The black Mayback whispered to a gentle halt beside the workers' entrance and Marco stepped out of the car to a welcome from the theatre manager, he being the only one who knew that Giuseppe Patrone was not the well of money from which the theatre had revived its drooping spirit.

"Sir, we are delighted to have you here this evening." The manager, a lover of the opera and all that is art, was emotionally indebted to Marco as it was his grand-father who had, in a sense, been responsible for the destruction of the theatre having held weapons there for the resistance during the War. The German soldier who touched the flame to the petrol-soaked seats did so, according to local legend, with tears in his eyes. The legend continued that after being congratulated by his senior officer for a job well done, the young soldier marched back into the burning theatre, mournful tones eminating from his soul as he sang himself into the flames.

Such was the passion associated with the theatre that it was difficult for the manager not to feel beholden to the man who had financed the rebuilding of Teatro San Giovanni and therefore also the rebuilding of his family's reputation. Both had been in ruins and now that one had risen from the ashed of war and waste, he hoped that his family's would soon rise too.

Marco liked the manager, as much as he liked anyone, and he stubbed his cigarette into the cobbled street with the toe of his shoe before exhaling the last of the smoke from his lungs, turning with a smile on his face and taking the manager's hand in a firm grip. Grip was everything, it showed intensity, or lack of it, and sinserity and the manager felt both and he felt three inches taller, substantial for a man of his deminutive stature.

Marco was led inside the door and quitely, out of the sight of others, the manager lead him to his private box. The box, resplendant in gold-leaf, mahogany and draping heavy silk curtains was a work of art. The brass handle on the balcony edge reflected the flickering candles and the hand-carved figureens surrounding the ope had taken the artisan carver eighteen months to complete. The curtain ties were braided by hand, the tieback made from 8mm unbleached cotton rope and features a loop and button type fastening, a monkey fist ball knot at one end threaded through and secured by an eye splice, made of the same length of rope, and decorated with a manrope knot at the splice. The work on every aspect of the box, of the theatre as a whole, was second to none and even the most devout spent-thrift would agree that it was money well spent. Marco turned to than the manager for his kind assistance and slipped a 500 Euro note gently into the kerchief pocket of the man's marine-blue Armani suit.

"I hear your son is wearing his way through football boots at a terrible rate. Please, from me, buy him a new pair," he whispered gently.

"You kindness honors me, Sir. If there is anything you need, please just let me know."

"My captain, tonight all I need is the privacy to enjoy this wonderful theatre so that I may be alone with the music and my sorrow."

"It will be done, Sir," came the almost comical reply and Marco gently bowed his head, highlighting his sorrow, thanked the manager again, and gently eased the door closed until he heard the solid click of a lock well attached. Now, he hoped, he had peace.

From the edge of his box, standing with a chilled flute of Champagne, he favored the French over his own native Prosecco, he glanced down below and watched while the seats filled with every size of bottom and the air with excited chatter. He pulled the gold cigarette case from the inside pocket of his suit, like the manager an Armani creation, which reminded him that he needed to buy his suits elsewhere if the manager was wearing the same as he was. The case had been a gift from Mauro, his first gift actually, and it was something that he had always treasured. He now felt the weight of it in his hand as he flicked it open and popped a cigarette into his mouth. Mauro was never one to go to the theatre but he would always accompany his brother if asked. Marco lit the cigarette and drew deeply before blowing a solid stream of smoke up towards the ornate ceiling. Smoking was banned in the theatre but the manager made special arrangements for Marco, that is to say, nobody would say a word.

Marco turned to sit down and picking one of the four seats available to him, he settled for the one away from the edge and settled down into the deep seat with a tired groan. He knew, more than likely, that he would spend most of the opera in peaceful slumber because the theatre was one of the few places where he felt perfectly safe. In his box he could relax, enjoy the opera, one of his true loves, and, if the need came over him, he could sleep. Having chosen the seat furthest back, there was no fear that people would see his slumber. However, it was to be Il Trovatore tonight, and that was something worth staying awake for. He would try.

The plans showed such great detail, not intentionally but very much by proud accident. The architect who worked on the rebuilding, Gianni Ermino of Ermino and Associates, he being the junior to his Father, had turned the job into a work of passion and he wanted the world to see his passion come to life in gentle progression on the website page of his company. The town council thought it a great idea and also felt that it would put pressure on the builders to complete the project that had now become global viewing. One of those who had downloaded the whole sequence was Regan and he now knew the theatre like the back of his hand.

He had received the text Gianni had sent to his 'Wife' while sitting in his hotel room and had moved quickly. As everything had been packed and moved out save for a small few belongings, shaving kit and the usual, he was able to check-out of the hotel without fuss. Once done, he moved to his car and threw his 'minute bag' into the boot. Everything he needed to get out of Italy, money, passports, small weapons and luck, was in that bag and he figured he would be needing it. He felt something prickle his skin and it was nothing but the sense of expectation and hope that the mission was near an end and that, if he could change the course of his life, would mean a new beginning too.

The drive to the theatre was quiet and without problem. So near to the end he did not want to race there, drawing the ire of the local police who would only love to check the boot of a car with a foreign national in it. A bag of guns being discovered by the police would end him in so many ways that he preferred not to think of it. He drove slowly and arrived unnoticed.

The area around the rebuilt theatre had been made a pedestrian zone by the mayor so that tourists could mingle amongst the market stalls and absorbe the history of the area without having to worry about the clatter of mopeds or cars. It was a good idea, for tourists who were not carrying guns, but for those who needed to, it disrupted things just a little. It was not so much of a problem for Regan who was able to mingle and mix with all types, but he was aware that people were beginning to ask questions about the number of killings occurring in the surrounding areas. Luckily, for Regan but not the Italians, deaths through crime were a common occurrence and the police, while on alert, would not be on as high alert as police in other countries. The amount of killing was just different. Regan slipped the car in between two others of similar colour and size and switched off the engine. He sat for a moment, gathering his thoughts and putting them into the relevant compartments of his mind. Once his mind was in order, with all thoughts and doubts pushed away, he steeled himself for the action to come. He had promised himself one more kill, so that would mean that the bodyguards, if they were there, were to survive, or at least given a chance to live. He made a pact with himself, just Gasco and nobody else. The killing had to stop.

Regan walked slowly, with an air of relaxed superiority, to the ticket desk and asked for a box ticket, if one was still available. He paid in case, barely nodding a thanks to the young ticket girl and began to walk away when he turned back, a slight quizzical look on his face.

"Is Mr. Gasco in his box? I am meant to meet him for a meal after the show and I have had a change of plans. I would dial his mobile, but you know what he is like. He always switches it off for the opera."

The young girl smiled her understanding and nodded, "Yes, Sir, he is in his box now. He arrived ten minutes ago."

"Thank you so much. I should knock in and let him know before the show so that he can change his plans for the evening, if he wishes. I know he hates to miss appointments, or for others, more importantly, to miss them. Tell me, I have a head like a sieve, what box number is he?"

The girl looked at her computer screen, tapped the keys a second and then replied, "Box 23, Sir. They say it is his lucky number."

Regan smiled and tipped his head in a gently bow of thanks. "I am sure it is."

The curved stairs, blanketed in the thickest carpet that had ever held Regan's feet, was a joy to behold. The intricate carvings, depicting angels and gargoyles intertwined, felt gently warm under Regan's fingers as he trailed his hand along the dark wood, climbing step by step. He had chosen the stairs above the lift wanting time to see ahead and not to be surprised by sliding doors opening to a pair of armed bodyguards.

His plan was simple; he was just going to complain. Having reached the top of the stairs the subtle sign on the wall pointed him in the direction of Box 23 and once past the gentle curve he could see the two guards standing at ease outside the door. Time to start complaining.

The taller of the two bodyguards heard Regan before he saw him. The irate voice, booming down the phone, was more of an annoyance than anything else and they had been assured by Marco Gasco that nothing, neither God nor Devil, should disturb his that evening. The second bodyguard looked at the other and rolled his eyes to Heaven.

"I am looking at it now, and the paint is peeling off the wood. You guaranteed this job for ten years and now look at it! It is shit." Regan had come within ten feet of Box 23 when he halted and started picking at the paint on the door beside Gasco's box. "What am I to tell people, eh? Welcome to our wonderful theatre, sorry the paintwork is so shit? What am I to say, tell me?" Regan looked at the two bodyguards and shrugged his shoulders in a half apology. The nearest to him raised his finger to his lips trying to get the agitated man to lower his voice and the second moved from his position at the door, towards Regan, with his hands outstretched, pleading for silence. Neither bodyguard notices that it was not a phone that Regan was speaking into.

Regan pulled his hand from his ear and drove the 'phone' into the lower ribs of the nearest bodyguard and depressed the button on the stun gun. It was small, black and looked like a phone so the two men had not reacted to the threat. By the time the first guard was crumpling to the ground, the second was zapped.

Regan caught the second bodyguard before he hit the floor and, taking the full weight of the man in his arms, dragged him to the next door, that was already slightly ajar, toed it open and pulled the man inside. He was back out and dragging the second man in by the ankles until he was lying beside his colleague, and had the job done in under sixty seconds. He stood over the two men for a moment and took a deep breath. He pulled a number of FlexiCuffs from his pocket and bound the two men. Each was then gently gagged; enough to keep them quiet for ten minutes. He needed only seconds, so his efficiency was wasted on his two new friends. He looked over the edge of the box, down onto the performers on the stage and stood for a moment. The music was mesmorising but he had a different performance to attent. He breathed deeply once more, and walked out onto his own personal stage.

He opened the door, having first gently knocked, and entered the box. His emotions were in check but there was no way to stop his mind from advising him that this was it, this was going to be the end of it all, the last kill of a career that had resulted in many a corpse.

The door clicked gently behind him as he shut it as quietly as he could. He was not trying to be silent for the sake of the kill, he just felt that slowing everything down would allow for him to, in a sense, savor the moment. He was inches from ending the hunt.

Marco turned and, even in the dimmed light of the box, he knew that the man who had entered was not one of his guards and, in fact, he was surprised that his terror did not scream from his lungs. He could tell, through the presence alone, that this was the man who had killed his brother and, it would seem, the two guards from outside the door of the box he was sitting in. He remained seated, thinking it would give the right impression. What that impression was, in that moment, he was not sure. He hoped it would be one of calmness.

"I am at a loss for words, I never thought that you would show yourself to me. I mean, I knew, I felt at least, that you would get me some day. To an extent, there is a certain relief that it is today and that it is here." The words were unimpeded by fear or haste. Marco sounded confident, regardless of how he felt. The silence hung in the air, unfiltered by the silent air-conditioners that kept each box at a comfortable temperature, suspended by an invisible sense of dread and expectation. Regan broke the silence.

"Both of us cannot leave this box alive."

"I didn't think so."

"You do understand why?"

"You have made that obvious in recent weeks, Sir."

"Have I?" The question was put gently, without threat or menace. Something was happening in the box that was not part of the plan. Nobody was dead yet.

"I killed your sister and your war on Italy has left quiet a few bodies, including my brother and some of my closest friends, on slabs in mortuaries."

"You did not kill my sister, Gasco. You slaughtered her."

The opera below was busily reaching its crescendo as Scene II spilled its sadness to the audience so captivated as to be immune to the drama occurring in the box above.

Marco's response was measured, chess-like in his need to maintain the calm that he felt might save him. "It got out of hand, Jack. May I call you Jack?"

"Tell me why she died the way she did. Tell me why it took two men to kill her and then to dump her on the side of the road." The quiver in the last words were difficult for Marco to interpret, did they mean anger or sadness. Was there an opening here for him to escape, or to over-power Regan. He didn't look like a man who could be over-powered easily. In the dark, Regan was a shadow with the bare semblance of humanity.

"We had it all, Jack. Kathy was going to take it from us. Out of nowhere she wrote a story on us while the police had barely a file on our activity. She was going to end our good times so we decided to end hers."

"You tortured her."

"Mauro did, and you made him pay for that. Can you not see that, Jack? We are both men of violence and our existence, while obscene to most, is necessary. You and I are killers, but we exist because we exist. If the world were full of people like Kathy, then there would be no need for killers like you, and no DNA for people like me. But that is not how it is, is it? I am here because of some twist of fate, some bend in the continuity of the self, and you are here for, I am sure, some similar reason. I mean, Jack, did you grow-up a killer? Can you remember a time when you didn't kill?" The words were heard by Regan, flowing through his brain into one of the compartmentalized rooms in his mind. He would be able to answer as the door to that certain room had been left ajar since Izzo died.

"I kill to protect," he paused an instant to see had he the strength of control to maintain his calm and then added "Marco." He had used the name of the man who had killed his sister, the man who was using his name as though they were friends. What Rubicon had been crossed?

Leanora was dying in Manrico's arms and the sorrow of the whole affair was floating from the stage into the hearts of the crowd, not a sound save those of tears coming from the audience.

"Oh, Jack, come now. You killed my brother to protect who? Society? Please, we may not like each other, have reason to detest each other, but let us finish this like gentlemen, lies do not become us."

"You speak like a gentleman but your words are without honor. You lack the anger, Marco, of a man who has been affected by loss. Your power, wealth, strength, everything you believe you have is nothing but a crystal butterfly. In fact, everything you ever had, everything you feel you now have is really only that which is on your person now. Everything else, and I do mean everything else, is gone. Your money, houses, all that illicit business, gone in the blink of an eye." Regan was slowly clarifying to Marco that he had taken everything and was doing this, staring Marco straight into the eyes, while gently twisting the silencer into place onto his pistol. This was not lost on Marco.

"That is a maybe, Jack, but I can start again, even if you have taken everything from me. We both can."

"Start again?" The tone had softened and Marco felt a surge of energy.

"Yes, Jack. Start again. Walk away from all of this killing and go and live your life. I can help you, Jack. I have more money that I could ever spend and I can set you up anywhere in the world."

"Anywhere in the world?"

"Yes, Jack, and you get to decide."

"A new identity?"

"Yes, a new Jack free from the bonds of this life you have now."

"You would do this for me?"

"So that I can live, Jack. I would do it so that I can live."

"We would never have to meet again?"

"Never." Marco was beginning to feel that there was a chink of light in the cave of despair and that Regan wanted to live as much as he did.

Regan slowly raised himself up from the seat his gun now aimed at Marco's head. He reached out, still looking at Marco, and gently opened the box door a couple of inches, silhouetting himself against the hall lighting.

"Our history?"

"Wiped clean, Jack. A clean slate."

Regan slowly lowered the gun and Marco slowly exhaled. He paused a moment then holstered the gun under his left arm.

"Good-bye," and he left, closing the door behind him.

Marco waited what felt like an eternity before pulling his cigarette case from his pocket and was not surprised to find how difficult it was to light a cigarette with hands that had cheated death.

Below, on stage, the opera was reaching its climax and the crowd tensely awaited the cruel ending, an ending they all knew and yet they anticipated it, awaiting its beauty like the night awaits the dawn. It came with a flourish.

Azucena arose in splendid pain on the stage and when Di Luna showed her the dead Manrico, she cried in triumph: *Egli era tuo fratello!* He was your brother.....You are avenged, oh mother!" The audience gasped and, at the same time as Azucena, the count screamed in despair *E vivo ancor!* "And I must live on!"

Marco, head in hands, exhaled the smoke from his lungs while still shaking and missed, because of the rapturous applause, the click of the door opening. This time, the door opened fully and the light of the hall flooded in displaying Marco for what he was, a shivering coward. Marco raised his head from his hands, cigarette still dangling from his lips, turned towards the black, polished steel of the silencer aimed at his head and just had enough time to shout "Oh, Dio!"

The roar of applause drowned Marco's shout in waves of emotion giving no chance for the muffled spit of the two bullets that hit him squarely above the bridge of his nose to be heard. The noise did not abate enough for the sound of the metal jacket being emptied into the broad chest, finishing with the last two bullets, sent with a depth of anger, hate and distain that only a brother made sister-less could send, into the right cheek of the already dead Marco. No mother would be asked to identify those remains.

Jack Regan, freed in that instant of hate and anger, stood over the bloodied remains of Marco Gasco and as the applause began to fade before the first encore, he looked down at the corpse while unscrewing the silencer on his weapon. He leaned over the lifeless body and pulled the hair until the head and ear were brushing off his lips. "She was my Sister, and I must live on."

Regan stood, checked his suit for blood, saw none on the dark woven cotton and turned to exit the box. Before opening the door again, he reloaded his pistol and replaced it into the holster under his arm. He was ready, again, just in case.

Something stopped him from leaving, the battle between the soldier and the brother that had been raging since he read the fax on the firing range. That seemed so long ago now and it was a battle that had dragged on for far too long. With Marco now dead he needed to end the conflict within himself, to put an end to the uncertainty that the whole Italian adventure had created for him.

He pulled the rope from all of the curtains and tied them together swiftly. The result was a piece of rope about 15 feet long and strong enough, he figured, to hold the weight of Marco Gasco. In fact, it really did not make a difference to the result that he wanted whether the rope held or not.

He quietly looped the rope around Gasco's neck, tying a quick hangman's noose and securing it under the bloodied chin. He then tied the other end to the brass handrail, securing it with a strong double-hitch knot. Quick, simple and effective.

Lifting the corpse up onto the handrail was slightly trickier than he had envisaged but he arched Gasco's back over the rail, arms hanging as loosely as the flopping head, and stood their for a second soaking in the sensation that he was about to unleash on the audience below. The brother had won the battle.

Regan held the noose in his left hand and pushed Gasco to the limit of balance, his hips just edging over the handrail. He then pulled his knife from his belt and, in one swift motion, opened the corpse from neck to belt line and then pushed Gasco over the edge.

Down below the applause was seeking the second encore, the rapturous audience oblivious to the crucifixion occurring above them, for that is what it was. Regan was going to leave the body in the box but as he was turning to leave, he remembered the autopsy report and the details of how Kathy was left impaled on a broken fence. Notwithstanding the fact that it was Mauro who had tortured Kathy, he decided that Marco was the head of the serpent and therefore required an ending equal, if not worse, than Kathy's.

Thirty feed below the box the audience was applauding the heroes of the stage and the atmosphere was redolent of times past in the theatre. The actors lived off the applause and the audience thrived on their false gratitude but the joy of both was equal.

The body slipped over the edge of the handrail and dropped down to the crowd below. The fifteen-foot drop ended with a sudden halt, the rope straining under the weight of the corpse. The rope did halt the downward path of the body but it did little to stop the content of the opened torso from spilling down onto the crowd below. The heated splatter of blood and entrails, jolted from the body, fell onto those directly below with equal distain for all. The response was immediate and the screams and hollers from those baptized in the foulness of Marco Gasco's insides, though only numbering in the tens, drowned the joy of the applause in a wave of horror.

Those covered in the foul mess ran, directionless but they ran nonetheless, hoping to escape any further drenching. Those lucky enough to escape crowded back away in an increasing circle of shock, looking up at the dangling remains of one who once dominated their society like a secret evil shadow. Then the bolts holding the handrail to the box failed.

Below Gasco's box, and slightly to the left, there stood an ornate copy of the local cathedral that held copies of the original scores of the theatre for all visitors to see through the glass frontage. During the day, when the theatre was open to tourists, the cathedral was wheeled to the front of the stage where its glass front allowed the visitors to view the old manuscripts through the protected glass. In the evenings, just before the crowds began to stream in, the cathedral was wheeled back into place under the box usually occupied by Marco Gasco.

Marco Gasco's filleted corpse landed on the model of the cathedral, the pointed central steeple passing through his chest and out his back, slowing his descent onto the rest of the model.

Muted silence filled the hall for just a moment before the audience absorbed the full horror of what had occurred. The screams that followed the initial shock were heard out on the street where, under the evening lights, couples were walking in the cool evening breeze. Two policemen, who were busy smoking and watching the young women walking though the square, rushed toward the doors of the theatre only to be forced back by the wall of people fleeing the horror that was within.

Above the melee, in the dark of Gasco's box, Regan looked down on his work for one moment. He allowed his eyes to record the body slipping down the spire below and, his appetite for revenge sated, he turned to leave the box. For the second and final time that evening he closed the door behind him with a gentle *click*.

Below, the applause had long since stopped.

43

Getting out.

When everyone else is losing their heads, lose yours too. That was one of the ways of keeping invisible. Someone would have noticed if he walked out of the theatre calmly and with an air of confidence free of panic. Maybe not those running from the gory shower that had just occurred, but maybe someone sitting having coffee and reading the evening newspaper. In Regan's book, it made no sense to be calm when the cloak of invisibility required panic and so, as he joined the crowds running through the doors, he grabbed the first female he saw that was unaccompanied and, taking her by the hand, yelled "come, I'll get you out of here." The young lady was too shocked to respond and welcomed the guidance of his strong arm.

They ran, one in fear the other out of necessity, away from the mass of people outside the front of the theatre pausing only for breath when Regan remembered that the lady was not expected to be at the same level of fitness as he was. He stopped and held her as she caught her breath.

"Are you ok?"

"Thanks you, yes. My God, that was horrible. What happened in there?" She looked up at the man holding her and felt safe again but that made her wonder why he was running.

"Suicide, I think." She had asked him the question in English even though she was obviously Italian. "I think he hanged himself from the ceiling, or something like that. It was pretty horrific."

She looked up again, sensing that something was not quiet right. His eyes were steady and he was not out of breath. She was thankful for his assistance but wary of his presence. There was just something about him.

"Were you in the theatre by yourself?" he asked carefully. "Should we go back to find your friends?"

He was careful and considerate, a real knight in shining armour, but that just made her more nervous.

"If I say yes, will you bring me back?" Her eyes peered intelligently at him and the sincerity of his offer melted away with his brief smile.

"I am afraid not, Miss. I need to go."

"Whatever happened in there you were behind it. Should I fear for my life?" Whatever fear she had displayed in running from the theatre, she was now displaying a streak of fearlessness. Regan approved.

"No, I am nearly finished. If I am left alone between now and the border, then I should not have to kill again." He figured that being honest was, if not the best bet, refreshing.

The young lady kept her composure much better that when she was in the theatre, maybe it was the herd mentality that made her panic then. Now, however, she stood before the man who had slaughtered another man in the theatre, slaughtered him like a pig and then threw him into the crowd.

"What happened in there? Why did you kill him?"

Regan looked down at her and decided that he would just say it. Maybe it would help me to hear the words float away into the air, or at least into the ears of someone disconnected from the whole bloody affair.

"He, that is the guy hanging from the balcony, killed my sister. He and his brother and their gang of thieves and murderers killed my little sister. They raped, tortured and killed her and threw her body on the side of the road for the crows and magpies to have their way with her." He continued to look into her eyes as he spoke and he saw no fear, she believed him. "I am a soldier. I used to hunt and kill terrorists and so, being what I am and feeling how I do, because of my sister's death, I came to Italy to hunt and kill those who killed her. All of them."

"Kathy Regan, the journalist?" she asked in response to the synopsis of events. She saw his eyes well up and she knew the man before was telling the truth and hurting badly. "I read the story in the paper, the story she wrote about the Gasco Twins. Are they the ones you," she paused a moment but did not take her eyes from his for a moment, "are hunting?"

"Yes," he replied quietly, almost a whisper, "they killed her and now they are dead."

The young lady continued to look up at Regan as her mind worked out what to do. "So, how is your plan working out?"

"I was going to kill him in his box and then walk away, melt into the evening like a wisp of smoke. Best laid plans of mice and men, however. When I had killed him, it just wasn't enough and the idea of hanging him over the edge just took over and I went with it. And now, here we are."

"I should just walk away, shouldn't I?"

"You should, it makes sense. I seem to attract trouble."

"Funnily enough, running around a country killing people does seem to attract trouble." She was attempting light-heartedness and he appreciated it.

"Well, thanks. You were a very professional distraction." He shook her hand as he thanked her and prepared to walk away.

"Maybe you should eat something before you run to the border. I mean, you should, shouldn't you?" She didn't know why, she just felt the need to help the man who had just caused mayhem in her town. Yet, that mayhem would lift the veil of silent evil that had masked the true sentiment of the town for years. In her own mind, maybe she just wanted to thank the soldier for, intentionally or otherwise, freeing her town. "My house is around the corner, I can give you something to eat before you leave. A "thank you" of sorts."

"Why do you feel the need to thank me? I just half frightened the life out of you and now you want to thank me."

"The Twins killed my husband five years ago. He owned a small plot of land near where Mauro Gasco lived and that bastard did not want anyone looking down on his land. They killed my husband because his little plot of land overlooked his garden. Nobody did anything about it. I know, fear is a great protector of those who commit evil, but someone ought to have said or done something. The police still call it "unresolved." Until today, I have been living in dread of my son growing up to avenge his father's death, such an Italian way of thinking. You have ended that fear, and for that I am eternally grateful."

"They cast a long shadow, didn't they?"

"Yes, but no more. The shadow of the Twins is gone."

Carter and Fields were close, they could sense it and it was getting close to the time that they would put an end to their silent chase and move in to kill Britain's unofficial "Most wanted." It had been a long hunt, not that of the two agents now sitting in their hired car going over the final parts of their hit. It had been a long hunt for the agents' colleagues and others before them. Jack Regan had haunted the British Army, killed some of its finest, but was still wandering the earth, a ghost of Ireland past. It was not proper that he was allowed to continue to live, not, in the minds of the agents, cricket. He had played the game, cheated death and lived and that just was not how things were to end. Carter and Fields were going to put an end to that.

Fields was listening to the output of the scanner that was hidden in the glove compartment, sliding the dial to pick up the various police frequencies that publically were unavailable but to the agents, and their bag of tricks, was. All he needed to hear was a report of another "outbreak of Regan" as Carter had called it earlier. That defined it exactly. The killing of the first Twin and the delivery of the body was a message delivered to the remaining Twin, a message whose intent was loudly understood whether the message was received or not. It shouted, "I am here, I am going to find you and I am going to kill you. Here's proof."

The plan had been simplified. Having tracked Regan to the hometown of the Twins, the intention was to stay out of sight until the second Twin was hit. They felt that the killings that they had uncovered to date, all of those related to the Twins' gang, had become more and more gruesome and, more importantly, more public. Such development of the killing spree allowed them to believe that Regan would want to finalise his mission in a manner matching, if not exceeding, the death of his sister.

Following Marco Gasco at a distance was necessary. Even before he had lost his brother he had implemented new processes of travel from point to point, even to the extent on using multiple cars and dummy routes. Fields had seen it all before and decided to sit back and watch from afar and Carter, bowing to experience, agreed.

Three days had passed, watching the house and the many comings and goings, and they had the feeling that they were not the only ones watching. That was not just a gut feeling; Fields has seen a tiny speck up in the sky on a number of occasions and had made inquiries back to London as to who else was watching the target house. The response was, at first, not surprising. London advised that it was not linked to them, so it had to be "our friends across the water." That did make sense as Fields did think that the Americans would want to catch Regan and bring him back to base and, by now, any agency worth its weight in peanuts knew that something was happening in Italy and that more than one country wanted to put an end to it.

Then, out of the blue, a contact from London confirmed that the Americans were not "droning" the area for Regan. That worried Fields. If the Agency was not looking for him then it had to be a third party.

Regan and Fields had been kept out of the loop of who and what Dark Eye was and that was just how things worked within their unit. The need to know was not needed and so they did not know that Jack Regan was an Envoy. Only Fields had heard the rumours of the unit, but nothing had ever been confirmed and he never thought of seeking confirmation. It was not something he ever thought he would need to know.

Yet now, somewhere in that itch that occurs in the middle of one's brain, Fields knew that something was wrong. They were watching Gasco, he was sure that Regan was in some manner watching him too, and someone else was watching them watching Gasco. Somewhere, somehow, someone was sending them information on Regan and that information had commenced at relative zero when they left London and had increased day by day during their stay in Italy. Key for them was the knowledge that Regan was hunting in Italy because someone had killed his sister. Once the killer had been identified then it was really a case of setting a simple trap for a simple terrorist. That was how the thought pattern went but not the thought pattern that was in Fields' head. He knew something was out of sync with the Whitehall way of thinking. Regan had killed members of the SAS, some said he did it with his bare hands but that was neither here nor there. Killing those guys was as rare as donkeys in the Grand National. There had to be more to the story and that sense that there was more represented the itch in the middle of his brain, an itch that could not be reached.

Fields was a thinker on his feet and his means of figuring out problems did not come from any University education, it came from the streets. That raw sense of what was real, what was happening, guided him in times of trouble and now, the guide light was on again. He knew that planning an attack that targeted and killed members of the SAS was not an accident. The casualty numbers were what you would expect from an indiscriminate bomb attack or, more likely, just bad luck. A kid terrorist does not have the wherewithal to carry out such a planned endeavour, he had to have qualified, capable and, as much as he respect the capabilities of the PIRA during the "Troubles" he did not feel that they had such ability. It had to come externally and whether that was Libya or the US, someone had trained one young Irishman to be a heck of a soldier. The question now was, are they still behind him? He never felt that the Libyans had the skill to train men to that level so it had to be the dark, unspoken secret; American backing.

Maybe he was taking the line of thinking too far, but there was what was most probably, a Predator drone up over his head watching what was happening below and that was not something that a rogue IRA man had at his disposal. It was what Special Forces had at their disposal, Special Forces of wealthy countries. He decided to stop thinking before he came to conclusions he did not want to face, but the seed of concern had been planted in the fertile soil of his mind and he knew, as he always did, that the plant that would grow from that seed would have a sour tasting fruit.

The car stank of sweat, smoke and boredom yet the two men were still very alert, listening to the chatter coming in on the scanner. Droplets of sweat raced each other down the side of Carter's face and he exhaled petulantly while slowly banging his head off the seat's headrest.

"Could we not have taken this in turns?"

"Why?"

"Well, one of us could, I don't know, not have to be here inhaling your stench."

Fields smiled while exhaling from his umpteenth cigarette of the day. "Yeah, well, you are no basket of rose petals either, my friend. The heat, and this shitty air-conditioning are not doing us any favours."

"You don't seem to mind."

"Been in worse. Smelled worse. Looked worse, actually."

"Worse than now?"

"Yup."

"Hard to imagine!"

Fields looked himself over, lowered the sun-shield to look into the mirror and laughed at what he saw. "You might be right, I could do with a clean-up. We should give it another hour or so and then call it quits for the day."

"Do you think this is the best way to track this guy? I mean, waiting for him to blow-up somewhere, killing some other fucker, does not seem to be the most straightforward way."

Fields rolled down the window of the car and flicked the butt of his cigarette across into the grass beside the footpath where it continued to smoulder. He reached for the pack on the dashboard and began to take another out. "It is like this, we need to keep out of sight. He needs to keep out of sight. The guy we think he wants to kill has kept out of sight until now and some fuckers up there," he pointed to the roof of the car but Carter got the gist, " is keeping us all in their sights. So, we need to keep watching until someone fucks-up and then there will be a sighting.....either by us, by them, by him or by others. It is all very clear!" he smiled while lighting another cigarette. "Someone always fucks up."

Carter rolled his eyes to Heaven and smiled at their situation.

Regan settled down into the deep, comfortable chair and allowed the cool breeze floating through the window caress the back of his head. The young lady was busy in the kitchen, pottering around efficiently as her efforts began to generate wonderful aromas. Regan had not realised how hungry he was until that moment and his stomach grumbled agreement. The young lady was talkative but not pushy.

"Where are you from, Sig. Regan?"

"I was born in Ireland and, actually, I don't know your name and was not polite enough to introduce myself. I am so sorry."

"I am Valaria. Valaria Baldini." Her head peeked around the corner and she smiled at him. "Food is almost ready, I hope you are hungry!" She then noticed the blood still on his clothes and hands and frowned at him. "Sig. Regan, please, there is a bathroom at the end of the hall and I will leave our some clean clothes for you. Please."

"Thank you." He pulled himself out of the chair and walked towards the bathroom before stopping and turning. "My name is Jack, it seems strange to be called Sig. Regan at this stage."

"Very well, Jack. Please go and wash-up, food is almost ready."

Regan leaned into the shower and turned the hot water to full before undressing and leaving his clothes on a neat pile on the floor. He noticed how clean and precise everything was in the bathroom, as it had been in the hall and the sitting room. But it was not stuffy, it was the precision of someone house proud.

He stepped into the shower and closed the door behind him. His aching body welcomed the hot water and he dipped his head into the spray allowing the water to wash his thoughts away for a moment. Each flowing trickle of water dragged anger from his pores and led it down the shore in the corner of the shower tray. Water always revived his spirit and today was no different and he allowed his thoughts to slow for a moment and to think of the young woman outside in the kitchen. She had, in what seemed to be a moment of madness, dropped her defences to all fears and allowed his problems to be hers. It made sense, he thought; as she had suffered in at the hands of the Twins too and shared troubles have a way of meeting. Whatever her reasons for jumping onto the train of his thoughts and actions she had given him a moment of normality in a storm of internal turmoil and for that he was grateful. However deadly Regan's intentions were when he put his mind to revenge, it was equally responsive to loyalty and so now the tentacles of his emotions would reach out and grasp Valaria's fears and frighten them away too. He was good at that.

She was not being disloyal, was she? Not to the memory of her husband, she couldn't be. Her time of mourning had been served well and she commanded herself not to feel guilty for the sense of happiness she felt cooking a meal for a man. It just felt normal, and she wanted to fuss over someone else other than her son, someone more her age. He seemed to be a fine man and it would just be nice to sit and talk to someone where the conversation did not float around the topics of football and the need for a puppy.

She turned the heat off on the hob and put the empty plates into the over to heat up slightly before serving the food. She was a good cook and she knew that he would enjoy the food. It did not strike her as strange that she was not worried about that which she already knew about Jack Regan. He was a killer of men, her husband had been a scientist who loved working the land. No connection between those two males types except for the twins, and now her. How strange.

She jolted a little when she remembered that she had to put out a clean shirt for him, she would leave it on the bed in the spare room and then step quickly into the bathroom and take his dirty clothes for the wash. It made her smile to herself that she was eager to fuss over a man.

Regan felt relaxed now that the hot water was doing its work but he was aware that he was expected at the table in a few minutes. He shut off the water and stepped out of the shower, reaching for the towel just as Valaria stepped into the bathroom to collect his shirt for the wash.

Regan stood half out of the shower reaching for the towel and stopped in his tracks, dripping water onto the floor and still steaming from the hot water.

"Apparently, I am naked," he offered as an icebreaker.

Valaria was as quick with her wit as Regan, "Oh, I am a doctor. I have seen it all before." She had, but she had never seen such external damage to a body in her years as a doctor. She did not want to stare at his nudity but the scars were a cause of personal and professional curiosity. He picked up on it.

"I have been through a few surgeries in my time, I am afraid. Some not as professional as others," he smiled as he picked up the towel and wrapped it about his waist. "I am sure science will find me interesting when I pass from this life."

"I am sure they will," she smiled, as she picked up his shirt, "but just not yet." She turned and walked out the door, shutting it quietly behind her.

Regan smiled to himself and towelled down before stepping into his trousers. He stepped out of the bathroom still towelling his hair when she called from the kitchen to tell him that there was a shirt in the spare bedroom on the left.

He walked in and put the towel on the chair to the left of the door and picked up the clean shirt. It was fresh but not new, obviously one of her husbands that she could not bring to throw away. He was buttoning it when he saw the picture beside the bed. Valaria's husband was a big man, and so the shirt fit well. Handsome with a broad smile, he was holding their baby in his arms and grinning with joy. It was a touching picture of a family beginning to take its place in a home and now that family was broken. The same men, he used that word very loosely to describe the twins, who had damaged his life, his family, had done the same to this young family. They truly had deserved what he had done to them, every second of it.

Valaria was filling a glass of wine when Regan walked into the dining room and she turned and smiled at him. He smiled back and inhaled the scent of good food deeply through his nose.

"It is a wonderful smell, and it looks good."

"Come, sit and eat and talk to me," she beckoned him to a seat and he sat down, shook-out the napkin and placed it on his lap. He blessed himself before reaching for the wineglass and he caught her smiling again.

"My mother used to slap my ears if I did not at least say a quiet prayer before meals and I did not want to impose grace on you so I thought I might have gotten away with blessing myself."

"You are an enigma, aren't you," she replied lifting her glass to her lips and sipping gently. "I do not know what to make of you, I mean I know you are a killer but you sit at the table and bless yourself like a nice, quiet alter-boy. Your body, and I apologise again for walking in on you, has been abused terribly yet your mind seems to work at speed. How is this so, Jack Regan?"

"Did you ever drop your shopping coming up the stairs of your apartment? The bag splits and a tin of fruit bounces down the steps and rolls to a stop at the end of the hall but does not break open or leak? The tin is not what it was, battered and bent as it would be, but it is still a tin of fruit. Well, I am a tin of fruit, I guess."

Valaria tried to stifle a cough and a laugh at the same time and failed miserably.

"Tin of fruit?" shed put down her knife and fork, steepled her fingers and peered at him through the gaps in her fingers. "I have heard many people describe themselves in my surgery but I have never heard one define themselves as a tin of fruit. And these people would be mad enough to think of themselves as tins of fruit."

Regan smiled the smile of a man at ease and he laughed at her surprise. "Yes, I know, I am not making much sense but it a way it is the closest thing I have to an explanation as to what I am. I think, though I may be wrong, it is easier on the ear to hear that I am a tin of fruit as opposed to a killer of men."

Valaria's smile eased a bit and she nodded in agreement. He could see the questions boiling up in her mind and decided to pre-empt them.

"It all started a long time ago, when I was a young man back home in Ireland. An incident occurred that I witnessed and, in some way, it changed me or it set something in motion in my mind and in my body. I lost the connectivity with friends and family and edged into a world of," he sipped slowly from his glass of wine as she waited intently for him to finish his words, "I don't know, actually. I want to say pain but I never felt anything. Physically, when I was injured, I didn't feel it because my body was on such a high. When that high was gone and I had to deal with the pain then it prevented me from dealing with the mental damage of what my life, my actions, did to my soul. Pain is the balance that I need to keep my emotions intact. Without pain I think, and if I allow myself to think, then I will surely tear myself apart with hate and remorse."

"And yet, now you are here," she added gently.

Regan was mesmorised by the young lady and the apartment. Both gave a sense of homeliness that he craved, or thought he did. Her eyes, soft and wonderfully brown, did not challenge him nor even flicker as he recollected his life to her. She just listened, in beautiful graceful silence she listened as the killer of men spoke like a child.

"I came because they killed my sister. The killed her and thought nothing of it, no concern or remorse. Now they can't think, feel or, more importantly, kill again. I made sure of that. That is what I do. In some way, everywhere I have been, I have killed those who have killed innocent people."

"You never killed an innocent? She did not mean the question to sound as a challenge and she regretted it as soon as the words left the lips that he was gazing upon.

Regan sat back in his chair, breathed deeply and closed his eyes. His mind, as commanded, pulled the names of his victims from the vaults and glanced quickly at them. One name floated to the surface, the face a bloodied mess with eyes blackened from the point-blank shot her face had endured at the hands of Regan's gun. He tried to push the image away, but it only caused others to rise.

"I have," he whispered, his voice exhausted with honesty. "I have argued with myself for years that I did not, but I did. I am not sure of the distinction of innocent anymore but it has changed. "

Valaria felt the room shrink as she waited for clarification from the man sitting opposite her and she was not sure if it was going to come.

"When I left Ireland I was certain that I had killed only enemies. I truly believed that what I had done, what I had accomplished, was justified. When peace arrived, I left. There was no need for me anymore."

"Did you make a difference?" It was not a loaded question.

"No. I did not. I thought that I had, but I didn't but you don't see that until years have passed and experience, life and death experience, shadows your soul. In the context of freedom, the search for freedom that is, killing creates new borders and prisons. To that extent, I created prisons when it was freedom I yearned."

"Who was the innocent?"

Regan took another sip from the wine, closed his eyes once again, and spoke with terrible clarity. "Her name was Anne. She worked in a laundrette that used to clean the clothing of some of our memebers, off the books. When they finished an attack, they would drop clothing to her, the stuff under the cover-alls that they didn't want to burn but were worried that traces may have embedded somehow into the fabrics. Well, Anne used to wash them, three times through the machines, so that if the boys were picked-up then there would be nothing on their clothes. It was her efficeiency that spotlighted her for the police. Every time they picked up one of the boys for questioning the clothing would be clean. Not a trace of gun-powder, nothing. They knew that someone had to be cleaning them and the path led to Anne.

"You killed her for cleaning clothes?"

"No, Valaria. I killed her because she helped identify the men in the unit and the SAS killed them. Then she fingered more, men higher up the chain, and the SAS went after them."

"And they died, so you killed her?"

"No. I intercepted the soldiers going to the house and killed them. She was picked-up afterwards and I was tasked with killing her. It was my leaving price."

"What on earth is a leaving price? You had to kill someone in order to leave the IRA?"

"Yes."

"Oh, God. You killed an unarmed woman?"

"I shot an eighteen year old girl in the face so that her mother would not have an open coffin. I looked her in the eyes and pulled the trigger. She did not say a word and her silence contained more courage than I could ever muster. She gave up those men because she was a child, a frightened child and I killed her for it."

"I wonder did she have a brother to defend her like Kathy has?" Valaria did not know what to say to Regan. It was clear that the killing, not just the one he admitted to, was tormenting his soul, or what was left of it.

"She had nobody. Her father was killed two years previously. Another story of horror from that God forsaken war." He seemed to have aged years in those brief moments, the face, weather worn and handsome, looked gaunt. "I did to that girl what the Twins did to Kathy. I just did not use the same method."

"No, Regan. It is not the same. Did you take pleasure from killing that girl? Did you? She challenged him, almost aggressively, because she saw what happening. The soldier fighting to stop his mind from unravelling and she wanted to help. She moved silently from her chair and went to him, took his head in her warm hands and held it to her body. He reached up and took her hand and held it, hoping the conflict within would not sneak out.

"I need this to end," his body began to shake, gently at first but then in violent jerks as the tears, poisoned with years of guilt and anger, were released by the warm hands that held his head to her body. The emotional damn, an eternity in place, had been breached. Valaria reached down and kissed Regan's head and held him tighter.

If the two agents had been watching the updates on the local news channel and not listening to the scanner they would have been alerted to the latest Regan activity long before they finally did. When it was picked-up it was too late, least they knew that it was too late. Yet, they drove quickly to the square in front of the theatre, carefully so not to draw attention to themselves, and parked next to a newpaper booth. Stepping out of the car both men could not resist the temptation to stretch before scanning their surroundings.

People were milling around the entrance mingling with the police and Caribineiri who both seemed interested in the case. A gutted corpse hanging from a private box in the theatre would draw interest from all sides of the investigative world, as well as just the curious onlookers. The uniformed investigators were attempting to clear the door to allow the firemen to enter, there was no other way to bring the body down, but their job was proving difficult as soon as the rumours of who had been killed spread.

Fields and Carter walked to the crowd and listend and looked, as they were trainined to do. The name that they heard, over and over, was Gasco. That was enough and they did not need to stay any longer to see what was happening. Fields stopped on his way back to the car and stood in the middle of the square. Carter thought that it was the wrong time for him to stop for a smoke and turned to repremand him. Instead, he saw what he was doing.

"There has to be a camera we can access to see where he went," Fields offered as way of explaning his sudden stop.

"Hundreds of people flew out those doors, Fields. We would need access to the file and to one of our sources to run it through the face-recognition software."

"I'll recognise him," came the flat reply.

Fields darted off across the square to a small restaurant on the corner. Above the door, aimed askew, was a security camera. He looked up at it and figured that the lens must be recording at least something coming from the front doors of the theatre and he raced in to speak to the proprietor.

"Good evening, Sir," his voice raised and panic filled, "I have lost my child in the chaos outside. Can I please see your security recordings? Please!" His voice was shaking with the concern that a father would have and the owner nearly fell overhimself trying to assist the frantic man.

"Come, come. In here, please," he beckoned, easing Fields into the back of the store with a concerned arm around Field's shoulder.

Once in the back room the large man efficiently pressed the correct buttons in order for the file to rewind back to the time just before the screeming started in the square. Fields was spouting gratitude while eyeing the screen carefully and the shopkeeper felt like he was the chief of police so grateful was the man beside him.

Fields watched carefully as, on the screen, people started to pour out of through the doors and into the centre of the square. More and more came, a flood of terrified humans eager to flee the gore. The image was perfect, so unlike the grainy, shakey images of the past. Digital imagery was making his job, in this moment, a little easier than usual and then....Fuck!"

"Do you see him?"

"No, sorry, I do not. Excuse my frustration, Sir. You have been so kind." The frustration was more a realisation that he could have turned to whoever it was had the "bird" in the sky, and asked them to look. Then again, he was not sure that it was a friend they could turn to at this time. Then, for the second time, "Fuck!"

"You found him!" The voice was excited and concerned all in one go and the response delighted the man.

"Yes, there he is!" Fields pointed briefly at the screen and then turned to hug the man. "Thank you so much. You have been so kind. Please, take this," he attempted to offer a wad of cash from his pocket but the man declined, insulted by the thought of taking money for helping a man find his child.

"Not at all, Sir. Go, please, and catch-up with your son."

Fields thanked him again and ran out the door looking for Carter and seeing him drive towards him. The car stopped and the passenger door flew upen for Fields to jump in and he obliged just as Carter floored the accelator.

"Well?"

"Left, down the street."

"What are we looking for?

"Would you believe a lady in a red dress? I don't know the connection but he walked her out of the chaos in the theatre and took her down that street."

"Jesus, Fields. Have we a hostage to deal with now?" Carter eased up on his speed, no need to draw attention to themselves while looking for the elusive lady in red and her Irish man. The twists and turns in the operation were making him dizzy.

"No, he is too smart for that and he is yet to figure out that we are onto him. Well, that is a hope more than a reality. Anyway, eyes open. She is bound to be living near here."

"Why, what makes you think that?"

"The image showed a well dressed lady with high heals. No woman would walk a distance in them bloody thing unless she really had to."

Carter smiled and then responded, "Maybe she drove here?"

"The signs on the walls and on the sign-posts, do you see them?" he asked exasperated with the unnecessary small talk.

"Yes, what do they say?"

"That one," he pointed to the wall across the street, "says "No Parking" and that one, repeated all over this area effectively says "Pedestrian Area, no cars.""

"Shit!" Carter was the only car in the area. So much for not sticking out.

44

Fishing

The crying eventually stopped, his river of pain had run dry for that moment. She did not let go, though, and he was glad of that. The feeling of being held, and not judged, made all the difference to him and needed it. He needed to feel wanted and, surprisingly, protected. He knew that he could not explain it all to Valaria but he got the sense that she already knew. Call it woman's intuition or, probably more to the point, a mother's intuition. Valaria understood that she was holding an injured man in her arms even if the wounds were not visible.

"I needed that." Nothing else was said and he did not move.

"I know, " she whispered, "we all do on occasion. Are you ok?"

"I had it all planned, as soon as she died my mind went into overdrive and I knew exactly what I was going to do. It is what I am good at and now, now that it is finished, I do not know what to do. I don't know how else I am to exist without the need to," he knew what he wanted to say but his mind and tongue were diabled but the warmth of her hold.

"What, Regan? What is it?" She was trying to cajole the anger and frustration from his soul. She had seen one man ruined, killed by the Twins, and she did not want to see the same happening Regan.

"I stay alive by killing, Valaria. As soon as I stop, then I feel I will die."

She lifted his head and looked sternly into his eyes, "You killed the Twins, you killed soldiers and, unfortunately, terribly, you killed innocent people. You are not going to let yourself be the final target. You need to find something new, someone new, to pull you out of this conflict. You need to leave others fight now. You need to," she looked up for inspiration and saw the picture of her husband holding a large fish, she didn't know the type, from the fishing trip he did while on honeymoon, "take up fishing."

He looked up at her; eyes still wet, but with a spark of life back in them.

"Fishing?" he asked incredulously.

"Shit, I know, I am sorry Regan but I think you know what I mean. This is a phase of your life that is now over. Maybe most of your demons are now dead, well the ones in Italy are certainly with their maker now. Know this to be true, you can change your life, accept the bad things that have happened and live. I lost my husband and you lost your sister. I have not stopped loving or wanting to love. You have to think that way too."

Regan allowed a smile to break the sturdy mould of his face and Valaria could see that she had gotten through to him. Sometime all a troubled soul needed was for someone to show them a different path. They did not have to walk the path with them; they just had to show them that there is always, always a different route.

"You are some lady, Valaria."

She blushed, slightly, and then laughed. It had been an eventful day and the stress had bled off. "You know, if our paths cross again, it would not be a bad thing."

"I kinda had the same though."

She smiled, leaned over and kissed him on the forehead. "You best get yourself to the border and set things in motion for starting a new life. If you are ever back here, and need a date for the theatre, here is my number." She handed him her card and he slipped it into his pocket.

"Thank you," he replied as he got to his feet and prepared to leave. "Thank you so much. Isn't it incredible how accidents have such strange results?"

"Regan, what happened in the theatre was no accident."

"I know, but it is probably the last one," he offered.

"Probably?"

"Baby steps, Valaria. Baby steps."

Valaria walked him to the door and hugged him once more before he left. He felt lighter as he turned to her once more to thank her and to say goodbye. Like most men, he preferred that goodbyes were quick and painless, but they never are.

He moved quicky down the steps of the apartment and was figuring his way to the border as each step passed. The "team" had, by necessity, broken and gone their separate ways. That was a shame, he thought to himself, because there is always a need for people like Bassi and Watson and, of course, Izzo. Izzo was dead, that was the part of the count that had not been expected and he still regretted thinking that an assault on the compound was a good idea. He had lost hold of the planning while attaining a grip on the need for revenge.

He walked through the side door of the apartment and out onto the street and within a few steps he had blended into his surroundings, the people walking the street, by removing his jacket and casting it over his shoulder. The car was three streets downhill from Valaria's apartment and he would be there in a matter of minutes and then out of the town. He needed to keep calm and make a regulated dash to the Swiss border. There, he had access to money, passports and Credibility. He would be safe.

He was too carefree. That was the simple tell, the giveaway that Fields was looking for. Italians are wonderful spirits but in the towns it is not possible to call them carefree. They worry about how they look, their clothes, make-up, hair, just about everything. The tall man with the fair complexion seemed to be carefree and for that reason alone, just as they were about to call off their drive around the pedestrian areas, he caught sight of the man he knew, in his professional soul, was Jack Regan.

"Christ, Carter. That's him. Eleven o' clock, jacket over the shoulder. Ease up."

Carter did as commanded and breaked; gently as he did not want draw any further attention to his illegally driven car. However, he did break on a bare patch of tar and, in the absence of other cars, the screech of tyre rubber on tar was louder that it would have usually been.

Regan did not react immediately but did slow his pace and stepped off the path, looked left and right as he crossed and decided that it was time to run.

"Fuck it, Carter! He is off, he caught on to us."

Carter dropped into first gear and floored the accelerator, literally hitting the floor and reving the engine to a low scream before shifting up into second and onwards.

Regan just felt it was wrong and that is why he moved. Credibility had warned him to be on the watch for two British agents who may, or may not, be in the country to capture him. They may have been driving a black Alfa Romeo, or Lancia. Not the specifics he needed to assess risk but Regan knew that if he saw something out of the ordinary, with two men involved, then he was at risk. Two large men in an Alfa, driving in a pedestianised area, counted as a risk and he ran. He was not far, and there were enough alleyways and stepped streets for him to confidently out run his persuers, or so he thought, until the first two bullets hit the wall two feet in front of his head.

Fields cursed. His first shots were off but he believed he had the drop on Regan and he fired rapidly from his Browning pistol. It was not the time for double-tapping a target and he unleashed the contents of the magazine at Regan as he was leaning out the window.

Carter's heart was racing. He was now in the thick of it with one of the legends of the Services chasing an enemy that had outwitted the best and brightest that their country could muster. He just had to keep the car straight and steady enough for Fields to get a round into Regan's body. One would do, just to stop or slow him down and then they would finish him. Jack Regan, the thorn in the British Army's side and festering wound of embarrassment for the Crown would soon be a smear on the pavement. He was certain of it.

Regan was certain of many things and being a smear on the footpath was not one of them. The bullets were peppering the aged stone of the old town walls and he was happy with that type of targeting. Shooting from a moving car on cobbled pavements was a factor that worked in his favour but the guy shooting was good, really good, to get the lead as close as it was getting. It was time to balance things a little and he ducked quickly into a sidestreet as two more bullets cracked over his head. The cover gave him a second to pull his weapon, take a deep breath and then stepped back out into the street.

Fields was just about to scream at Carter to swing the car left after Regan when the man stepped out onto the street fifty yards ahead of the Alfa as it shuddered to a screeching halt. Carter had seen Regan step out too but, more importantly, he had seen the raised weapon. The first two bullets smashed throught the windscreen, followed by two more into the hood, the dance was repeated and then that brief moment when the mind tallys the number of bullets fired and knows that there are more to come.

No more killing, fuck them. I am not going to kill again today. At least, that is what Regan was trying to convince himself. Two shots through the windscreen to make them crouch down, two into the hood to damage the engine and repeat. Eight shots and then he disappeared back into the allyway. He was not going to kill any more men today.

The Alfa's engine spluttered to a halt just as Fields and Carter exited from each side. Fields took position behind the opened passenger door with his pistol raised looking for a target that had already flown. Carter was sitting behind his door checking his weapon before raising himself onto one knee and poked his head, preceded by his weapon, around the door. He was half expecting a bullet to assault his head but it did not happen to him nor to Fields. He exhaled with relief and then looked over at Fields.

"Now what?" he asked, unsure of what was to happen now that they had lost the car and their cover.

"We have our orders, Carter. We follow him." He stood up and looked at the crowd of people starting to use their phones to call the police. It was really time to get out of there. Nobody was going to approach them, they were visably armed, but calls were being made. "Grab the bag from the boot and let's go."

Regan was not running, he did not need to. In an instant he had disabled the car and pinned the two men down. How they had found him was of little interest in that moment but they were coming after him. That he was certain of.

He walked down the street efficiently and carefully. He had darted down one of the side streets and then slipped into the human traffice on one of the larger streets close to where his car was. He was still invisible.

Carter grabbed their bag from the boot and turned quickly to Fields. "What about the car?"

"Step away."

Carter did as he was told and started to jog towards the street where Regan had been. Fields followed for a moment before turning and firing two shots into the fuel tank of the car. The effect was immediate and the car erupted into flames.

"Now, Carter, run." He did not have to explain his command, as the sounds of multiple sirens were getting closer.

Regan got to his car and and could hear the sirens too. He glanced over his shoulder and saw a pall of smoke rise from where he had been and smiled to himself. It was not the first time.

He eased into the car, started the engine and, before moving onto the road, he checked his mirrors. There was a gap in the traffic and, back and to the left, at a distance of about eighty meters, he was sure he saw he two new friends. It was time to drive like an Italian.

Carter had run like an Olympic sprinter to try and catch Regan but he was following his nose and not a line of sight. He figured that by moving towards traffic he would find his target because Regan had to have had a car. It made sense to Fields too but he was a little behind, not as fit as he had once been.

They were sure that the police would stop and quickly check the flaming car to ensure that nobody was in it. However, that was not going to give them much time. The witnesses there would be giving the police their descriptions and the direction in which they ran. By now the radios would be screeching about two foreigners running around the old town, armed and dangerous. Italian police were efficient at shooting first and asking questions later and, in these circumstances, Fields could not blame them.

He caught up with Carter in time to see him throw the bag on the ground in frustration and knew that they quarry had been lost.

"Dark blue Fiat, heading North," panted Carter before picking up the bag and starting off again. Fields called him back.

"We need to take one of these and get after him. Show me the bag."

Carter obliged and he pulled a small, black pack out of which he took a small black fob, the size of an electronic key, which acted as a scanner which, using a three billion hopping code, opened the door of a BMW feet from the two agents. Fields had expected a five-minute wait but luck was on hand. The decoder had bounced onto an unencrypted alarm and killed it. They jumped into the car, Fields driving this time, and turned out onto the road and off in the direction that they saw Regan drive.

Regan, in full combat kit-out, would have opened the car quicker but that was not important now. He was speeding out of the town towards the mountains in the distance and from there he would have, he hoped, a clear run to Switzerland. He just needed to keep calm and ensure the tyres stuck to the road. He was trying to stop his mind from racing and was struggling. He needed to think but thinking made him angry.

He moved in his seat, a brief distraction, and tried to concentrate on what Valaria had been talking about. She was a wonderful woman and he wished he had met her in another life. The more he thought about her the more he felt he should turn the car about and race back to her apartment. He was not sure why, it just seemed like a good idea. Sometimes, and those times are rare, it is necessary to follow the heart and not the mind but Regan was one who was always controlled by his mind. For once, he wished otherwise. To be back in those arms, to desire that warmth of affection again, was a siren on the rocks of his soul. He could not go back, not now. Maybe, if things were to change, he might have a chance to go back and see what the theatre was like in the company of such a woman. It would be nice to go to see an opera without killing someone.

That was a stupid thought and one he allowed into his mind to try and break the line of thinking. Being facetious was a valant attempt to stop the bubbles of anger and frustration that were again growing inside. The anger was coming back.

He needed to be free of it all and, it seemed, he felt like he had a good chance of getting to the border. Once there, he would lose the car and with his bag on his back, he would cross the border and get to one of the safe-spots designated previously by Cinderella.

"I am sure that he will not expect us to have a car already. We may have a chance of catching him off guard." Fields was speaking hurridly as he glanced at signs for directions. None of them said "Regan this way."

"If we catch-up, what is the plan?" Carter asked as he checked his weapon for the umptheenth time.

"Blow the wheels out, hope he crashes and then empty our lead into the car. It will take a few seconds and then it will be over. I am not sure that we want to deal with him outside of the car."

"Because?" Carter asked before realising that it was a stupid question.

"Because he is prepared, he is better trained and because he warned us to leave him alone?"

"When?"

"When he decided not to kill us. He fired through the centre of the windscreen and then into the engine block. He was capable of better. It was a message that said, "Leave me alone.""

"Maybe we should listen to such messages," Carter offered.

"We wish. Like Regan, we have no choice in what we do. Puppets on strings."

"I never liked puppets and I hate that analogy. Analogies always mean trouble."

"Analogies or not, we are in trouble. We need to get behind him, shoot out the wheels and hope that Lady Luck is riding with us in the back of the car."

The anger had not taken the grip he had expected it to take and instead the dark cloud of depression crept in. It did not ever feel like a cloud to Regan but more of a heavy spirit circling his mind and squeezing it tighter and tighter. He knew what it was, when it came and when it would go but that never made the sense of depression any easier to deal with. For some reason, today, and not any of the previous days, the spirit was squeezing tighter than ever. He tried to reason with it, telling it that it was only interested because he had allowed himself to be vunerable with a woman but the spirit would not listen. The spirit screeched at him, the weight of sound worse than the sense of futility that permeated his soul.

"Fuck off. Not today," he shouted with venom.

The screeching got louder and louder and he screamed at it to leave him alone. His screaming intensified as he fought the feeling of impending torment and then, in the blink of an eye, it was gone.

The glass in the rear window shattered into a thousand pieces as two bullets careened through the glass and imbedded themselves in the dashboard just to Regan's right. His moment of screaming madness and drawn his attention from his mirrors and his pursuers had found him.

"Hit the fucking tyres, Carter. We need him off the road!"

They had taken the correct road and were driving at speed when Carter saw Regan's navy Fiat up ahead on the motorway. He seemed to be driving erratically and Fields wondered if one of his shots had hit the target earlier. He had not had the time to check for blood on the footpath but had felt that he had missed with all of his shots.

Regan's car began to speed up but Fields figured that the stolen BMW was equal to the challenge and he was right.

Regan was back in control and he floored the accelerator, the response, unfortunately, not as hoped. Speed was not a priority in the Fiat and Regan knew that he would have to out-drive the men behind him or shoot them off the road. Either choice was a challenge and he know that the Fiat was not built to out-power a BMW but nor were the men behind him built to take an Envoy out of the game. Up ahead he saw the answer.

Traffic was not favourable to the tactics that Fields wanted to use on the road. Though not heavy, there was enough traffic on the two lanes to disrupt the chase and Regan was utilising it very well indeed. He had just passed through two cars, one in each lane so he was driving on the dividing line, and then hit the breaks for an instant. The two cars breaked more intensly than Regan's and almost collided with each other. With both cars breaking and slowing Fields had to do the same as there was no way through for the wide German car. Each side of the auto-strada had concrete dividers so he could not mount the verge. Regan had just made himself a few valuable seconds.

Regan saw the size of the gap increase for just a few seconds but it was all he needed to get the distance he required. He was closing on the articulated truck just ahead of him and he drew his weapon in anticipation of the plan he had just formulated in his mind. His pursuers were not the only one thinking of tyres.

The driver thought he was doing well and keeping within the tight time-scale imposed on him by the late delivery and his taco-graph. He was not, and had not yet, broken the speed limit and was destined to reach the border by late evening. That would do and he could stop, eat and rest before finishing his journey. His load of tyres were a replacement for a huge batch of faulty tyres delivered two weeks before to Germany and the manufacturer was intent on getting the replacements to the car manufacturer earlier than promised. The driver was pushing the speed a little higher hoping that his taco-graph would not be checked this day. It would be.

Regan pushed the Fiat a little harder and moved up along side the trailer containing hundreds of tyres. He noted the speed was increasing and thought that the driver of the truck was taking a risk. It did not matter now as Regan planned on stopping him.

A quick glance into his rear-view mirror and the driver saw the blue Fiat at first speed up and then ease-up along side without passing. Surely, he thought, the car had enough power to pass him and he paid no further heed. Regan's plan was simple but simplicity did not always mean success.

One of the two cars finally passed the other and Fields was able to speed past the two of them and chase Regan. The dial on the speedometer raced past one hundred and sixty kilometres and beyond and began to close the gap on the Fiat. Fields was sure that he would have Regan within a mile, two at the most.

He didn't hear the gunshot or the bang of the tyre but instead he felt the trailer lurch. The dread of an impending topple sat in his stomach and he was correct. The two bullets had penetrated the thick outer wall of the outside tyre on the trailer and caused it to disintegrate in an instant. Further bullets were not required as the exploding tyre parts caused the tyre directly behind the first to explode too. The right-hand side of the trailer dropped heavily onto the bare rims of the wheels and the driver made an automatic adjustment to the left. The speed and momentum of the trailer caused it to veer to the left, and the driver tried to compensate to the right, then the opposite side as the fishtailing began. There was no way to prevent the inevitable and the driver lost control of the truck just as the Fiat finally passed him. He was unaware that the driver was responsible for a second set of tyres not making it to the German car manufacturer. The trailer leaned fatally over onto the left again where it seemed to be suspended by invisible wires, held for an instant from disaster before toppling over onto the concrete dividers.

Fields could not believe what he was seeing. The fishtailing trailer was just ahead and Regan was passing the truck. He had to get through and he floored the accelerator causing the engine to scream in anger as it tried to respond but it could not go fast enough to avoid the trailer. Fields slammed on the breaks, thankful for his seatbelt. Without the chance to look, he hoped Carter had his on too.

The weight of the trailer slamming onto the concrete had the expected effect. The doors burst open and a hail of tyres exploded out of the trailer. Regan's plan had worked. Hundreds of tyres bounced uncontrolled across the motorway smashing windscreens and denting roofs and bonnets. The truck skidded on for a hundred yards before coming to a stop, a trail of bouncing black behind it.

The driver opened his eyes when he felt the movement stop and he exhaled heavily. He was not sure what had happened but whatever it was, it was not good. The sound of screeching tyres on asphalt assaulted his ears and he waited for the inevitable thump of cars colliding with his trailer. This time, however, it did not happen. Regardless of the fact that he had lost his second load of tyres he still managed to count his blessings that he was still alive. He whispered a quiet prayer of thanks and then, after unclipping his belt, he manouvered himself free from the wrecked cab.

Fields cursed his luck again. A small mountain of tyres and a large wrecked trailer and rig now blocked the road and a build-up of cars was now beginning to back-up behind the two agents' car.

Carter was quickest to react and he ran and started pulling the tyres aside to make a path for them to get through. The driver of the truck had just staggered out of the cabin and was being attended to by other drivers who had stopped and so Carter and Fields felt no obligation to go to his assistance.

Looking up from his manual labour, Carter figured that the trailer was not blocking their pathway fully and that once a portion of the tyres were removed they would then be able to give chace again. The road was going North and he knew that Regan wanted to get out of Italy and back to whatever secretive hole he had crawled out of. That being the case, he would aim for Switzerland and was sure that Regan was doing the same. Fields, for once, was thinging the same thing.

Regan had allowed himself a flicker of a smile when he saw the swarm of tyres bouncing on the motorway. A pang of guilt made him pull over for an instant to see if the driver had survived. In had not expected the truck to topple over, only skid to a halt and block the road. The fact that it had toppled over both alarmed and amused him in equal parts.

He stepped out of the car and looked back thankful that he could see the driver now standing outside the battered cabin being assisted by other drivers. He was still on his feet so hopefully it was just a case of nerves. A truck toppling over would have that effect on a driver.

Fields looked up after throwing the umptheenth tyrer across the road and saw, in the distance, the man they were chasing standing at his car looking back at them. He could not see Regan's face but believed that, in the same position, he would be laughing too. He stood for a second looking up the road at the man he had to kill and wondered aloud was it going to achieve anything.

"You said something?" Carter shouted across.

"Just wondering, Carter. Trying to figure out what we are doing. Look at him, he is up there looking at us and sure as fuck laughing his ass off as we clear up his mess."

Regan turned back around, sure that the driver was fine, and got back into his car. The mountains were not too far away now and, though the petrol gauge was hitting the red zone, he was sure he would be in the foothills in no time. There was a good chance of this working out even if he had to abandon the car close to the border and hike.

The dark spirit of depression attacked again and once again it was without warning. He should have been happy, amused even, with how he delayed his pursurers.

Chapter 45.

Killing English.

Fields and Carter saw the smoke rising on the mountain ahead of them. The twisting ribbon of road would take them to the spot where the car was burning and then back onto the trail of Regan. As with nearly every aspect of the operation to date the plans had slipped out of their pockets and into the piss-pot each time the name Regan was mentioned. Now, up a mountain, in open spaces with high-powered rifles, the likelihood that Regan would give them the slip was thin. At least, five kilometres from where the car was burning, that seemed like a reasonable expectation to Carter. Fields, driving at that moment, had other thoughts. He was feeling that bloody churning in his stomach and he knew that it was fear. Not fear of the unknown, just pure fear. Combat numbs the body and mind to allow the sense of fear to stay in the pit of a soldier's stomach but Fields was not afraid of combat, he never was. He was afraid of Regan.

Why he had been drawn to the mountains was no mystery to Regan. He needed an escape, not an airport run or an airlift out of the country but a proper escape and he felt that the mountains offered that. He would be able to live in the mountains for a few weeks, months if necessary, and gather his thoughts on how he was to proceed with the rest of his life. Dark-Eye was no longer an option and he was a hunted man, a hunted man whose fire had, with the death of Marco Gasco, burnt out. Now, with nothing to drive him forward, he had parked the car into a culvert on the twisting road and turned off the engine. Like a writer he felt that whenever a blank page hit him he needed to keep on doing something until inspiration reached out to him again. He sat, hands on the steering wheel, and stared into space allowing the events of recent days and weeks to rush over him. He had had his little war and now he was expected to pay the piper. Well, the piper who wanted him to return to the United Kingdom to face trial was now making his own way back to there with no intention of ever mention the name Jack Regan again. Watson was a good man, a man he had trusted with his life and now he needed him again. That was not going to happen. He continued to stare into space.

His mind was skipping gears and he needed to slow things down. By identifying what positives he had, he would be able to create a plan that would keep him moving. By keeping on the move, he would keep the two English men off his back. And that, in the short-term, was the first thing he had to deal with. Dealing with them meant that he would have to draw them in and kill them, turn back to being the hunter and let them know how it felt. *Yes*, he thought to himself, *why was he running from them?* They were good, talented to an extent but they would never have been considered for Dark-Eye, not the young one at least. The fire had not gone out at all, it was still a smouldering ember and now the thought of becoming the hunter again sparked the amber and it lit into a flame in his chest. His head no longer was resting on the steering wheel and the loose grip he had had on the wheel now tightened and he raised his head back up straight. Time to draw them in. Time to kill, time to be free.

He stepped out of the car, stretched his muscles and breathed deeply, sucking the fresh mountain air deep into his lungs. He knew that there had been moments in the previous days were the dark thoughts pertaining to his own death had hung from the dusty rafters of his mind waiting to be disturbed. It was a fight that he would always be engaged in, trying to keep his hands off his own neck. Now, however, he had the urge to be a soldier and he was ready to start hunting. A new wolf was to roam these mountains in search of prey.

He clicked open the boot of the car and pulled out the holdall he had held in reserve. He had everything he needed in there for a rapid get-away. It was, in effect, his "one minute bag", i.e. if he had to drop everything and take only that which he could gather in a minute, what would it be. For a soldier, that was an easy question; food, matches, cammo, ammo and a gun. With Regan, it was slightly different as he had money and multiple passports too. And his knife.

Carter was young but he was a professional. He figured that something would happen at the car because it was burning. It was a signal and Fields saw it for what it was too.

"He is drawing us in, Carter." The words were not tired but they were heavy with concern. "He is drawing us in because we are chasing him. We should have left him alone."

Carter eased the car to a stop upwind from the burning carcass of what was Regan's car. Nothing seemed out of the normal, except the burning car, but then again, they were dealing with a pro and pros do not do obvious.

"How do you want to deal with this?"

Fields looked past the car and into the trees, took a deep breath and released it slowly. "He is gone into the trees and he wants us to follow. Oh, this is not the day I want to fucking die."

Carter stepped out of the car and looked up into the trees. There were no visible marks on the embankment that showed that Regan had clambered up and into the trees. No sign whatsoever that he had been there at all, except for the burning car. Now, standing under the clear blue sky, the sun drenching their shoulders and backs as they looked up into the trees, the two British agents did not need to voice their concerns any more. The sense that a Grimm's fairy tale was about to unfold in the dark forested mountain weighed on their thoughts.

He was watching them. If they had been tuned to the frequency that he worked on then they would have figured that he was close. He was back to being the creature that had killed the kidnappers in Colombia's highland forests and the Italian forest had adopted him as its own the moment he had sat under a large fir tree, took account of his situation and, as he had done in Colombia, become one with his surroundings.

He had taken a moment to review what he was wearing and found it suitable for requirement, with a few changes. He drove the blade of his knife into the tree and spread the bark and flesh of the tree by simple twisting of the blade, the sap would flow out in small streams and it would be put to two uses. Firstly, he spread it onto the areas of clothing that attracted the most sweat, and therefore would smell, as only humans do. It was the first step to removing the human aspect of the being that he was becoming and it was the most necessary. The trace scent of pine would not raise a flag in a forest, the salted onions of old sweat, even in trace form, would be picked up by a trained nose and he was giving credit where it may not be due to the two agents who had decided that following Regan was a good idea.

The next step was to apply the camo-paint but as he was twisting the top off the the first stick of paint, the olive green, he saw a snake slip into a mud-hole just down the slope. So long as he did not disturb the snake, not knowing what it was but figuring it to be an adder, he could coat himself in the mud and be, in his new surroundings, invisible. He moved carefully to the hole and, after checking for the snake, removed handfuls of the dark mud and applied it generously to his head, face and torso. His cargo pants were black already so he added patches of the lighter clay to those, having pulled it from an embankment and softened it in the water. Slowly, but surely, he was becoming more and more invisible, more and more at one with his surroundings. The two agents had caught a glimpse of him earlier in the day and that image was set in their mind, it was near impossible to change that image in their heads until they optically received the updated version. That version now was a completely different animal and not one that they were going to see unless he decided to show himself, and that was not part of the plan.

Fields was fitter than his young companion and was not alien to his surroundings. He had been raised in forested lands and grew up fishing and hunting in the woods near his home. He had often spent nights tracking animals to two obvious conclusions, the first being the capture of the deer and the second the lashing of his mother's tongue for being away for nights without warning or updates. This was long before the advent of mobile phones and so parents either trusted their children to come home, or they did not. Mrs. Fields felt she had raised a wolf, such was his love for the woods, but still she felt nervous when he was late in returning home. Still, however, his bounty was welcomed on the kitchen table, bounty that on occasion was bigger than the hunter. Fields carried home his first deer two nights after his tenth birthday, which he has spent out in the rain tracking his prey.

Now, in thin air and dry woodlands, Fields did feel at home but his insides still knotted at the thought of hunting Regan. He admired the man, but feared him too. Yet, acknowledging the skills of the man they were about to hunt, he felt a little better being in the environment similar to that in which he had hunted as a kid, and not too different from the other European forests where he had honed his skill as a soldier. Regan did not know that the skills of one of his hunters were as good, if not better, than his own but, then again, Fields did not feel the confidence that his skills ought to given him. In that moment, standing in the amongst the trees, the sky darkened, thunder clapped its start to the hunt and lightening exploded against an old tree somewhere deep in the forest. It began to pour rain and deep amongst the trees connected but not in view of each other, three men stared momentarily up through the leaves and branches and into the dark grey sky. The rain, in that moment, did not consider itself sufficient to clean souls, the actions of man and God where only capable of that.

Petersen leaned against the large opened door of the hanger looking out into the rain. He had never seen sheets of rain and he kept his head inside the doorframe for fear of soaking the cigar that was clamped rigidly between his teeth. The heated smoke wafted up his nostrils, through the nasal passage and back out his mouth in a circular motion not lost on him. He was chasing his own tail in an attempt to give Regan enough room to clear the area. The two Englishmen had gone in search of them but Regan, he knew, would be off the grid in seconds if he needed to be. All credit cards, passports, electronic devices and dwellings would be cut, burned, broken and vacated. A simple bag on his back, no weapons unless he had a pick-up store, some money in his pocked and his wits. That is all that he would have and it would be more than he would need to disappear. Petersen suspected that after the brief chase through the streets that Regan came across a car with an open window or door and just automatically took advantage of that good fortune. That was over two hours ago and, thinking like a soldier, he would have made a trip to the least obvious border post or port. In real terms, knowing who was following him, that could mean anything. The hunters would expect him to go to an obscure port, and so that is where they would look. So, maybe he went to the airport in Rome. You never knew, as was proper, which way a Special Forces soldier was going to go. That was why they were special.

He hoped that his excuses and stalls had given Regan enough time to disappear for good. It killed him that the young soldier was now being set free but that, maybe above all things, was what he really needed. He used his skills and instincts to create within himself the prowess of a human killing system. Petersen reigned in his thought process for a moment and thought about that, those three words – *human killing system.* That is what Regan was; a thinking, feeling, emotional human who had the ability to kill, and to keep killing while maintaining his humanity. Petersen didn't know that the human aspect of Regan's psyche had begun to erode from that instant in Rome when he had to cast his eyes onto the battered and abused remains of his sister. The anger that severed the ties to humanity and allowed the soldier to become less human, was the same sense of justice, that search for justice and the need to right the wrongs as he perceived them, that made him more human. It was that confusion of self and need, desire to kill versus the righteous kill, that was tearing the young man apart. Petersen needed to save his fellow soldier; it was just that the method he was going to use was neither what he expected nor what was to be expected of a soldier. To save the young man who meant so much to him, he was going to have to kill him.

Fields had trekked carefully for just over an hour before he slowed to a silent stop. Carter, lacking the skills that Field's had developed from his youth, tried his best to keep up and to keep up silently. It happened, however, with every step that Carter took, that every twig and stick he stepped on cracked and every noise he made, from the twigs snapping to the obscenities muttered when he fell, were the equivalent to a fire-cracker in a confession box. Regan would know where they were and Fields knew, he sensed, that the man they were hunting was watching them. It is that creeping of the skin on the back of the neck, the tingle on the soft flesh inside the elbow and on the back of the knee, those little unmistakable signs that let you know that there is someone watching, someone out there whose intentions are yet undeveloped. Decisions being made with every crack of the twigs and sticks that Carter broke.

Field's could not find a trace, not a footprint nor a bent branch, trampled foliage, nothing. They had walked for over an hour and were now descending again, into what seemed like a broad valley. He could hear what he thought was a waterfall and the foliage was denser as the trees were more spaced out. The trees were different too and as he fingered the leaf of one tree he picked up, not for the first time, the scent of pine. Not the chemical aroma of a car-freshener, but the fresh, lively nose-tingling scent of pinesap. Fingering the leaf he had just pulled from the tree between his fingers, he looked around at nature's giants surrounding him. The large oaks, as ever, exuded strength, power and a gentle calmness as the breeze ruffled the leaves. They never exuded pinesap.

Carter was becoming more and more frustrated by his inability to keep pace with his older colleague and that, coupled with his new-found ability to make noise when he needed to be silent, had him cursing Regan. He had not had a clean shot in the town but if he had, he would have taken it. He was not the type to be running up and down mountains looking for a man they should have been able to kill on a number of occasions in the past. In reality, he was a well-trained desk-jockey; he could shoot straight and was pretty good with a knife. However, shooting straight and being pretty good at anything was no use to him now. His belief that the enemies of the state were always going to be on the receiving end of a Predator drone had softened his edges and he was completely out of his depth in the mountains. He was unaware still, unlike Fields, of the fact that the man they were chasing was, in fact, hunting them.

He stopped for a moment to catch his breath; jealously admiring the fitness of the mountain goat he called his colleague. He had developed a stitch in his side and raised his hands over his head to relieve the pressure and to help drag air into his lungs. He could see Fields ahead in the distance inspecting something on a branch and thought that maybe; finally, he had found a trace of the man they were hunting. The scent of pine wafted under his nose and it made him smile, it reminded him of the inside of his new car. A gentle thud on the ground behind him froze him to the spot. He thought of calling for Fields but, instead, he fought the desire to urinate. He lost the battle when he heard the whisper behind his right ear.

"Shhhhhhhhhhh, not a sound. It is the hunter I want, not the bait." The voice was calm, clear and whispered like the wind through the leaves. "I am not going to kill you, do you understand?"

Carter believed him, the whispers sounded sincere, about as sincere as the butt of Regan's knife as it connected silently with the base of his skull and knocked him out cold.

The wind ruffled through the leaves again and the gentle sound calmed him. Yet, he knew that something had happened, a void had been created and he felt it draw him to turn around. He drew air deeply into his lungs, more to steady himself than to breath, and he turned noiselessly.

There was no sign of Carter, but he knew that. To an extent, it would have been preferable to see him slumped on the ground but now he had to go and find him. He was going to have to respond to the silent directions of the hunter. The tables had been well and truly turned and that is when it dawned on Fields that for all the skills he had developed as a child and as a man, in hunting the creatures of the forests, he had never tracked and killed a man. It was obvious from Carter's disappearance that Regan had.

He began to walk towards the point where he had last seen Carter and carefully retraced his steps. He was not as noiseless as he had been as he no longer saw the sense in trying to elude the hunter who was, in all probability, watching him now. He continued to walk.

Carter came to in darkness and in pain. His mind raced to the conclusion that he was dead, then discounted that immediately. He was alive, just not sure where he was. The pain was centred on the back of his head and it then, though the mist of fussy thought, dawned on him that the pain was the result of Regan's technique of knocking people out. It was a crude technique, but effective. Light started to filter through his lids as he tried to open them but he figured that the numbness he felt was because Regan had probably punched him in the face a few times before leaving him. He had not. Carter was tied to a tree, his body bound to the trunk with young ivy vines, so many vines that it seemed that the tree was consuming him.

Fields walked past Carter and did not see him it was only the grunt from the awakening Carter, a grunt that nearly made Fields jump out of his skin that made him turn to look twice at the tree.

"Jesus Christ, Carter?" he asked incredulously. "How the fuck did he do this to you?"

Carter grunted again, unable to speak with the vine rapped around his face and in his mouth. He saw Regan appear behind Fields and grunted a warning as loud as he could.

Again, it was the scent of pine that alerted him just as Carter grunted his warning, but he was too slow to do anything, too slow to even react. The hunter had caught him. A split second after his senses warned him of Regan's presence the polar opposites of cold steel on his neck and the warm breath falling on his skin behind his right ear told him that he was now in the presence of Jack Regan. A large arm slid under his left arm and, snake-like, moved up and gripped Fields' neck just above the point where the blade of his knife was touching his skin with shivering tenderness.

"Leave me alone." The voice whispered like a turning page but was filled with anger and malice, each sentiment being held in place by a thread of sanity. "Leave me alone, Fields. I have not done anything to hurt you or your noisy friend, yet." Each breath burned the back of Fields' ear as his captor took careful flows of air into his lungs between words. "I am home. This is where I belong and you will leave me alone. Do you understand me? You will leave me alone." He spun Fields around with one swift pull of his powerful arm, Fields' spin halting with him facing Regan eye to eye.

All the concerns issued from the pit of his stomach to his mind, those self same concerns that had caused him to shiver at the thought of the hunt had just been justified in the court of fear where he now stood accused. The sight of Regan standing inches from his face moved him in every direction of terror. From head to toe, he dared not look down to see if he was in fact wearing some form of footwear, the young man before him was mottled greens and browns of the forest mixed with the paints and ripped camouflage cloth. If he looked slightly to the left or right of the man he disappeared. It was a level of camouflage so professional that nature would learn a lesson, the application of years of

Darwinian development that taught the young man how to work nature to make him disappear. The eyes bored out through the mud and paint, two grey-blue diamonds flashing hatred and, he allowed himself to think, a level of fear. Could he work on that to save his life and that of Carter?

"I could smell you. I could smell the pinesap you rubbed on yourself to mask the sweat. I used to do the same when I hunted as a kid. It worked on deer."

"But not on you," the reply felt almost physical and it was a statement more than a question, as if he was wondering how to remedy the fault while still using the guise.

"I could smell the sap on occasion but it only registered when I was standing amongst the oak trees. Then I knew we were no longer hunting." He hoped his words were coming out confidently even though he thought he should have dressed the same words in reverence.

"No ivy vines on the pine trees. I needed young ivy to tie your friend up."

"Oh, I see. Is he hurt?" It wasn't a hostage situation but he was treating it like one. Keep the conversation positive, give the hostage taker a chance to see the positive and in this case the fact that Carter was alive was a big positive. The response ended the charade.

"What if he is? You are not in a position to do anything from what I can see. Your gun is in a leg holster, not the right place for a manhunt. Your friend's gun is in the bushes twenty meters behind him and I have a knife. Wait, let me balance the odds." The words were said mockingly to the man shaking in fear before him but, nonetheless, Regan sheathed his knife and turned the belt around so that knife was sitting in the small of his back. Not impossible to get at but it would be harder to get at than it would be for Fields to reach for his holstered pistol.

The two stood silently staring at each other, the gauntlet having being cast to the ground between them. Regan, tall and powerfully built but invisible except to those standing inches from him. Fields, smaller and visibly shaken.

They stood facing each other as the rain began to dance on their skin again, heavier than before. Regan felt the rain penetrate the thick layer of mud and paint he had applied to his body. The paint was waterproof, the mud was not and it started to run down his skin in rivers of brown. To Fields the image was more grotesque that the professionally applied camouflage; it made the man before him seem more at one with nature, more of force of nature. And nature had no feelings.

"How is this to end, Regan?" The words, swamped by the rain and false courage, came out louder than they needed to but he didn't care anymore he wanted out of the whole game.

Regan stood statue still, his eyes flickering as they scanned Fields for telltale signs of impending movement or threat. He was not going to be caught out now and knew that he could cover the ground to Fields quicker than the aging agent could draw his weapon. That, for the moment, was as far as he could think. Beyond dealing with Fields and Carter there was a mental wall being formed, a wall that he could not penetrate at this time.

"It ends with you living, or dying."

"You don't see me as having a chance in this fight?"

"No." It was a matter of fact answer to a straightforward question.

The silence regained its footing and only the sound of the rain remained between the two sets of staring eyes. Regan was trying to focus his thoughts on getting out of the forest intact. He had promises to fulfil and those debts of honour would not be paid by his death, at the hands of the British agents or by his own hands. He needed to move.

Fields felt lost. He was going to lose whatever happened. Regan had had enough and moved, quickly and violently.

Fields didn't see it coming, he had been hypnotised by the gently dance of the rain into feeling almost comfortable. When Regan moved he was spellbound and could not react, it was almost a relief.

Regan drove Fields across the rain soaked ground until they crunched into a tree. Fields' lungs deflated and would not be let re-inflated as Regan's forearm was nestled comfortably under his chin, pinning him to the ancient tree trunk.

Both men were shaking, one in complete and utter fear of death, the other in uncontrolled realisation and anger. Wisps of steam floated from Regan's head and shoulders as if the rain was boiling on touching his skin and his eyes seemed to crackle with anger and intensity.

Holding Fields firmly against the tree and feeling nothing coming from his prey to suggest that he was about to struggle or fight, Regan reached round his back and drew his knife once again. Fields eyes bulged when he saw the blade hang before his eyes and he briefly struggled before accepting his fate.

Regan eased his weight ever so slightly off Fields' neck, just enough to let him breath and giving him enough room to place the blade firmly against the flesh of his neck. He was now inches from Fields' face.

"You could have left me alone. Why didn't you?" The voice was so calm as to be almost gentle but the weight of the knife blade on the skin of the man held by him gave no comfort to the gentle voice.

"I am just doing my job. It is just a job."

Anger fractured the timbre of the calm voice and the knife eased through the first layer of skin.

"It is never just a job, never. You started this, your job made this." It was not lost on Fields what "this" was. Regan's mind was trying to disconnect from the past and the realisation of the present. Regan, the hunter-killer, was "this."

"I didn't ask for this, you gave it to me. You gave it to me when you killed those kids at the truck. You made this. You fucking made it and now you want to take it. Now you come hunting me. Me! You fucking think that I am here to be caught? I am here because you fucking made me and you don't even realise it."

"It has to end, Regan." The answer was a scream.

"I KNOW! I FUCKING KNOW!" The knife slid slightly deeper and fear and blood seeped out.

"You are killing me, Jack. That blade is going deeper."

"You came looking for me but you didn't get me where it suited you and now I have you where it suits me. Leave me alone," the weight on the knife eased, "leave me alone or I will come back for you and give you a war, a war on my terms. No rules."

"Ok, Jack, I hear you," the words were strong and solid and did not, surprisingly, revealing the terror that they masked. "I won't look for you again, you have my word."

Regan lifted his weight from Fields but kept the knife to the flesh. He leaned forward menacingly and whispered once more into Fields' ear a simple reminder of what would happen, "No rules."

The knife traced across the skin of his neck as his eyes watched the young man's hand return the blade to its sheath. Then, in the drenched blink of an eye, Regan was gone. Fields, his back still to the trunk of the tree, did not move. He barely allowed himself to breath, as he feared that Regan would change his mind, come back and drive the blade of that terrifying knife up to the hilt in his chest. His fears were unfounded, Regan was well gone.

Fields finally found the courage to move and felt the weight of the world lift off his shoulders as soon as he did. Regan was gone, and he was now, at least for that moment, safe. He was done with the service as much as he felt the Service was going to be done with him once the news of this failure reached home.

He picked himself up physically and emotionally and went to free Carter from the binds that held him. They had been soundly beaten and lucky to be alive and, it dawned on him, completely lost in the forest.

Carter was terribly shaken by the events; his youthful exuberance and arrogance had dissipated with the rising steam from the wet foliage. Regan had frightened him to the core and the man that Fields cut loose was not the young man who had been sent to hunt Regan. His eyes were red from crying, his right cheek puffy from one of the blows received from Regan and he stood in the rain, snot dripping from his nose, like a chastised schoolboy. Fields felt sorry for him.

"Have we had enough?" Fields knew the answer before we got it, the eyes that were staring blankly at him told the story in booming tones.

"What was that?" he asked meekly. "What is he? They fucking told us he was just a former IRA thug with connections. Connections with who? Satan!? Jesus Christ, Fields, I thought I saw movement to my left, over there by those rocks," his hand was shaking violently as he pointed, the rain unable to sooth the fear. "I thought I saw him and then he was gone and I wanted to call you but then everything went black. He wrapped me like a fucking Christmas present."

"I didn't fare much better myself but at least he spoke to me, while nearly sawing my neck off."

Carter could see the blood smudged around the slight wound on Fields' neck and wondered what he had done to stop Regan from completing the cut. Both men knew that they were blessed beyond belief to be still alive.

"He told me to back off, Carter. He told me not to look for him again or he will come looking for us.

The two men stood staring at each other as the rain continued to pour down. The heavy drops and darkening skies could not wash away the fear nor hide it and the unspoken truth between the two men had a weight that no words could match. They would keep the promise made in those woods, a promise that allowed them to walk away from the fear.

They turned, supporting each other arm in arm, and trudged back in the direction they hoped would lead them out of the woods.

A short distance away, looking down on his former prey, Regan wiped the raindrops from his eyes and felt a balance return. They were leaving, and now he had to do the same.

Chapter 46.
The final shot.

The chopper skimmed in relative silence over the thickets of pine trees, the thin air having little effect on the engines. Built to make less noise than its counterparts, this Pave Hawk was not going to alert the enemy with its noise unless it crashed. It seemed, however, that crashing was, if not an option, then a possibility.

"Sir, we are flying on fumes. I need to turn back."

Petersen was staring through the clear afternoon air looking for something that would identify Regan in the woods, if he were in the woods. The rain had stopped and, if he was running through the meadows, it was conceivable that the heat of the ground would mask his heat signature that the technician was looking for. "Just give me five more minutes, Captain. Just give me that."

The voice came back calmly, "You have two, Sir. Then you jump or come back with me. Those are the options."

President Malcolm's lack of clarity had made the options crystal clear. The President had been intentionally vague, as he had to be under such circumstances where every word was being recorded. Petersen and decided, as a leader of men should, that if Regan was to be removed from service, then it was best if it was he who did it. He had unlocked his rifle from the store, the inquizative look from the Gunnary Sergeant not tempting an answer to the question 'Now why the Hell do you want your baby?' Petersen was tied to Regan in a way he could not explain and he was not going to allow anyone else take him in. It was not reasonable, he knew that Regan was not the kind of man who was going to accept the orders from a President that he could not respect. In addition, he agreed with how he thought Regan would think. However, he didn't want the young man to be removed from duty in the manner in which the President so explicitly did not mention for fear that the recorded call would be used against him in the future. Petersen didn't like his President, and hated his politics even more.

The Predator Drone had permission to scan the Italian countryside because it was on a training mission with two Italian operators. The Italian Government was thinking of purchasing a number of the drones to act as eyes in their war against Organised crime. When the request came from on high, and not the request that was made to Petersen, and landed on the desk of the other agency looking for Regan on the President's behalf, they used the cover of the training mission to act as back-up to the intel mission working on the ground and through the Web. It did not take them much time to figure that someone of their ilk was working in and around the large town of Garibaldi. Of course, the drone did not pick up on the killings but the analysts did. The papers were full of details now and the unit, working out of an office in Rome, was now on the trail of a man, or men, who had killed with ease around the town and countryside of Garibaldi. The information was now live-streaming and the Drone had been repositioned to follow any action that the expected to materialise.

Petersen was now in-country and waiting for details to arrive when he was buzzed. Picking his phone from his pocket he saw the number was blocked and that meant only one thing.

"Petersen."

"Your boy is on the move, heading to the mountains. He is just over one hundred miles North of your base, heading North-East. We have a Reaper on him but she is being called home in half an hour. She has been up for twenty-three hours and on the edge of her endurance. You need to be here now to pick-up the slack when she is pulled."

Petersen looked over to the team in the Blackhawk, a team that had been on standby for eight hours. He raised his hand and rotated it clockwise and the pilot gave him the thumbs-up signal.

"Our engines are turning and we will be off the ground in two minutes. We should be there in forty minutes."

"I will let you know his whereabouts just as we pull the Reaper."

"Can't you hold it there. If I am not mistaken, the endurance is 24 hours. Give me a break here, Chief."

The Section Chief laughed silently on the other end of the line. "My friend, when experienced pilots are guiding my babies, then they can stay up for 25 hours. She has been harassed by two new pilots, Italians, who think they are on a Playstation. She is coming down in 20 minutes, thirty at the most. Four and a half million dollars a baby, I am not going to kill her unless you have that in loose change to replace her."

"Chief, I am on the helicopter now on we are moving. Thanks for your help and best of luck with your new pilots!" Petersen did not expect to hear from him again.

The pilot had pushed his Pave Hawk all the way and he had managed to arrive on the general scene just a short ten minutes after the Reaper and turned for home. The Section Chief had been good to his word and had sent the details to Petersen via the coms on the chopper. The news was not good, however, and now Petersen knew that Regan was being chased. The odds were, generally speaking, stacked against Regan but that was not a new scenario for him to work in.

Petersen directed the pilot to the general area where he thought Regan would now be, which was quite easy taking all factors into consideration. He would run to the trees. That was a certainty, along with the fact that Petersen knew that he was now going to shoot his young friend. Landing and chasing were not an option. Not with the men he had at his disposal and especially not against the man he was to chase.

Petersen knew better than to question a pilot who was already breaking all the rules to have him flying around the Italian mountains looking to shoot a man.

"Got him!" The technician nearly jumped off his seat to point out the opened door. ""Three o'clock, low." With all the technology on the chopper, he had seen the figure running in the meadow while reaching for his Zippo. Such is life.

Petersen's heart jumped with joy and then threw itself off a cliff of dispair when he realised what it was he had to do and that realisation hit just as the two minutes were up.

"Ok, we are outta her Sir."

"Captain, just one shot. Ten seconds is all I need."

"You take the shot but I am turning in 10 if you do not."

"Roger that, Captain." Then time slowed to a creeping treacle.

His finger began to weigh onto the trigger and his right eye seemed to blend into the sights. The image of the back of the young man he had helped to create was now in his sights and his orders were orders. He knew that if he held fire for another few seconds then Regan would be out or range of his weapon and the chase would have to continue elsewhere. Or he could pull the trigger and end it all now.

Regan saw the trees rush towards him. The trees offered cover, a sanctuary from the eye of his friend and hunter, though he was not aware that his mentor was so close, so dangerously close. He felt the safety begin to embrace him and the fear that was being hosted in the pit of his stomach was now beginning to release itself from his hold. He was nearly there and his body knew it and pushed him closer to the line of trees and to escape.

Petersen had made up his mind. He was not going to let Regan be hunted by anyone else. He was not going to allow a circus atmosphere to develop around the one he saw as the son he never had. He also didn't want a *Rambo* situation to happen around the tourist mountains of the Italian North. As fictional as Rambo was, no police force or national Guard equivilent wanted to hunt a special forces soldier. It was, on a number of levels, the wrong thing to do. No, he had to spare the young man by taking his life. Was that not the right thing to do? He had completed his hunt for vengeance and now, contrary to the expectation that he would be allowed back into Dark-Eye, he had no options left. Either be cut loose, and Petersen would do that except the President had made his point clear that the book had to be closed on this little adventure, or be killed. Options were few and far between for Petersen and the range of his shooting capabilities and the time the helicopter had left in the air were both decreasing by the second.

All of the facets of this mission, the reality that had applied itself to the myriad of actions that had occurred over the previous weeks finally culminated in a frantic few moments where the life and death of a perfect soldier were decided with the twitch of a muscle in his arm. A twitch which pulled the tendon in his finger. The result, the trigger finger squeezed gently and a gout of flame blew out of the muzzle.

Petersen had done what he had not wished to do and now, in the miliseconds that follow such decisions, everything slowed. The thump of the rotor-blades seemed to slow to such an extent that the ears were trying to convince the brain that the chopper would not be able to support itself in the air at such a low turn-rate. Petersen's mind leapt, not to the thought of the path of the bullet and its ultimate target, but to how helicopters always seemed to be a part of Regan's key events. Northern Ireland, the assault on the terror compound in Cleveland and now this. The projectile had already well commenced its trajectory, its spiraling trip to the target.

The 750 gram Hornaday A-Max very-low-drag bullet fired from Petersen's .50-caliber McMillan Brothers Tac-50 travelled the distance to Regan in just over a second, a distance covered of just over 900 meters. From inside the chopper, firing that kind of weapon at a target of 900 meters, the chances of success were generally slim. It was the reason that most snipers could not shoot like Petersen. He had stopped counting his kills after an incident during the Battle of Debecka Pass, he had attained 25 hits during that four hour battle and did not want to count any further. Killing was never a competition, it was a matter of life, his, and death, the target. It was as personal a set of relationships he had had in his life, each man he killed took a little of the soul of the man who had done the killing. It was how it was and it was not something that he could explain to his wife nor to those academics who like to speak to soldiers after the shooting had stopped.

Now, he had fired once more, in anger, at a target that, not for the first time, had been running away from the shooter. He had raised his eye from the telescopic sights in time to see the result. At the same time, in line with what he had just advised, the pilot turned the chopper and headed for base, flying on kerosene fumes.

He stopped running. Something in his head, heart and legs told him that he had run far enough. The trees were now but a few meters from him and he would have loved to be back in the embrace of trees again, back were he felt safest and free from all of the events that he had endured from when this life, this life of a hunter-killer, had began in Ireland all those years ago. He stopped, relaxed and took a deep breath.

The impact punched him off his feet, the air forced from his lungs and his head spinning in pain and confusion as he fell forward, slowly or so it seemed.

His arms did not rise to shield him from the impact of the sun-dried earth and instead he hit the ground with a muffled thud. There was no pain, a sign that something was well and truly wrong. There was no pain but there was the smell of the warm grass and, for an instant, the warm wetness on his neck reminded him of his dog from his childhood licking him joyously as they rolled in the grass together and chased through the woods. Then, as if the joy of that life, and the realisation that his dog was long gone, were tears in the sun, the images evaporated and he was left lying on the ground where he had just fallen. He could smell the trees, could still smell his dog and now, in addition to those sentiments, he could taste a part of his past too. It was not the dust from the heated ground that flavoured his lips, it was his blood, pooling in his mouth and around his lips as he tried to cough. Pain followed, like sheets of rain on a barn door, it could almost be seen, and it definitely could be felt. Such rain chills to the bone and he knew that he was thinking too much about the rain because he felt his legs and arms grow cold. The sun could not melt through that coldness, not on this day nor on any other summers' day. It was the cold of leaking blood and nothing could take that chill away. In that moment, a thought raised its hand in the classroom of his mind and asked the teacher, *after all the blood you spilled, did you never think of saving some?*

The answer was a simple 'no.' After years of understanding that death was part of the Opera in which he was a player, the acceptance was never real. Now, his life seeping from his back and, he believed, his chest, mouth and nose, the sense of acceptance was lost and he wanted his dog. He wanted someone to hold his hand and knew that the path to the final journey was to be taken without the comfort of a loved one. His hands were cold and the blue sky was darkening, a rushing twilight even though the sun was high in the sky. It made no sense to him. *Why was the sun shining and twilight spreading at the same time?* It almost seemed funny that he was experiencing a climatic wonder as strange to him as sun-showers of his youth in Ireland that seemed, at that time, almost ridiculous beyond belief. Sun and rain, Catholic and Protestant, Christian and Muslim. All things could co-exist in nature but not always in the hearts of men. How strange life was.

Question after question sped through his mind in a flurry of unanswered desires. Twilight encroached further into the stream of thought that he was floating in and then it all stopped. The questions seemed answered, the pain eased, the coppery taste of blood in his mouth sweetened and, from the edge of the trees, the rustling of twigs and bushes announced the arrival of a she-wolf and her cubs.

She halted momentarily and sniffed the air, growling at her cubs to stay behind her as she tried to understand the scent of man in the air. She saw where the scent was coming from and, sensing no danger from the prone figure in the grass, she trotted carefully towards it.

The cubs did not need a second invitation and sprang out of the bushes, released from the confines of trees and plants and into the meadow, following their mother.

The wolf sniffed around the man carefully, poking her nose into his cheek before licking his ear and head. The wolf did not know why it nuzzled the man, it just did. As the man lay bleeding in the fading twilight nature had found a way to hold his hand and the last sensation that Jack Regan felt was his dog, licking his neck after a day in the sun.

THE END

Printed in Great Britain
by Amazon